Lady's Time

Alan V. Hewat
several music
fiction has app
Review and M
in Vermont wi

"The heart of *Lady's Time* is its evocation
of New Orleans life at the crack of the
Modern Age. Hewat brings the city so
alive you can nearly smell it. With a
remarkable cast . . . *Lady's Time* makes
the birth of jazz as real and strange as a
vivid dream."   *Los Angeles Times*

"This is a novel one cannot imagine,
which makes reading it a bizarre and
interesting experience . . . Hewat
expresses not only a deep love and
understanding of the roots of blues and
jazz, but also a healthy respect for
voodoo. These two qualities lift the book
out of the realm of ordinary historical
fiction."   *The Boston Globe*

"An ambitious and in many ways
charming book, likely to give pleasure to
anyone who likes ragtime and New
Orleans . . . Mr Hewat's prose runs
along, lively and smiling, as so much
ragtime – 'sunshine music' – does."
Washington Times

Alan V. Hewat

Lady's Time

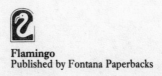

Flamingo
Published by Fontana Paperbacks

First published in Great Britain by
William Heinemann Ltd 1986

This Flamingo edition first published
in 1987 by Fontana Paperbacks
8 Grafton Street, London W1X 3LA

Flamingo is an imprint of
Fontana Paperbacks, part of
the Collins Publishing Group

Made and printed in Great Britain by
William Collins Sons & Co. Ltd, Glasgow

For Doug and Lydia

Contents

The author gratefully acknowledges the assistance of fellowship grants from the Massachusetts Council on the Arts and Humanities and the Vermont Council on the Arts in completing this work.

PART I:
SAND SPRINGS
1903–1916

Chapter One

Burnin' the Iceberg

On the day that her son drowned, Lady Winslow awoke before dawn, as was her custom regardless of the season. "If you let the sun sneak in on you," she told Leon many more times than once, "you will be lost in time, and then whatever will you do, pray tell?"

Over her flannel nightdress she pulled on a dressing gown and tied it tightly around her middle, and pulled heavy woolen socks over her feet and ankles, and went downstairs to the kitchen, where she lit the hanging lamp and loaded the woodstove from the box Leon had filled the previous evening. She fetched a bottle of milk from the cold box and poured a cup's worth into a small saucepan which she set in the middle of the stovetop, beside the kettle. Humming a scrap of whimsical melody, she stood and let the stove warm her for a minute and then turned and went into the parlor to light the coal stove there; as she left the kitchen she hunched her shoulders against the cold, to which she had never been able to accustom herself but which she indulged as one of the costs of her happiness. While waiting to be certain that the coal ignited she opened the lid over the keyboard of her piano and touched a couple of the keys softly, as if in tender greeting. Then she returned to the kitchen and made herself a cup of chocolate and stood at the window watching the day arrive.

During the night a snowstorm had come and passed, and the day that dawned was clear and freshly whitened. The evergreen trees surrounding the clearing were fleecy and the ground seemed to bulge like a freshly plumped pillow. "La," Lady said, and softly bit her lower lip in wonder at this complete and unexpected transformation of the world. As a child she had never seen snow, and now, though she was somewhat wary of its silent power, her appreciation of its ability to smother an entire landscape never failed to move her. "It's like a flood," she explained once, "with all of its rage taken away."

She called to Leon from the foot of the stairs, and when she heard his feet on the floorboards overhead, she said: "Look outside, darling, and see what you see." The sun had just broken the horizon beyond the woods outside Leon's bedroom window, and low shafts of light streamed through the tall pines. The ground glistened like treasure. "Oh boy," Leon shouted. "Snow, Mama. Oh boy." "Hurry and come fill the basin," Lady said. "Isn't it a morning to see, though?"

While Lady fried a small piece of ham in a skillet and stirred a bowl of pancake batter to smoothness, Leon performed his morning chores, which on this day included shoveling the snow from the steps and digging paths to the road in front of the house and the privy in back. Leon was a slender, energetic boy of twelve who had not yet come into his growth but was clearly about to, judging by the size of his feet and hands, which were already considerably larger than his mother's. His complexion was ruddier than Lady's and his lower lip was thicker, but he had inherited her dark, somewhat plaintive eyes and her heavy black hair, and there was no mistaking the affinity between them. Standing on the small porch outside the kitchen door and stamping and brushing the snow from his clothes he said, "Mama, I dreamed last night I was flying over a place I've never seen."

"That must have been exciting, darling," said Lady, who had

not had a dream since the night following her mother's burial and did not regret the loss of them. "Now, if you will fill the woodbox, the basin is warm enough to wash your face and hands in, and try to comb your hair down flat. It's most unsightly to see, poking out every which way so."

"D'you know what Mister Calhoun says about my hair?"

Lady looked sharply at him. "What?" she said.

But Leon looked away, suddenly shy. "Nothing," he said. "I forget. Listen, it's such a swell day, can I go now?"

"You may go when you have eaten your breakfast, my darling, and not a minute sooner and you know it. Kindly sit yourself and save your sass and sweet-talking for the little gals at school." She set his plate before him and then rolled her eyes upward as Leon attempted to load the whole piece of ham into his mouth. "La, this child," she said. "Leon, darling, will you ever eat sensibly? If you swallow before you chew, that food is just going to lie in your stomach in a big lump that will get bigger and bigger until it tears a hole in you. Do you want that to happen? Do you?" Leon met this with a look of exaggerated skepticism, and Lady giggled. "Well," she said, "do it out of consideration for my own sensitivities, then. I find it altogetherly distasteful to see you acting so, like a wild animal with no manners. Oh, and by the by, I need you to perform an errand for me on your way to school."

"Oh, Mama," Leon pouted. "Oh gee, I'll *never* get there. I'll be late. I will. I'll be late to school." He washed down the last of his pancakes with a huge swallow of milk. "Can't I just go?" he said.

"I said it was on your way," Lady said. "I simply want you to put your head in at the inn and ask Mister Vaughn whether he would be so kindly as to come for me here. I was going to walk over and meet him there for a drive into town, but I believe the snow is too deep for a pleasurable stroll today. Will you do that for your poor little mama? Will you please?" She batted her eyes at him until he smiled. "Oh, all right," he said. "I guess so, if you don't mind if I'm late to school."

"That's my sweet boy," Lady said. "That's your mama's darling."

When Leon had left, bounding away up the road, she stood at the parlor window and sipped hot chocolate. Outside, the clearing opened onto the lake road, on the other side of which was a narrow stand of trees and underbrush, skeletal without their summer foliage so that the lake was visible from the house. Its icy surface covered by the newly fallen snow, it looked like a whitewashed wall against which the trees were only shadows of themselves. "La," Lady said softly. The pure whiteness of the day made her feel joyous and secure. She turned to the piano and sat down on the lowbacked chair before the keyboard, set aside her chocolate and rested her fingers on the keys. After a few seconds they began to play, a gentle, meditative ragtime piece whose simple cadence and undemanding melody expressed something of the tranquility she found in the world on that bright morning.

At The Sequantus House, the manager, Henny Vaughan, huge in a bearskin coat and hat, stamped through the snow to the stables. He was exhilarated by the crisp morning and the opportunity it presented him to do Mrs. Winslow a kindness, that perplexing woman who in her resolute independence always asked so much less of him than he was prepared to offer. He knew that although disinclined to walk through this much new snow she would make the effort nonetheless to keep to their arrangement—simply, in his opinion, for the perverse sake of her blessed autonomy—but this time he would surprise her, by leaving early and intercepting her before she'd even dampened her boots. "Why, Mister Vaughn," she would say, feigning astonishment, "there was no need for you to come for me. I am not such a fragile flower, you know. Still," she would add, "it is most kindly of you, I'm sure." If he were bright enough then, he might say something in reply that would cause her to laugh with the soft, liquid sound that always caused such confusion in him, when she settled in next to him in his sleigh.

Henny was a tall and solidly built man whose nature expressed itself in an air of graceful authority, by whose exercise he excelled at the hosteler's trade. He treated both his guests and his employees with the unaffected, respectful dignity of an instinctive diplomat, and everyone who dealt with him was warmed by his forthrightness and serene charm. Like many people who shine in the public performance of their professions, however, he was in private a shy man, and especially so in the company of women, whose presence put him constantly on his guard. Not long before the turn of the century, he had been married for a short time to a beautiful woman slightly older than himself, who kept a suite at the Strathcona Court Hotel, where Henny was the night manager, and whose wealth and social standing far surpassed his own. On her insistence the marriage ceremony was performed in private and kept a secret, a condition to which she made him pledge his word, with the promise that it was only temporary and had to do with her inheritance. Then, a little less than two weeks after they were wed, she left him. She disappeared with all of her possessions, leaving no message behind to explain away Henny's unhappy disbelief. Honoring his pledge, he kept his despair to himself, even when his wife was killed the following summer during a lovers' quarrel with a prominent man who, after he shot her, hanged himself from an apple tree on his estate in Tuxedo Park.

The scandal never touched Henny, but that was a meager consolation for the feelings of shame and betrayal he bore, and the suspicion, which he could never confirm, that she had used him only to fulfill the purpose of some whim or woman's fancy; and although he never consciously decided to avoid the company of women, the discomfort he felt whenever a woman turned her attention upon him was sufficient to ensure that his relationships with them were insulated by a cautious formality. Even with a woman like Mrs. Winslow, whom he'd known now for about a dozen years and whose attributes of charm and loveliness seldom failed to set off a ripple of pleasure in him, he could not shed the habit of keeping himself on guard, though there wasn't a woman in the world, he knew, from whom he required less protection.

Henny whistled tunelessly through his teeth as he harnessed the fat black gelding called Blackbird and hitched it between the shafts, then filled a nosebag with oats and stowed it beneath the seat and fetched an extra bearskin rug from the bench at the back of the stable. The sleigh was a cutter, low and light, with a high, curved dashboard in the front and a seat just large enough to hold two grown people, fitted snugly side by side, and it rode smoothly on the snow, with a hissing sound from its runners. Leaving the stables, the horse settled immediately into a comfortable trot as he descended the sloped, curving driveway of the inn and then turned left onto the lake road. To Henny's right the lake seemed immense in the featureless whiteness of its frozen surface; the mountains beyond it to the north and west looked as distant as the moon, though in the clarity of the chill morning air Henny had the impression that he could distinguish the outlines of individual rocks poking through the snow on their peaks. He drove past the turnoff where the road to Sand Springs left the lake road and headed into town, a little more than a mile away, and clucked and called to the horse, "Did you ever see such a morning in all your days, old feller?" Ahead, the road dipped toward the shore and then straightened and entered the woods, where it passed the clearing where Mrs. Winslow and her son lived in their little white cottage. Henny was about to slow the gelding to a walk when out of the side of his eye he saw a small figure slide out upon the lake, waving its arms and yelling like a wild banshee, and a second small figure jumping up and down on the shore.

They were boys, thickly wrapped and hatted in cold-weather woolens, and the lad on the lake slipped away from the shore, with his arms windmilling and his feet churning up wakes in the fresh snow, and just as Henny apprehended that it was young Leon out there on the ice, a pattern of gray lines emerged in the snow around the boy and in their midst, like a table overturning, a segment of the lake's cover burst up and tilted forward and Leon dropped from sight. Unweighted, the breakaway segment righted itself and settled flat, bouncing gently and turning a blue-gray color as lake water seeped into the snow on its surface.

"God in Heaven!" Henny cried, standing up in the sleigh and hauling back on the reins so harshly that the horse squealed and reared up on its hind feet. Jumping from the cutter, Henny threw off his coat and then his jacket and raced in great, bounding strides past the second boy to the shore and into the water, his boots smashing through the ice until he was in almost up to his waist and had to beat and pry at the frozen surface with his hands. "Leon," he called out. "Hold on, lad. I'm coming for you, Leon." He kept his eyes fixed on a point just beyond the spot where Leon had gone under and drove himself toward it with frantic effort, his ears resounding with the roar of his fear, and his hands and feet burning from the freezing cold of the water, which enveloped and resisted him as he advanced into it, making his progress nightmarishly slow. When the water reached almost to his shoulders' height he had to join his fists together and raise them high above and behind his head in order to summon the power to smash through the ice before him. "God damn you," he shouted thickly, realizing that after he'd advanced another two or three steps the water would be at the level of his head and he would have to dive beneath the ice to continue his search for Leon. His joints were stiffening in the icy cold and his muscles were losing their will to respond, and it occurred to him that to dive would likely cost him his life. He knew that the lake harbored strong, deep currents generated by the underground streams which fed into it; he could only pray that the boy hadn't been carried off by one of them. "God damn you," he said again, this time almost sobbing, and heaved at the ice from beneath, lifting a large, arrowhead-shaped section away from the endless white platform. In the water he uncovered there, Henny saw a mittened hand floating.

He shouted once in surprise and triumph and hauled at the

hand, and Leon floated out from under the cover of ice. Henny drew an exhausted breath and turned and, towing the boy like a dory in his wake, beat his way back toward the shore. When he'd returned to waist-deep water, he got both arms under Leon and lifted him up. The boy was as limp as a butchered lamb and the skin of his face was a solid gray hue except for his lips and eyelids, which had turned the indigo shade of a moonless night. Henny squeezed Leon in his arms, shook him and shouted his name, but there wasn't so much as a flutter of response in the child, and Henny despaired to see that Leon's eyes were only dismal white crescents laying dull as pulled teeth behind his thick, dark eyelashes. Slime hung from the boy's nostrils and his lips were curled up at the corners in an ominously peaceful smile. "Jesus, Mary and Joseph," Henny groaned, "he's done for."

He thrashed out of the shallow water and as soon as he was on the shore turned Leon over, grabbed him by the ankles and lifted and shook him, bouncing him head-down like the handle of a churn. On the fourth or fifth bounce, water began to rush out of the boy's mouth and nose and splatter in the snow, and Henny dropped to one knee and laid Leon, chest down, across the other and pressed his hand down upon the child's shoulderblades. Other matter joined the water escaping Leon's mouth, little green and pink lumps forced out by the pressure of Henny's big hand, and then, praise be, the child made a sound. It was only a single feeble cough, accompanied by an almost imperceptible shiver that conveyed no more displacement in the atmosphere of the day than an insect's sneeze, but Henny detected it and rejoiced. Immediately he rose to his feet and ran stumbling on his numb feet to his sleigh, with Leon cradled in his arms. He laid the boy's small form out on the seat and covered him with both bearskins and jumped in after him. Standing like a charioteer behind the dashboard, he whacked the gelding across the rump with the free end of the reins and yelled at it, "Move, God damn your black hide, move." He failed altogether to notice the second little boy, who at that moment was racing as fast as his short legs would carry him back toward the Sand Springs road, crying in terror.

Lady had not intended to stay at the piano for any longer than the few minutes it took to complete the simple, cele-bratory rag her fingers had chosen to play; then she would go upstairs to her bedroom and brush out and pin up her hair and get dressed in order to be ready to leave with the innkeeper when he arrived. It was a Thursday, one of the two days of the week that she gave piano lessons in the room above Alfred Cal-houn's barbershop, and there were six pupils scheduled for in-struction, four of them children and two women, one of them an elderly widow whose company Lady especially enjoyed, for the woman was spunky and unashamedly proud of the little she was able to accomplish in her exercises, and not at all bothered by the plenitude of music that would forever exist beyond her fingers' grasp. Neither was she intimidated in the slightest by the ordeal of passing through Calhoun's shop on her way to Lady's studio, a gamut whose passage had proved too daunting for so many prospective female students over the years. At one point Lady had undertaken to bring her instruction to these women in their own homes, to spare them the fright of encoun-tering the hostile barber and his crowd of louts, but in their own parlors the women had been more concerned with receiv-ing Lady in a proper fashion or attending to domestic matters than with their lessons: "Excuse me, Mrs. Winslow, but I have to check the oven. I shan't be a minute." "Are you quite sure you won't take some coffee, Mrs. Winslow? I made it special." "Could you say that again, Mrs. Winslow? I'm afraid my mind was outside. My wash is on the line, and I fear it's going to rain." In her own studio they ceded her the authority to direct them, and it seemed that when they left at the end of a lesson they were as heartened simply by having left home to acquire their new knowledge as they were by the accomplishment of an exercise mastered. Further, those women who had dared Cal-houn's shop usually arrived at the studio upstairs feeling espe-cially bold, and eager to attack their lessons. "You may find this

11

next passage to be somewhat difficult at the written tempo," Lady would caution. "Let's try it," the student would respond. Alfred Calhoun, that hateful man, had enlivened Lady's days in more ways than he could possibly have intended.

She was halfway through the second strain of the rag, a thematic inversion of the opening melody, and thinking of nothing in particular, when her hands faltered in midphrase and then, before she could stop them, introduced a new theme so unexpected that she repeated it twice through before its air seeped into her memory. "No," she cried, and stood up so suddenly that her chair toppled over. "No no no." She drew her hands up to her bosom and anxiously turned to the window, as if expecting to see something cataclysmic emerge from the lake or the trees outside; but the scene she beheld there was as bright and silent as before, its tranquility undisturbed except by an occasional soundless puff of white among the evergreens as snow sifted down from one branch to the next below in a glistening shower of ivory dust.

I did not hear that, Lady thought. *I could not have heard it.* But her hands led her back to the keyboard, where they sought out the theme and played it for her again. Her left hand dove deep into the bass clef and walked up and down there with a hobbling gait, and the fingers of her right hand settled just above middle C and fashioned a series of minor chords and dissonances, and she closed her eyes and saw heavy gray mist swirling in blocks like giant stones tumbling in undersea currents, and she heard a voice call out slowly in low tones so sorrowful that her chest ached at the sound of it, calling: *"Poor Alice. Oh, poor little Alice."*

Tears filled Lady's eyes and spilled slowly down her cheeks, and she said, *"Leon,"* in a low, shivering voice and listened for his answer in the music. She repeated her son's name over and over again, summoning her concentration to drive out the churning gray miasma of her fear and listening while her fingers tormented the keyboard like a cat playing with a wounded bird, seeking his voice, the living voice of her skinny boy, who had been her love and protector since the morning he was born in a room with a stained ceiling, filled with coal smoke and the hawk wind blowing up from the river and rattling the window in its frame, where she had wept to see how pink he was, her Leon. Now she couldn't find him. Now he had been taken from her by a sound and a voice that she was certain she'd escaped, calling to her from a time in which she had ceased to exist. *I cannot follow him*, she thought. *I must not*. Fear and weariness slowed her fingers; the music softened.

Then, praise be, she heard him. A tiny palpitation, a minute disturbance in the chill, liquid vision forced upon her by the music, brushed against her, and she let her breath out in a grateful sigh and turned her head toward the window just in time to see Henny Vaughan, wearing a shirt and trousers stiffened by ice and with his hair and mustache white with frost, leap from his sleigh and fall to his hands and knees in the snow outside her front door. Shaking his head slowly from side to side, he pushed himself to his feet and turned and reached down into the sleigh, and from the seat he lifted a large, shaggy brown bundle which he clasped to his chest as he began to stumble toward the house.

In her confusion, it seemed to Lady that she was floating beside herself, watching and following but not feeling the floor beneath her feet as she walked to the door, or the doorknob in her fingers as she pulled the door open. "Mercy," she said, and stepped back as Henny tripped on the sill and fell to his knees in the narrow hallway, releasing his bundle onto the floor. "The water," Henny said in a barely intelligible groan. "In the water." He tried to get to his feet but succeeded only in toppling sideways against the frame of the parlor door, where he rested, still on his knees, with his shoulders heaving and his hands trembling and water forming pools on the floor around him. His face was spotted with vivid red and white patches and his lips were purple, but Lady paid him scant attention as she closed the door and moved without haste to examine the bearskins.

The heavy brown fur was damp and cool and exhaled the odor of an earth closet, and as soon as she touched it with her hand Lady understood that it was Leon's body buried inside the skins. She unfolded them carefully and saw that his hat and one of his mittens were missing, and that his eyelashes were spiky with water and vomit clogged his right nostril and his skin was the color of pewter. He was as silent as the snow. "Oh my baby, my boy," she said, and she began to undress him where he lay, flinging his sodden clothing in every direction. When he was naked she could see that all of his pinkness had been washed away and he was as distant from her as the frozen mountain-tops, and when she picked him up in her short, strong arms and began to mount the stairs she didn't feel the weight of his flesh but only a volume of cold air which she was somehow able to embrace and contain. "Go to the kitchen, Mister Vaughan," she said over her shoulder to Henny, whose teeth were chattering like hailstones. "Go and warm yourself at the stove. I'll see to you presently."

Upstairs, she laid Leon out in his own bed and fetched extra blankets to pile upon him, and she stood for several minutes at his bedside stroking his pallid forehead and feeling the cold breath of his skin upon her palm. Fear and resolution twined together like serpents inside her; she was alone and vulnerable again, she knew; her times had called to her in the low, groaning tones of huge iron wheels turning, and she understood that if she wished to recover her son from the process that now concealed him from her, she would have to ignore the inevitable cost and answer back. Moving with the slow care of a sleep-walker she turned away from Leon's bed and went downstairs.

In the hallway at the foot of the stairs, Henny Vaughan was seated on the floor and trying feebly to remove his boot. Without speaking, Lady knelt to help him. His boots were soaked through and heavy as sand, and she tore a fingernail to the quick while removing the second of them, but eventually she got them both off him, and his socks as well. "Come along, Mister Vaughan," she said, rising from the floor and holding out a hand to him. "You'll never restore your good health sitting here. Come on." He grunted and shook his head, and she bent down over him and put her hand under his chin and raised his face so that she could look directly into his eyes, which drifted in and out of focus. "Henny Vaughan," she said, "if you don't stand up this minute and follow me into my kitchen, I swear I shall never invite you there again, do you hear me? I *need* you to walk with me, for I could never carry you myself. Do you hear?"

Henny rolled sideways and got to his hands and knees. "All right," he said thickly. "I'm all right." He gathered himself and lurched to his feet and then she was able to guide him into the kitchen and seat him on a chair before the stove.

She opened the stovetop and fed more wood into the fire. Then she went back to the hall and got one of the bearskins, which, after loosening his shirtfront and removing his collar, she draped over Henny's shoulders. From the small enclosed porch outside the kitchen door she got a bucket and a hammer and, though wearing only socks on her feet, descended the back steps to the pump, where she knocked away the night's accumulation of ice and filled the bucket. Returning to the kitchen, she dragged a galvanized washtub from the corner, poured into it a measure of cold pump water from the bucket and then emptied into it the contents of the big kettle which had been simmering on the stovetop since before dawn. Henny was grunting softly and rocking back and forth on his chair, clasping the bearskin tightly around himself, and Lady knelt in front of him and rolled his trouser legs up above his ankles, then tugged the washtub into place before his chair and set his feet into the warm water, eliciting from him a gritted moan. In two more trips to the pump she fetched enough water to fill every pot, kettle and saucepan in the kitchen, and as many of them as fit there she set upon the stovetop, with the rest arrayed on the floor nearby. Then she went to the cupboard and, standing on a chair in order to reach to the topmost shelf, took down a bottle of apple brandy and poured a cup full. She had to peel back the bearskin from around Henny's head to get the cup to his mouth, but it took no persuading to get him to swallow the liquor and when she returned with a second cupful his head was up and he was able to take the cup in his swollen hands. He swallowed, coughed and said, "I'm grateful to you, Missus Winslow," and she was heartened to see that the scarlet and white patches on his face had begun to fade and blend to a more evenly distributed color, and that his eyes had regained their focus. "And I to you, Mister Vaughan," Lady said, "but I cannot linger here with you, I'm afraid. If you want to rest, please come upstairs and use the bed freely."

There were bricks stacked two-high beneath the stove, and she wrapped four of them in a towel and headed for the stairs. "Is the boy all right?" Henny asked.

Lady stopped and considered for an instant. "I'm listening for him. At the moment, it's all I can do," she said, and went up the stairs.

Throughout her ministrations to Henny, Lady had continued to feel as though she was floating in a warm, liquid atmosphere whose density deadened all sensation, so that even the pressure of her fear was unspecific and lacked urgency. Now, having pulled back the bedcovers to set the warm bricks around Leon's still, small body, it seemed to her that she was quite detached from her son as she noticed how very remote he appeared. Reaching to touch his narrow chest, her arm seemed to extend into a distance almost beyond sight, and when her fingers encountered his skin it took seconds for the icy message of his flesh to return to her. She watched her hand stroke the boy's stomach and legs and marveled at how cold and hard his familiar body was, like milk frozen in a glass bottle. She arranged the bricks around him and pulled the covers to his chin, then she knelt beside the bed and, turning his head to the side, placed her ear against his. She heard nothing that she had not already heard in the murmuring of her fear. The boy was alive still; the tiny palpitation she had first felt at the piano still fluttered against her senses, but it might as well have been a

16

breeze tumbling along the far shore of the lake, and Lady understood that she hadn't the power to grasp it or to turn it to her own use.

She put her mouth close to his ear. "Leon," she whispered, "Leon darling. Baby boy, if you can come back to your mama, please do it now, darling. I'll never give you up, I swear, but please come back. Don't make me follow to find you, Leon. Don't make me go where we cannot protect each other." Her voice fell into a singsong pattern as she whispered over and over, "Mama needs you, baby; please come back to Mama, please." Around her in the little bedroom the daylight was harsh and brittle, and filled every corner like a siren's howl, but Lady's eyes were clenched shut, searching in the swirling silver mist of her fear for the source of the tiny displacement which told her that her baby boy was still alive.

She halted her entreaty when she heard a footstep on the stairs, and sat back on her haunches and brushed her hair away from her face as Henny appeared in the doorway. He wore the bearskin on his shoulders like a tribal robe, and in his hand he carried a steaming cup. His trouser legs were still rolled to his calves, and his feet and ankles were a bright pink, the feet of an immense bird with pale yellow claws. Dazed by the effort of concentration, Lady stood up. She realized that she had forgotten about the innkeeper altogether, as if months had passed since she'd left him in the kitchen. She stared blankly down at his bare feet, wondering whether she had ever before seen any creature with toes as long as his.

Henny coughed and pointed with the cup at Leon. "I've made coffee," he said. "How is the lad's condition?" His voice was labored and slow, and he leaned heavily against the doorframe.

"Praise be, he's alive," she said.

"That's something, then."

Looking down, she noticed that her robe had fallen open and she busied herself at folding it closed over her nightdress and tying its cord. "Yes," she said absently, "I'm quite certain he's still alive. I am afraid, however, that he . . . I mean to say that I cannot . . ." She drew a breath and put her hands to her cheeks and looked with longing sorrow at Leon's face, lying like a pearl in the nest of his black hair. The color of his eyelids had faded to the blue of snow shadows and his nostrils looked as frail as dried petals, so delicate that her heart slipped in her chest.

"Perhaps warm liquids," Henny said. "He's likely chilled to the very core." He took a careful step away from the doorframe, holding out the cup.

"Yes," Lady said, "perhaps." She took the cup from Henny and raised Leon's head with her hand and pressed the cup's rim against his lower lip, prying a narrow opening in his placid smile of unconsciousness.

"I took the liberty of adding a drop of brandy," Henny said. "For its stimulating property, you know."

"Perhaps," Lady said again. She tipped a bit of the hot liquid between Leon's lips; it drained slowly through his teeth as if sinking into hard-packed sand, and when it was gone from view she poured in a little more. There was no response from the boy, but she didn't really expect any.

"It's not enough," Henny said. He knelt beside her and took Leon's jaw in his hand and pressed in on the boy's cheeks until Leon's mouth opened. "Lord, but he's cold," Henny said. "Come on then, lad, drink up and tell us how you feel." Lady poured in some more coffee until the cup was empty; disappearing unimpeded down the boy's throat, it might as well have been leaking out of a hole in the back of his neck.

In the early afternoon Henny, declaring himself restored to health although his hands still shook, drove to the inn to telephone for the doctor, wearing rags around his feet because his boots were too wet to be worn. Intending to return to the Winslow house, he was pulling a pair of dry trousers up his legs when he fell into a dimensionless sleep which lasted until just before the following dawn, when he opened his eyes and said, "He was dead before I could find him, the poor tyke." Weeping softly, he kicked off his trousers and rolled into his bed and slept until noon; he dreamed that the lake was on fire.

Doctor Curtiss appeared at Lady's door in midafternoon, carrying his worn black bag. He poked and squeezed Leon's body, thumbed his eyelid open and held a small piece of reflecting glass under the boy's nostrils. Resting his hand on the front of Leon's neck, he sighed. "There's a pulse, Mrs. Winslow, but not much more. No comfort for you in that, I know," he added brusquely. He was a taciturn man with a gruff voice and an oblique way of expressing his compassion, which was vast and indiscriminate. He took a square-bottomed bottle and a teaspoon from his bag, wiped the spoon clean with his thumb and filled it with a viscous brown tonic which he poured carefully into Leon's mouth. "Doesn't even swallow," he said with quiet anger.

Lady stood calmly beside the doctor, watching politely but with an uninvolved air, as if he were merely performing a domestic task such as turning a rug for her. She had not asked Henny to call for him; she understood that there was nothing that could be done for Leon in his present condition, that she could only wait until a particular moment announced itself, and concentrate through her fear so that she would be certain to recognize its signal. When it came to her, probably after nightfall, she would have to embark alone into time, on the journey she had forbidden herself for so long, knowing that there was no alternative to which she might appeal, for the consequences of this day were now fixed, as inevitable, she realized, as its dawning. She attended to the doctor's efforts with the neutral regard she had taught herself to employ with all men. "Man doesn't care if you listen to him as long as you look lively his way while he talks," she recalled a little bird of pleasure telling her once. "If he talks joking, just laugh and say, 'Aw, Daddy,' and if he talks serious scrunch up and look gravely till he's done. Maybe he won't whup on you so bad if you do." The memory didn't startle Lady; it was merely another side of her fear. The little bird's name was Baby Luana, she recalled; a puffy-faced blond girl with bruises on her fair skin. "Study on the master's ways," Baby Luana had said, a lesson from the women in her family.

"I can come back tomorrow," Dr. Curtiss said at the door. He scowled, frustrated by the impenetrability of suffering. "The boy's in grave condition," he said. "Don't delude yourself. If you'd like, my wife could come. I know you're alone here. Someone with you, if you like."

"You're very kind," Lady said automatically, "but I prefer to look after him myself. There is—" She hesitated. "Perhaps time will provide a remedy."

"Hm. Do you pray, Mrs. Winslow?" He shifted from foot to foot.

"Why, I suppose I do, Doctor," Lady said. "I suppose I do."

"Try not to be afraid," the doctor said. "Easy thing for me to say. I'm sorry. Good day to you." Lady opened the door for him and he glared out at the brightness of the sunshine and snow, and hefted his bag as if he wanted to hit something with it. Lady watched from the door while he climbed aboard his sleigh and clucked to his horse. He didn't look back at her or wave as he drove away.

It was an early winter twilight, the sun falling far to the south and the clear sky gradually turning silver and then indigo, in whose light the snow seemed in its whiteness to rise and swell like yeasting dough. Lady set things straight in the kitchen, emptying the foot tub and the saucepans, and replacing the brandy on the cupboard shelf. At one point she went to the back steps and listened into the woods for a minute. The silence was unqualified; there was nothing there to guide or arrest her. She reentered the kitchen. *I'm only dithering*, she thought.

She went to her bedroom and sat in front of her mirror and brushed out her hair with long, even strokes until it hung undivided down her back, as thick and dark as the sound of her fear; then she gathered it and rolled and twisted it into a symmetrical cluster which she pinned into place against the top and back of her head. She rouged her lips and brushed a preparation of frankincense and mastic into her eyelashes, to thicken them. While she was performing the familiar tasks, she felt at last that the sense of separation from herself, which she had endured since the morning, had begun to diminish, and with it the low, groaning pressure of her anxiety, the feeling of fat serpents uncoiling through her. She dressed herself in a black gown with a straight skirt and white lace at the collar and cuffs, which were cut just above her wrists, leaving her hands free, and by the time she had finished there was a silence in her to match the stillness of the woods outside.

She went to Leon's room then and lit the oil lamp on the table beside his bed. "It's all right, darling," she said softly, peering down through the yellow light at his pale, lifeless face. "Mama's going to bring you back. Don't fear, baby. It's all right." Tugging at the footboard, she moved the bed away from the wall and into the center of the room; then she went to the kitchen and returned with four saucers and a pitcher of cold water. She placed a saucer on the floor by each corner of Leon's bed and filled each saucer from the pitcher. When that was done, she set the pitcher aside and backed away from the bed to the door, and stood in the doorway staring into the room, trying to remember things she wasn't certain she had ever known. She felt quite hollow now, empty and silent; if struck, she would resound like a big drum, *padoum*. The memory she was seeking did not come, but an exigent feeling in her hands and wrists guided her back to her own bedroom and to a black, stave-sided trunk with a domed lid, which stood against the wall near the window.

She raised the lid and inhaled the musty odor that fled upward into her face, and then lifted out the shallow tray. The inside of the trunk was as dark as a well at twilight, so she fetched a lamp from her dresser, and by its light she could see a few forgotten items scattered about the trunk's bottom: a black straw hat, a photograph, a shoe, a pair of gray gloves, a buttonhook, a little rabbitskin pouch tied at its neck with a thin leather string. Without hesitation she picked up the pouch from the trunk, set it on the floor, then put the tray back into place and closed the domed lid. The musty odor remained in her bedroom, but it reminded her of nothing. She picked up the rabbitskin pouch and the lamp and set them both on the dresser; glancing at herself in the mirror, she noticed how calm she appeared, how expressionless her face. The lamplight had turned her skin a pale golden shade. The rabbitskin was brown and somewhat stiff, but she untied the leather string without any trouble and dumped the pouch's contents out on the dresser top.

On the lace doily before her, inscrutable and somehow ominous, lay three twists of paper and a gnarled root whose shape was vaguely human, with a long string looped around its waist. Now the silence in her was given shape by the appearance of a new tone, high and distant and plaintive. Lady put her hands to her face and pressed her palms tight against her eyes, and began to breathe rapidly as if she was about to weep. Quietly, in an uninflected voice, she said: "Mama." The sound in her began to thicken and grow, a keening sound full of desolation and loss, of exile far from the habitations of the human heart, the sound of a battlefield after the guns have been silenced and the living have trooped away. "Sometimes," Old Patanouche had told her a long time ago, "dead folks can be extremely difficult to get their attention. It's no good just to walk up and say, 'Hi, look here,' 'cause sometimes they will and sometimes they won't, and that's that. A dead person's so free, they don't reckon they have *got* to pay any attention to anything except themself unless and until they decided to, and no way a living soul is going to make them do otherwise. You have got to be *patient* with the dead, and tolerating. Do you understand what I'm talking about?" "What do they look like, the dead?" she had asked. "Hmp," the old woman had snorted, "it doesn't matter none about looking. Dead don't signify by looking. Oh, maybe a little shank of lightness here and there, but mostly not." "I don't like that," she had said. "It's scary when you can't see." "That's the very reason you have to prepare," Patanouche had said. "If you're scared you don't see but the scary things anyhow. You've got to don't *be* scared."

Lady dropped her hands from her eyes and smiled at the memory. The old woman's wizened brown face was clear before her now, as nearby as her own face in the mirror, and as familiar. She remembered that she had said to Old Patanouche, "I'm scared of dying, I think," and the old woman had rolled her eyes and shaken her hands in the air and said, "Ah'm skeered a'dyin', Ah'm skeered a'dyin'," in a tiny, singsong voice until she had had to laugh. Then Old Patanouche had looked at her with kind, patient eyes, the most comforting eyes she ever knew, and asked, "However did you get to be such a *timid* child? I'll tell you something that most folks don't know, and that's that dying is the best and nicest part of being dead, and if folks *did* know that, they'd want to be dying all the time, account of it's so nice. Dead gets restless and bothersome but dying is altogetherly a pleasantness. That's why it doesn't come to anything if you try to call the dying, child, 'cause there's no place they want to be except where they're going, it's such a peace, and if you try to interrupt them they get terribly pained at you and just go on their way. Sooner or soonest you can always catch up to a dead person, but you can't with a dying, and that's that. Fear the pain of living, dear, if you've got to fear anything." She'd leaned forward so that her face was close, and she had smelled the cloves on Patanouche's breath and seen the tiny veins of gold in her dark brown pupils. "You still skeered?" Patanouche had asked in her tiny voice. "I don't know." "You're not thinking you want to be dying now, are you?" "Is it as nice as angel pie?" she had asked. "Hmp, maybe nicer," the old woman had answered. "You come with me in the house now and we'll drink some chocolate and be proper ladies before your mama needs you at home for the folding." Lady realized that the old woman must have put a herb of forgetfulness into her chocolate that afternoon, for the memory of their conversation had stayed hidden from her until this moment; she realized too that what had stayed her from the urgency of panic on this terrible day had been not her deadening fear but the knowledge of this, that she had to wait until Leon had finished dying before she could commence the business of bringing him back.

She opened the twists of paper then and saw that they contained little clumps of green and brown dust, the powder of crushed herbs and petals, and she put a pinch from each clump into the water of each of the saucers on the floor around Leon's bed. Then she took the human-shaped root—a male, she noticed, the stump of a thorn swelled in the fork between its legs—and tied it to the bedpost at the southwestern-facing corner of the bed, and when she had done that she pulled a chair beside the bed and sat and put her hand next to her son's cheek and waited for him to die.

The tiny palpitation which had signaled the presence of life in Leon disappeared finally shortly before midnight; to mark the event each of the saucers exhaled a bubble of blue steam the size of a lark's egg which floated up and burst against the ceiling, leaving a mark like a toeprint there. Lady stroked the child's face and bent and kissed his forehead, and then left the room and went downstairs to the piano. As she seated herself on the lowbacked chair she murmured, "This is what I have to do," and noticed that the mild trepidation she felt was qualified by a sense of nostalgic anticipation. There was a tingling in her wrists and shoulders that she had not felt for many years, and even before she set her hands out upon the keyboard the details of familiar faces started to appear to her. As soon as she touched the keys, she heard a low, drawling voice say, "Bring 'em in from the alley now, child, and let 'em roll," and she could smell the spices and smoke and the river air of New Orleans, and in the composure of her concentration the notes began to rise from the keyboard into her fingers and she started to play the music she had left behind in time, the music of her blues.

The blues. The slow-flowing, late-night music that Brick

used to play when he came home from work after midnight and sat in the dimly lit parlor bent over the old sea captain's piano with the leaf-shaped spots on its sides, where the sea air had eaten into it, and the yellowed keys which were the same color as Brick's teeth. The first time she heard him playing that music it woke her from her sleep and she looked across her little room and saw the mist rubbing against the windowpanes and thought that the music was the sound of the mist itself, gray and swirling and forever shut away in the cold night outside the windows. There was in the city then a wraith in the body of a boy who had been halted forever at the threshold of manhood, his skin the pale, translucent color of milk glass and his hair like white silk, and he was blind and deaf and could not speak and ceaselessly wandered the streets of New Orleans on bare feet that never stumbled or bled, accompanied everywhere by the sound of the child's harmonica he kept pressed against his toothless gums, his lips nibbling around its tarnished carapace like the rippling skirts of snails. That sound was known in every quarter of the city, and whenever it was heard people shivered and crossed themselves or drew hexes in the dust. The wraith was called Blind Jibba, and it was said of him that he had been a bugler at the battle of Shiloh, where the explosion of a mortar shell had blown him into a condition of solitude from which no one had ever been able to call him back. She had seen him once; he had passed through the schoolyard where she was playing and had turned his face toward her as he went by, so that she could see his eyes, which were the color of boiled potatoes, and at that instant a voice calling from his sound had made her begin to weep unconsolably. She had run home and flung herself into her mother's lap, but even her mother, sweet little Mimi, had been unable to comfort the desolate terror she had felt then. The blues Brick played reminded her of Jibba and his sound, but Brick added other, consoling voices to it, so that it was more like Brick himself, like his gentle, mournful voice, and did not frighten her so. Its weary melody balanced pain and healing, and its deep-flowing rhythm was like the rhythm of time itself rolling toward the dawn of another day, so that it opened out from the arid misery of Jibba's sound with wry promise. She'd gotten up from her bed and gone to the parlor and seen Brick in the shadows there, his head hanging forward over the keyboard and turned to face her, and in the amber light cast by the lantern that Mimi had left burning for him at the foot of the stairs she saw that Brick's eyes were closed and his wide mouth was pulled back at its corners in a placid, reminiscent smile.

Without pausing she had walked slowly to his side and placed her left hand on top of his, which was so large that she didn't cover even the space between his wrist and his knuckles, and he neither changed expression nor opened his eyes but kept on playing, with his left hand pumping a slow, powerful rhythm that was like the flowing of the river and his right hand plucking the chorded songs of a sorrowing choir singing about misery and hope. Her hand rode on top of his like a voyager on a raft, and she could feel the brown, lazy power of the rhythm surge through her palm and her wrist all the way to her shoulder, and as she recognized that the music was addressing her in a way that seemed altogether familiar, she closed her eyes and smiled.

That was the night she had begun to discover the secrets of music, and she stayed there at Brick's side with her hand riding on his until dawn approached and the mists outside the window began to lighten and she could hear her mother stir overhead. Brick stopped playing then and said, "That's enough, child. I can teach you what you need to know in the daytime." "I never heard music like that in the daytime," she said. "Well, there's sunshine music and nighttime music," Brick said. "There's music for every hour of the soul here and hereafter, I reckon." "Will you teach me every kind?" she asked. Brick looked at her gravely and said, "I will teach you the music you will need to know, little Alice. The rest will come to you soon enough."

In her parlor Lady smiled at the memory of the tickler's face, so like a hound's countenance with its sad, watchful eyes and long, creased cheeks, and his reassuring voice which spoke with the same rhythms and accents as his blues. Now, as it had on that first night, music surged up from the piano into her hands and wrists all the way to her shoulders, with a tonality reminiscent of the thick ocean sound of Brick's old, stained upright, but this time it was not Brick's music but her own, the blues of her own life, that led her on as she commenced her search in time, looking for her baby, her Leon.

Chapter Two

Snowy Morning Blues

I never did have a daddy, you know, and my mama passed along when I was just past sixteen. She was murdered by a man whose face I saw in a dream but never could find alive on earth. And I'll tell you something: I've seen a lot of this old world in my time and no matter where I went, from Sand Springs to Shanghai and all over the globe, I've looked for that man all my life.

Now, Mama always said she was going to tell me about my daddy. "Soon, darlin', soon," she'd say. "It's right on the tippy-top of my tongue. You and me will sit down proper and I'll tell you all about your people and you'll be proud." When I was small, no more than a crumb crusher, she told me his name and how he looked, so tall and handsome. His name was Anthony Mayhew Winslow, so elegant. Anthony. "Like Mark Anthony," Mama told me, "that was Queen Cleopatra's beloved in the Egyptian times." His people lived on the Arkansas Delta and he died a hero in the autumn floods, trying to save a colored family who'd been trapped by the waters on the roof of their house. My daddy gone, before I was even born, and then Mama too, so you see, I never really had past times in the way of history and all. I've just been making myself up as I went along. Spontaneous composition, you might say. Running the changes.

Mama played piano, and I've been hearing the music since before I was born. She used her own name, Lady Winslow, and she played ragtime in the old-fashioned style, slow and formal with a rich sound and a stately measure. She sure played fine. She came all the way from New Orleans. The land of dreams, you know, and she never lost that certain way of talking. The first time I was ever in Chicago I was maybe twenty-one and just off the circus band, it was back in the speakeasy times. I was playing that hot jazz then, you understand, with a little group in a South Side spot. I was just learning my trade, playing *Fidgety Feet* and *High Society*, those old hot chestnuts. One night Louis Armstrong walked in. Oh my, we fell right off the stand. He wasn't so much older than us but, Lord, that man was a hero and an inspiration. If ever music walked on feet, those feet wore Louis Armstrong's shoes, ask any musician you meet. He spoke to me and my ears rang, I'll never forget it. I was on cloud nine. He said, "I *hoid* you figuratin' there, brother. It sounded nicely. Mm-hmm, most nicely." His voice was high and soft, and I said to myself, My Lord, that's just how Mama talked. That same accent, that same sound, from New Orleans. I tell you, it put me in a terrible confusion. Consternation in syncopation, ah-ha.

Mama raised me by herself. She had a studio where she gave piano lessons, upstairs over a barber shop, and two days a week in the winter she went to Carlowsbridge and demonstrated sheet music in a department store there. Carlowsbridge was the county seat and the nearest thing I ever knew to a city when I was a boy. The town we lived in was a little place called Sand Springs. That was where I did my growing up, so you see, I'm just a country cousin after all. We lived outside of town, Mama and me, in a pretty little house in the pine woods, right next door to a big resort inn that was named The Sequantus House—Sequantus being the name of the lake—and Mama played her ragtime for the guests there. Summer was the busy time for us, when the rich people came up from New York and Philadelphia and Albany and Hartford, and some from as far

29

away as Baltimore, you know, for the scenery. Mama did an hour at noon in the sitting room by the terrace and then a longer recital in the evening around sundown in a little white bandstand on the lawn by the edge of the gardens. Seven days a week and no union man sitting on the clock. Those were peaceful times for us.

We were inn people, at least as far as the townspeople were concerned. It always struck me odd how they'd go on about the difference. Here I was, going to school in Sand Springs and running with the Sand Springs kids, and then when I got a little bigger I played on the town baseball team, and they'd say, "Oh, this here's Leon. He's from the inn," as if I was visiting from the moon or someplace. But that's how it was in a small town like that. If your granddaddy wasn't born there you were an outsider, and that's that. Sand Springs was the only town I'd ever known. I was a babe in a basket when my mama brought me there. But it was, "This here's Leon. He's from the inn," all my days. Sometimes they'd make fun of Mama's accent, too. You know how it is, kids scrapping in the schoolyard, they'll say anything that comes into their heads. They'd say, "Ah declayuh, whah's yore mumma talk so funny, Winslow?" One time a boy named Roger Calhoun said she talked like a nigger. I whipped the bejeezus out of him for that, blacked his eye and bloodied his nose, and he never said that again. If I'd had a gun, I'd have shot that boy, that Roger Calhoun. His daddy was the barber who owned the shop where Mama had her studio, and he was a hateful man, a loudmouth and a bully. He beat his wife and kids and cursed everyone in sight. Just a nasty man, he was. You had to walk through his shop to get upstairs to Mama's studio and when you did he'd stop whatever he was doing and stare at you as if he couldn't decide whether to cut you or shoot you, then when you were through and on the stairs you'd hear the crowd of idlers that loafed around there start laughing, and you'd know Calhoun or one of them had said something lowdown about you and it'd make your ears burn. I never did understand why Mama kept her studio there, but between you and me, I think she did it to put Calhoun in his place, knowing how uncomfortable it made him. She talked sweet but she had a feisty side to her, Mama did, and she could size up a person and give as good as she got.

Calhoun told me one time I had hair like nigger wool. I didn't even know what he was talking about, you understand. I'd never ever seen a black person then. We were uptight and lily white, all right, ah-ha. But I recall I was too ashamed to tell Mama what he'd said. She came out of the South when it was still fighting the Civil War and black people's lives weren't worth a plugged nickel in most white folks' eyes, but she was the most tolerant woman you'd want to meet. And she forbid me, absolutely forbid me, to use a word like nigger. The only time she ever struck me was once when I said nigger. I never saw her so upset, and I hardly knew why. Well.

Besides Mama, the only people I can remember who'd put Calhoun in his place were Uncle Pedey Donker and Henny Vaughan. Uncle Pedey was the oldest person in Sand Springs, had well over a hundred years in his tank. Next to him, Methuselah was a latecomer. His family claimed he'd fought Indians on the Ohio frontier with General William Henry Harrison, old Tippecanoe and Tyler too, and I believed it well enough. I thought he was a swell old bird. He didn't talk much, and when he did he didn't make much sense sometimes, and he smelled awful rank on a hot day, but he had all that history in him and I thought that was something. He and Mama liked each other, too. They used to flirt with each other in a nice little way, you know, saying kindly old-fashioned things. Uncle Pedey called Mama the Fairest Flower. One time he caught hold of my sleeve and told me, "Boy, the fairest flower blooms by tender light. You'll always be good to my lady, won't you?" I said, "Yes sir, Uncle Pedey, I will." Yes sir.

You used to see Uncle Pedey all the time in Calhoun's shop, sitting asleep back against the back wall in this broken-down old armchair, fighting those old battles in his dreams. He used to shout things in his sleep, things like "Women to the rear!" and

"Fire on the right, boys!" By and by, he'd wake up and tell Calhoun what a poor excuse he was, say, "You're a dog, Alfred. You're a bitch's whelp," and Calhoun would get so steamed you could see the smoke coming out of his ears. Got his goat every time, and every time Calhoun came back at him, Uncle Pedey would just cackle and pretend he didn't hear a thing, and that made Calhoun all the madder, which was just the point. You couldn't get a better show at the Bijou than Uncle Pedey and Alfred Calhoun.

Now, the only reason Uncle Pedey spent so much time in the barber shop was that that's where Henry Donker spent *his* days. Henry was Uncle Pedey's keeper, you might say, his companion. He was a great-grandson or grandnephew or somesuch and all he did for an occupation was to squire the old man around, which meant he parked him down in that old armchair while he kept company with the boys who hung around Calhoun's, the town loafing society. They drank whiskey out of pint bottles and read the pictures in the *Police Gazette* and swapped gossip and lies till suppertime. You know the kind I mean. You find those loafers in every town from Timbuktu to Kalamazoo. Henry Donker was a halfbaked-looking joker with a frog face, who wore a checkered suit and owned a Model T Ford, and he fancied himself to be so debonair, ah-ha. He got around, all right. Every Fourth of July he dressed Uncle Pedey up in this old blue uniform they had for him, that had no medals or insignia, just blue cloth and brass buttons and a wide-brimmed hat, and took him down to Carlowsbridge to ride with the veterans in the parade, and when it was over he brought him back. That's how much Henry got around, and compared to the rest of Calhoun's crowd that made him a world traveler, but he was the original square from nowhere and poor company for that nice old man.

Fourth of July in Carlowsbridge was a wonderful celebration, just wonderful. They had games and races and firemen's contests and a horse show and all kinds of food, my, I can't remember it all. Barbecue and strawberry pie. There was usually a sideshow with freaks and wild animals in pens, and a band concert playing patriotic tunes that'd make a dead man stand up and salute, it was so spirited, and then in the evening there'd be the fireworks, and that was the grandest thing of all. Color and noise that just filled up the sky, mm-hm. We kids used to go down first thing in the morning, it was a nickel ride on the trolley, for the baseball game between the Carlowsbridge team and our Sand Springs nine. In fact, the last time I went, I was playing in the outfield for the Sand Springs team. I hit a double with two men on base and knocked them both in, and we won the game. That was a lovely feeling, all right, that sweet sound when I hit that ball. I loved baseball when I was a boy. I could hit the ball a mile and, mercy, I was fast on my feet, too. And you know, that was the same day my mama was killed. It was 1919, right after the end of the First War. Mercy. Lord of mercy. The Fourth of July.

They always had the big parade at noon, with bands and floats and politicians, service groups. I guess anybody could march in it that wanted to waste shoe leather, because it seems to me there were always as many stepping along as there were watching from the sidewalk. I remember I marched myself, with a group called Major Horace Parrott's Military Boys' Band. That was where I got my first instruction on the clarinet, you see, learning the *Double Eagle* from Major Parrott, when I was ten, eleven years old. Mama tried to teach me on the piano, off and on, but it was too frustrating for both of us. I couldn't get the hang of it and didn't particularly care to, but I thought the Boys' Band was a swell idea. You know, the uniforms and all. They had little red uniform coats with gold braid on the shoulders, you see, and white hats, just like the Marine Band, and I figured that was fine as could be. Well. Major Parrott was this old windbag who'd been a tuba player at some army camp or another in the time of the Cuban War. That "Major" business was just something he'd made up, I'm sure. He used to talk about Sousa and Gilmore as if he was tight like this with them, but his idea of music was two-part and on the beat, two, three, four, everybody play loud, and at practices we spent more time marching than we did playing. He had an assistant, a boy named Lyle, who used to jump in and tap your fanny with a stick if you got out of step, but nobody said anything to you if you started playing in D when everyone else was in C. But we did get to wear the uniforms on the Fourth of July, and of course I took my little licorice stick home and practiced until the birds fell down from envy, ah-ha, look at me now. Thank you, Major Parrott.

The veterans marched right up at the head of the parade, right behind the politicians. They set Uncle Pedey in an open carriage, a landau with the top down, usually with a couple of other old warriors who were too far along to walk, and they'd take turns waving to the people, flashing their gums for the folks, and then when they got to the fairgrounds they'd hoist them out and haul them up on the stage with the politicians and the preachers and make them sit there for the speeches. Old-fashioned speechifying was a fine art in those days. You'd get one of those big-bellied old congressmen or a good Chautauqua orator and he could go on for hours, make your head ring. They had lungs like Caruso, those fellows, and they could turn a phrase and then play variations on it as good as any jazzman you ever heard. Spend an hour just telling you the sky was blue, fifty different ways in a voice like a trombone. Of course, Uncle Pedey and the other old vets slept through a good part of it. They all had some sidekick like Henry sitting behind them to make sure they didn't fall off their chairs or get up and start shufflin' and scufflin' and cause a scene, which they almost always managed to do anyway, and when they did it was the best part of the show. One old boy stood up one time in the middle of a preacher's blessing and sang *Abe Lincoln's Pappy and Stephen Douglas' Ma* all the way through, six or seven verses. They couldn't shut him down. That was a risqué tune left over from long, long ago, you know, and it had everybody blushing to hear it like that.

Uncle Pedey used to throw his ear trumpet at people. He

had one of those brass ear trumpets, practically as old as he was. It was all bent and dented, looked as if it had been chewed on by a goat. He got up and fired it at the mayor of Carlowsbridge one year and popped his hat right off his head. Another time he started waving it around like a sword, and when Henry tried to head him off Uncle Pedey clobbered him right on the chops, ah-ha, right in front of everybody. Henry Donker wore a fat lip for a week. I did like that old fool. I always figured if I had a granddaddy I'd want him to be just like Uncle Pedey. I guessed he knew exactly what he was doing, putting on the world. When you're old you can do that, you know. I do.

They finally took that old ear horn of his away from him, after he almost killed the president of the Sand Springs bank with it in Calhoun's one day. Harold Wales was the man's name, and he used to come in for his shave first thing every morning, before he unlocked the bank. One morning Uncle Pedey hollered out, "Curse you! Feel my steel!" in his sleep, dreaming those old dreams, you see, and he grabbed up his horn and threw it as hard as he could. It hit Alfred Calhoun right behind the knee and his leg buckled. Calhoun upset the shaving basin all over Wales' lap and would have cut his head clean off if he hadn't had the razor down and been wiping it off just then. He turned around and stomped on the ear trumpet, flattened it out like a penny postcard, and raised hell with Uncle Pedey for the rest of the day, which Uncle Pedey pretended not to hear, and they threw out the horn and never gave him another one. As far as the old man ever said so, he never did miss it.

Now, Henny Vaughan was one man Calhoun never gave any lip to. He had the barber buffaloed and hogtied, and when he went into the shop for his Thursday trim it was, "Yes, Mister Vaughan," and "No, sir, Mister Vaughan," and all those other clowns kept still and minded their manners while Henny was in the chair. Henny had that stamp of authority written all over him. He was a big, chesty man who always dressed well and looked spruce, smelled of Bay Rum and tobacco. Big shoulders, big hands, and he carried himself the way a big man does when he's strong and confident, you know, wrapped tight and in control. He pulled me out of the lake when I was drowning one time, and he was the nearest thing to a daddy I ever had or ever wanted when I was a boy. The happiest day of my life was the day he told me he was sweet on my mama and asked me for my permission to marry her. It never happened, and I mourn for that still. I do. I loved them both so much.

Henny Vaughan ran The Sequantus House, the inn. He didn't own it, you understand. A family named Peterson did, and just about everything else in the county too. The Petersons had mills and a wire factory and a big estate where they lived in a house that looked like a king's castle, with big stone towers you could see from the Carlowsbridge road, and they were as rich as kings. Almost everybody in Sand Springs worked for the Petersons one way or another, and they used to talk about old Antioch Peterson as if he was the Man himself. He was long dead and gone, but the way they talked about him around Sand Springs, it was as if he'd just stepped out to grab a taste and was coming right back to take the next chorus. I saw Mister Edgar Peterson one time in my own parlor. He was old Antioch's son, and when I was little he came to visit one afternoon and sat down in the parlor and chatted with Mama like as he was a neighbor come to call. I was somewhat impressed by that, but Mama said it wasn't such a much, you know, and they were just talking inn business, she said, because he owned the inn. She said I shouldn't mention it about and I don't think I ever did. Edgar Peterson wasn't well spoken of, not like his daddy, though I recall he struck me as a kindly man with a soft voice.

Henny had a voice like a big old baritone saxophone with that nice Harry Carney sound, so deep and smooth. He'd grown up in New York and his daddy had worked in hotels before him, and he knew the business top and bottom. I used to follow him around the inn every chance I got, and there was nothing about the place that if it broke he couldn't fix it with his own hands and knowhow, no matter if it was the generator or the plumbing or a button come off the bellboy's uniform. The Petersons may have owned that inn, sure enough, but it was Henny's place and everybody knew that, because he lived and breathed it, and when I was a boy I wanted to be just like him. And he was always so nice to me, took me right under his wing as if I was his own and gave me the run of the place and answered all my questions. By the time I was sixteen, that last summer, I'd done just about every job there, starting out as a little message boy carrying notes around for the guests on a silver tray. I had a little uniform I wore and one of those little round hats with a strap under my chin, like the Philip Morris fellow, and I carried the messages and went up and down the halls ringing the bell for the dining room seatings. Mama said I looked like an organ grinder's monkey in my little outfit. But I worked in the kitchen and in the yard, too, and all over that big old place, and I was happy as could be, you see, because I was working for Henny Vaughan.

I remember one summer my job included having to go up on the roof and raise the flag every morning, and then bring it down in the evening. There was a little platform where the flagpole stood, way up on the roofpeak above the entrance, five stories up, and to get there you climbed up a ladder from one of the storerooms in the attic and through a trap door. It was like being on a mountaintop, where you could see for miles out across the lake and the hills. That was a thrill. I liked to sit up there in the evening with my back against the flagpole and watch the sun go down, see the lake get all smooth and silver and the hills turn purple, and then the fireflies would come out, millions of little lightning bugs like stars in the fields, mm-hmm. The bellhops would light the paper lanterns in the gardens and I could watch the guests strolling around down below, wearing their light-colored summer clothes, looking so fine, oh my, and I could hear my mama's ragtime, ringing sweet as a bell, so clear at twilight time. Then someone would strike the gong on the side terrace, and that was the signal that the day was over, officially, you know, and Mama would finish up with a little blue-sounding cadenza she always played and everyone would go indoors and play cards or read or whatever the rich folks did after dark. But every so often I liked to stay up there until the last light was gone out of the day and there was nothing but me and the stars, and nobody else around outside the inn except back by the garages, where the chauffeurs sat around in their undershirts and drank beer and told their stories or tried to sweet-talk the kitchen maids into taking a walk in the moonlight along the lake shore. But I was floating along up there above them, all by myself alone, and I did like that feeling.

You know, when you die, or more likely while you're dying, you experience that floating feeling, and it's really quite peaceful. It's restful and pleasurable and there's no pain. I did that, you see. Yes, I did. When I was a boy back there, and no more than twelve, thirteen years old, I fell through the ice on the lake and I was a goner. By the time Henny found me and pulled me out I'd passed right over to the other side, and then Mama brought me back, using some herbs and an old voodoo root from New Orleans. Now, that's something not everyone lives to see. I'll tell you about it.

It was early in the morning and I was supposed to be on my way to school. I was supposed to go by the inn and see Henny and give him a message for Mama and then I was supposed to take myself in to school and do my reading and writing and 'rithmetic, you understand, and no messing about. But it was one of those days when I just couldn't get down to it, and I was cussing and fussing and dawdling all along the way. There'd been a nice little snowstorm overnight and that was always a magical time to see, when it was all fresh and shining in the sun, still lying on the trees and no tracks in the road. You felt like as you were the first person to put your feet on that ground, like an explorer from the days of old, or old Commodore Peary looking for the North Pole, you know, whipping up the dogs and eating seal blubber. But then when your feet

38

got cold you could go home and Mama'd give you a cup of hot cocoa, and that was even better than seal blubber.

Now, it was a good three-mile walk to school for me along the lake road and then down the Sand Springs road, and if I went on up to the inn that added a little more to the trip, so I took off early that morning, all wrapped up in my boots and mittens and my little wool cap and scarf, because it was a cold morning. When I got out to the Sand Springs road my little friend Ripley was out there waiting for me by the corner. His house was just down the way and we used to walk in together. Ripley Threadgill. His daddy was a motorman on the trolley that ran between Sand Springs and Carlowsbridge, and I used to think that was an exciting thing to do, and Ripley was a timid kid and I used to boss him around and get him into scrapes because I was bigger, you know, and more adventurous than him, and then he'd go home and his daddy would fan his britches, ah-ha, as if he was a regular little scoundrel. Poor little old Ripley.

So I said, "Ripley, let's go take a look at the lake and see how the ice is this morning." It had just started freezing over a couple of weeks before, and we had strict orders, I mean strict, to stay off it until our folks said it was okay, but with the new snow lying on it it looked so solid and smooth, and we went down to the shore there beside the road and I tested it with my foot, and it felt all right to me. The snow was all powdery and light on it and the ice was slick as could be, and after I'd run my little foot back and forth on it without really stepping out onto it, I went ahead and pushed off and did a little skid, almost like as it was an accident, you know, saying, "Whoops, how'd that happen?"

Well, Ripley was being his timid self and saying, "We shouldn't ought to do this," and, "We're gonna be late to school," whining like that, and I was showing off for him, cutting up, so I got back up on the shore and took a running start and jumped out on the ice, whee, waving my arms and whooping and slipping off as if I was going to slide all the way across the lake, only when I got to maybe ten yards out from the shore and I started to slow down I started hearing cracking noises. Uh-oh. All around me, like eggshells, rat-a-tat, and before I could figure out what to do about that, all of a sudden the ice turned sideways on me and I was in the water with no place to go. The last thing I recollect is that I was lying on my back pressed up underneath the ice, floating, you know, with my face shoved against it like a one-eyed cat peepin' in the seafood store. The water felt like fire on my skin and I must have taken a mouthful as I went in, because my lungs and my belly were burning too, and in my head it was roaring like a locomotive. Everything got very gray all around me and started turning darker and darker and fading away, and I remember I felt a rising sensation, as if I was being lifted up very slowly, just drifting up through a cloud, and then I heard a soft tone, sweet and musical like a little silver chime ringing.

Now, everything has its note, you know. If you take and strike a tree you'll get back a sound and that sound is that tree's note. You blow across a bottle, you get the tone that belongs to that bottle, and no other bottle sounds quite the same. That's why a player will spend years looking for the right horn. That's why you have to trim and shape your reeds, because you're looking for that note, that tone, that sounds best to you, and somebody else's tone just doesn't wear comfortable. The only way I can explain what happened to me then as I was getting away under the ice is to say I heard my note, my very own, and then I became my note. That's what dying was like for me. I became a sound.

It was pure and perfect, my note. It had no echo and no distortion, no overtone, no measure. It was just the essence of one note, drawn as fine as a hair, fine as the dust you see in a sunbeam, and it filled me right up and carried me off. It spread me across the universe. I melted. I didn't have any weight or shape or size. I was everywhere. I was the *sky*. Mercy, but it was a bliss, and not so much as a tiny bit of pain or fear or confusion.

And then it all changed and it got very rough for a while. Very rough and painful. I felt as if I was being dragged over sharp stones and pounded on by big hammers, felt a huge weight pressing on my chest. My note just broke up and disappeared, and there was an awful rumbling going on, like an avalanche, and hot lava running down my throat, things clutching and scraping at me, hellacious things that I couldn't get away from because I was lost and had no idea which way to turn. Everything was black and in the blackness were things I couldn't see, because they were as black as everything else, but I knew they meant to do me harm. It was a nasty time, and all I wanted was to get back on my note. I don't know how long it lasted. It could have been a minute or a month, you know, because time had gotten away from me altogether, but after a while it started to fade away and then my note popped back into view again, said "How d'you do," and I was so happy then.

But it was different, you see. This was a different stage, a different movement, because I didn't just feel my note but I could look at it, too, as if I was floating along beside it and it was leading me someplace. Everywhere around me it was gray and white and empty and my note was a little blue line that ran off into the distance, out beyond where I could see, but as I floated along after it the light changed and took on a rosy color and a smoky texture. It seemed to swirl and throb as I drifted through it and my note seemed to thicken and blur, and it looked as though it would be soft to touch, but I still had no body, nothing to touch it with. And then it split apart, all along its length, just like that, and where there had been one note there were two. One of them was still my note, but the second was not, and it began to wind around mine and weave back and forth, making harmony and pulling my note away from its line, so that it became a melody. The two notes wrapped themselves around me and tickled me and spun me around, and I could feel myself tumbling, and when the second note danced away I followed after it and coaxed my own note along with me. I ran to keep up with it and my breath got short and heavy in my chest. The sound of my breathing filled my ears, and the sound of my pulse got louder and louder behind it. The rhythm of it pounded on me, pounded, pounded, pounded until I had to shout, and that's when I woke up, shouting.

I found myself in my own bed, in my little room upstairs, and it was nighttime outside my window and the lamp was lit. My bed had been moved away from the wall, out into the center of the room, and Mama was sitting on the edge of it, squeezing my hand and looking so concerned. She was wearing one of her gowns and her hair was up on top of her head, the way she did it when she went to play at the inn, but she looked softened and weary and her lower lip was swollen, like as she'd been chewing on it, and there was no mistaking how worried she'd been for me. "Merciful glory," were the first words she said, "I have you back."

"Oh, Mama," I said, "I dreamed I was flying. Was I sick?" You see, I didn't remember the ice at all. I felt very sleepy and my mouth was dry as if I was coming off a fever, and my fingers and my toes ached somewhat in that way that's almost pleasurable to feel, and I didn't have a notion how I'd come to be there then.

"You were a long, long way away from me, darlin'," Mama said. She bent over and hugged me for a long time, and then she pulled back and stared at me with a funny look on her face. She looked as though she was listening to something far away, and she said, "Did you see any faces in your dream? Did you see any people?"

"I don't think so," I said, because I was in too much of a confusion to put it all together. All that I could say was, "I was flying."

Then Mama said a strange thing that's never been any plainer to me in all the years I've thought about it. She said, "They've found us now, darlin', but I swear they'll never take you from me. It's my pain they're after," she said, "and I swear upon my heart they can have it, but they'll never have you." And then she turned her head away with that same listening look on her face and she raised up her shoulders and pulled her neck in, as if she was waiting for a blow to fall on her, and when I dropped off to sleep she was still sitting there, looking just like that. I've had fifty years to think about it, you know, and I don't know to this day who they were or what they wanted with my mama's pain. Truth be told, I don't think I'll ever find out.

Chapter Three

High Society

Some people say you don't belong in Sand Springs until you've buried three generations of your family in the cemetery up behind the Congregational Church. Put that way, it makes us sound quaint, but there's a grain of truth in it. The fact is, there aren't that many people who've wanted to come here and settle since our grandparents' time. Hasn't been any reason to. Still isn't.

You see, when we say that Mrs. Winslow was an outsider to us, that doesn't reflect against her. It's a statement of fact. She wasn't born here, didn't have people from around here, she wasn't a Sand Springs woman. She lived up by the lake, in the Collins house. Collins was a Connecticut man, an artist, had some money from his family. He wanted to paint by the lake, so he built up there. Hired Asa Tilden, Orrie Tilden's father, and they built the house together, Collins and Asa Tilden. Good job they did of it, too; stone foundation, clapboards and a shingle roof. Two stone chimneys. His second year there we had a short winter. We were cutting hay in November and didn't get a solid freeze until after New Year's. The lake never did ice over in the middle that year. Didn't snow much, either, but it did rain. Rained an awful lot. Collins caught pneumonia that winter and died of it. Then Antioch Peterson bought up the property as part of the same parcel he put the inn on.

Mrs. Winslow bought it from the Peterson Trust. Edgar Peterson didn't give it to her, she paid cash money for it, notes and gold coins. She brought them to the bank in a valise and they passed the papers in Harold Wales' office. The house was hers, free and clear. None of us had ever seen a woman with that much cash money before. Some of the things that were said about her then, that was why. That and Edgar Peterson's car.

It couldn't have been easy for her, living out there with just the boy. She made her own way and we respected her for it. Even Alfred Calhoun came to respect her, though it would have killed him to admit it. If she had an enemy in this town, it was Alfred Calhoun, right from the first day she came into his shop, but that wasn't her doing. It was Alfred and his cussedness. She just wanted to rent the room upstairs.

It was something to see. She marched right in without hesitating for a second, and before Alfred could say anything she was there in front of him with her head up and her hand out. Said, "Mister Calhoun, I am Missus Winslow. Good morning to you, sir, and good day," with an accent we'd never heard in these parts before. When Alfred held back his hand she grabbed it anyway and gave it a solid pump. Then she let go of it and he gaped at it as if he'd just discovered an extra finger there. We'd never seen the like. She was an awful pretty woman, short and on the plump side. Had big dark eyes and dimples when she smiled, too, but that wasn't what drew your eye to her. It was the way she stood, as if she was taller than she was, and the way she looked a man in the eye, businesslike. Not hard, but serious. We weren't used to women who could deal with men like that. "I am told, Mister Calhoun, that you have a room to let," she said.

Alfred Calhoun had said time and again that any damn woman who ever set foot in his shop would get tossed out on her bustle, but now he just cleared his throat and shuffled his feet and looked flustered. Mrs. Winslow waited on him a bit, and when he didn't speak she said, "I require a studio, Mister Calhoun. I give lessons on the piano, and it's necessary that I have a studio in a central location. You can imagine how pleased I was to hear that your room upstairs was available. Could I see it please, Mister Calhoun?"

Alfred kept giving her little sideways glances, as if he was shy, and when he did speak it was in a softer voice than any of us could recall. "Well, ma'am," he said. "Well, it's—" "It's right upstairs, isn't it?" she said to him. "Yes, ma'am, it is," he admitted, as if it was a hard thing to say. She smiled at him then as if he'd just done something wonderful for her. "Why," she said, "that's just exactly what I'd heard." In her accent the word came out *hoid*.

Calhoun snuck a look around then to make sure no one was having a laugh at his expense, but he couldn't muster up the gumption to come back at her with his usual meanness. She was watching him closely, you see, and when it looked like he was working up to it she just headed him off. Asked, "Is the room locked?" "No, ma'am," he said, "it is not locked, but—" "Then I can let myself in," she said, "and I won't take you from your business. I'm certain you are a busy man, Mister Calhoun. Is that the way there?" She pointed to the door in the rear of the shop, next to Uncle Pedey's chair. "Yes, ma'am," Alfred said, "but—" "Then please continue doing whatever it is you have to do," she said. "I thank you." And she marched right off toward the stairs.

When she got to Uncle Pedey, though, she stopped and tilted her head to him and gave him a big smile. Said, "Good morning to you, sir, and good day," in a friendlier way than anyone had spoken to the old relic in years.

Now, the minute she'd set foot in the shop Uncle Pedey had sat bolt upright in his chair like a rooster at daybreak and opened his eyes so wide they nearly fell out in his lap, and when she spoke to him he smiled back at her pert as could be.

If he'd had any teeth in his head, he'd have shown them all with that smile. And he spoke up loud and clear to her. Said, "Peter Benjamin Donker, madam. Forgive me for not standing, but age has shamed these limbs of mine."

"Why, don't give it a thought, Mister Donker," Mrs. Winslow said back to him. "Your gallant manner stands tall in your stead." She held out her hand for him and he grasped it between his own bony paws and grinned like a fiend. "Madam," he said, "you are the fairest flower to grace these fields since Jonah was a cabin boy. I am at your service."

She withdrew her hand gently from his. "I would not hesitate to call upon you, Mister Donker," she said, and gave him a smile that actually made the old man blush down to the roots of his whiskers. When she had passed through and up the stairs he slumped back down in his chair, but the fire stayed on his cheek, and he hooted, "By damn, that's a woman, boys." For a little while you could almost see the young man he must have been.

The rest of us who were there held our tongues, though. We just watched back and forth between the ceiling, where we could hear her footsteps, and Alfred Calhoun, who was looking around like a man whose pocket has just been picked. After a minute, Bob Marshall made a noise that started out like a snicker, but it turned into a cough when Alfred rounded on him with a look you could strike a match on, and then we all got busy with our newspapers and *Police Gazettes* until she came back downstairs.

She didn't waste any time dickering. Said, "It needs a cleaning, Mister Calhoun, but I shall see to that myself. I will put a carpet on the floor and curtains on the window, and that should keep the music from intruding upon you. My intention is to use the room only on Tuesdays and Thursdays and only during the daylight hours, however I shall pay you the full weekly rent for it. Will two dollars be sufficient?"

Alfred flared his nostrils at her and looked apoplectic and said nothing, but she nodded as if he'd spoken. "Very well, then," she said, "let's make it two dollars and fifty cents. I shall pay you each Tuesday morning for the following week." She dug in her purse and came up with money and held it out to him. "Is it settled, then?" she said.

Calhoun made a show of reluctance but he took the money and said, "It is settled," in a miserable voice. He glared at her like a wet hen. All he got in return was a smile. "I'm very pleased," Mrs. Winslow said. "I shall be in to clean it tomorrow and have the furnishings sent around on Friday. If you need to reach me, I shall be at the inn. I trust the arrangement will be no inconvenience to you, Mister Calhoun." She took his hand and pumped it once, and said, "Good morning to you and good day." Waved to Uncle Pedey and then she was gone. Left us shaking our heads and fanning our cheeks like maidens under the mistletoe.

Alfred Calhoun just stood there for the longest time. Stared at the money in his hand and ground his jaws till the muscles at their corners swelled up like walnuts. Finally someone said, "Well, Alfred, it looks like you've got yourself a musical conservatory here," and then we started to laugh. There was a justice in it that we couldn't deny. Alfred Calhoun had been browbeating our women for as long as he'd been in Sand Springs. He abused his own wife and slandered the entire sex. So it was satisfying to see him overwhelmed that way by one small, pretty female who had the gumption to stand up and look him in the eye. It was. We had a good laugh on Alfred.

He stood there and took it, too, and it didn't please him a bit. After a while, though, he closed his fist around the money and shook it at the door. "God damn it, boys," he said. "God damn it, don't you see? I had to take it. That's a Peterson woman. That's Edgar Peterson's whore, damn her. She come to town in his car and she's working at his inn." Uncle Pedey chose that moment to snort like a stallion on the rut and sing out, "The fairest flower, lads, in all the land." Calhoun turned on the old trooper and shook his fist at him, too. "You stupid old coon," he said. "I'd have taken the two dollars for it. Hell," he grinned, "I'd have taken a dollar!"

"If you thought it was Peterson money, Alfred, why didn't you hold out for five, or ten?" Bob Marshall asked him. All Alfred said was, "You son of a bitch."

Even in the beginning, not everyone believed it was Edgar Peterson's auto that she arrived in. It looked like his, all right, but we saw so few autos in those days that one looked about the same as another to us. We only saw it the one time, when she stepped out of it at the inn. It left her there and that was that, a black auto. A woman who had enough cash to buy a house outright would have had enough to hire an auto. It was the cash, now, that got people talking. What kind of woman has that kind of money? we asked ourselves. The answers weren't flattering. But then, once we got to know her we put that kind of talk aside. She was a widow, after all. We figured the money was settled on her out of her husband's estate, and most of us clean forgot about the car, until the recent business with the detectives and the accident. What Orrie Tilden saw and heard up in the woods. But that's getting ahead of the story.

Alfred Calhoun kept on talking badly about her, of course. "Widow?" he'd say. "That hussy's never been a wife." But that was Alfred. He'd nurse a grudge all the way to the grave. If it ever came down to it, we'd have taken her side against him any day. Alfred Calhoun was a hard man to like. Still is.

We liked her. She always seemed cheerful and never too busy to stop and say hello and how d'you do. She had a friendly manner and a way of speaking you might call musical. Her voice was pleasant and once we got used to it her accent didn't seem at all strange. She dealt fairly, too. She sold us so many pianos Lou Berde should have made her a partner in the store, and then she taught the women and kids to play on them, but only those that wanted to and could afford it. Fair enough. It spruces up the parlor considerably, a piano. Before she came along the only people here who had them were the schoolmistress and Harold Wales. Schoolmistress had to know how to play, that was part of her job. As for Harold, nobody ever heard him play a note.

But that's off the point. The point is, she got on fine here. The boy, Leon, was a good boy, and that spoke well for her too. He went to the town school, played with our kids, grew up tall and strong and hard-working. No airs to him, and no more sass than you find in any boy. He could run like a deer and hit a baseball halfway to Carlowsbridge, and by the time he was sixteen he was playing on the town team, outfield and first base. But for all that, they weren't town people, either one of them. We never knew her as anything but Mrs. Winslow. There wasn't a person in town who was close enough to her to call her by her first name, Lady. They were inn people, her and the boy. Not town people; inn people.

Those that don't know any better always make the mistake of thinking the inn's part of the town, but it's not so. They're worlds apart. Sand Springs people work up at the inn, that's true. Work down in Carlowsbridge, too, or wherever else Petersons want them to work, and then they come home to Sand Springs at night. It wasn't always that way, but that's the way it's been since Antioch Peterson came and went. Hadn't been for Antioch Peterson, we'd all be farmers still and probably a damn sight happier, too. But then, maybe not. Antioch Peterson gave us plenty to think about, and plenty to see.

Antioch Peterson built the inn, The Sequantus House. He didn't live long enough to set foot inside it, but it was his inn, make no mistake. Still is. Built it with its back to the town, facing northwestward out over the lake. His inn. He damn sure didn't build it for us. Built it for his rich friends and the people like them. We can watch them driving through town on their way up there, straight out Main Street all the way to the lake. They ride through in big touring cars with nigger drivers, don't even look at us as they go by. Big fat people, stiff as statues. We eat their dust all summer. Get out there, all they do is sit and play cards and read the New York or Philadelphia newspapers that come up on the train a day late. Sometimes they get up off their chairs and walk around in the gardens, but the thing they do most is just sit. Lord knows, they didn't get rich that way, sitting around reading day-old newspapers. If that was all it takes to get rich the crowd that hangs around Calhoun's would be Rockefellers.

Antioch Peterson built the inn and then brought in people from outside to run it, just like his farm and factories and everything else. Vaughan the manager and the French cooks and the young Scotsman who gives the golfing lessons and the other fellow who runs the boats and Mrs. Cleary the housekeeper, they all came from outside. We got what work was left over. Washing dishes and toting bags and laundering the sheets and mowing the lawn, that was our lot. The kind of jobs where the rich people can pretend they don't see you. Alfred Calhoun hasn't been right very often in his life, but when he called those jobs nigger work he had it on the button. Right from the beginning, Antioch Peterson made niggers of us every chance he got.

Before he came we were farmers and always had been. Our grandparents, and their parents before them, carved their farms out of a rocky landscape in hard seasons and left them to us. The history of this place is told in the stone walls they built, miles and miles of them. More stones in those walls than there're acorns in the trees, and all those stones came out of the ground our families cleared to work. Pulled them out of the ground like surgeons pulling shot out of a wound and stacked them up mile after mile in walls a Chinaman would envy, and they still didn't get them all. Made no difference if you only had a single acre that'd been worked a hundred years, at least once a week you'd bust your plow on a rock that wasn't there the day before. If you're a farmer the earth's supposed to be your partner. Around here it was more like a chiseling brother-in-law, mean and full of secrets. It fought back at you every day of your life, sunup to sundown. We kept on fighting it because it was what we'd always done. It was what we had.

Then Antioch Peterson came along in the early spring and

beat the land flat. Took four hundred acres that nobody in his right mind would ever have thought to use for anything but hunting or hiding in, steep hillside land covered with thick woods and shot through with boulders, and in a month he whipped it flat. A God-damn month. Everything we'd ever done, everything we'd ever known, was wrong. That was Antioch Peterson.

Since before that winter there'd been talk that somebody had been buying land on the hills east of the river, between Sand Springs and Carlowsbridge. Then as soon as the thaw came they laid a rail spur up from Carlowsbridge along the east bank of the river, across from the road, and one night two freight trains came and parked right alongside that acreage and sat there, hissing and grumbling until just before dawn, when they started unloading.

A bunch of uniformed men wearing sidearms and carrying lanterns and clubs jumped down and started blowing whistles and shouting and beating on the sides of the boxcars, making a God-awful racket in the mist that rises off the river there. The first thing they did was get the machines unloaded off the flatcars. We'd never seen machines like those, tall black engines with huge iron wheels and fireboxes on them like blast furnaces, and covered with pulleys and straps and chains. All manner of scoops and plows hanging from them front and rear, and devices that looked like big iron jawbones with jagged teeth, spikes and augers stuck on them. Hellish-looking machines, like factories on wheels.

Then there were the workmen, an army of them. All sizes and shapes and colors. They'd ridden in the boxcars. Most of them were dressed in city clothes and shoes and none of their stuff looked choice or cared for. For every one of them who was built for laboring there were three or four who seemed sickly or feeble and flinched when the sunlight fell on them. Of those that spoke at all, some talked with foreign accents or in foreign words, but most of them just stood around and said nothing to anyone. They were dregs, immigrants and colored men. They had dented hats and torn shoes and no teeth. Antioch Peterson must have emptied every flophouse and park bench in New York to recruit them, and until the uniformed men told them what to do they just stood in the gravel beside the trains, scratching under their clothes and spitting on the ground. Before the sun had cleared the trees that morning they'd been given food and coffee and turned loose on the land with orders to clear and level everything between the river and the farthest hills, and they did.

They ate and slept in a camp right there beside the track. Those that washed themselves did it in the river. From sunup to sundown they cleared brush and felled trees and blasted stumps. They pulled roots and dug rocks, and between them and the machines they knocked down and chewed up everything on those hills that wasn't soil. The birds and animals fled as if they were running from fire. If a man among them sickened he was taken away in a wagon. He wasn't replaced or heard from again.

None of them complained or tried to quit, either, and for good reason. The second morning a couple of the foreigners started shouting at each other while they were standing in line outside the food tent, yelling in their own language and shoving each other around. Whatever it was about, they worked it up to punching and wrestling on the ground, and one bit through the other's ear and the other gouged the first one's eye and there was blood flowing. Everyone else pretended not to notice. Finally one of them got his hand on a stone and dented the other's head. Stood up and dusted himself off, spat on the loser, looked pleased with himself, ready to take on the world. One of those uniformed men stepped up and put his pistol next to the fellow's head and shot him, just like that. Blew his brains out. After that there was no fighting or complaining, precious little talk of any kind. Most of them seemed to be silent by nature anyway; the rest kept themselves silent as if they'd taken a vow. It made for more unpleasantness. A tree fell and squashed a man flat because nobody'd spoken to warn him. A section of root from a dynamited stump pierced a man's chest because nobody'd said, "Duck." The dead were taken away on the same wagon as the sick.

We could see it all from the Carlowsbridge road, the whole show. That was when we started watching the Petersons. Seems like we haven't stopped since. If there's one thing we know about, it's Petersons and their kind. They never tried to hide a thing from us. Guess they thought it didn't matter if we saw or not. We didn't exactly stop and stare, because of those guards, those thugs in uniforms he had, but we watched, all right. We watched those city men and those huge machines. They toiled like ants, and they skinned the land. Peeled it bare, as if it was a carcass. Then they cut the tops right off the hills and filled the gulleys with them, so those acres sloped with a nice, gentle roll right down to the river's edge.

Lord, we didn't know what to believe when we saw what he'd done. Here we were, we'd been breaking our backs on this land for two, three, four generations. It was what we knew. He made it look so damn easy the way he shoved it around with his silent army and his machines, as if it was nothing but sand. When they were finished they loaded the machines back on the flatcars and the men got back in the boxcars and between night and morning they went away. Gone. And the seedlings were already raising their heads to the sun.

Then he came. Antioch Peterson.

A new train came up the spur, only two cars, and he stepped down and before he had both feet on the ground we knew it was him. We'd never seen him, his name was only a rumor to us, but there was no mistaking him. He was a big man, a massive man, big as a bear and booted to the knee. There was a crowd of men with him, managers and foremen and architects and accountants, and when he marched away from the train and out across his new meadows they followed along like geese, taking three steps to his one. When he paused, they clustered around him and nodded and cackled and wheezed at everything he said.

He'd designed it so that the hills rose like sloping steps away from the river, and when he reached the highest of them he turned and looked back down on it all and he said, "By damn, I do like it. I like it fine." People who were there said you could hear his voice clear across the river, said it rumbled like an engine. They said the sun behind his big square head made him look as if he was ringed with fire that morning, and when he gestured with his hand you could feel the wind of its movement. His architects and accountants scribbled in little notebooks and his foremen kicked the earth, and when he pointed down along the river his tannery began to take shape, and further along his woolen mill and his wire factory. He spread his hand out toward the horizon where cattle would fill his fields, and with his index finger he drew the roads and railroad tracks and electrical wires to come. Then he turned his back to the river and looked down into the glen behind the farthest hill and with both hands he molded and shaped his castle, and the next time he came it was there, just behind the ridge of the hill, so that all we could ever see of it from the Carlowsbridge road was the peak of the roof and the tip of the tower. He could stand there on the tower then and take it all in, from the lake in the north to the factory smokestacks in the south, and know it was all his.

That was Antioch Peterson.

When his factories opened we left the land and went to work for him without a second thought. We figured, you see, it was the way to learn his power. He'd chosen us and our land and he'd shown us his power, and we were flattered and thankful for the demonstration. We figured, working for him we'd find out the secret of that power, share in its rewards. We never did, never have. Some folks are still looking for it, though, looking for him. If you ask how come we know so much about the Petersons, that's why. Sand Springs has spent two generations' time keeping a watch out for Antioch Peterson.

When he died all of his holdings passed on to something called the Peterson Trust. None of us knew what a trust was, of course, but we looked for him in it. Figured it was probably a collection of parts that, if you put them all together, would measure up to him. Walk with his long, swaggering stride, talk with his bellowing voice. We watched his managers, his foremen, his farmers, all those he brought in from outside. His farmers, yes. We belonged to this land, knew it waking and sleeping, but did he hire us to tend his fields and stock? No sir, it was outside people. Germans and Swedes, big blond people who didn't smile much or sing, and he gave them houses on his acres and a schoolhouse for their children and a chapel with a German-speaking pastor. He took us instead to work in his castle, cooking and cleaning, and in his factories and his inn. We hoped it was because he believed we were too good to work the land any longer. We were likely for better things, we hoped. For a time we didn't call it nigger work. Then we did, but by then he'd been paying us regular wages and we'd gotten used to taking our pay. He'd given us a streetcar line that ran right past the gates of his mills, too, and an electrical generating station to light our houses and a telephone exchange and so many other things that tied us to him. When he died we looked for him in all of them.

All we ever found were pale shadows of him. For instance, there was the manager of the Peterson Trust, a man named Mr. Fitzroy Bobwit. He'd been one of the geese stumbling over Antioch Peterson's footprints when he'd walked his land that first time. Bobwit had Antioch Peterson's purse strings, but that was all. He was one of those thin-lipped little fellows who's forty years old at birth and never gets any younger, a little bald noggin and eyes dry as dust. Used to come up from the city twice a year to visit the Peterson properties and look over the books. Had an office in the tannery where they filled his inkwell every morning even when he wasn't there. Had a meanness to him, but not power.

More to the point, there was Henny Vaughan. The manager at the inn. First time we saw him we thought there might be something of Antioch Peterson there. He was a big, broad fellow with a deep chest, big hands. Had a look about him. The same square-sided shape to his head, same strong chin. Not the same power, though. There was weight to Henny Vaughan, and strength, but not power, not power enough. Vaughan's eyes tended to be cool and watchful, where Antioch Peterson's had been hot. Vaughan's voice didn't roar in our ears. He was a manager, and that was all.

And finally, there was Edgar Peterson, and he was the least of them. And that takes us back to Mrs. Winslow.

PART II:
NEW ORLEANS
1887–1902

Chapter Four

Devil Dance Blues

In the morning before daybreak, while the night mists lingered upon the streets and alleys of New Orleans in swirling clouds tinged with perfumed sweat and coal smoke and the vapors of brandy and river mud, Mimi Beaudette would wrap her shoulders in a black shawl and put her little straw hat on her head; after taking a last look in at her sleeping daughter and uttering a brief specific against any malign spirits that might be abroad at that hour, she would drag her shallow wooden cart from the pathway beside her house and tow it away to the wealthy quarters where the rich white people lived in brick mansions behind tall wrought-iron gates. Her cart had big iron wheels that clattered on the paving stones and an iron axle that chirped like a piccolo in the damp early air, a sound which sang to little Alice every morning in her sleep and made her smile as she burrowed deeper into the soft, spring-scented pillows of her bed.

Mimi Beaudette was a washerwoman and seamstress, a small, chubby Creole woman with skin the color of walnut shells and strong, stubby hands which had been discolored by the dyes and tinctures and caustic soaps of her trade, and every morning she called at the kitchens of her rich white clients. There the housemaids awaited her with bundles of soiled linens and faded silks, spotted muslins and stained calicos and matted velvet and raveled lace for Mimi to cleanse and restore. "See, darling," she said to little Alice, pointing to a dark red stain the size of a cabbage leaf on a linen tablecloth, "now, this here's a claret, that they drunk so much of it they lost the feeling in their fingers and the glass fell down from their hand, and somewhere there's a coat sleeve or a trouser leg with as much of it again. And look there"—her finger moved along to a cluster of purple spots—"that's ripe cherries, where they set down the pits." She touched a purple spot with the tip of her tongue. "Mmm, cherries and sweet cream. La, the rich folks, how they do."

By now the sun had risen above the rooftops on the other side of Angelus and the mists had turned to thin vapor; chickens scratched in the dirt street and ships' horns were groaning on the riverfront, and on the next block a clarinet student was attempting a scale, without tone or tempo. Mimi did her washwork in the fenced-in yard behind her little brown house, out in the open where the chinaberry and the smoke tree grew out of ground that had long ago turned yellow under the rinse of soapy water tipped from the washtubs and the black iron cauldron which simmered in a shallow pit on a bed of burning coals, and the sounds of New Orleans swam in the humid air all around.

Mimi's work table was constructed from four bleached planks nailed together and laid across four short-legged sawhorses; beneath the table squatted an apothecary's inventory of jars, cans, pots, packets and casks containing hard and soft soaps, vinegar, turpentine, potash, quicklime, pearl ash, glue, soda, Poland starch, hartshorn, chalk, potato water, ox gall, ammonia salts, oil of vitriol—all manner of herbs, extracts, lotions, acids and powders, her allies and her weapons in the daily contest she waged against the traces of human carelessness and excess. "*Dirt*," she snorted to Alice, pronouncing it in the local way: *doit*. "If it was nothing except *dirt* your mama could go dancing every afternoon and fish fry on the weekend. If it was only *dirt* I could scare it off saying BooHoo, like I chase a chicken off of the stoop. Darling, if you're rich you never touches *dirt;* you got the servants to keep the dirt away. You take this here now." She indicated a sallow patch on the same tablecloth. "This isn't dirt; it's grease, and most likely from the fat goose, account of it's so pale to look at." She groped under the table until she found a cube of white chalk, which she grated with a short-bladed knife over the stain until the stain was hidden beneath a layer of white dust. Then she covered the dust with a piece of brown paper. The flatiron which had been sitting up beside the fire proved too hot to her thumb's test, so she set it to cool on the end of the table while she dabbed at the cherry stains with a sponge moistened in citric acid. Then, when it had cooled sufficiently, she drew the iron across the brown paper three times, peeled back the paper and brushed off the chalk dust. The grease stain was gone from the linen tablecloth. She sprinkled the claret stain with a mixture of lime and spirits of ammonia, rinsed it in cold water and sprinkled it once more, then gathered up the tablecloth and dropped it into a soaking tub. Turning to the cauldron she picked up a wooden paddle and stirred the heavy pudding of cotton bedsheets simmering there, then moved on to another tub to begin scrubbing a bright damask shawl.

Mimi worked without haste or hesitation, trudging back and forth across the yard with the rolling, short-legged gait of a strolling porcupine from table to pump to tub to cauldron, always in motion as she rubbed and scrubbed and beat and twisted, stretched and ironed, wielding her paddles and sticks, her dolls, her hooks, her brushes and spoons, hopping up onto a three-legged stool to reach high over the clotheslines strung between the top of the fence and the ends of the skinned poles planted in the yellowed ground, and bending low to poke the coals beneath the bulging cannibal cauldron, and little Alice, her fair skin shaded by an old straw hat, padded happily along behind her or sat among the fallen blossoms beneath the chinaberry tree looking up at the empty garments dancing on the clotheslines, and the linens and sheets and curtains which billowed and snapped like shining sails in the clear, golden sunlight. The sound of her mother's voice purred in Alice's ears to divert and reassure her, spoken low and gentle as downy foam in the soft, plangent accents of Creole New Orleans, the sound of a banjo with velvet strings plucked by the warm breezes that blew all the way from Africa to the Caribbean Sea. "Your granddaddy was an island Frenchman," Mimi told her, "with teeth so strong he could bite through iron, and when my mama was a little girl she sat on a satin chair at the Opera and saw a lady ride upon a dromedary that came from all the way to Abyssinia. La, but the times was better then." Her recollections of the better times were recounted without rancor, and if the present was a burden to her she bore it altogether cheerfully, and palliated its disappointments with chuckling and song.

> The Queen of France has golden hair,
> And tiny feet and skin so fair;
> She sits at her table in a silver chair,
> Tipi ton ton my darling.

She sang softly to Alice in the backyard, silly rhymes about birds and animals and kings and queens, things of a sort never seen on the dusty little street called Angelus, and sometimes she would stop in the middle of a task and take Alice's hands in hers, and together they would dance around in a little circle on the dust and patchy ocher grass, smiling and singing in the sunshine.

> Ti ti ti
> Ton ton ton
> The gray goose flown away

At noon they went indoors and took their dinner from a pot on the stove and then Alice would nap in her bed upstairs while Mimi, the brim of her straw hat tugged low over her face, would sit in the yard on the canebacked kitchen rocker and smoke a pipe of tobacco before returning to her work. Some streets away a brass band marched along, playing one of the old

French quadrilles, and was answered by the big black dog who lived on the sidewalk in front of Tom Clare's saloon and barked like a bass drum.

New Orleans then was a dream city built upon the black mud where the brown serpent river bent around a corner of the South, where the earth was so moist that the dead were buried above the ground and their spirits passed nearby so close that a person could feel them move through the humid air, as an unexpected chill breath on the cheek or the ear, as ever-present in the atmosphere as the music of the cornets and trombones and the smells of coffee and crayfish, the crepitating scents of Spanish spices. Time ran over itself in layers in the liquid air of New Orleans, for there was no place to set the past aside; nostalgia got mixed up with ambition and it was often harder to forget things than to remember them. As much as she was able, Mimi Beaudette ignored the spirits and kept her mind concentrated on her life in the present. "They only bears their past unhappinesses," she said of the spirits, "and I've got you for my happiness today, Alice darling, so fine and so fair." But occasionally she was beset by uncertainty and would trundle around the corner to Piro, to consult the Haitian-born conjure woman called Widow, who interpreted perplexing dreams and read the future in a pile of knucklebones, visits from which Mimi invariably returned scoffing, restored by indignation to good sense. "Woman say she sees stains of red like blood," she'd snort, "and didn't I come from spending half the morning lifting Burgundy wine from off of Missus Vavasseur's silk bodice where it fell? Blood, la. The old hoodoo says it's the future, but darling, it's every day of your mama's life, today after today. I believe I'll let me worry about the future when I know it's going to be anything differently, and that's when. La, that Widow, how she do."

Little Alice was a happy child in her mother's back yard, with no reason to believe that her life would not always be the way it was there where the black cauldron steamed and the laundered sheets waved in the sunlight and Mimi waddled back

65

and forth on the yellow ground chatting and singing in her quiet, toneless way. The only disturbance in their life together was the rain, for when it rained in a sudden, noisy downpour blown up from the Gulf, Mimi would have to scurry and hop to gather down the drying wash and rush it to the shelter of the narrow back porch, and in those moments Alice could feel Mimi's attention turn away from her and sometimes, for an instant, she would experience the silence of loneliness like a chasm opened in the ground beneath her feet; but then, with the wash gathered and protected, she and Mimi would stand together on the porch and Alice could lean her head to the side and rest against the softness of Mimi's hip and smell Mimi's scents of soap and steam and kitchen smells and be comforted again. While they watched, the rain churned the soapy ground to a lather and foam bubbled up like clouds and spread itself across the yellowed earth and pale grass in shallow drifts, and when the storm had passed and the roosters began to crow all over the city to announce the return of the sunlight as if it were a new dawning, the froth on the ground would dwindle away, leaving behind tiny, glassy bubbles clinging to a leaf or a blade of grass or the leg of Mimi's stool, until they vanished, *pip,* in a twinkling. "Where do they *go,* Mama?" Alice asked when she was very small, and Mimi said, "The angels picked them, darling, and put them in a basket to take to the queen, and then the queen baked them all together in a pie and all the angels had angel pie, which they found most deliciously, thank you." "I want some," Alice said. "I want some angel pie." "Someday, darling," Mimi said. "Some fine day you shall have your angel pie. You'll ride in a carriage and eat your angel pie, and all the gentlemen will bow and smile to see you so." And she squeezed little Alice around the shoulders and they smiled together at the thought of angel pie, while the sunshine returned to fill up the back yard with its warmth.

But Alice couldn't sit forever beneath the smoke tree and the chinaberry, and in time, though she was a timid child and small for her age, she was enrolled at the Ursuline Sisters' school to learn sums and spelling and the names of the saints and Presidents, and it was there, in the dusty yard behind the school, that she saw Jibba for the first time and for the first time encountered the bleak and inevitable lessons of loss and solitude. She was standing at the side of the yard, shyly watching some older girls skip to a schoolyard song:

> "Here come the lady with her face so gay,
> Here come the gentleman to take her away,"

when she heard and felt the distant keening that was the saddest sound in that city where every night in every quarter a man or a woman could be heard singing the blues, calling back to self-respect from the swamp-darkness of an abandoned heart. All the little girls in the schoolyard fell silent and clustered close together with their eyes wide and excited. "It's Jibba," one little girl said, "Blind Jibba. Look at how he is. Ain't he sad?"

Alice looked and saw him turn the corner and commence to cross the schoolyard toward her and the other little girls, and at first he appeared to be only a small white boy dressed poorly in a torn shirt and dirty trousers, a forlorn boy no bigger than some of the little girls in the schoolyard and not much bigger than Alice herself, but as he came near she began to appreciate how strange and interesting he was, for the paleness of his skin was as luminous as the night mist beneath a streetlamp and he walked with the shuffling gait of an old, old man at the end of the day, with his bare feet drawing trails in the dirt of the schoolyard and flickering like ocean phosphorus in the dust they raised. His face was a boy's face, though, smooth and unmarked, with the skin pulled tight over his cheekbones and his brow, and his head was like a baby's round skull bobbing unsteadily at the end of his thin, blue-veined neck, surrounded by floating filaments of silky white hair. His face turned constantly this way and that, back and forth and up and down, anchored by his left hand which pressed against his mouth the small, tarnished mouth organ by which Jibba expressed his loss and isolation in tones so profound and unmistakable that Alice felt a trembling in herself even before he passed near enough to her that she could feel the chill that emanated from his skin, and then he turned his face directly to her and she saw his thin pink lips nibbling the edges of his little harmonica and his opaque eyes with their color of boiled potatoes and the sound he expressed surrounded her with a layer of silence like a cocoon of sleep in whose core she heard two names spoken in sorrow, and she began to weep.

Jibba passed on trailing dust and chilled air through the schoolyard, and Alice, stricken by a dread greater than she had ever imagined, ran home and flung herself headlong into her mother's lap, and when the consolation she sought there remained out of reach of her unhappiness she wept all the harder. Mimi took her daughter's face between her hands and read the message of sorrow in Alice's eyes and felt the rhythm of fear stir in her own heart. "What did they do to you?" she exclaimed. "Don't they know my baby's not supposed to weep so?" "Oh Mama," Alice sobbed, "oh Mama, I heard your name from far away." "How?" Mimi said. "How did you hear it so?" But Alice was too distressed to speak, for in her own ears her voice sounded so distant and lost that she could not bear to hear it, so she only wept while Mimi gathered her in her arms and held her on her lap, rocking on the old canebacked kitchen rocker there in the sunshine and safety of their back yard, until Alice's sobs lengthened into the exhausted breath of sleep. Then Mimi lifted her carefully in her strong little arms and carried Alice upstairs to her bed and stood beside her there. When she was sure that Alice was at peace she brushed the salt traces from her daughter's soft cheeks, and then she left the house and hurried around the corner to the conjure woman on Piro.

The conjure woman called Widow was tall and hollow-cheeked, with eye sockets like charred holes and long-fingered hands that she carried with their thumbs tucked under so that they resembled the clawed feet of a climbing lizard. Her parlor was dark and smoky, with a faint smell of burning hair, and

Widow sat expressionless on a straightbacked chair on bare floorboards in the center of the room while Mimi paced and spoke indignantly. "I never called for a spell on nobody in all my time, Widow, and you're the one that knows it," Mimi said, "but now somebody's calling one on my sweet baby girl and it's touched her in her heart where I can't reach to pluck it out. I make my own way and treat everyone kindly as kindly can, and that fair child is innocence itself, so it's not deservingly to her or to me to have this happening. Where's the deserving in it? You tell me, where?"

The conjure woman leaned forward in her chair and stretched out her arm and dropped a half-dozen knobby gray objects the size of wrens' eggs on the floor by her feet. These were her bones, said to be the knuckles of drowned French pirates from the time of Lafitte, and they settled at odd tilts and angles on the worn floorboards where for several minutes she scrutinized them silently from above through half-lidded eyes. "Woe, Mimi Beaudette," she said finally in her deep, slow voice. "Woooe, Mimi Beaudette." A chicken that Mimi hadn't noticed before came out from behind the conjure woman's skirts and walked without haste to the kitchen. "What is it?" Mimi asked. "What did you see?" She tapped her foot impatiently and one of the bones on the floor moved slightly.

"Sit down and be still," Widow said without raising her eyes from the floor. "You upset the reading."

"Eh, la," Mimi said, but she sat herself on the black iron chair by the conjure woman's left side and tried to appear interested in the jumble of knuckles.

Widow dropped two more bones among the others and sighed through her nose with a rattling noise. In the silence that followed, Mimi thought she heard footsteps on the ceiling overhead but she didn't turn her head to look. Widow sighed again and said: "The child don't turn to me, Mimi Beaudette."

"What do you mean, she don't?" Mimi asked.

"I mean the child don't come clearly to my call," the conjure woman said. "Most likely there's another that's holding her from me, only without showing itself better I can't collect who it is." "Oh mercy," Mimi said. "No no," the conjure woman said. "It's nothing ill in it. I see no spell on the child."

"Then what?" said Mimi. "What makes her so fearful?"

Widow closed her eyes and turned her head sideways and cupped her long hand behind her ear over the bones and listened. "I'm hearing things," she said. "Things she heard. Oh my. Oh my my. Oh."

"What?" Mimi said.

"Jibba," Widow said. "Jibba called her. Jibba called to . . . no no, oh my. I hear it now. Jibba called *you*, called Mimi Beaudette, calling to you through her. Calling your name, and woe. Oh Mimi Beaudette, take care. Jibba calling you, calling in sorrow, calling your name."

"Me?" said Mimi. "What's it about me?" The news startled her but in her relief at learning that there was no spell on little Alice she was puzzled rather than frightened by it, for as a sensible person she had never seen cause to fear Jibba.

"Child heard your name," Widow repeated, still listening to the knuckles.

"But I know that," Mimi admitted. "She told me she heard that. I'm her mama, no?"

The conjure woman took her hand away from her ear and held it up in a staying gesture. Mimi leaned forward on her chair to get a better look at the bones, and saw that a fat brown palmetto bug was trying to climb one of them; she wondered whether that was part of the message the conjure woman was receiving, for the bone was moving slightly as the bug scratched at it. "Heard another one's, too," Widow said. "Another name calling through her, in sorrow and harm. Take care, Mimi Beaudette, there's harm in it, harm to you."

"La, what name?" Mimi asked skeptically. Having lived her life fairly, she was confident that she had made no enemies who would want to harm her, and she felt no urgency in the conjure woman's warning. The palmetto bug lost its grip on the bone and toppled over onto its back, and lay waving its legs in the air. "I keep honestly to my own affairs," Mimi said.

Widow opened her eyes and turned her head to face Mimi. "Trot," she said.

"Pardon?" said Mimi, sitting up in her chair.

"Trot," said the conjure woman. "That's the name that was calling, was Trot." From overhead a scraping noise sounded, as if a heavy piece of furniture was being pushed with effort across the ceiling.

"Poo," said Mimi conclusively. "I never knew any Trot or any name like Trot, so that's that."

"That's the name," Widow said simply.

"Are you certain, Widow?" Mimi said. "Trot's no name to me."

Widow pressed her lips together in an expression of impatience. "Why do you come to me, Mimi Beaudette, when you always don't want to hear?" she said. She reached down and picked up two of the bones from the floor, rubbed them between her palms and held them to her nose and took a deep breath of them. "I'm saying the name is Trot and it's a harmful name to you," she said. She let the bones drop back to the floor, where one of them landed on the palmetto bug and injured it. "I'll tell you something else, too," Widow said. "Put your hand out over here." She grabbed Mimi's wrist and guided her hand to a spot in the air directly above the knuckles and the bug, whose legs were waving feebly. "Open your hand," Widow directed, and when Mimi obeyed she felt a sting of cold on her palm, risen from the bones below. "Mercy," she said, jerking her hand away. "You see?" Widow said. Mimi closed her fingers over the cold spot. "La," she said. Her heart fluttered in alarm and she touched her bosom; the spot of cold, no broader than a pinprick, pierced her bodice and settled on her breast.

"You already know your Trot, all right," Widow said. "You're only too stubborn to recollect it, Mimi Beaudette."

"That's foolishness," Mimi said, rubbing the cold spot

through her clothing. "You're tricking with me now, Widow." The scraping noise overhead came to an end with a single, emphatic thump, like the lid slamming shut on a large box. "If I ever knew any Trot, I guess I'd be the one to remember I knew it," she said, feeling indignant again.

The conjure woman bent down and began picking up the bones from the floor. "I don't do no tricking," she said sullenly. "You can't trick with what you hear, unless you think the child was tricking you too. She heard it before I ever did, you know." She stood and moved to the window and dropped the knuckles into a glass jar on the sill; the palmetto bug stayed on the floor, scarcely twitching now.

"If that's so she'd have told me," Mimi said, standing up and stepping carefully over the bug. "The more I think on it, Widow, the more it occurs to me that she's probably just took sick with a colic or touch of the ague, and I'm bestly going home and dose her with nutmeg. Unless you wants any laundering done I'll pay you Friday." She smoothed down her skirt over her hips and prepared to leave. "Look here," she said, "I'm grateful to you for learning there's no spell on little Alice, Widow."

The conjure woman turned by the window and faced Mimi, shaking her head slowly, as dark and spare as a bargeman's pole. "Take care for yourself, Mimi Beaudette," she said gloomily.

"I live my life the way I live it," Mimi said, taking hold of the door latch. "I can't be fearful for that, can I? I can't do different." As she left the house a chicken ran out from under a side table and ate the palmetto bug.

Mimi paused on the sidewalk; in the near distance she could hear a funeral in progress, with the brass band playing *Flee as the Bird,* the cornets yearning for glory and the bass drum, muffled in shroud cloth, thumping the slow pace of the procession with a sound like the final jerk of the gallows rope. "La," Mimi said to herself, "that Widow, how she do."

When Mimi got home to her little brown house Alice was

72

still asleep in her bed and Mimi, after feeling the child's fore-head and discovering no fever there, let her sleep on through the rest of the afternoon and the evening in the hope that Alice would dream away her fear; but when she herself was on her way to bed, Mimi paused at the door of little Alice's bedroom and saw by the lamplight that Alice's eyes were open and star-ing at the ceiling with a distant and pensive expression that Mimi had never seen on her daughter's face, and when she called softly to Alice the child turned her head and stared at Mimi and her round, dark eyes widened suddenly as if in ter-ror. Mimi drew a sharp breath at the thought that Widow had been mistaken and the child was indeed under a recurring spell, but in the next instant Alice smiled delightedly and said, "Oh Mama, I was so *sad,* wasn't I?," and Mimi realized that the look on her face was only one of wonderment. "Yes, darling," she said. "Oh yes, you were."

"I cried and cried and cried," Alice continued in amaze-ment, for in her child's way she had already forgotten the hurt that had caused her tears, so that when Mimi asked her then whether she recalled why she had cried so, she answered, "I don't think so, Mama, but I cried and cried. Wasn't I sad?" The child laughed then and Mimi was so gratified by the reas-surance she felt that she was scarcely troubled at all when, as she was undressing, she discovered that the cold breath of the conjure woman's bones was still in her breast, a tiny drop of ice not far from her heart. She decided that it was just another of Widow's tricks and, irked, she resolved simply to ignore it until it went away.

"I'm not a grieving person," Old Patanouche said to Alice one day. "There's nothing to be learned from grieving except sorrow, and I don't see the need to be studying on *that* when there's so many other folks that seems to enjoy it altogetherly. But sometimes a person can't help from worrying, and I do worry for the sake of your mama because she's a good person acting ignorantly. Do you know what I'm talking about, child?"

"No, *Gran'mère*," Alice said solemnly. "Is Mama sorrowing?"

The old woman looked indignant. "She's not taking the care to *avoid* her sorrow," she said, "even though it sits so close by her heart." Several weeks had passed since Alice's encounter with Jibba in the schoolyard, and the child's memory of the events of that day had dwindled to a shiver, but Old Patanouche still nursed the message of Jibba's prophetic lament, and the cold spot in Mimi Beaudette's chest nagged at her like an unwarranted reprimand. She had been in her kitchen when Alice's dread had announced itself to her; in a broth of rainwater and turtle's milk the old woman had been boiling camellia stems to prepare a healing poultice for a young girl in the quarter whose fingers were frozen by a dropsy into the talons of a roosting bird, when the wooden spoon in her hand had suddenly begun to writhe and hum in a fashion that she'd recognized with alarm, for it signified the arrival of another child's petition for assistance in preparing against the hostile and incomprehensible forces of adult time and circumstance. Removing the saucepan from the fire, Patanouche had hurried to her parlor and seated herself at the table there and listened intently while the blind wraith foretold Alice's grief. She'd cupped her hands upward on the tabletop and Alice's tears had gathered in the creases of her palms and then turned to frozen splinters as Mimi Beaudette had received the message of her fate from Widow's knuckles and taken it obstinately to her bosom. Then, when night had fallen and Mimi had retired unrepentant to her bed, Old Patanouche, the ally of the children, had carried Alice's crystallized tears to her kitchen and, picking carefully among her herbs and charms, she had set about the task of summoning the child.

"Mama says there's no point to worrying about tomorrow," Alice replied. "She says tomorrow's going to come if you worry or not, and she just lives her life today after today. She says I'm going to be a rich man's bride."

"Hmp," Patanouche grunted. "Is that what she says?"

"Yes'm," Alice said, proud to take her mother's part. "Does she say anything about the past times?" Patanouche asked.

Alice thought for a moment. "She says her daddy was an island Frenchman," she said. "I know who her daddy was," Patanouche said. "That's not sufficiently enough to stop me from worrying about her."

Alice fretted. "Can't you make it all safe for her, *Gran'mère?*" she asked.

"How? How am I going to do that?"

"Don't you know things?" the child said.

The old woman let her face go slack in a stupid expression and waggled her jaw from side to side. "Ah knows how ter bake de cheery pie," she said in a singsong voice, "an' Ah knows how ter pluck de chicken dry. That's the things I know, dear." Alice giggled. "That's not *all*," she said. "There's nothing else that will help a woman that don't allow she needs help," Patanouche replied. "A person's sorrow comes to you from out of the past, and you got to look fairly to the past to prepare against it. Mimi Beaudette's not looking fairly anyplace. She's all alone and she chooses it to be that way, alone, and for that I can't do nothing for her."

"La," said Alice, relieved. "Mama's not alone. She's got *me*, and I'm her pride and joy." But the old woman only grunted noncommittally and the child was left feeling slightly mystified, the way she always was by her conversations with Old Patanouche.

Old Patanouche was a familiar figure in the quarter, a tiny, mouse-brown woman shriveled and bent by her years, which were said to number well over one hundred and to have encompassed several lifetimes. It was said of her that she could remember back past the Spanish times, even to the time when Bienville himself had come along the river in his dugout with his company all dressed in animal skins and had claimed that crescent shore for his king by thumping his staff three times upon the ground until the earth had answered back to him, *padoum*, with a note like the sound of a huge golden bell struck by a cannonball. It was known that Old Patanouche traveled constantly back and forth between the present world and the world of the spirits, and for that her intercession was much requested by people of the quarter who sought the roots of their earthly troubles. Unlike many of the sorcerers in New Orleans, however, she made no claim of clairvoyance, nor would she permit her skills to be employed for casting spells, although the means and materials of spelling were known to her and on occasion she could be persuaded to prepare a love-philter or a potion of healing forgetfulness if she were convinced that the circumstances of its usage were benign.

At one time certain hostile people in the quarter had put it about that she was a zombie, for it was reputed that she never slept and, further, that zombies were sometimes seen dancing in the coalyard beside Old Patanouche's little cottage at the closed end of Angelus, but that was a thing which was often said about Caribbean people, and the evidence of her alert and lively kindness sufficed to refute the rumor. Mimi, who had watched the old woman come and go along the street for years, told little Alice: "She's just a sweet little old human person that knows the mysteries, is all. You don't ever have to be scared of her. La, Miz Patanouche," she called, waving. The old woman stopped and turned to face them, blinking slowly in the sunlight. "Good morning, Mimi Beaudette," she said. "Good morning and good day to you." She had a soft, light voice with a faint rasp of huskiness in it and she stood like a squirrel resting on its haunches, with her hands lifted and folded together in front of her bosom. "Miz Patanouche, this is my little Alice," Mimi said. "Darling, say howdo to Miz Patanouche and please to meet you." The old woman smiled and said, "Hello, Alice dear." Amid the lines and deep seams of her face her eyes twinkled like the eyes of a child on Christmas morning. But Alice was timid and pressed her toes into the dust and turned her face against Mimi's hip and wouldn't speak to the old woman, who laughed and said, "That's a lovely child, Mimi Beaudette. I know one day she will be my friend. I love the children so."

But Alice never said a word to Old Patanouche or paid the old woman any mind until several years had passed and she had seen Jibba in the schoolyard and heard his mournful message. Not long after that, as she was returning home one afternoon from running an errand for her mother, her eye was caught by something interesting at the end of the street, and instead of entering the narrow path that led around the side of the little brown house to the back yard Alice went along to get a closer look. Angelus was a short street which came to a dead end against the barrier of the tall board fence that enclosed the coalyard where the zombies danced, and the last house on the street was Old Patanouche's cottage, a little gray dwelling not much bigger than a hencoop set in a dirt yard surrounded by a few scrawny shrubs and patches of wild-growing herbs, all within the boundary of a low picket fence. The sight which had attracted Alice's eye was an orange cat dancing on its hind legs in the street in front of the old woman's gate.

The cat's head ticked from side to side as the animal hopped from one hind foot to the other, with its forelegs dangling out before its stomach like a lady holding up her skirts and prancing to the playing of a seesaw country fiddle, though the only music to be heard was the distant clamor of a spasm band riding a lumber wagon through the streets to advertise its appearance that evening in one of the city's parks. So altogether preposterous was the animal's jig that Alice could not help laughing aloud and clapping her hands; but when she was near enough to be able to count the cat's whiskers the animal spun around once and flattened its ears and, with a single bound, leaped clear over the top of the coalyard fence. Then Alice heard another voice laughing along with her own and she turned and saw Old Patanouche standing behind her gate, chuckling and tapping her hand against the gatepost in the rhythm of the cat's dance, and Alice was seized by the old woman's merriment and, gathering up her skirt in front of her, she began to mimic the dance of the orange cat in the street. Old Patanouche stepped back from the gate and did the same thing but without actually hopping the way the cat had hopped from foot to foot, and they laughed and danced there in the afternoon sun until they ran out of breath and had to stop. Then they stood gasping and giggling and smiling into each other's eyes and Alice, who was still too shy to make friends with the other little girls at school, could tell that Old Patanouche was going to be her dearest friend and that thought so pleased her that she began to talk as if resuming a conversation that had lapsed only an instant before.

"That was so *funny,*" she said, "how that cat was doing. Cats can't do that, can they? Cats can't dance."

"Well dear, what did you see then?" Old Patanouche asked. "I saw the cat," Alice said. "And was the cat dancing?" asked Old Patanouche. "Yes," said Alice, and then she added, "*no*. Cats can't dance." "But you saw it," the old woman insisted. "I don't *know,*" Alice hooted, delighted with the game. "Don't you know if you saw it?" "I did see it," Alice said. "I did." "Then you do know," said Old Patanouche. "But," said Alice. "Hm?" said Old Patanouche. "*But cats can't dance.*"

The little brown woman smiled and shook her head. "You'd best come inside and let me make you a cup of chocolate, Alice Beaudette," she said, "for it's too confusing out here. You do like chocolate, don't you?"

"Oh yes," Alice said. "It's my favorite."

"You see?" said Old Patanouche. "I knew that and I didn't even have to see it. Do you know how I knew that?" "No," Alice admitted. "Neither do I," the old woman said. "I just knew that I knew it, and I did." She took Alice's hand in her own, which was warm and dry and creased across its palm like a monkey's paw, and led the child into the little gray cottage, and Alice wasn't at all timid; she felt somehow that the tiny, mouse-brown woman with her soft, light voice and sparkling eyes was no less a child than she, engaged in some enticing game which required that she wear an elaborate costume of old age, and Alice could imagine no greater pleasure than to be Old Patanouche's playmate that afternoon.

Inside the cottage there were only two rooms, a kitchen and a parlor, and both were filled with things that Alice had never considered. The parlor was suffused by a muddy brown light, like the den of a creature who lived in the riverbank, and the air was cool and smelled of flowers and cloves. A carved chifforobe with mirrored doors stood beside the door and a big leather rocking chair stuffed with horsehair was placed near the window. The floor was covered with a carpet of woven straw, in the center of which a round dining table was attended by four straightbacked wooden chairs, and in every corner of the room and on the windowsill and beside the doorways saucers of clear water had been set out to amplify the voices of the spirits when they came to call. But it was in the spaces between the furnishings that the odd things rested which Alice had never considered before: bits of string and yarn, paper flowers and parts of china dolls, tiny wheels and clock faces and shapely stones and shells and pieces of colored glass, gourds and tambourines and bunches of doorkeys strung on metal rings big enough to slip over Alice's shoulders. And feathers. Old Patanouche's parlor teemed with feathers of every size and shape and color, tied up in sheaves or fans, strung together like the bushy tails of foxes or simply lying about in clusters and piles which whispered and turned over at the passage of a body or a spirit's breath. As Patanouche led Alice into the room the rocking chair by the window began to rock gently and a brown feather flew up and hovered just above the cracked leather seat, but before Alice could take alarm Old Patanouche rushed across the room making shooing motions with her hands and talking commandingly in a language the child had never heard and the feather drifted away and settled to the floor and the rocker, after giving a final, emphatic heave, stopped and was still.

Patanouche turned back to Alice with a wide, welcoming grin and as she beckoned the child to the rocking chair Alice noticed for the first time that the old woman hadn't a tooth in her head. "Come and sit now, dear," Patanouche said. "This will be your chair all the times whenever you come to call here, and I told them that." "But there was nobody there," Alice said, hesitating. "Are you being timid now?" Patanouche said. Alice

shook her head solemnly. "No," she said. "Oh no. Only sometimes," she admitted, "it's scary when you can't see things."

"Hmp," Old Patanouche said, "you can't see the fishes in
the ocean, nor neither all the Frenchmens in France, can you?
Are you scared of them too?" "No," Alice said. "Well then,"
Patanouche said. "In the time being you pay heed to what is,
and let me worry about the rest for you. Can you do that?"
"Yes'm, I suppose I can," Alice said. "Suppose?" Patanouche
said. "You're not supposed to suppose. A child like you, you're
supposed to be *learning,* and not supposing. I'll do the supposing around here, thank you kindly Miss Alice dear, and right
now I'm supposing you're supposed to sit yourself comfortable
in your chair whilst I suppose us up a nice cup of chocolate the
way us ladies are supposed to like it to be, I suppose." And
when Alice climbed into the heavy rocker and settled herself on
its cushion she discovered that she had only to incline her head
in the slightest way in order to start the chair rocking in a
rhythm as soothing to her as the sound of Mimi's voice, and
immediately she felt as drowsy and secure as she had ever felt
beneath the chinaberry tree in her own back yard where the
drying linens danced on the clotheslines and the rain sowed
angel berries all around.

From that day forward until just before the eve of the new
century little Alice visited regularly at Old Patanouche's cottage, and as she had suspected on that first afternoon the old
woman became her dearest friend and most welcome companion. "I only hope you're not a bother to the old lady," Mimi
said. "You mustn't be a bother to her, darling." "No, Mama,"
Alice said. "But what do you *do* there?" Mimi asked. "She isn't
teaching you the mysteries and like that, is she?" She leaned
back on her heels and cocked her head suspiciously. "Oh no,
Mama," Alice answered with a smile. "We just talks and plays
and drinks chocolate like ladies. *Gran'mère* says there's no mysteries that's worth learning anymore anyways. She says there's
so much to learn in this world now that a body can't be both-

ered to fuss in the other world, she says. Mostly we just talks and talks."

"Eh, la," said Mimi, "but what do you talk about?"

Alice wrinkled her forehead and tried to remember the details of her most recent visit with her friend, which was never an easy thing to do, for their conversations seemed to consist of little more than riddles and rhymes, fancies too innocuous to recall. These were the simple devices by which Old Patanouche intended to prepare the girl for the times that would follow her mother's death, and in instances where she understood that her instruction might perplex the child, Patanouche carefully applied to Alice's chocolate the benign herbs of forgetfulness, sealing away her lessons as if in envelopes of memory that would be opened only when time dictated. Thus when Alice tried to recollect the old woman's words, she could usually do no better than draw curlicues with her toe in the yellow earth of the back yard and say simply, "Oh, stories."

"It's not harmful things, is it?" asked Mimi. "That's a sweet old lady, I know, but if she's telling you harmful things you should tell your mama about it."

"No, Mama, it's just things," Alice said. Then, remembering, she added brightly: "She told me the story about the two princesses, that one was dark and one was fair and they both was happy ever after all their days even so, and it made me laugh."

"That's nice then," Mimi said, and turned back to her work without further worry on the matter, for even though she loved her daughter dearly and was watchful in her concern for the child, still she viewed Alice with the diminishing eye of an adult and was forborn from appreciating the full dimension of the child's character. "Please don't face yourself into the sunlight like that, darling," she warned gently. "Your skin is too fine and fair for the sunlight, I do fear, and will darken and turn coarsely, la, your fine French skin. Kindly find a shade now, that's my darling, and wear a hat when I call you to help me fold. Don't the time pass though?" she said as she fetched the flatiron, for the afternoon was running on and there was still mending as well as ironing to be done. "I expect we'll be seeing Mister Brick any moment soon, and won't that be pleasing?"

Brick had been visiting Mimi and Alice in their back yard for some weeks now, ever since shortly after Mimi had taken the cold spot to her bosom, and sometimes he called early in the afternoon and stayed until evening and sometimes he just stopped by on his way to work at Countess Welcome's, but it seemed that he made it a point to look in on them every day and Mimi was awakening to the realization that in his relaxed way he was courting her, which she found most pleasurable to consider. He would amble into the back yard, walking in his slow, measured way, and greet her in his deep, kindly voice and then, while she resumed the steady rhythm of her work, smiling to herself as she moved among her pots and tubs and clotheslines, he would seat himself on a straightbacked chair in the sunlight. Tilting the chair back on its back legs, he would nudge the brim of his Panama hat up until the sun shone full on his freckled forehead and into the deep creases that ran from the sides of his nose past the corners of his easy-smiling mouth, and he'd sit there by the hour in the yard, smoking his thin, dark cigars and calmly chatting the afternoon away. Except when he turned his head to cough or clear his throat, his absinthe-colored eyes never left Mimi Beaudette, and the rhythm of his conversation, which seemed to roll like a log in slow-flowing water, matched the tempo of Mimi's labors and seemed to lighten the burden of them. Alice noticed that many of the things he said caused Mimi to grin and roll her eyes and pat her hair and sometimes to laugh and say, "Oh, *la*," and if she was near enough to Brick's chair Mimi would touch his shoulder or his knee in a gentle, shoving gesture, and if she was not so near she would turn and look at him with a faraway look like a sailor scanning the horizon of the sea, and he would smile at her with a wide, lazy grin and Alice, though she hadn't heard the words he had spoken, could feel his charm and the happiness it caused in her mother.

"Mama says he could charm the birds out from the trees," she told Patanouche shortly after Brick's visits had commenced, and Patanouche nodded and said, "That's a very kindly man to know."

"I think he's fearful nice," Alice said. "He says he could teach me to play on the piano maybe." "Do you want to learn that?" Patanouche asked. "I don't know," Alice said. "I don't know if I can." "But do you want to, dear?" Patanouche persisted, watching Alice with a sudden close interest. "Oh *yes*," Alice said. "I think that would be ever so nice to do." "Then you shall," the old woman said, bending over a stunted shrub.

Alice was helping Old Patanouche tend her yard. The river had swollen and overflowed its banks and levees that spring, bearing all manner of squirming and poisonous swamp creatures into the city. Copperheads and moccasins had been seen in the parks and cemeteries, and only the night before, in an alley near the shrimp wharves, a teamster had broken a wagon wheel driving over the tail of an alligator whose body was as thick around as a fat man's. To keep any of these invaders from entering her dusty yard and bringing mischief with them, Patanouche had prepared a mixture of quicklime and ground cayenne in a small bucket, which she and Alice were pouring in a thin line along the ground just inside the picket fence. "If it's just a cat that comes in," the old woman told Alice, "he can simply turn himself 'round and dance right out again, and I can see to that, but snakes is sometimes more than what they appears to be, and is best staying out altogetherly, I believe." Carefully she plucked a small orange caterpillar from the stem of the shrub and set it on her shoulder; in a few seconds it turned into a butterfly.

Alice was staring at her own hands and failed to notice the transformation. "Don't you think my fingers are too little for playing the piano, *Gran'mère*?" she asked.

"I think you're all over very little yet, dear," Patanouche said, "and that's why I love you so. But hands can do whatever you choose to suit them to and if Brick says he can teach you piano playing then you just listen close to him and you'll find a way to do what you have to, I'm certain." The butterfly flexed its wings slowly and the old woman bent her head to the side as if she was listening to it; after a minute she nodded twice and it fluttered away in the direction of Piro, as Alice went on studying her small, chubby hands, turning them this way and that.

The previous afternoon in the back yard Brick had beckoned little Alice to stand in front of him. He had let his chair down and leaned forward with his elbows resting on his knees and smiled at the girl in his lazy fashion, with his pale green eyes somewhat sad and regretful the way they always were, and he had taken Alice's hands in his own and said, "What shall we be making of you, little Alice? What do you know to become?" His hands were dry and leathery and fit around Alice's like shells, and Alice liked the warm feeling of them and said brightly, "I know sums and times tables."

"She can read and spell, too," Mimi said, looking up from her ironing. "She spells something fine, I declare." She bore down on the iron with a grunt, and from a distant quarter came the sound of a trumpet and a trombone in rising dialogue.

"I can spell 'orange,'" Alice said, "and 'elephant.'" In the accent of New Orleans the words almost rhymed: *O-rong; Elly-phong*.

"And see how fair she is," Mimi added proudly.

Brick turned Alice's hands over, examining them back and front. They were small, pale copies of Mimi's, short-fingered and plump, with their tips like little pink bubbles and their backs as rounded as sausages. Brick's hands were broad-backed and his long fingers looked as though they had been assembled from carefully milled segments; they folded and unfolded like carpenter's rules and the pads at their tips were flattened and worn smooth. Mimi, watching the examination from her table,

84

giggled merrily. "Is it fortunes?" she said. "Can you tell fortunes, Brick?"

"Mighty small fortune in these hands," Brick said gently. "Mighty small hands." Alice noticed for the first time that he talked from the side of his mouth. "I have ten fingers," she said, "and ten toes."

Brick held out his own right hand between them and spread his fingers like a peacock exhibiting its fan; his fingers seemed to radiate from his palm as long as sunbeams, and Alice placed her own palm against his and saw that when she fitted her wrist to his, her fingertips scarcely crossed the deep, dry crease of his lifeline. He turned his head to the side and coughed once, sharply. "Ump," he said, drawing a breath. "You do have a slight of growing to be done, little Alice. Those hands you've got now won't hardly bridge two black keys without dragging on the white between." Then he closed his hand over hers again and held it tightly without speaking for a minute or so, until Alice felt a tingling in her wrist. It was not an unpleasant feeling, just a small rippling where the bones met, but it surprised her and in confusion she pulled back against his grasp. Brick released her hand immediately and smiled at her again, broadly and with something of proud discovery in his habitually sad eyes. "Aha," he said. "Fortunes always do come more direct from the heart than the hand. Would you like to learn piano playing, little Alice?"

"I don't know," Alice answered. "I don't know if I can. Could you teach me that, Brick?"

Brick leaned back in his chair again and the sun struck lights in the polished copperplate of his hair. "I reckon so," he said in his slow, reassuring drawl. "I reckon that might be the best thing to do."

"My baby's going to be a rich man's bride," Mimi chirped, setting aside her iron, "for she's as fair as the Queen of Madagascar." Alice laughed and raised up on her toes and spread her short, chubby arms. "Tra la la for the Queen of

Madgigascar," she sang. "Tra la la," Mimi echoed, and they giggled and curtseyed to each other like tipsy ballerinas while a river breeze blew over the back yard and made the yellowed grass nod and the sheets on the line billow like big Gulf clouds in the summertime.

Brick smiled contentedly at the sight of them and the feeling of the warm afternoon sunshine on his face, for he was a night-working man and the fortunes of daylight always came to him as a pleasant surprise and added to the well-being he had come to feel since he had introduced himself to Mimi Beaudette and begun the routine of calling on her and her daughter in the soapy yard behind their little brown house, where Mimi worked in calm, practical rhythms so suited to his own. It had been something in her rhythms which had first attracted his attention to her when he'd used to watch her in the early morning from the window of his room upstairs above Monette's barber shop, next door to Tom Clare's saloon, where he kept a bed and a wardrobe, a table and two chairs, a runty coal stove that never quite drove the damp out of the walls and a small upright piano with yellowed keys and pale, leaf-shaped spots on its top and sides where the salt air had infiltrated, for it had belonged to a sea captain who had kept it in his cabin aboard ship and employed it as a companion during periods of insomnia. Like the captain, Brick slept sparingly and was soothed in his wakefulness by the company of the instrument, which carried in its sound the consoling sonorities of deep water flowing.

Brick usually left the Welcome Mansion during the darkest hours of the early morning, when the mists and the stillness of the passing night separated the sounds of the city into isolated pockets, individual voices detected in the indefinable distance, like the faint, hollow percussion of water dripping slowly in a cave. People in the streets at that hour avoided one another's recognition and faded quickly in and out of the fog; in the bucket joints, they sat apart from each other with their heads in their hands, or slept on their forearms, drooling cheap liquor onto their coatsleeves.

Brick had his own key to the barber shop. Just inside the door a lantern hung from a nail and he lit it and used it to guide his way past the three barber chairs anchored like monuments on their swivel bases before the long mirror, in which as he passed he could see the pockets of shadow consuming his eye sockets and the deep creases in his cheeks and around his long ears and nose. He looked like an old, tired hound with tanned skin and rust-colored freckles spattered on his cheeks and forehead as if he had been caught outdoors in a rain of chocolate. Some of the other ticklers called him Spotty Dog, and Beau Davy had even composed a short blues by that name in his honor, but mostly he had always been called Brick, which was short for Bricktop, in reference to his coppery hair.

At the rear of the room there was always a basin of water on the stove, ready to be heated when the shop opened in the morning, and he usually stopped and splashed some on his face to rinse away the smells of whiskey and smoke and perfume that hung so thickly in the Countess' parlor. Then he'd light a long, thin cheroot at the gas jet beside the hat rack and continue on through the door at the back of the barber shop and up the worn, narrow stairway to his room. If he was feeling chilled he would drop a few coals into the fire in his stove, then pour himself half a tumbler of whiskey and sit on his narrow bed with his long legs stretched out and his head and shoulders propped against the wall and sip the whiskey and smoke his cigar and wait for the ragtime music he had been playing since the previous twilight to depart from his head and hands. He extinguished the lantern and stared at the two small windows which overlooked Piro, where the fog reflected the streetlamps' glow with the faint, cold light of shaved ice, and eventually he either fell asleep or, more often, got up from the bed and went to his piano.

He would sit on the straightbacked chair before the piano with his head drooping forward on his long neck so that it hung directly above the keyboard and wait with his fingers resting lightly on the keys until, of their own accord, his hands began to stir and play. His left hand pressed the deep tones at the bottom of the instrument and found a note or passage of notes which contained the sound most suited to his feelings and then the right hand would fit that sound to a sentence, in a rhythm that was Brick's own rhythm, slow and easy-flowing, and a melody would emerge that was like the lazy, reassuring sound of his own voice talking out his sorrow and fatigue, until he arrived at an acceptance of them or at least a new way to address and examine them. The piano guided him through the times of his life and the times which had led up to his life, illuminating the connections and spreading the present into the past, although sometimes he found himself caught up in corners of memory for which he had no reference, inscrutable constructions which he eventually concluded were not of his times at all but were simply left over in the piano from the times of the sea captain who had died before his proper hour, stabbed on the dockside where he had intervened in a quarrel between a seaman and a stevedore. Mostly, though, the piano spoke to Brick and his own times, with the consoling remedy of the blues, and sometimes he could smell the dust of West Texas where his father, a freed slave, had raised him after his mother, a copper-haired woman with Cherokee features, had been shot by Confederate refugees, and sometimes the sea air of Galveston where he'd learned his trade. Sometimes it was only the smells of New Orleans, of cigar smoke and perfume and river mud and catfish frying. He played softly when he played in the early morning, with no more than a feather's pressure of his long, flat-tipped fingers, and people passing in the street outside couldn't be certain, if they heard him at all, whether it was music they were hearing or merely the movement of the mists, until dawn made the fog chalky and the barber's boy let himself in downstairs and began to sweep out the previous day's clippings. Then Brick would stop playing and go back to his bed and sleep out the morning without dreaming.

The habit of this ritual had occupied Brick for longer than he could recall when he first noticed the piccolo chirp of Mimi's iron axle singing in the fog outside his windows like a small bird on the sill, and he cut his music off in the middle of a phrase and stood up from the straightbacked chair and went to the window, puzzled that the resolute privacy of his nostalgia had been invaded. He looked down on Piro through the dwindling mist and saw the little Creole washerwoman turning the corner of Angelus across the street and setting out to collect the consignment of her day's labors, dragging her shallow wooden cart behind her, and the peaceful measure of her trudging steps, the slight, steady bob and roll of her shoulders beneath her black shawl rose up to him in his second-story room like the music of his blues rising into his fingers from the familiar worn keys of his piano, and although his puzzlement did not diminish as he watched her until she disappeared into the haze, Brick found himself smiling at the serenity he felt.

He was interrupted in his playing again the next morning, and again he went to the window to watch Mimi pass and felt the same calm pleasure ascending in him, and the morning after that he anticipated the shrill call of her rusty axle, summoned it with a trilling of the highest keys and then listened for its reply, which fell in snug harmony upon the notes his fingers had chosen. Before the month was out he greeted her in the street and introduced himself in such a natural and pleasing way that neither of them was surprised in the slightest by their encountering each other thus, and before the seasons finished changing, Brick and his weathered piano moved into the little brown house on Angelus and for the first time in his solitary, peripatetic life he found himself at the heart of a family. The suddenness of this change in his circumstances amazed him, and all the more amazing was the sensation that its arrival had been inevitably summoned, that this unexpected turn in his life had been imposed upon him somehow by another person or power, as if he were an instrument under the manipulating pressure of another's fingers. He was so content in his new surroundings, however, that he resolved not to jeopardize his happiness with worrisome speculation, but rather to embrace it and be grateful for as long as it lasted.

For all the peacefulness he enjoyed in the little brown house, though, Brick's insomnia did not desert him altogether. There were mornings, to be sure, when he came home and went straight to the bed he shared with Mimi and eased between the sweet-smelling sheets; turning onto his side and drawing up his knees because the bed was too short to accommodate the full length of his legs, he would fit himself against Mimi, who slept tightly curled like a burrowing animal in hibernation, and breathe the familiar mixture of kitchen and laundry smells she carried in her hair as she stirred drowsily against him, and he would touch his lips to the shallow cup of sweetness at the nape of her neck and fall immediately into the sleep of his contentment. But there were as many mornings when he lingered in the parlor downstairs, detained by an exigent feeling in his wrists and hands, until his music rose up from the piano into his fingers and the boundaries of time dissolved around him.

Mimi never awoke to the music he played during the early hours, because he was not playing it for her, but the very first time he sat down to address his reveries in the new surroundings of the little brown house his hands fell straightaway upon the new strain which had recently appeared among the characteristic phrases of his perpetual dialogue with the tarnished keyboard, and before its melody had passed, little Alice descended into the amber light at the foot of the stairs and came to stand by his side. It was a tentative, unformed air, both sweet and sad and not exactly of his own times but not apart from them either—so that he had known that it was not one of the sea captain's leftovers—and it had come unbidden to his fingers on the morning of the day he had taken Alice's little hands in his in the back yard. Though he hadn't been able to decipher its message he had listened attentively to it, and when it had reappeared spontaneously on the next night he'd recognized it, and the night after that had anticipated it and made a place for it within the designs of his own familiar figurations. By the time he moved into Mimi's house the air had come to ride securely upon the rolling of his own rhythm and its voice sang a high, steady harmony to his own, and as soon as Alice came into the parlor and placed her hand on top of his, and he felt the music of his life's blues flow through him into her, Brick understood that the little air had been sent to enunciate a connection between them, and he guessed that that connection constituted an obligation by whose observance he might justify and safeguard the happiness of his life there.

"I will teach you the sunshine music first," he told her as dawn approached and Mimi began to stir into wakefulness overhead, "because that is the ragtime, and it's the music the people will enjoy to hear you play."

"But the nighttime music is so pretty and sad," the little girl said softly.

"There are so many things you have to know before you can use the nighttime music, child," Brick said, "and you cannot call them up before their time. Wait on them, little Alice. Soon enough they'll find you, and when they do they'll never leave you alone again."

There was more than a year to come before the dawning of the new century when Brick began instructing Alice in the ragtime, and from the first he was surprised to find her such an adept pupil. It was true that her hands were small and often indecisive on the keyboard, but she was enthusiastic and seemed naturally attuned to the secrets of harmony and rhythm, and her familiarity with the keyboard blossomed far more quickly than, to judge by the example of her mother, he would ever have guessed possible, for although Mimi Beaudette was measured in her life by the fundamental tempos of her own innate practicality, her musical sensibility extended no further than her Tra la las and toneless little back-yard tunes.

Brick thought he remembered having heard once that Alice's father had been a musician, one of the many classically schooled Creole symphony players whose livelihoods had been taken away when the last revision of the city's Race Laws had stripped them of the social and economic privileges of their European heritage and left them with no opportunity to exercise their proud talents except by marching in the brass bands or attempting the ratty spasm style of the black musicians whose sweaty, elemental playing, haunted by the blood and terror of their times, writhed constantly in the New Orleans air. Monette's barber shop was a gathering place for a group of the unhappy Creole players and there had been scarcely a day during his residence there that Brick had not awakened to the sound of their voices rising up like sour fumes from the shop downstairs. "They took a violinist," the Creole musicians would say, "and made a fiddler of him, la." Having known exile all his life, Brick sympathized with their distress, but their complaining strained his patience. *They have to make their peace with what is,* he thought, *and get on along with living their lives, or they're only going to make themselves crazy.* It occurred to him now that one of their voices might have belonged to Alice's father, but he couldn't recollect the specifics of what he might have heard about the man, and it was a matter that Mimi adamantly dismissed from discussion. "Eh, la, that's all from the past now," she said, "and what's gone is gone. I got so much that's better to occupy me today, and no time for those that's departed or either those to come, praise be." To emphasize her present happiness she gave Brick a quick hug around the neck that almost knocked him from his chair and followed it with a kiss on his long, seamed cheek. "You the darlingest man," she said close by his ear. "Let's you help me fold those curtains there real quick and then we tuck ourselves upstairs a while and be pleasurable, so long as Alice is visiting by kindly old Miz Patanouche."

"Brick says even if he doesn't know where it comes from that I am most musicianly," Alice told Old Patanouche. "I've been learning a new tune almost every day in the ragtime style, and other things besides." She held out her hands and flexed her fingers. "Do you think my fingers are ever going to grow any, *Gran'mère?*" she asked.

"Things are always changing, dear," the old woman answered. "You know that's so." She stood before her big-bellied stove that squatted like a bullfrog by the kitchen wall and slowly stirred the milk she was warming for their chocolate.

"Brick's got fingers so long he can cover twelve white keys without even stretching," Alice said. "If I have to do that far I have to do it from here to here, like this." She pushed aside a small jar of speckled beetles and demonstrated on the tabletop the distance her hands had to jump to cover twelve white keys; pleased by the illusion of the gesture, she played some silent figurations there.

Old Patanouche's kitchen was as crowded with unusual things as her parlor. There were little piles of peeled sticks and thorn branches on the floor, and bundles of dried grasses and flowers tied up with string. The cupboard shelves and countertops tilted this way and that at crazy angles and held all manner of jars and bowls that somehow never slid away or spilled their contents which included, besides the beans and rice and other common foodstuffs, roots and herbs and little shriveled things with shiny green skins, and hard gray objects that could have been either pebbles or human teeth, the beaks of chickens and geese and sea birds cut into squares, cats' whiskers and squirrels' ears which had curled up into themselves like furry seashells, tongues from various birds and animals, and claws, skins, scales and eyeballs, and tiny human figures fashioned from bread dough, which had the habit of turning over when you couldn't quite see them from the corner of your eye. An iron kettle and a black stewpot bubbled quietly on the back of the stovetop, and on the table, next to a jar of salt and a pair of rusty scissors, a pig's foot lay on a wrinkled rectangle of butcher paper.

"Here's your chocolate all ready now, Alice dear," Old Patanouche said, holding out the special china mug which imparted the most particular flavor to Alice's chocolate. "Be careful to let it cool—"

"—so it sweetens your tongue," Alice interrupted in a slightly impatient tone. "I'm sorry, *Gran'mère*," she hastened to add, for the old woman's eyes widened in surprise, "but you *always* say that and you always have said it, and I know it by heart."

"I suppose you're tiring of it now," Patanouche said calmly. She turned toward the door and beckoned the child to follow her. "Come come, let's sit ourselves in the parlor like proper ladies and take our ease." And as she followed Old Patanouche into the neighboring room, it occurred to Alice that in fact she no longer did feel the same delight that she had felt for so long in her visits to her old friend; she had heard all the stories and riddles so often that some time ago she had stopped bothering to listen to them, she realized, and more and more in recent weeks she found that she had to make an effort to pay attention while the old woman rattled on in her garrulous way, lest she hurt Patanouche's feelings. Even the look of Patanouche had altered in Alice's mind's eye; she no longer seemed as comfortingly sleek and mouse-like as before, but, sadly, appeared withered and sere in an odd and almost repellent way.

As Alice settled into the old rocking chair, Old Patanouche smiled gently at her and said, "You're not hardly my little child anymore now, are you, dear?"

"Oh, *Gran'mère*," Alice replied in a distressed voice. "Oh, I've been so happy. Can't you make it stay like this? Can't you?" She felt quite confused and helpless at that moment.

The old woman's soothing smile didn't leave her face, but she shook her head slowly. "Some things do change in ways that were settled for us long, long ago," she said, "and there's no way to hold them from coming, you know. The things you started feeling in your body back then this autumn are changing you in your spirit, too, and, child, there's so much more to come."

"Why don't my hands grow more?" Alice asked obstinately.

"Now now," Patanouche said. "They are growing, and you can't deny it, as fast as they only can."

"Will they ever be as big as Brick's, do you think?"

"Brick is Brick and Alice is Alice."

Alice pouted into her mug. "They won't," she fussed. "They won't ever. I hate my hands."

Old Patanouche sighed. "Your hands will always have the skills they need to have," she said patiently, "and you know that's so, or else Brick never would have come to teach you. See here." She reached into the folds of her old, worn skirt and, to Alice's surprise, plucked out a speckled hen's egg and in the same motion tossed it toward Alice. "Eee," the child exclaimed in alarm, and then, "Oh *la*," as, with a swift, instinctive dexterity whose like she had never divined, her hand darted up and snatched the egg from its flight directly in front of her face. Amazed, she stared at the speckled shell. "Why," she said, "Why, *Gran'mère* . . ." and began to giggle. She hadn't even spilled her chocolate.

"You see?" Patanouche said, and she too began to laugh, and for several minutes they sat there in the old woman's mud-brown parlor laughing together like crows in a cornfield. But as they calmed and the thrill of Alice's amazement began to subside, a sad and serious look came over Old Patanouche's face, and before Alice could pronounce any of the questions that were bubbling in her throat the old woman waved her hand in a gesture which made the child feel suddenly lax and docile, and said softly, "I have to go away from you, child."

Somehow this news did not disconcert Alice, and she only nodded and drank her chocolate in small, judicious sips from her special china mug while Patanouche continued in the quiet, husky voice that was so sweet to Alice's ears. "You are my most special child, Alice Beaudette," Patanouche said, "and in the times you need me most, I'll never be far away from you, but now you must go and grow your own way without me. Now, I taught you the things that will set you on your path, and I'm going to pray they keep you safely in your time. I have a special present for you to take along with you." She stood and shuffled into the kitchen, and Alice sat peacefully in the big leather rocker, which swung back and forth in its slow measure that was as comforting and familiar to her as the rhythm of Brick's music, and after a while Old Patanouche returned and handed Alice a little pouch made of soft, brown rabbitskin and tied at its neck with a thin leather string. "There are some things in this that you will have to use," the old woman said, "and when the times come to use them, you will know how. I want you to take it home with you now and put it in a place where nobody can find it, and for the time being you can bestly forget it until you need it, and then you will find it again, all right?"

Alice nodded but did not reply.

"Did you finish your chocolate?" Patanouche asked, and Alice nodded again and held out the emptied mug. "That's my good child," Patanouche said, taking the mug from her. "And now it's time for you to get on home and help your sweet mama with the folding," she said. The rocking chair stopped rocking, and as Alice stood up from it a wisp of vapor rose up from a saucer on the floor near the chair's foot and changed into the shape of a bird and flew out through the closed window to the sunshine outside.

Old Patanouche took Alice's hand in hers and led the girl to the door. "I believe I'll call on some old friends of mine for a while," she said. "I always do enjoy it so, to visit with old friends during the gay times."

"Mama says the evening of the new century is going to be ever so gay," Alice said brightly. "I can't hardly wait. I expect to go to the fair and stay up all night long, and perhaps I'll see the two-headed goat and the Chinaman. Mama always goes to see the Chinaman. Won't I have fun?" She placed the rabbitskin bag inside the broad-brimmed straw hat Mimi made her wear to protect her skin from the darkening rays of the sun and settled the hat on her head, and Old Patanouche pulled the door open.

"I'm certain you will, dear," the old woman said. "Now give

me a kiss good-bye," and as Alice bent to touch her lips to the soft, wrinkled cheek she noticed for the first time how much taller than Old Patanouche she had become, and it made her feel proud and somewhat protective. "I love you ever so much, *Gran'mère*," she said.

Old Patanouche reached up and touched Alice's cheek, and for the last time she smiled her gentle, merry smile into Alice's eyes. "I know that you do, dear," she said, "and I love you too. Now get along." By the time Alice had stepped out into Angelus and turned to secure Patanouche's gate, the old woman had returned to her parlor and begun to darken and seal her house in preparation for her New Year's sociability.

Three nights later, not long after the huge iron wheels bearing the new century had turned their measure, Mimi stood up in the parlor of Lizzie Bocage's cousins' house and announced that she would have to depart. "It's been the loveliest time," she said, "and I pray that this new century is going to bring us all a peace that the old one never did, but I can tell you, my dears, of one thing that will not change, and that's how a body has got to keep on working, for if it has been as noisy and gay over in my white people's quarter as it has right here, then I sigh to think about the messes I must face this morning. White people are surely messy all the time, you know, but never so messy as when they have themselves a gay time." Several of the women said amen to that and Mimi giggled and said, "La, the white folks. Sometimes I wonder if they don't have extra holes on them that the spills run out from." Everyone had a good laugh at the thought of that, and Lizzie Bocage realized that they were all a trifle tipsy from the fruit brandy they'd been drinking. "I'll walk with you, darling," she said to Mimi, but Mimi waved cheerfully and said, "Oh no, la, don't disturb yourself, Lizzie dear. I'm wishing a good evening to one and all, and good night."

Outside, the revels had diminished to distant murmurings, for the rockets had all been fired and the anthems played and the street fairs were closing, and the fog and the season's chill were reclaiming the streets. The paving stones glistened dimly underfoot, like eggs in oil, and in the gutters clusters of bright-colored shredded paper huddled limp and damp. Hats and shoes and pieces of clothing were strewn this way and that, and as Mimi passed a lamppost she had to step around the smashed remains of a chair that lay about its base. She turned the corner and entered the narrow connecting street that led from Beaudoin to Piro, and as she did she was startled by a peal of laughter which flared up like a trumpet's call in a darkened house nearby. Anxiously she put her hand to her bosom and touched the tiny cold spot that she had ignored for so long, so diligently that she had never quite been able to forget it, and for an instant she stopped in her tracks, for it seemed to her that she had felt the spot stir beneath the flesh of her breast. She took her hand away from the spot and stared at her palm in the dim, hazy light, but there was nothing there that she could see, and after a minute she shook her head willfully and said, "Mercy, what foolishness," in a loud voice and, drawing her shawl more tightly about her shoulders, she resumed her passage down the narrow street. Then, just before she reached the corner of Piro, she heard a deep, familiar voice speak to her, softly saying her married name.

"*Mimi Vraicoeur*."

Mimi stopped and turned completely around in the heavy mist. "Who is it there?" she called out scarcely louder than a whisper. "Who is it?"

"*Ti Mimi*," the voice sighed, and she turned her head to the left and looked back along the way she had come, and there, approaching in the chalky fog, she saw the shadowy outline of the tall figure of Vraicoeur, the tormented man who had been her husband until one night in his madness he had tried to strangle her and the child she carried in her. For all of the will she had applied to it in the years since that night, still she had never been able to forget the resigned, torpid feeling of acceptance that had stolen so quickly into her as his long, beautiful fingers had pressed around her neck, trapping her breath inside her where it turned to a fire that made her blood boil in her eyes and ears, and then the icy deluge that had rushed into her chest when he'd suddenly released her and clasped the sides of his head and fallen to the kitchen floor, because without thinking how to do it she had managed to grab up the heavy iron skillet from the stove and lift it in a driving arc until it collided with his skull, just above his ear. She had run out into the back yard and hidden on the ground in the darkness beneath the smoke tree and waited, choking down her sobs as she fearfully embraced the unborn child within her swollen belly and whispered, "There there. There there, baby darling. There there," over and over until through the dense, dangling branches of the overgrown smoke tree she saw Vraicoeur outlined in the frame of the kitchen door, his nose raised and his head turning this way and that like a dog sniffing the wind. She'd held her breath then, and heard him call out to her, calling her name. "Mimi Vraicoeur," he'd said in his deep, anguished voice, "*ti* Mimi, little wife." "No, baby darling," she'd said silently to the child. "Please, no. He shall not take you, no." And Vraicoeur had cocked his head in a dog's listening gesture, with one ear raised to the wind, and she thought for an instant that she had spoken aloud and he'd heard her, and she would have screamed then in her fear, but in the next instant Vraicoeur had turned and gone back into the kitchen. When at last she'd found the courage to leave the shelter of the smoke tree and creep back to the house, Vraicoeur was nowhere to be found, and the next day word came into the quarter that he'd been arrested after a fight with a group of colored musicians and taken away, talking craziness and covered with blood. With all of the stubbornness of her will, Mimi had persuaded herself that he would never come back, and as much as she ever could she had forgotten about him and the bad times he had caused her, and gotten on with her life and the life of her child.

Now he stood before her, a long, scarlet-lined opera cape hanging behind his heels as if he was spilling fire from his shoulders, and in the dim, misty light she could see that his handsome, golden-skinned face, with its long, shining jaw and the widow's peak that lay on his forehead like a dagger's point, was swollen with his madness as it had been on that awful night. His dark eyes stared out at her from within his derangement without the humanity of depth or feeling and when he spoke, softly saying, "Mimi. Ah, Mimi," his voice was as remote and mechanical as the shrill chirping of the rusty axle of her cart, crying in the street before dawn.

"Obregon," Mimi said. "It is you, isn't it." She blinked hopefully, searching his face for a sign of the sensitivity that had once animated it, the softness that had been there when he had been a boy and the pride of his family. "You have been away such a long time," she said. "Did they harm you, Obregon?" He took a step closer to her and she could smell on him a rotting odor, like swamp mud. "Oh, Vraicoeur," she said, despairing, for it occurred to her then, smelling that odor and seeing his opaque eyes, that when they had taken him away, after the madness had taken him over and driven away his kindness, they had killed him, and that the Vraicoeur who stood before her now, looming so tall that it seemed as though he was staring down at her from high overhead, was a zombie. *He has spent all this time finding his way back from the dead,* Mimi thought, *back to me.* She began to weep quietly. "Oh, Vraicoeur," she repeated.

"Don't say that name," he said, his voice low and toneless. "Vraicoeur is no more."

Interpreting his words as a confirmation of her thoughts, Mimi wrung her hands in despondency. "Oh, *la,*" she wailed.

"Vraicoeur was a white man," Vraicoeur said. "That was French Vraicoeur, and look what it got him, eh? Look, Mimi Vraicoeur. See here." He flipped back the wings of his cape in a scarlet explosion and held up his hands in front of Mimi's face, and Mimi saw that his left hand held a gleaming straight razor folded into a bone handle. She cringed away from it, but he whispered, "No, *look!*" and this time she saw that his fingers, which had always been so beautiful to see, for they had been slender and straight and strong, were all bent at odd, painful angles and knotted as though he had grown extra knuckles in them, and the ends of two of them, and most of a third, were missing altogether. "Oh, *Vraicoeur*," she gasped.

"No," he said harshly. "No Vraicoeur, no more. White blood did this to Vraicoeur, white blood in him. Burning in him, white blood did this."

Mimi started to turn away toward Piro, but he grabbed her by the shoulder and held her to his side, and his cape fell over her, enclosing her in darkness where the muddy, fetid smell of him was so thick that she felt as if she was drowning. He bent his head down and whispered to her, "I seen my white blood in me, Mimi; burning out the black, I seen. I seen it happening in fire and pain, in me, in you. I seen it in the *child*, Mimi. Why you think I done what I done? You think, they think, all think I'm a crazy nigger. They wrong. I know. I *know*. I don't bring you pain, woman; I free you from it. Set free all pain. All pain." He snapped his free hand sideways and the blade of the razor flipped out of the bone handle, and from beneath the suffocating cape Mimi saw it sparkle in the mist; the cold spot in her bosom began to expand unbearably, like an exploding star, so that even before Vraicoeur had taken the sparkling blade and with a sudden yanking motion had pulled it across her throat and her blood and her breath burst out in a rush through the opening he made there, her heart had stopped as if frozen, and she never heard Vraicoeur say, "Call me now by my slave name, little wife. Call me Truehart." In the accent of New Orleans, he pronounced it: *Trot*.

Mimi fell in a clump at his feet, and her little straw hat rolled away and her hair spread out in the gutter and mingled with her blood and with the colored paper streamers there. Vraicoeur stood watching her with a listening expression on his face for several seconds, and then he dropped to his knees and put his hands in her blood.

Chapter Five

Flee as the Bird

Just before the dawning of the fourth day of the new century Alice, sitting in the straightbacked chair at the foot of her mother's coffin, began to dream in sounds, in low, groaning tones that filled her through and through and made her think she must be in a cave deep below the ocean, where nothing lived but giant gray stones rubbing back and forth against each other while the cold currents rolled around them. Then, in the midst of their slow, mournful grinding, she heard the piccolo chirp of her mother's cart, distant and dwindling the way she always heard it fade into the mists when Mimi turned the corner onto Piro at the start of the day, and from somewhere high overhead the desolate note of Jibba's mouth organ falling down upon her like the wounded cry of a bird who has collided with a star and been hurled back to earth, trailing a plume of blood from its smashed beak and shrieking the anguished song of its life. Closer and closer it came to the very center of the top of her skull, and she raised her hands over her head to shield herself and was about to release her fear in a scream when Brick shook her awake.

"You're sleeping with your eyes open," he said, "and it's time to waken now." He spoke softly but his voice was tight and his eyes cut watchfully toward the parlor door. "Someone's here," he said. "You go on upstairs quick and brush out your hair the way your mama always likes to see it." Alice blinked the sleep away and as the room took shape around her she could see that all of the candles around the coffin had burned out except one near Mimi's left foot, and that one was guttering low below the casket's rim, leaving her mother's body deep in shadow, shrunken and shapeless like the dust she had become. Brick guided her to the stairs with a gentle pressure of his hand, paying no notice to the creaking of a footfall on the step outside the front door but speaking a bit urgently when he said, "Go ahead on up now, child, and quick like I told you. You brush it out good, your pretty hair."

She started to climb the stairs but stopped and turned around on the fifth step when she heard another footfall outside. Brick had moved to the door and was standing with one shoulder braced against it and she saw that he held a small pistol in his hand. "Brick?" she said, but he didn't hear her, for at the same instant the person outside knocked heavily. "Who is it there?" Brick said, cocking the pistol with his thumb. A thick, slow voice answered, "Ashes to ashes an' dust to dust, if the women don' get you the whiskey must. Lemme inside there, tickler."

Brick let the hammer down on the pistol and placed the weapon handle-first in the back pocket of his trousers and opened the door to admit a wiry black man in a cheap black suit and, following at his heels, a shuffling, shabbily dressed boy who was fatter but no taller than Alice and who carried a hammer in his hand. Out in the street behind them the night mists were lightening to a smoky blue. The wiry man looked up and saw Alice on the steps and he blinked his yellowed eyes and said, "Mornin', little missy," in his deep, slurred way. "Mornin' an' bad day, I knows, 'cause I seen 'em all like this before, but we'll take your mama over easy an' slow. I condole with you." The boy didn't look up; he kept his eyes directed toward the floorboards behind the man's heels, with his mouth pushed forward into an O as if he were about to whistle a tune. Alice didn't recognize the boy but she knew that the man was Weeping Daniel, who drove the hearse for Mr. Julius LaRivière the undertaker and was called by that name because he had trained his horses to cry big tears at the graveside. He accomplished this by splashing onion juice in their eyes, and now his handsomest pair, the ones he used at the most significant and expensive buryings, were so well practiced in the mourner's art that Weeping Daniel had only to flick his fingers in a certain way in front of their faces in order to fill their eyes to spilling.

Brick closed the door. "Go on now, little Alice," he said gently to the girl. "It'll soon be time to go." The girl nodded and climbed the stairs to her room. The gaslight beside her mirror was still lit from two nights before and as she pulled the soft-bristled brush through her hair she was able to stare into her own eyes. Her hair was black and hung in shallow, even waves all the way down her back to the tops of her legs, and she tried not to think of anything while she brushed it, stroke after stroke in unbroken rhythm, hearing the voices of the men in the parlor downstairs, which was all there was to hear.

Weeping Daniel was saying, "'Fore we close her in, don' the child want to look in for her final farewell? They always wants that." And Brick answered him talking low with his voice rushed by tension the way it had been so uneasy for the last three days, saying, "Leave her be now, Daniel. She's had her two days and three nights for that and nothing else, and it's done."

She's gone ahead, Alice said silently to herself. *Oh sweet Mama dear.* There was nobody's hand on the brush but her own.

"Tickler, I've borne this witness more times as a boar got whiskers and it's a fact they always wants the one last look," Daniel said.

"Get on with your job, I tell you, or else go back and send someone that'll do it and not be plaguing me with this delaying," Brick said.

"All right, all right," the driver said. "Come along, boy,

104

what you gawpin' at anyways? Put that down and start out by movin' them candlesticks over to by there, out the ways." Alice turned her hand over and brushed out from underneath, tilting her head to the side, still looking nowhere but into her own dark eyes in the mirror. Her fine French hair, Mimi always called it. French eyes and French skin and fine French hair; someday, little Alice, you will ride in a golden carriage and all the gentlemen will bow and smile to see you. Several minutes passed, and then Alice blinked as the sound of hammering filled the little brown house like spirits knocking on every wall. With every blow her image in the mirror shivered, but the steady, soothing rhythm of her brush refused to let itself be upset by the sound of her mother's coffin as it was nailed shut.

Three days before, at the rising of the new century, she had been awakened by a voice calling to her from within her sleep, calling, "Poor Alice, oh poor little Alice," and she had sat up in her bed and begun right away to concentrate as she had never tried to concentrate before, drawing all of the parts of herself together in the effort of locating and identifying the change that she knew had come over her during the night in the stillness of her shadowy little room. Outside, the night mists were white against her windowpanes, and in the stairway beyond her door glowed the amber light of the lantern left burning on the bottom step, and she knew by the way the echoes of her concentration rattled through the little brown house that she was all alone at the center of a spreading pool of solitude.

The previous evening it had been happy laughter which had jingled in every corner. Mimi had stood on a chair in the middle of the parlor floor and pulled the ends of Brick's white bow tie straight across the wings of his stiff collar. "La," she exclaimed, "but the darlin' man do look so handsomest. See, little Alice, see how *proud* it make him so." She ran her dappled little hands along the shoulders of the black tail coat, picking and smoothing as they went, and giggled her delight into Brick's face while he smiled his calm and gentle smile for her and Alice clapped her hands. "Oh Brick," Alice cried, "you look like a king from the days of old."

"Better than kings," Brick said. He took Mimi by the waist and hoisted her down from the chair and then stepped back and shot his shining cuffs and flourished his long-fingered hands in the air like a conjurer. "This tickler looks like a *musician*," he said with wry pride. He nodded to the girl. "Little Alice, would you kindly play that sweet waltz we've been learning you?" Alice blushed and put her hands to her mouth and shook her head. "I cannot," she giggled. "You do it."

"No," Brick said. "You must be the professor, for I have to dance with my queen." He took Mimi's hand and bowed down before her, and she returned his bow and then curtseyed, her black eyes shining. "La," she said in loving wonderment. "If you kindly, professor," Brick said to Alice.

Alice settled herself atop the pillow which, placed on the seat of the straightbacked chair, permitted her to look down upon the keyboard of the weathered upright that Brick had brought with him when he had moved in with them. Her hands commenced slowly, as they always did, and she frowned as she strained to recall where the right notes lay among the keys, while Brick and Mimi gravely followed her measure and began to turn together on the worn parlor floorboards. As the melody came clearer to her fingers Alice sneaked a look at the two adults from the corner of her eye. They were as oddly matched as a stork and a broody hen; plump little Mimi scarcely reached up to Brick's chestbones, but they waltzed together most effectively and, watching them, Alice felt the tempo that flowed from Brick as he stepped and spun and she let him lead her along, going a shade faster and then faster still until her wrists began to tingle and her fingers stumbled in the cracks between the keys. Brick grinned at her as he twirled past. "Don't play no blue notes tonight, little Alice," he chuckled. "Leave those blues in the alley tonight," and he picked up the pace by another step-measure and then another, until he had whirled Mimi's feet right off the floor and the tails of his coat were flying free behind him. The setting sun lit rosy lights in the windowpanes and Alice stopped playing and jumped down from her chair and started to spin around singing the tune of the sweet little waltz faster than her hands could ever have played it, faster and faster until all three of them staggered to a stop, laughing like dogs in the yard.

Brick's employer, Countess Eulalie Welcome, had ordered Brick's New Year's evening clothes in September, for she was a woman who believed in the virtue of anticipation. "If I makes my arrangements oily enough," she said many more times than once, "then I got the time for the mistakes an' the excuses an' all the billydamn that jump up in my face evvy night of the year an' in the end it *still* gonna come rightly the way I want it, an' my dear, that is the only ways it ever falls in this house." So in September while everyone was still dressing in white against the summer's heat she summoned a theatrical costumer of long acquaintance; Mr. Strap, her enormous major-domo and hard man, drove out in the Countess' own barouche, which had been modified in the springs and axles to accommodate the weight of her personal dimensions, and fetched back Monsieur Pettiplain, a tiny, long-nosed Creole who perched like a newly hatched bird in the open carriage, surrounded by the nest of his fabrics and laces.

The Countess sat in the only place the public ever saw her sit, the big horsehair chair in the parlor of her mansion, directly before the crimson drapes which she always kept drawn shut behind the arched windows that Basin Street regarded as it passed outside her gate. Some of the other madams were not so particular about privacy. Josie Arlington, for instance, was forever given to shouting, "Let 'em see!" and flinging wide her French doors so that her business could pour out into the dusty street as if she ran an establishment no tonier than any barrelhouse on the back of town where they took the doors right off the hinges and the screwmen from the levee and the sapmen from the turpentine camps drank varnish and cut each others' bellies open with razors. But Eulalie Welcome accorded her clientele the privilege of discretion and herself the prerogative of mystery, and her downstairs windows stayed closed and covered at all hours in every season. "Only my gennamens sets a wink into my parlor," said Eulalie Welcome. "The rest is riff an' raff, an' can go wherever they goes to look at what they wants to see."

Like her carriage, the Countess' horsehair chair had been fortified and enhanced in its dimensions to suit her bulk, and she filled it to its limits and summoned her employees one by one to be measured by the costumer. "Thishere's my little Charlotte, Pettiplain, that's just mad to dress herself in green or yella," she said. "Only you can see she's already got her a yellerish cast out of her blood, so green or yella is only gonna give her the color of tropical fever." The Countess puffed meditatively on her long-stemmed pipe, which the little birds said she filled with crushed Mexican chilis, and put forth her pronouncements in a bulldog voice, while Pettiplain hopped birdlike from foot to foot as he measured up and down and around the girl who stood quietly with downcast eyes and did not dispute with her employer. "Was the Countess thinking of purple, perhaps?" the costumer chirped. "Poiple?" the Countess said, surprised. "Why, I suppose not, not poiple. I'd have said claret before I said poiple." "Claret of course," agreed Pettiplain, pecking with a short pencil in a tiny black notebook.

"Thishere's my Araby," Countess Welcome introduced another of her young workers. "My my," said Pettiplain approvingly, for Araby was striking in her appearance. The Countess continued, like a auctioneer: "Araby is built full an' fair through the chest an' shoulders, which the gennamens likes to gaze upon. A gown for thisun ought to be cut to approve their gazing but in a altogether decent way, an' that means no slackness, hear? I like a risin' through the chest all right, only it's got to be foimly so."

For the male employees there was nothing to discuss in the matters of color or style, for all were to be outfitted in opera clothes: cutaway coats, wing collars, stiff shirtfronts, white ties and waistcoats. Nonetheless, the Countess had her stipulations concerning details: "The soivin' mens got to be left a trifle loosely in the knees an' the shoulders," she dictated, "for bendin' an' liftin' that they do. An' cut the tickler's sleeves a couple inches short an' don' let it pinch him up the back, 'cause he got to be able to touch 'em *all,* top an' bottom." Brick smiled at the sound of that; he liked the Countess. "She's a fair person," he would tell Alice later on, "and fair's about as good as you can expect from someone who's not kin."

Brick was nowhere near the flashiest tickler in New Orleans in those times and that held against his reputation somewhat because flash constituted a considerable portion of the tickler's art; it seemed as though every nightfall turned up a new favorite, some dimpling sport who flung his hands high into the air while he played and displayed a jewel in his smile as he splashed pell-mell through his specialty pieces, vying for preeminence with new tempos, new figurations and breathtaking haberdashery. By dawn his sound would have proclaimed his name through the District, and for the better part of a day or more the pleasures of every parlor would be his to command until the next prodigy arrived and papered him over. But Brick was reliable and steady-flowing and Countess Eulalie calculated him to be no less an asset and fixture in her house than the crimson draperies or the priapic Cupid at the top of the stairs. "You play it so comfortable," she told him once. "I be the foist poison to tell you I ain't musicianly. I got a voice like a ol' hound an' in my ear I can't tell the difference 'tween a hawk or a handsaw, but there's one thing I can always do without mistakin', an' that's when my parlor is all full up with gennamens an' liddaboids I knows without lookin' if the feelin' for pleasure an' joy is in that room. An' that's why you are my tickler, Brick dear, on account you never yet has failed to put my parlor in a relaxation frame of mind."

In an ordinary year the New Year's celebration ranked low among the feasts of New Orleans and many folks would have ignored the occasion altogether, but for the turning of the new century anticipation ran high in the city and elaborate festivities were planned in every quarter. Many of Eulalie Welcome's competitors were hiring extra musicians and entertainers for the evening, trumpeters and kick dancers and the like. Miss Lulu White had engaged for her Mahogany Hall a string quartet which was said to be connected in some way to the Beaux Arts Academy, and Chalcedonia Penniman would be presenting an Italian tenor who had only recently toured the opera houses of South America. Hilma Burt's ivories were to be tickled by the teenaged sensation Ferd LaMenthe and the blues singer Mamie Desdoumes, both, and at Germany's Buddy Bolden and his band would play their spasm music, hot enough to make a corpse turn its head. But Countess Welcome had chosen to stand staunch by her steady Brick, shined up and looking "handsomer as the king of Spanish Mexico" Mimi exclaimed to Alice while they dusted him off one last time and handed him up his high silk hat before he angled away into the evening, walking with his long and easy-striding gait and pausing at the corner of Piro to turn and tip his topper to them one last time. Though the hour was early, the night's dampness was already beginning to congeal in mist, and above Brick's head the streetlight wore a discreet corona.

Out in the city the sounds of beginning celebration swam through the humid air, with drums and laughter and rockets flaring and dying away. Trumpet calls sliced the gathering darkness like silver swords cutting silk; the clear marble tones of clarinets tumbled overhead and the steady upright pacing of ragtime measured every streetcorner. From Piro Alice heard voices and a clashing of cymbals. "Can we go yet, Mama?" she asked. "Naw, you go first," Mimi answered, for even on this, the night of the turning of the century, she had her work to do: in a pot of green copperas and logwood dye she was boiling white linen gloves until they turned black. "Stay in the street, though, so as I'll find you," Mimi said, and Alice skipped out the door into Angelus' dust. She cut a glance down to the closed end of the short street, where Patanouche lived, though she knew she wouldn't see the old lady there. Patanouche was well along on a visit to the spirit world; having sealed her tiny house and blacked its windows with herb smoke and incantations, she'd levitated to an empty plane midway between her parlor table and the ceiling above it, and at present she was floating there on her back like an otter in a stream, greeting and socializing with her innumerable acquaintances among the departed and incorporeal.

On Piro a street fair was setting up, with lanterns strung overhead and small tents and booths along the curb. Cooking fires had been lit and the scents of gumbo and hot oil, of fried dough and catfish batter and spices and fruit, competed for place in the night air among the sounds of voices and music and hammers and saws. In Tom Clare's saloon and the barber shop next door smoke hung in the air as thick as silt in the river and the lit cigar ends glowed like alligators' eyes. At this early hour the street itself belonged to the children who raced this way and that, calling out in bird voices and watching everywhere with round, dark eyes. Their mothers watched from the windows or gathered by their doors in small groups to gossip in quiet harmony, humming and chuckling and touching each other's sleeves as they leaned close and commented, explained, prophesied.

"Loo, little Alice." Alice looked and saw three women break their circle and turn toward her, their faces kindly and inquisitive. The woman who had called out, Mrs. Bocage, held her hand raised up by her shoulder in a signaling gesture. "Little Alice," she called, "is your mama coming out tonight?"

"Yes'm she will," Alice answered. "She said she'd come along presently."

"You see her, you tell her we be waiting for her, hear?" Mrs. Bocage said. "You know who I am, child." Hers was a homely face and sad, lined with vertical creases which had been worn into her cheeks by the passage of tears that she'd shed for her dead children and lost husbands, so many of them gone that she was known in the quarter as the Orphan Woman and many folks turned away from her, fearful of contagious misfortune. Mimi was one who admired her, though, because for all of its repeated assaults grief had not soured her nature or made her hard, and Mimi took comfort from Lizzie Bocage's melancholy kindliness. "I will not hear a cruel word that's spoken about her," Mimi scolded one day when Alice brought home a schoolyard jibe about the Orphan Woman. "The woman has been struck by suffering for time after time and she is still the soul of sweetness. If ever there was a saint that walked on earth it is Lizzie Bocage."

"Yes'm, I do, Miz Bocage," Alice said. "I'll tell her what you said." "That's a sweet child you be now," Lizzie Bocage said, and she and her friends closed their circle again. As Alice passed on she heard her mother's name in their conversation but she had no particular interest in stopping to listen, for she presumed that she knew whatever she had to know about Mimi.

On the other side of the street a small crowd of children surrounded a chicken which was telling fortunes by turning over pieces of paper that had been scattered inside a hexagram drawn in the dirt, each piece of paper inscribed with a symbol relating to one of the three primary topics: money, love and death. Beyond the children, watching silently, the lean, dark figure of the conjure woman called Widow loomed like a charred signpost. Her yellow-rimmed eyes raised up from the ground and came to rest on Alice, and Widow blinked slowly. Old Patanouche had once told Alice that Widow was nothing but a zombie caller, but Mimi seemed none the worse for visiting her, so Alice saw no reason to be fearful of the conjure woman's stare. The girl smiled shyly, and without giving an answering change of expression, Widow let her eyes return to the chicken.

A rattling of hand drums sounded from further up the block and was followed by a sudden billowing of fire as two barrels of pitch were ignited at the corners of a raised platform. Shadows trembled on the house fronts behind the stage as the flames pawed the air, and from every corner of the street the children raised up like starlings taking flight and converged upon the platform, where a tall, muscled man wearing only a loose pair of trousers had begun to juggle first three, then four, then five blazing torches. Throwing them high and spinning into the misty air and dancing about beneath them as they fell like comets into his hands, their tails of flame turning his tanned skin to brass, he twirled on his toes, dropped to his knees and jumped back onto his feet again, all the while laughing in loud, barking cries in time to the drums played by two mulattoes in the street beside the stage. Lines of shadow rippled like eels between the muscles of his chest and shoulders. Now the crowd of children began to thicken with the arrival of grown men and women. Many of them were familiar to Alice as residents of the quarter but there seemed also to be as many strangers, and many of them costumed and masked or hooded so that their faces and figures, even their gender and skin color, were altered or altogether obscured. It occurred to Alice to wonder how many of them were spirit visitors, for Patanouche had told her that on occasions like this, when human activity was so noisy and gay, the near-dwelling spirits felt it safe to mingle in the earthly crowds, and she drew her breath sharply and held it when two cloaked figures passed close by her left side, for she was certain that she had looked as deeply as could be seen within their cloaks and spied nothing there but fog; then they stopped and turned beside a lantern and two human faces filled the shadows of their cowls, and Alice let her breath out in a sigh.

Firecrackers burst in an alley and a fat woman across the street shrieked in surprise and then laughed uproariously and began to dance from side to side, swaying like a haywagon. The woman wore a green-and-orange-patterned gown and a wide-brimmed hat trimmed with peacock feathers and in her hands she held a gin bottle and an almond cookie cut and decorated to resemble a man on horseback. As if summoned by the impulse of her dancing, the notes of a brass band floated near; someone had just propped open the doors of the Responsibility Association Hall on the next block, freeing the strains of a sprightly quadrille to tumble out into the street, which was becoming more thickly crowded by the minute. The fat woman's dance carried her wider afield and she bumped heavily into a small, dapper man wearing yellow shoes with new cork soles who grabbed her gin-bottle hand and waltzed her around in a circle. When he released her, laughing and flashing a silver tooth, she spun away and backed into a second man, tall and light-skinned with a widow's peak like a dagger point on his forehead. He wore an opera cape which reached nearly to the ground and when he lifted his hands to fend off the fat woman the inner lining of the cape flared scarlet, and there was no joy in his expression when he harshly shoved the woman away from him, so hard that she staggered and her eyes popped indignation, and she would have given him the rough edge of her tongue except that by the time she got herself turned around to face him he had disappeared into the crowd, melted away like a snake in tall weeds.

Alice turned her attention back to the juggler, who had climbed onto the top of a wooden packing crate which had been stood on one end on the stage and was lashed around with thick longshore hemp. The juggler had thrown away all of his torches except one, which he was rolling back and forth along his neck and shoulders where the dark, pitch-fed flames framed his head like a lizard's ruff, and all the while his feet kept dancing, cocking and stomping in the language of the crisp, evocative rhythms of the hand drums, rhythms that the slavers thought they had buried two hundred years before on West African shores but which had followed along anyway in breath and blood across the sea. Bone rhythms. People in the crowd moved their heads and their shoulders in time to the rhythms and many tapped or shuffled their feet on the paving stones, and the children jumped and danced and did their best to second-line the juggler's steps. This was a Creole quarter where the African strain had blended light with French and Spanish and Indian blood, but the ancient rhythms had their powers still and the honeyed faces in the crowd could be seen to ripple in approving response to the ancestral messages proclaimed by the drums.

The juggler kissed his torch once, twice, three times and blew a phenomenal plume of flame out over the heads of the crowd, and they craned their faces up to it like sunflowers and when it vanished they looked back at the juggler and saw that he had disappeared.

For an instant the hand drums were silent. The brassy quadrille swaggered alone along Piro. The children shrieked laughter and ran behind the stage and peered beneath the raised platform, and the faces of the crowd turned to each other with pleased expressions of wonderment. Alice clapped her hand over her mouth and backed away a step. "Say, where he gone to?" a voice said beside her and Alice answered, "I don't understand." Only in dreams did people disappear so; in the tingle of fright her first thought was to find her mother and have the mystery of it explained away with a giggle and a little rhyme, but before she could commence to seek for Mimi there sounded a loud knocking, three times from the packing box on the stage and with the third knock the drums resumed their clattering. Though no one could be seen to touch them, the ropes around the box dropped away to the platform and the lid of it fell open with a smack and there, inside the box, stood the juggler wrapped in an indigo cape with a white dove perched on each of his shoulders. The crowd exulted in laughter and applause, and the juggler bowed so deeply his forehead touched the stage. The doves fluttered away overhead, where darkness now commanded the sky and pressed the mists down close to the earth, and the juggler danced off the back of the stage. The packing case was pushed aside, and a bearded man wearing checkered trousers stepped up to the front of the platform and began to denominate the virtuous properties of a patent medicine, and Alice sidled away through the scattering crowd, looking around for Mimi. Something ominous was whispering to her timid heart.

On the opposite sidewalk young men were testing their strength, trying in turn to lift a boulder by the iron ring that was set into it, and not far from them a hollow-cheeked Cajun was handling bayou snakes with his mouth. A girl Alice's age was selling marzipan out of a tray, little tinted birds and bunnies, and everywhere all around the street fortunes were being told, by chickens, by goats, by an entranced child wearing feathers, by an old woman shaking a gourd, by a phrenologist in a frock coat. A fiddler accompanied a dog that danced on its hind legs and a two-headed calf was tethered to a lamppost. A parlor window was lifted open and emitted the sighings of a string quartet as fresh as iced lemonade. Out of a doorway a man in opera clothes stepped and paused on the stair; he was joined by a woman in an emerald gown who smiled at him and took his arm, and together they descended in stately fashion to the sidewalk.

Through a gap in the crowd Alice caught sight of Mimi and Lizzie Bocage smiling together and her heart lifted happily to see them. Mimi wore her favorite brown dress, cinnamon-colored with a fine lace collar and cuffs, and a little brown straw hat balanced like a snuffbox on her thick hair. Alice started across the street toward the two women but was halted by the passage of a rushing line of dancers costumed as river creatures. Then a rocket burst overhead, turning everyone the pale color of the fog, and she was jostled by two old men who lurched along with their arms around each other's shoulders, singing together in the old patois, their voices slow and rasping like the bellies of tortoises dragging across a stony shore. A sudden thrust of cold air blew through the night and caused the lanterns to sway where they hung and the colored streamers to wave; a tumbleweed clump of shredded paper rolled over Alice's foot and in the street nearby a man's cape caught the breeze and snapped open and she glimpsed scarlet dancing like flame behind his heels. Laughter rambled out through Tom Clare's doorway and the sound of a piano playing a stomp tune.

Mimi was nowhere to be seen and Alice stood, still and perplexed, looking around until her attention was arrested by the sight of a troupe of acrobats dancing on their hands to the music of a flute; while she was watching them a shiver passed through her chest and her ear detected a tiny prickle of noise in the night's clamoring which made her think of Jibba's sound, high and distant and as insubstantial as the taste of a single tear, but before she could consider that, her concentration was scattered by the explosion of three pistol shots fired close at hand in rapid succession. Sudden fright churned the crowd around her into a swirl and in Alice's head an awful throbbing commenced. "Mama," she cried out in terror, and then again, "Mama!" Moving with the awful, slow weight of a dream, she tried to push through the crowd toward the direction of the shots, convinced that they signaled tragedy.

After an eternity of effort she came to an opening where the crowd had drawn back and formed a circle, and, expecting to encounter a scene more drastic than she could imagine, she forced her way to its inner edge and stopped there, puzzled. In the center of the circle stood a red-faced policeman holding in one hand a rattling old pistol and in the other, by his shirt-collar, a terrified dark-skinned boy of six or seven years. "Where'd you get this, boy?" the policeman shouted, shaking the boy right off his feet, but all the child could provide for an answer was to stammer and roll his eyes and begin to cry shrilly. The policeman glared belligerently around at the crowd, who had already begun to forgive the boy his prank, which had evidently harmed no one. "Who knows this boy?" the policeman demanded angrily. "Who claims this child?" Something disheveled in the officer's expression suggested that he had been celebrating this evening himself in the saloons along his beat. The boy had features and coloration more African than was usual in the quarter and had probably strayed from one of the uptown wards; nobody spoke up to identify him but a woman's voice called out, "It's just a little child. Don't handle him so," and another said, "Wasn't no harm done by it, mister. Just let it be." The policeman squinted around suspiciously as other voices joined in to petition for the child's release and the boy, sensing that the tide of sentiment was turning in his favor, played to the crowd by weeping more piteously. Finally the policeman acceded; he gave the boy a final shake and dropped him with a cuff across the back of the head which sent the child sprawling. "I'm keeping this for evidence against you if I ever catch you misbehaving again," the policeman said, brandishing the pistol. "I'll have you into the Waifs' Home so fast you'll think you been struck by lightning, you hear?" He pulled back his foot to fetch the child a kick but before he could deliver it the boy scurried off on all fours among the legs of the crowd, which broke apart and resumed its eddying flow along Piro, leaving the peace officer posed on one leg like a piece of fountain statuary. Alice's fright left her as quickly as it had come and when she turned around she saw Mimi nearby.

Mimi was alone, standing at the foot of the steps which led up into the Responsibility Association Hall, with her face lifted dreamily into the golden light and rollicking brass music that spilled out of the open doorways. Alice saw Mr. Tervalon, the shoemaker, stop in front of Mimi and tip his derby hat and say something pleasant, and Mimi answered him with a smile and a burst of chattering whose cadences were clear to Alice even though she couldn't actually hear her mother's voice in the din of the street, and Alice felt reassured and suddenly lazy and paid no mind to the glimpse she caught of another man standing not a dozen steps away from Mimi, just outside the beam of golden light, though it was plain to see that the man's attention was focused on Mimi with an intensity that shimmered like a candle flame. It was the tall man with the knife-blade widow's peak and the scarlet-lined opera cape, watching Mimi with a reptile stare, his eyes dark and hooded and his jawline shining silvery like a railroad track in the moonlight, and when Alice reached her mother's side he disappeared, so, and Tervalon was tipping his derby hat once more and backing away in the direction of a vendor whose clothes were covered by pieces of mirror glass, who sold flavored ices from a pushcart.

Mimi greeted Alice with sparkling eyes and a hug around the shoulders. "Are you having a fine time?" she chirped. "Did you see the Chinaman yet? You know, that man can spell himself back into the times before Jesus. I always enjoys it to see the Chinaman." Alice told her mother about the juggler and the other things she had seen and Mimi remarked that if the eve of its arrival could be taken for an omen the new century would surely be a wondrous time for them all, and she patted little Alice's cheek with her chubby hand and gave the girl a penny for ices. "Lizzie Bocage is just gone and went indoors to fetch a shawl for her shoulders," Mimi said, "for she is easily taken by the chill. When she returns she and I are intending to go visit by her cousins on Beaudoin. Do you want to walk with us?"

Alice considered it for an instant but shook her head. "I think I'm sleepy, Mama," she said in a small voice, for the laziness she was feeling had crept into her limbs and eyes, and the sounds of the street were running together and forming a haze in her ears. Mimi leaned close and looked at her carefully and nodded, clucking softly to herself. "Too much excitement, darling, too much, I can see. You are still a child, no?"

"I fret for her lots of times now," she was to say to Lizzie Bocage as they were on their way to Beaudoin. "She is so timid and childlike it makes me wonder whatever's to become of her."

"She's a beautiful child," Lizzie Bocage murmured comfortingly, "and so fair in her skin, my. She could pass, I declare. That's something to think on for her."

"Oh mercy, no," said Mimi. "Passing, you got to leave everything behind you. She might as well be dead to me then and gone forever, and I couldn't ever—" She cut herself short at the sudden recognition of whom she was saying it to, for Lizzie Bocage, the Orphan Woman, had buried five of her own in coffins no bigger than shoeboxes. "Oh, Lizzie dear, I didn't mean. . . ," Mimi said. "Oh *la*, how did I say such a thing to you?" She touched her friend's sleeve, and Lizzie Bocage eased her with an understanding smile and patted her hand. "There

there," she said, "the child's got a fine life of living to come for her."

"Brick swears she's talented some at the piano playing, only he says her hands are so small," Mimi resumed. They had turned onto a narrow connecting street which was empty of revelry, and the sounds of the city's celebrations faded abruptly, as if they had removed to the opposite shore of a large body of water. The two women's footsteps echoed off the paving stones and stirred up little puddles of mist in the street. "It's time for her to start growing, Lord knows. Her blood broke in her the early part of autumn and I keep looking and looking for the other signs to follow. Her daddy was a tall man, very tall."

"That's a late blooming rose, is all," Lizzie Bocage would reassure her. "You have just got to trust in the working of time to bear it all out the way it suppose to be." "La," Mimi would answer hopefully, as they reached the corner of Beaudoin and crossed the street to Lizzie's cousins' house, where a fine parlor gathering was in progress.

"This night is just too taxing for any person, I think," Mimi said to Alice. "That Tervalon, he's feeling so gay he asked me did I want to go along with him see the parade on Canal Street. The *erotic* parade, me. Oh la, the men, how they do. When Lizzie comes back we'll walk you home, darling. You're not feeling ill?"

"No, Mama," Alice yawned. "It's only sleepiness. I can take myself home. I can do that." Mimi stroked her hair. "Well," she said, "I know you can. I only don't know what's inspiring Lizzie Bocage to be so long gone. But you always was my sensible child, so give Mama a kiss and I'll tell you all about it in the morning."

Alice touched her lips to her mother's soft brown cheek and smelled the familiar mixture of kitchen and laundry smells in the fine hairs at Mimi's temple. "What will you tell me, Mama?" she said. "Why, whatever there is to be told, darling," Mimi said. "Whatever there is to be told." Inside the Responsibility Association Hall cornets and trombones chased each

120

other up and down like dogs and cats in a summer garden, and as Alice turned the corner onto Angelus a steam calliope hooted in the distance from somewhere near the river. She looked back but the crowd was too thick for her to wave to her mother and she yawned and continued on to the little brown house halfway along the street, where the lamp cast an amber light in the stairway.

The turning of the century. In other cities far away—in New York and Philadelphia and Boston and Cincinnati and Chicago—men with shining white faces were raising goblets of French champagne and bellowing out bully prophecies of progress and dominion. "To the American Century, gentlemen," they boomed in voices flavored by expensive cigars and the assurance of their passion to succeed. The very passage of time, the arrival of the promised future, belonged to their domain; time was an engine, a dynamo, a machine with huge iron wheels whose turning they intended to acquire the authority to control, by guile, by industry, by the power with which they had been blessed in this republic and the sight of the Almighty, and the boldest among their bold fraternity felt that they could stand firm upon any piece of American earth and sense in their marrow the massive turning of time's driving wheels.

Alice still regarded time with a child's innocence of change; to her it was all nothing but a matter of sunrise and sundown, of day relieving night, and while each day might contain its novelties and diversions, she perceived in her life no accumulation of effect. Each discovery weighed equally among the rest, undistinguished by either precedent or consequence. It was something Brick remarked in her piano playing. "You get the notes just fine as can be, little Alice dear," he said, "but you've got to be thinking about the *flow* that makes every note feel as if it just spilled out of the one before it and is on its way to the one that comes after." She knew what he meant; it was the feeling that ran all the way up to her shoulder whenever she rested her hand on the back of his while he played, but it was nothing she could take from the keys with her own hands, and nothing she felt the lack of when she played. The importance of it eluded her altogether, and as long as she touched all the right notes she could please herself and Mimi, who laughed and clapped her hands every time Alice played a new piece for her, and said, "La, but I have broughten the cleverest child into the world." The memory of Mimi's laughter and the sure anticipation that it would chime again tomorrow made Alice smile to herself as she settled her head on the goosedown pillows that Mimi made certain always smelled fresh as a spring morning, and the smile stayed on Alice's lips while she slept amid the turning of the century.

But in her sleep that night, time called to Alice and drew her into its flow, calling in a thick, slow, alligator voice that had no tone or inflection, "Poor Alice, oh poor little Alice," and when she opened her eyes and sat up in her bed she was full of the realization that nothing anywhere was what it had been when she had gone to sleep, for not merely was the little brown house empty around her but she was alone, all alone, even beyond its safe confining walls, and the weight of her concentration as she tried to measure the difference between those two states of circumstance pushed her back down upon the pillows, staring though the darkness at the ceiling overhead.

Just before first light, while the fleecy mists rubbed against the windowpanes, Lizzie Bocage appeared in the bedroom doorway wringing her long, mournful hands, and Alice turned her head and saw the Orphan Woman's despairing face with the gulleys worn there by the tears which had flowed so often and heard her say, "Poor Alice, oh poor little Alice," and Alice stared at the Orphan Woman without blinking or speaking aloud and thought, *How different it will all become now.*

At the Welcome Mansion the celebration of the new century lasted until past dawn, and by the time Brick shut the lid on the German grand piano and departed the house the news of Mimi's death was in the streets, passing from the late revelers to the early risers, so that Brick heard its message without being directly told it, and when he got to Angelus and the little brown house he saw that Mimi's flat-bottomed cart with its iron wheels and the axle that chirped like a piccolo still stood in the narrow path beside the house, with its handles lifted as if to ward away the sadness. He went into the parlor and set aside his silk hat and his tail coat and took off the white vest and the tie and collar and laid them all on the sofa and seated himself at the old sea captain's piano, and although the midwinter sun had begun to pierce the mists and dry the glistening damp from the paving stones and the house fronts his hands found darkness in the keys and he bathed his sorrow in the nighttime sonorities of the blues. The desolate chords flowed urgently out into the morning, proclaiming bereavement to the quarter in tones of lamentation so unconsolable that they penetrated everyone's heart, and the dogs hid under the houses and even in the reveling places like Tom Clare's saloon the high-draped street boys who had vowed to jolly the New Year all the way to Pentecost fell silent and drew crosses on their breasts. Old Patanouche felt the pain of it where she drifted among the spirits and she looked anxiously down at little Alice, examining the child until she felt what Alice herself felt, which was the placidity of acceptance, and the old woman said farewell to the child then. In her parlor her body recomposed itself into the form of a small brown wren which quit the house by the chimney; for several minutes it fluttered purposefully back and forth from corner to corner where Angelus joined Piro, scattering dust and tiny feathers, and then flew away to the north.

Mimi's corpse was driven home from the morgue by one of Julius LaRivière's assistants later that morning. Brick left the house and Alice stayed upstairs in her bed while Lizzie Bocage and the assistant mortician washed and dressed the body and laid it out in the parlor, in a rough pine coffin set across two of the sawhorses which had supported Mimi's table in the back yard. It took six basins of water to wash Mimi's long black hair, which had fallen loose as she died in the gutter and had mingled with dirt and blood and streamers of colored paper, so that by the time she was carried back to the little brown house on Angelus her hair was crusted and tangled like a river bird's nest and Lizzie Bocage had to wash it and rinse it over and over before she could brush it out and plait it and roll it, weeping tenderly all the while for the violent fate of her friend. They dressed the body in a black gown with a lace choke collar high enough to cover the rudely stitched gash on Mimi's throat where the razor had parted her flesh and her life had run out, and then LaRivière's assistant rubbed rouge onto Mimi's cheeks, for her color had dwindled to the green of early spring, and they crossed her hands on her bosom, and the first thing Alice noticed when she came into the parlor and stood looking down at her mother was that in death the spots and stains on Mimi's chubby hands had faded away altogether, which would have pleased her mother, she knew.

They placed tall candles around the coffin and two straight-backed chairs at the foot of it, and for three nights and two days Alice sat there while the people from the quarter came and went. Sometimes Brick came to sit in the chair beside hers and sometimes he went away; there was an agitation in him which he could not quell and his sorrow made him restless, but Alice never stirred. Lizzie Bocage ushered the condolers through the little room, taking care that they did not brush against the candles, presenting them and their sympathies to Alice, who hardly noticed their familiar, saddened faces or heard their halting words of apology and commiseration uttered in ripe, drawling English and the soft, plaintive accents of the old Creole tongue. At one point a preacher arrived, a white-haired man of medium stature who stood on his tiptoes when he raised his voice to God; when he had finished praying at length he took Brick by the arm, addressing him as Brother, and began to enumerate the amenities of an orphan's home with which he was connected. Brick pushed the man's hand away and stalked angrily out of the house, and Lizzie Bocage persuaded the preacher not to follow, but rather to visit the yard behind the house, where food and drink had been set out upon the bleached white planks where Mimi had sorted and folded the rich white folks' fabrics.

On the second morning two white policemen came to the house and told Brick that the man who had killed Mimi was still at large in the city. After they left, Brick went away and when he came back he had a pistol in the side pocket of his coat which he kept touching as he sat beside Alice, who stared straight ahead at the coffin even while she slept. The white pine boards were dappled with knots and whorls, veins where pitch had flowed; the board ends were cut rough and stubbled with splinters and the nailheads ringed by the dimples left by careless hammer blows. Alice spent the time considering the totality of the coffin wood, drawing lines of connection between its surface features, fixing them into constellations and imagining the forces which held them so, apart and together, and the forces which might disjoin them and give them new shapes and dimensions. She remembered the time when Old Patanouche had pricked the end of her index finger with a penny pin and squeezed a drop of Alice's blood into a saucer of water. Alice had cried out at the pain and put her finger in her mouth, and Old Patanouche had said, "Oh hush now," and spit lightly on the corner of her shawl and touched it to the pinprick and the pain had gone immediately away. Then the two of them had bent their heads close together above the saucer where the drop of blood hung suspended in the water, its shape suggesting a map of the continent of Africa that Alice had seen in a book at school. Old Patanouche had tapped the rim of the saucer gently with her fingernail and the drop of blood had begun to turn slowly, altering its shape like a billowing cloud in the afternoon sun so that it became a cow's foot, an overturned wheelbarrow, a fat bird with a crocodile's head, a garden spade, a procession of gentlewomen wearing plumes in their hats. "Is it my fortune?" Alice asked. "Oh tell, *Gran'mère*, what will I be." But no sooner did she speak than the drop of blood broke apart and disappeared in the water. "Hmp," the old woman had grunted, and she'd leaned back in her chair and looked at Alice with an appraising expression, narrowing her sweet, round eyes and sucking in her mouth at the corner and staring at the child until Alice became quite uncomfortable under her scrutiny and cried out in alarm, "What? What is it? What did it signify?" The old woman had relaxed her face then and smiled her gentle smile and, shaking her head, she'd said, "Don't ever be fearful of me, dear. Trust the workings that I have to do." It was the night after that one that Alice had come into the parlor like a sleepwalker and placed her hand over Brick's while he played and felt for the first time the power of his music's flow.

By the third night the quarter's condolence had been properly spent and only a dozen or so mourners remained in the back yard behind the little brown house, sipping whiskey or lemonade and listening to a trio of small dark boys who stood shoulder to shoulder on the yellow ground near the clothesline pole and sang *Flee as the Bird to Your Mountain* and *Nearer My God to Thee* with the harmony of angels until a light rain began to fall and white foam bubbled up in patches like feathers on the ground and people took that to be a message from Mimi Beaudette's spirit and as quickly as they could they left. Later that night Alice began to dream in sounds.

In the morning she tied back her hair with a wide black ribbon and when the hammering ended and Brick came to the bedroom door and said softly, "It's time, little Alice. We have to take her now," she was calm and ready for the slow ride to the burying ground at the poor people's cemetery. Mimi had been a woman practical enough concerning matters directly at hand but in her life she had paid little heed against the future and no mind to the hereafter, and she had quit the world belonging to neither church nor burial society, so that there would be no priest and no parade to guide and accompany her final journey through the streets of the quarter where she had lived and died. Instead, she lay in a crude pine box on the dusty bed of LaRivière's third-best wagon, his paupers' wagon, with a small fat boy sitting on the closed coffin lid humming a slow hymn in short breaths and miming with his hands the manipulations of a slide trombone.

Alice sat in the middle of the driver's seat with Weeping Daniel on her left side and Brick on her right, looking down on the worn-out black horse with the patchy hide and the unbalanced ears who shuffled rhythmlessly along the damp dirt streets that led out of the back side of the quarter to the hill where the cemetery was hidden, on ground high enough that the dead could be buried in the earth. The fog around them was beginning to catch the sun's gold but the houses they passed were shuttered and mute, lumpish and damp with dew, like pieces of the night mist congealed and rooted to the earth. In the distance the cocks were beginning to crow and somewhere someone was playing a trumpet in a rising phrase, repeated over and over; but in the wagon carrying Mimi along, the only sound of consequence was the piping voice of the boy in the back, humming an old blue hymn. Alice glanced back over her shoulder at him and Weeping Daniel saw her look. "Ump," he said in his sour, slurred way, "boy think he's a brass band on a picnic. Think he's Frankie Dusen in the park. Suppose to be learning the undertaking trade, learning silence and condoling, an' he's got more noise in him than a electrical telephone. Boy"—he raised his voice—"there's nobody's dancing here today."

"Let him be, Daniel," Brick said mildly. "He's only a boy."

The boy finished out his chorus before he answered Weeping Daniel, explaining in a patient voice, "Ain't dancin' music; it's buryin' music." "Don't you be negatizing me," Daniel complained over his shoulder. "Ain't nothing 'cept a boy going *pee-pee-pee* and I told you to stop it now, or the next sound coming out of you's gonna be the sound you make when you're long gone without the time to say good-bye."

Brick leaned forward and looked across Alice at the driver. "Daniel, I'm finding little comfort in listening to you complain so," he said.

"Ump," Daniel said, switching the reins from his left hand

to his right. "Bad times, tickler, bad times." It was not exactly an apology, but there was no defiance in it and Brick accepted it with a nod. He started to say something but his voice was taken from him by a spell of coughing that tumbled up from his chest, so sharp in him that he bent forward around it, clutching his chest with both hands, and his eyes filled with tears. When it had subsided he cleared his throat with a deep, dredging rasp and spat something the color of the morning mist into the street beside the wagon. Nobody spoke for several minutes, until Brick, his eyes dry and his breath coming easy to him, lit one of the thin brown cheroots he favored, and then Daniel said, "Hoo, tickler. Sounds like when we get up there"—he nodded in the direction of the cemetery—"you might be asking are they holding a place for you there."

"I've got a place," Brick said. "I've always got a place."

"Burying place?" the driver said. "You got a burying place?"

"Living place," Brick said.

"Lay you down someday, just the same. Got to have a place for to lay you down."

"I do my living sitting up, Daniel," Brick said, "and wherever there's black and white to put my fingers on, that's my place." He looked down at his hands and spread and flexed his fingers. They were long, and flattened at the tips, and when he played they never rushed or fumbled on the keys but moved with the precise articulation of jackknives. Alice looked at them and then up at Brick's kind, homely face and felt a soft jolt of alarm, for she remembered suddenly all the times she had listened to him coughing and realized that it was not a quirk but a condition in him. For the first time she wondered whether he had in him the time to teach her everything she would need to know.

"Huh," Weeping Daniel said, "musicianer, huh. I seen the kind of places you do your living in."

"Music doesn't mind where it's played," Brick said, "or who hears it."

"Maybe so," Weeping Daniel said, his voice rising. "Don't

be thinking it's gonna take you anyplace special though, tickler. We all come out the same place in the end."

"I've heard that said."

"Same hand cuts you down as me. Rich or poor, black, brown or white. If you ramble or if you sits at home, butcher gonna find you and cut you down all the same, amen. A-*men*. The things I seen, missy," he said to Alice, who had turned her head to look at him not because of what he was saying but simply because the sound of his voice was interesting to hear when he lifted it out of its habitual complaining murmur; the talk of death animated it and gave it a musical tone. "The best leaves grieving hearts behind," he told her. "It's never too soon to be preparing for that, you know. Someday you'll be taking this ride."

"I don't see how it will matter to me then, Mister Daniel," Alice said.

Brick smiled. "At least you won't have to listen to all this mess," he said.

Frowning, Weeping Daniel popped the reins and clucked to the horse. They were nearing the cemetery now and the road had begun to incline uphill, which made the animal reluctant. The driver looked at Alice from the corner of his eye. "You're not such a child as you look, are you?" he said. She answered simply: "My mama is gone."

"Huh," Daniel grunted. "You gonna take up raising her then, tickler?" he asked. As it returned to the affairs of the living his manner was becoming sour again.

Brick coughed lightly, and Alice said, "Brick is teaching me things I need to know." "Just like the papa," Daniel said. "No," said Alice, speaking softly, reasonably. "I never had a papa. Just a mama and now she's gone and not coming back again. I'm alone now."

"But you got the tickler," Weeping Daniel said. Alice turned her face to Brick and smiled at him. There was sadness in her eyes but her heart was as calm as it had been since the turning of the new century had brought time's changes to her.

"For a while," she said. Brick returned her smile and it seemed as though they understood each other perfectly. "Long as you need me, little Alice dear," he said. "Long as you need me."

"Hallelujah," said Weeping Daniel. "Coming to the burial ground."

That night Alice returned to her bed for the first time since her mother's death and dreamed an intricate dream in which she had to cross and re-cross the city by streetcar, changing trams at every stop until she reached her destination, which was a wrought-iron gate in the middle of a featureless white stucco wall. Though she did not recognize the place, she did not knock or call but grasped the gate's handle, an iron ring, and pulled the gate open. Before she could pass through the wall, however, a shadow fell over her and something with soft, strong hands grasped her by her wrists and lifted her off the ground. That was the point at which she left her bed and, neither awake nor asleep but balancing both states within herself, went downstairs to the parlor. Brick was sleeping there, sprawled on his back along the short brocade sofa with his legs stretched out like buttresses to the floor and his pistol not far from his hand. Mimi's murderer was still at large in the city and on the second day of mourning a message had come to Brick from the conjure woman called Widow, saying that the assassin, if permitted, meant to harm little Alice too; Brick didn't traffic with the spirits and forces himself, so he had no way to verify the message or to alter the fulfillment of its warning, but he armed himself nonetheless with the small handgun and swore himself to watchfulness which he was able to sustain until, finally, fatigue washed over him more strongly than even devotion could ward off and he was just able to lock the doors front and back and draw the shades before collapsing onto the sofa in the drifting bliss of sleep.

As she entered the room Alice noted that he was asleep but recorded it only as a feature of the house, along with the drawn shades and the gaslight burning on the wall and the lifted cover of the piano keyboard, and she moved across the worn parlor rug still feeling the grip of the soft, strong hands around her wrists. She went to the piano and sat on the pillow on the straightbacked chair and spread her fingers across the worn keys and waited and after several minutes her left hand began to move among the bass notes and to establish a rhythm flow there that was not like anything she had learned to play in all the months that Brick had been teaching her bright little waltzes and nursery tunes but, rather, was like Brick's own music which she had felt beneath her palm on that night when she had first come downstairs into the darkened parlor and rested her hand on his: his late-night flowing music that rippled and rolled like the wide brown river outside across the city. Then her right hand began to flourish among intricate, angelic chords full of strength and sorrow and to pull the chords unstrung and chase melodies between their notes like the wheeling flights of sea birds darting in and out of the thunderheads that leaped so quickly up from the Gulf on a summer day, and there in the space between sleep and wakefulness Alice began to feel the music in her hands and shoulders and to feel the power of the forces of rhythm and harmony that gave the music shape and dimension and the heart's message. She felt as though her hands were riding Brick's hands again while they played his music, but the knowledge of that neither frightened nor confused her because it signified that she could ignore the workings of her own fingers and give herself up to the music and its flow, and so, while her hands went on playing, she slipped back into sleep and was lifted again by the hands of her dream and carried high into the midst of the constellations of the night sky, where she was not afraid.

While Alice dreamed and played that night and Brick slept soundly on the sofa, the man who had killed Mimi returned to Piro, a tall, golden-skinned man who wore his hair cut long and brushed to cover his ears, which had no lobes, and a widow's peak like a dagger worn on his forehead. He was cloaked in an opera cape which hung nearly to the ground behind his heels, with a scarlet lining, and it had been his intention to come for

Alice immediately after he had dispatched Mimi, but his plans had failed to account for the power of Mimi's blood which, when it spilled out of her throat onto his hands, had induced in him a reverie of strength and pain in whose spell he had wandered as if blind through the streets, howling ecstatically, for two days. Then, exhausted, he had climbed on top of a large wooden crate in a storeroom at the Cotton Exchange and slept around the clock. He awoke to find his hands clean of blood, and without remembering why, he began to trace his way back across the city to Piro. He relied primarily on his sense of smell to lead him on, for his eyes were subject to the distraction of confusing and incongruous images, and he did not trust them.

The last and most distressing of these visions was of a brick wall blocking the end of Angelus where it joined with Piro, which had been erected in his way by Old Patanouche as a final gift of protection for Alice. The assassin saw the wall clearly enough, but he also smelled his destination in Alice's blood nearby and, unable to turn back from the scent, he surged unhesitatingly after it. The blow he received when he collided with the wall split his forehead open in a diagonal gash from the point of his widow's peak to the tapered end of his eyebrow and knocked him staggering in a circle. He cried out in rage and, goaded by the blood-spoor taunting him from the little brown house halfway along Angelus, drew his razor from his sleeve and rushed against the wall again and again, growling in his throat like a dog and beating on the bricks with his hands and feet and knees. His razor snapped in two and the blade fell into the street and his hands broke and bled. The growling in his throat rose to a wail and on the other side of Piro in Tom Clare's saloon a group of street boys who were finishing out the night with a sleepy game of Spanish poker for low stakes dropped their cards and shuffled warily outside, and stood in a cluster blinking apprehensively at the spectacle of a tall man shedding blood from his face and hands who scurried back and forth from corner to corner across the entrance to Angelus, waving a razor's bone handle and howling and punching and kicking at the early mist in a ritual dance of madness and private despair so consuming in its violence that it shamed them to silence; when it was concluded, when the man fell on his back in the street and his cape spread out around him in a scarlet pool like spilled fire and his eyes turned up in his head and his howls were reduced to plaintive whimpering, the street boys fled to their homes like conspirators in a failed plot.

The police came then and stripped the man's cape from him and bound his hands and feet together behind his back and while they were considering the best way to carry him off someone who lived in the quarter suggested that they use Mimi Beaudette's old laundry cart which was standing unused in the narrow pathway beside her house. A policeman fetched the cart and they dumped the assassin onto its flat, shallow bed and hauled him away to the precinct station, and as they passed Lizzie Bocage's house the piccolo chirp of the cart's iron axle woke her and she rushed to the window in tearful confusion. Looking out into the mist she searched for the sight of her little friend trudging off to the rich white wards to fetch up their spills and stains for another day's work, and it wasn't until she beheld the short procession, of three policemen and a wagon with a trussed body in it, that Lizzie Bocage let out her breath and unclasped her long mourner's hands and sighed, "The poor darlin'. Poor little Alice, sure enough." The procession passed near enough to her window that even in the thick mist she could see the angry faces of the white policemen and the unconscious, ecstatic face of their prisoner, whose feet were bound up with his hands so that he curled backwards like a scorpion stinging itself on a flat rock, and Lizzie Bocage recognized him and sighed again, for it was Vraicoeur, who had once been Mimi Beaudette's husband and was little Alice's father, whose madness had been such a misery to them all.

Chapter Six

Tickled to Death

In the pages of Tom Anderson's *New Orleans Blue Book*, the classified guide and directory to that district of the city that was popularly called by Alderman Story's name, Countess Eulalie Welcome's Mansion was listed by its proper title, The Velvet Palace, and said to boast, "more Mirror Glass than graces the Grand Hall of Versailles Palace, and more Interestingly Positioned." "From this House every Gentleman departs bearing a Smile and a Song," promised the advertisement, which had been dictated to Tom Anderson's secretary by the Countess herself. "An' that song," she admonished her pretty little birds of pleasure many more times than once, "had best be, 'His Pockets Is Empty, la la, but His Heart Is All Swole Up,' an' my meanin' is with happiness an' joy, else you gonna see me toin inta one no-count Countess. Ah-hah, ain't that right? You don't want that nohows, liddaboids, no you don't. You wants to keep my nature sweetly disposed like a puppy chile on a pork chop. I prefoys to be ever so sweetly disposed in my nature, you see." She nodded her huge head decisively and, like a breeze dancing over a wheat field, little ripples of flesh rolled across the broad surface of her shoulders and bosom; the half-dozen little birds thus addressed returned her nod dutifully, with their expressions prim and alert the way she liked to see them looking, for they were always anxious to nurture her approval. "The altoinatives is too unpleasant to talk about in woids," the Countess had assured each of them, and they knew better than to debate her word on the matter.

Countess Eulalie was a massive woman, so ostentatiously indolent in manner and amorphous in form that it might have been supposed that she'd been carelessly designed not by the usual Power whose function it was to construct the human form but rather by some primitive artisan employing materials no more animate than jute sacking and goose feathers, but the vigilance of her spirit was acute and comprehensive within the reaches of her domain. Although she seldom left the huge, reinforced armchair that squatted like a horsehide citadel before the crimson drapes which flanked the entryway to the lavish room she called her parlor, the little birds of pleasure believed that her scrutiny extended into every corner of the three-story brownstone Mansion. They attributed to her the powers of a restless and versatile demon, who they said could see around corners and through the solid oak doors and could hear the conversations of their dreams and smell the night sweats of their souls. The manifest instruments of the Countess' authority over her affairs were two: her voice with its hard, sarcastic rasp; and Mr. Strap, who was her major-domo and hard man, a giant, gray-faced mulatto with thick, pitiless hands, who was known throughout the city as a man without mercy whose only pleasure came from reinforcing his employer's discipline.

"There are stories you'll hear about Strap and the things he's done that will make your gizzard roll over and cry mercy," Brick told Alice, "but the man's no concern of yours. You're a tickler now, girl, and you have the power of the music, wait and see. Play the music like you can and the Countess, she'll respect it, and Strap never does do anything the Countess don't want done. Those two go back a long, long time together, it's said. Listen to this." He cocked his head over the keyboard and played a melody that Alice hadn't heard before, fast-moving in its way but lowdown still, and with an ominous tone. "Tony

Jackson made this up," Brick said as he played. "It's all about Strap. They say the Countess came to N' Orleans in a flat-bottom boat, came up out of the bayou seated on a stack of alligator hides taller than a man's head, and Strap steering that boat with a pole. Say they ran it up against the levee there above the Black Bottom, and Strap jumped out and lifted that woman up with one hand and set her on the dry land, and with his other hand he heisted out those 'gator skins, and they walked side by side to Basin Street and when they saw the Mansion, Countess, she said, 'That'n's mine.' And that was that. I can't tell you if it's true or isn't, Alice dear, but I'll tell you this: that Strap is a hard man and a powerful one, and he totes a razor up the sleeve of that old frock coat of his that he doesn't use to shave his ugly face, but you don't have to pay him any mind at all, you hear? Of course," he added, smiling in his lazy way, "you shouldn't be playing this little piece around the Mansion, neither." Alice nodded as she watched his hands and recorded the piece in her memory while it played itself out with a bass figure that sounded like sardonic spook laughter, and she knew that she would recognize Strap, all right, and that she would not fear him.

Brick shifted the music back to the middle of the keyboard then, and commenced a ragtime strain which was slower and considerably sweeter than the Strap tune. He played it once all the way through and then flicked a look at Alice out of the corner of his eye, and without a word spoken aloud between them he slid aside to the end of the bench they shared and the girl moved to its center and picked up the music, just as he'd left it for her on the keys. "Um-um," Brick said softly, watching her fingers pluck the notes of glowing harmony and bobbing his head in time to the walking rhythm. "That's mighty nice-sounding, Alice dear, mighty nice. But remember what I told you that one time, how you mustn't push against that little falling figure there, you know the one I mean. Let it ripple like a brook, and they'll all take their notice of you. Um-um. A pretty little chromatic fall like that, why, I've seen it stop a man's breath in his throat, it's so sweet when you hit every note and make it *sparkle* that way. Um, that's right; that's it like that, and *there*. Play on through it now and bring it home. Um-um." His low, gentle voice followed along beside her throughout, always in time to the music, and flowing and blending into the spaces between the figurations of melody like sunshine in a cypress grove, and the little parlor filled up around them with the warmth of the music they shared.

On the morning of the day after they'd buried Mimi in the paupers' ground, Alice had awakened from her dream of flight to find herself still seated at the old, salt-stained piano, and the feeling of soft, strong hands still gripped her wrists and the last echoes of Brick's blues still tingled in her fingers, but the little brown house had been cleansed of sorrow and fear, and with the tonal feelings she had harvested while she'd played in her sleep, Alice had banished the past and driven away her childhood to a hidden place beyond the hard, flat light of the winter morning outside the parlor windows, and she was eager to begin whatever it was that would commence that morning, five days after the turning of the new century. She'd called to Brick in a low voice and he had sat up immediately on the couch and flexed his long fingers with their precise articulation of spiders' legs, and the two of them had smiled with unexpected complicity into each other's eyes and fallen to their business in a fashion so instinctive that it was as though they had been practicing it together for a lifetime.

The straightbacked chair before the piano was replaced by a bench upon which they could sit side by side, and from that day forward they met there every day in the early afternoon, after Brick had risen and smoked his first cigar of the day and eaten his waking-up meal, which consisted of bread dunked in cold coffee that had been sweetened with molasses. The ritual of instruction to which they dedicated themselves never varied in its order: first Brick would play, summoning forth the messages of time and melody from within the struck-steel heart of the old instrument, and then, while he sat at the end of the bench and commented and explained in an amiable, attentive way, Alice would extract their essences with her fingers from the cracked, discolored keys and examine them with her concentration until their form and their nature were clear to her. For several months things proceeded at a halting pace, while Alice shed the errors and habits of distraction that she had adopted as a child. But even as she struggled, she concentrated on the music with the patience of a scholar deciphering the language of a vanished race, and probed each scale and every harmony over and over for nuance and variation, and eventually the lessons passed from Brick to her as effortlessly as summer clouds passing across the face of the moon. In time they discovered that the voices of her playing had become all but indistinguishable from his voices, and her rhythm rode upon the deep, rolling flow of his life's rhythm then as trustingly as her hand had ridden the back of his on that night so long before, when she'd been a little child and his music had called her from her bed to stand beside him in the amber light of the parlor before dawn.

Outside the little brown house the seasons folded over upon each other and the mists of New Orleans congealed and dispersed like the dreams of exiles and orphans. Though Alice did not notice, the traces of Mimi Beaudette vanished from the neighborhood; in the back yard Brick had pulled the clothesline poles from the soapy ground shortly after the burial, and broken up the planks of Mimi's table for stovewood; a washerwoman from another part of the quarter had come and taken away all the pots and jars and sacks and little boxes which contained the soaps and dyes and chemicals and tinctures, and the tubs and tools and the squat black cauldron as well, and when the rains came that first spring after Mimi's departure the ground no longer expelled white froth and angel berries to twinkle and burst in the returning sunshine near the chinaberry and the smoke tree; Mimi's shallow wooden cart with its complaining axle rotted away to gray punk and lacy rust in the alleyway behind the precinct station because the police and everyone else forgot it was there; and scarcely anyone in the quarter recalled the sound of its piccolo chirp except Lizzie Bocage, who still mourned her cheerful little friend and was sometimes hauled upright in her bed at dawn by the certainty that she was about to hear that shrill, piping signal of the washerwoman's progress through the mists.

But the music had enclosed Alice within its deep, sustaining currents, so that the only changes she noticed in those months were the increase of her hands' assurance and the growth of her heart's familiarity with the voices of the keyboard. The only sort of time that mattered to her then was the duration of each note as she considered it upon her fingertips, and so diligently did she tend to her studies at the old piano that the world forgot her altogether. Even the spirits who hung about in the city's vaporous atmosphere could not discover her, because her manner forswore both speculation and nostalgia, either of which would otherwise have attracted the spirits' attention to her, and when she went out in the morning to perform the errands of the household while Brick slept, the inhabitants of the marketplace in the quarter scarcely noticed her as she approached and forgot her as soon as she had passed, for in her concentration she was as remote from them as a star in the daytime.

It wasn't until another winter had come and then commenced to drain away northward that Brick was satisfied that the music was solid and steady in Alice, so that the first part of his obligation to the girl had been fulfilled, and then he knew that it was time he began to talk to her about the other matters. "You do that so well now, don't you?" he said to her one afternoon while he watched her play an intricate, tumbling ragtime piece that was full of the sound of falling feathers and wind-driven petals. "I suppose I still could always want for your fingers to grow a slight, but that's no mind to you anymore, for the quickness you've got in them is a blessing on you." Her hands were still plump and conspicuously smaller than his, but they danced and darted like minnows along the keys and struck every note on its center, and she had instinctively devised alternative fingerings to compensate for her limited reach, and stylistic tricks that were most pleasing to the ear. "I see you discovered how to bridge that chord up top there near the end of that strain," he said approvingly. "That little hop you use does give it a nice bit of opening, and it does fairly tinkle in the hearing of it, I declare, um-um. I don't have to tell you about that anymore, though, do I, dear? You know what you can do now, and it's as strong in you as it's ever going to get." He waited for Alice to finish the piece, and then said, "Let me have it back now for a bit," and he moved to the center of the eroded old keyboard and took up a new voice from the keys, and began to tell the girl about the Mansion and the Countess and Mr. Strap, and as their story unfolded Alice began to move back into time.

And not long after the spring had raised up into summer that year, her time broke open before her and she began to consider the future, for she was visited by the realization that Brick's life was passing from him. One early morning she was awakened by a noise she had never heard before, the hard, hollow sound of a single dissonant chord, bitter and plangent in the cottony darkness, and in the first instant of her wakefulness she thought of Jibba, whose distress was always abroad somewhere in the city, but then, as the sorrowing tone faded in her ears, she understood that it was Brick's voice, calling to her not from his throat but from his fingers with the spontaneous urgency of a sob. Quickly she slipped out of her bed and wrapped herself in an old robe which had been Mimi's, and descended to the shadowy parlor, and in the dim amber light cast by the lantern at the foot of the stairs she saw her gentle instructor bent away from the keyboard of the comforting old nautical piano, with his fist pressed hard against his chest and his dear, patient face knotted in a rigid expression of pain, and she suddenly noticed for the first time what she had been forbidden by the rigor of her self-absorption from recognizing before; that the coppery sheen was fading from Brick's hair and the freckles on his creased forehead had lost their ripe chocolate luster and lay upon his sallow skin like flakes of dry mud;

that his neck seemed to have lengthened and his flesh had taken on the brittle look of old silk threatening to burst on the sharp, visible edges of his bones; and that in his absinthe-colored eyes, so calm and encouraging, the smoke of his constant pain drifted with a greasy sheen. For the first time since her mother's death, Alice was aware of the chill currents of fear in the close air of the little parlor. She saw that Brick had brought pieces of the night's mist into the house with him, gray patches that clung to his back and shoulders like dead leaves from a frozen tree, and she fetched a shawl and placed it over his shoulders and held him tightly from behind, alarmed at how thin he had become, how frail within her embrace, until the spasm which had caused his wracked, dissonant outcry released its grip and he breathed easily again.

Alice helped him across the room to the narrow sofa and covered his legs with a comforter and fetched him a china cup of herb tea, and while he lay back along the sofa and inhaled the vapors of the herbs, she took his place at the weathered keyboard and let his interrupted blues play themselves out through her hands. When they were done and silent she looked back at Brick and saw that he had set the cup aside and was sleeping, but as she stood up from the bench he opened his eyes and smiled at her in the old, lazy way that had always charmed her, and said, "You tell my life better than I could myself, little Alice dear." Later that morning, while Brick slept in Mimi's bed, lying on his side with his legs pulled up so that his feet wouldn't poke through the covers at the bed's foot, Alice opened the big wardrobe trunk that squatted in the shadows at the end of the hallway upstairs and took out two of her mother's black dresses, and carried them to the parlor, where she measured them to herself and began to prepare them to wear to the Mansion.

Brick kept on working at the Welcome Mansion throughout that summer and into the fall, performing with a stringent self-control which forbade his illness to impinge upon the measured flow and tone of his music even though it gnawed at him constantly now, with the slow, unappeasable appetite of a shadow advancing before the afternoon sun. "Tickler's been lookin' a slight peaky lately," the Countess remarked to Mr. Strap one morning while they sorted and counted the receipts on the pantry table. "I hopes it ain't nothin' 'cept seasonable." Though she knew nothing about music itself, the madam was acutely attuned to its effect upon the moods of her parlor, and in her appreciation of his skills she regarded Brick almost superstitiously. "Speakin' frankly 'tween you an' me," she told Brick one night, "this bidness ain't so much different from the others. It's jus' sweat an' jizz an' clean towels on the commode, ah-ha, that's no secret. Only, when I sets down in the parlor 'midst the gennamens an' the liddaboids I gets a queenly feelin' that I loves to feel. I don' understand how you does it, Brick darlin', but you makes it all bind together in your way, an' I'm grateful to you for that." Like any person who lives by her own rules and design, the Countess harbored within her hard-eyed autonomy certain small pockets of self-deception, sufficient to prevent her from acknowledging in anyone's company but Strap's the increasingly apparent evidence of Brick's deterioration. For his part, Mr. Strap gave no indication that she had spoken at all, but kept his impassive yellow eyes fixed on the tabletop where his long, thick fingers divided and stacked the bills and coins and gentlemen's markers with the unhurried motion of grazing oxen.

In that city, where sound flowed with the profusion of a martyr's blood, Strap bore silence like a shield hewn of stone. Every gentleman who ascended the marble steps from Basin Street to the Mansion's mahogany door was confronted in the narrow vestibule by this cadaverous giant and endured the test of his icy scrutiny before passing through into the house, for it was the major-domo's public function to ensure that no prospective patron be admitted to the parlor who might by his character or demeanor violate the genteel atmosphere which Countess Eulalie cultivated there as her stock in trade. "If a gennamens wants to go ruttin' 'round the place like a tomcat," she had let it be known many more times than once, "let him go do it by Hilma Boit or the Joimany lady's, or one of them colored houses. There's places aplenty for lowdown tomcattin' in this town an' I don't grudge 'em a whisker, but none of 'em's in my parlor, an' that's well known by one an' all. The ignorant ones is reminded of it by my Mister Strap."

Garbed in impeccable evening wear and armed with the force of his silent gravity, Strap directed the traffic in the vestibule with the gesturing of his massive hands, and his decisions, once rendered, were as incontrovertible as nightfall itself. Despite the widely fostered opinion, however, he was no mute, and on those rare occasions when he was either provoked or inspired to speak, his voice would issue forth in a sepulchral whisper, scarcely louder than the sigh of air escaping around a closing door, in an effect which those who had heard it swore was even more menacing than his silence. "That's a *hard* man," Brick repeated over and over. "He chews up pig iron for breakfast and spits out razor blades on his plate." He modulated into a major key and a strolling tempo, and continued to describe the Mansion to Alice.

Behind the vestibule was the entry hall, lit by a glorious chandelier which hung over the foot of the curved, carpeted stairway that flowed to the dim hallway and fragrant chambers above. The right-hand side of the entry hall was taken up by the arched portal opening into the parlor and its splendors, presided over by Countess Welcome from her heavy, cushioned resting place, which was deliberately positioned just inside the archway so that she might intercept and examine every person who entered or departed from the room. The Countess clothed herself by custom in plum- or raspberry-shaded silk gowns, cut long enough to permit her the luxury of going barefoot unobserved, and she wore her hair in dangling ringlets tinted with Egyptian henna; when she extended her swollen and somewhat waxy hand for a gentleman's touch of greeting she displayed no fewer than a dozen polished diamonds upon her wrist and fingers and another in the canine tooth on the left side of her mouth, which was the side she smiled from. But the opulence of her person constituted no more than one detail of the vast, elegant parlor with its velvet-faced walls of scarlet and its soft maroon carpet. The ceiling above the room was high and dark, divided into coffered squares, and it supported a pair of huge crystal chandeliers more glorious than the one in the hall outside. The oiled woodwork surfaces of the moldings and frames in the angles and corners of the chamber had been carved throughout in a profuse glossary of scrolls, grooves and leaves which swallowed the lamplight as it fell upon them and reissued it burnished like fingerworn golden coin.

In the wall at one end of the room was a fireplace the size of a general's tomb, surmounted by a blood-veined marble mantelpiece and a gilt-framed mirror as big as a banquet table. The parlor's chairs and couches were deep and solid, covered in crimson velvet and black braid, and the tables and sideboards had been wrought from lustrous mahogany and were freshly set each day with runners and doilies of spotless linen and lace. Polished marble replicas of classical statuary occupied the niches and alcoves, and in the spaces of wall between the heavily draped windows hung oil paintings depicting scenes of field and forest in a calm, academic style. And in the corner of the parlor at furthest remove from the entry arch, a German grand piano rode upon the maroon carpet like a cherrywood ark in a sheltering port.

"The first time you see that piano you'll think it's as big as this house," Brick told Alice, "but when you count the keys you'll find no more than the eighty-eight you have right here, set one upon the other as close together as these. Your hands will know their way, don't fear. But strike easy on it until you've learned its nature, because when you reach right down in the heart of it, it will give you back a sound that's as big as the symphony, and Countess doesn't want that kind of noise. She likes a nice, relaxing tone of music to be going in the room, where everyone can chat away pleasantly without raising their voices, and if you ever really turn loose on that old piano it raises a shout they can hear all the way clear to Algiers. Ease back on it as you go, and let the light show through." The piano had been constructed in the Black Forest, and when he had first gone to work at the Mansion Brick had discovered in the sonority of the instrument deep pockets of darkness which lent a maudlin taint to even the sprightliest compositions, and which had taxed him through several weeks of arduous restraint, until he had finally dispelled and replaced them with the sunny brightness of his own ragtime; but even then, and throughout the years that followed, his relationship with the instrument remained watchful. "It's like riding a fractious horse that you never quite broke," he explained. "You have to concentrate all the time, and you don't ever dare let go and give it its head, because the Devil himself don't know where it might run. For an instance, you take the blues now. Many's the evening when things start to go idly after midnight, and the Countess' little ladies will start wheedling you to play them a blues, because it sits plumb in their nature to root up sorrow and take it for their own. But I'm warning you right now, the blues in that big old box are cold and sorrowful as the blues from a tomb, and so altogether full of pity and sadness they'll turn a woman's face to the wall, and if you ever put that kind of a feeling into her parlor, you'll see Countess turn foul as a sailor and start calling for that yellow-eyed son of a bitch, Strap." A wisp of the Strap tune drifted up from his left hand. "Of course then," Brick added, "you don't have you no blues yet to play, do you?" He started to smile but just then his sickness reared up in his chest with its claws grasping, and he grunted and turned away from the keyboard and snatched up his handkerchief and began to cough into it.

Brick's spasms shook the piano bench and Alice could feel the iron taste of his pain in her own throat. She knew that when he took it away from his mouth his handkerchief would be spotted with blood, but when she reached out her hand to comfort his shoulder he shrugged it away, saying, "Play," in a strangled gasp, so she turned back to the keys and let the music wash through her without sorrow, and finally the spell passed from Brick.

For a minute or two he sat beside her with his head down and his shoulders folded forward, listening passively while she drew out the bright skeins of ragtime melody and embellished them with the little twists and filigrees of his style, and when she had finished he stood with slow effort. "I reckon I'll take some rest now," he said, breathing shallowly and speaking without emphasis. "You want to work some in the middle of that, where it turns around. More happiness in it. Countess always wants happiness." He turned and shuffled toward the stairs, his body bent inward around the hot ember of his pain.

Alice waited silently with her hands folded in her lap until she heard the quiet sigh of Mimi's bed accepting Brick's weight overhead before she resumed playing. Outside the windows of the little parlor the light was wintry, and the winds were sour and tended to taint the city's music with the toneless rustle of dead stalks, but the ragtime Alice played flowed like warm honey through her hands and palliated her apprehension and her sorrow. Before much longer, she knew, it would be time for her to begin the journey of her destiny by following the music out of the little brown house on Angelus.

Brick's condition dictated that; his sickness was beginning to sow its poison even into his wrists and his long, calibrated fingers, and more and more the signals of the infection could be detected just beneath the surface of his playing, sharp-edged stones of discordant fear and malice, over which the easy-paced flow of his ragtime was suddenly stretched shallow, its calm rendered perilously fragile. Soon he would be denied even the protection of his gallant will; his pain would begin to thrust itself up through the imposed serenity of his ragtime as it had already started to rend the gentle reflectiveness of his early-morning blues, and then the tone-deaf Countess, even in her loyalty, would no longer be able to ignore its shrill intrusions, for it would bark amidst the murmuring civility of her parlor like scornful laughter, exposing the venery beneath the veneer of genteel commerce she so rigorously imposed upon that chamber. In the rooms upstairs erotic engravings hung about the walls, and mirrors were positioned above and around the soft, sighing beds; there were satin-lined manacles in the rooms upstairs, and harnesses of silky calfskin with brass buckles where they joined, and small rosewood paddles waxed to a jolly glow. At the head of the stairs strutted a bronze Cupid with an erection like a plough handle pointing to Heaven, and at the furthest end of the third-floor hallway, beyond the linen closets and the attic stairs, hid an unfurnished room with padded walls and an upholstered floor imprinted with traces of blood and carnal juices, where an admiral of the Brazilian fleet and his brother the Archbishop of Jacarezinho were said to have once spent three days fucking themselves to death to satisfy a wager that had gone unsettled since their adolescence. Upstairs in the Welcome Mansion the brazen odors and canine sounds of debauchery frolicked like bear cubs, but—such was the force and insistence of Countess Eulalie's determination—neither gesture nor utterance ever so much as implied them in her parlor.

Brick's music had long been one of the guardians of the Countess' parlor illusion, and he knew that as well as she did, though he regarded his talent far more practically than she. "It's nothing more than a matter of keeping the room in tune," he explained to Alice simply. "Listen to the music as it comes back to you from around the room and you'll hear just how the room is taking it. If it sounds like things are slowing it down, you just push on the tempo a little bit; if the folks are too noisy and the music can't get through, that's when you soften the music and pull them back to you, and then bring it back up to where it should be; but if you hear them acting too soft and sad, don't play any louder, but just raise up into one of the sharper keys that prickles up the spirit. Countess thinks it's something magical, but it's all in your ears and your concentrating, and it's all in the music, too."

Alice kept on listening, then, even when she knew a piece from every side, and she tested the softer sounds and the sharper keys until they were secure in her hands and in her comprehension. She understood that once she had received the last portion of Brick's music and he had none left in him to keep his pain submerged, then the music itself would be the guide and protector that Brick had been for her throughout the months since her mother's death. As evening fell she would dress herself in one of the pretty, high-necked black dresses which she had taken from Mimi's trunk and prepared to suit herself, resewing the seams at the waist and bodice, where she was narrower than her mother had been, and lengthening the hem, for she now stood slightly taller than Mimi; Alice had shortened the sleeves, too, to ride above her wrists, and added gatherings of white lace to the cuffs and the collar so that she would not present a somber appearance. Gowned, she would wrap her shoulders with a woolen shawl and go out into the twilight just as the damp mist was beginning to seep into the streets, and without fear or hesitation she would follow the music's trail to the tall, black-iron gate guarding the paved driveway that curved around the kitchen garden and past the stables to the Mansion's kitchen door.

Brick had told her that her knock would be answered by the cook, who, assuming that Alice had come to seek employment as a little bird of pleasure, would shake her head curtly and cluck and mutter to herself concerning the time and the world in which mere children sought such means as this to relieve themselves of their childhood. Hardly a day passed that the cook did not admit to the house another aspirant to this sinful milieu; tinkling like cracked brass or braying like little donkeys, winking and sashaying like painted princesses of Gomorrah— only occasionally shamefaced and fearful and dragging their toes—there was in the cook's estimation no end to them and their dreadful eagerness. The cook, a thin, flour-dusted woman who smelled of coffee and catfish, found it necessary to labor constantly at prayer while she worked in her kitchen, and she knit her hands before her bosom as she conducted each child through the pantry and the dining room to the Countess in the parlor.

When Alice followed the cook through the pantry she would encounter two or three of the little birds lounging there, eating chocolate candies and primping each others' hair, and as she passed through they would begin to speculate in whispers, appraising her appearance with idle wisdom and estimating the willingness of her skills; their whispers would follow her into the dining room and the parlor like filaments of yellow smoke, haughty and sour.

But when the time came, Countess Eulalie looked Alice straight in the face without distress or undue curiosity, and the cook's disapproval and the suppositions of the little birds of pleasure in the pantry were banished by the clear-seeing gaze of the madam's tiny eyes. "She doesn't appear to be any slight livelier than a piece of old cheese," Brick had said, "but she's a smart and a feeling woman, and she won't mistake you or be unkind." And when Alice said to her, "Countess Welcome, my name is Alice Beaudette and I have been sent to play piano for you tonight," there was neither scorn nor condescension in the Countess' rough voice as she answered straightaway: "I has me a tickler already, chile, that suits me jus' fine, I thank you."

"Brick is ailing too poorly to play tonight," Alice said. "I have come to play his music in his place."

Recognizing that the moment she had been dreading had finally arrived, Countess Welcome sighed profoundly, for she was irked at herself for not having prepared against it. "I has me a substituter that I calls on in that case," she temporized, and squinted to see whether the lie had any effect.

But Alice only nodded calmly, as if acknowledging the logic of the answer. Brick had said: "Straight off, she'll tell you that she's got a substitute, but that'll be just to hold off until she gets a measure of you, so don't let on that you know it isn't true. Let her collect her wits and then play your music, and she'll be happy enough when she hears what she's got."

Alice could see that the Countess was brooding, and after a minute she spoke, to keep the woman's attention. "I play all of Brick's music the way you like to hear it played," she said. "I play the ragtime and the light pieces, and I play in all the keys, top and bottom." She spoke in her most serious and composed manner, with her voice soft and low and as easy-going as Brick's in its inflection because that was the way of the music that had brought her to the Mansion, and the Countess heard that and was perplexed. She winced, her tiny eyes receding as the folds of pale flesh on her brow bunched together like powdered clouds. "Plague take us all," she rumbled softly.

"Yes ma'am," Alice said.

"The tickler ain't your papa, is he?" the Countess asked, tilting her head inquisitively.

"No ma'am," Alice answered. She met the Countess' gaze directly on, with her head high and an assurance in her pretty eyes which was most impressive.

"You a fair-complected chile, soitainly enough. I suppose you keeps from the sunlight."

"My mama and papa were French."

"Mp," the Countess grunted, raising a penciled eyebrow. "Ain't we all, in our ways." She pursed her lips to phrase another question and then thought better of it, and instead she sighed again and considered Alice silently, as inscrutable as sand, while in her thoughts she weighed the commercial possibilities suggested by the girl's appearance. The child was comely enough, she saw, as pretty as any of her little birds, with fine hair and a thin nose and skin so fair that in an environment less discriminating than New Orleans she might pass unchallenged for white. Too, she bore herself with natural and imposing dignity, although with her practiced eye the madam detected, she thought, a wraith of hesitancy flickering in Alice's eyes. That suggested vulnerability in the girl, a trait which the gentlemen always found most tantalizing in a little bird of pleasure. But what was its value in a tickler? Her inability to grasp a ready answer to the question made Countess Eulalie uneasy, and she tapped her waxy fingers restlessly on the arm of the horsehide chair. "How old are you, chile, for a fact?" she asked.

"I am sixteen years old," Alice answered without hesitation, which increased the sum of her years by a couple. "She'll tell you you're too young no matter what you say," Brick had said. "Too young, hell. She's got all those little gals of hers down in the parlor, which some of them are no older than you *used* to be, and they do those things night after night that'd make a street dog cry shame. Don't mind her when she says that. She's still just holding off."

The Countess shook her head slowly. "It's too young, I swear it is," she grumbled, but her voice lacked conviction. "I jus' couldn't be soitain of how they'd take the sight of it," she mused. "Your tickler's always got to be austere an' dignify in the parlor, an', ah-ha, look at you now, how you look. There you stands, all puppy fat an' shinin' like springtime on the rosebuds. I jus' don' know. It ain't altogether the custom, an' I jus' don' know."

"Wouldn't you care to hear me play?" Alice asked, trying to regain the madam's attention.

Countess Welcome squinted and looked her up and down some more. "You looks quite gravely, done in black," she allowed. "Is that your mama's gown?"

"It was hers," Alice said.

The Countess wrinkled her brow sympathetically and then looked away, turning her meditative gaze upon the dark, opulent room around them. Upstairs the little birds of pleasure twittered and preened, preparing in their way for their evening's pantomimes of gentility and lust; before much longer Mr. Strap would appear in the parlor, silent as bone, to inspect the crystal decanters of brandy and whiskey which stood arrayed in little jeweled avenues on the mahogany sideboards, and fill the bucket-shaped silver humidor on its carved walnut stand with a fresh supply of port-cured Cuban cigars. The chandeliers would be lit soon, and the split logs in the vast fireplace set to blazing, and the Countess' gentlemen clients would begin to arrive,

courtly and commanding. As night deepened in the city outside, the room would acquire its characteristic hum of dignified
comportment, and the gentlemen and little birds would address
each other as civilly as diplomats and ladies at a palace tea. And
where, fretted the Countess, was the sweet golden music that
would bind it all together?

She shifted slowly in her chair, like a walrus on a rock.
"Sickness, sickness," she muttered, glaring at the silent piano in
the corner beyond Alice's left shoulder. "What can I be runnin'
here, anyways?" she groused in her bulldog voice. "This one's
eye close up on her, an' the other one bleeds outta her nose.
This one got a prickly feelin' on the neck, an' that one toin
spotty all over her charmin' parts. Liddaboids never did got the
sense to look after themself; I got to been doctor an' noice to
'em both, an' now I got me a failin' tickler too. I mought as well
close it down an' go into the infoimary bidness instead, alla this
billydamn keep comin' up so frequent." Her hand flew up from
the arm of the chair and slapped back down with a solemn,
resigned thud. "Aw, what it matter what it is," she said. "Ain't
no good if I don' have me my tickler. Tell me, chile: is it
thought to be a poimanent condition, what he got?"

"He expects he just needs some time to rest from it," Alice
answered, and for the first time that evening her voice acknowledged uncertainty, because for an instant the protection of her
music seemed to fall back from around her, and she remembered Brick and the way he had looked when she'd stopped by
his bedroom door just before she had left, with his agony pressing him down into Mimi's little bed with such unrelenting
weight that he'd barely been able to turn his head toward her to
acknowledge her departure. The image of it tainted her tongue
with the iron taste of pain, and her throat quivered as she began to wonder whether he would still be alive when she returned to him, and the concentration to which she had trained
herself for so long threatened at that moment to shatter like a
clay pipe dropped on a stone hearth, when the Countess surprised her by asking: "Are you afeared of sin, chile?"

The question restored Alice's concentration even while it made her pause, for it was not a question for which Brick had prepared her, but reminded her rather of the catechistic riddles the Ursuline sisters had posed when she had been a child attending their school, whose answers she could never recall. Finally she said carefully, "There's no sin in music, so far as I've ever heard it said, and none in playing it either, so I don't suppose any sin can harm me as long as that's what I'm doing, Countess."

"Hoo," said the Countess, and smiled in surprise. "My my, but that's prackly philosophical. I dunno if it's austere, but I'm passin' soitain it's philosophical. Is that how you plays your pianna, little Miss Alice Beaudette? Like a philosophy?"

Alice held up her hands for the madam to see, and turned them this way and that in the maroon twilight of the opulent parlor. "I play like a tickler," she said, feeling the music strong in her again. "A tickler is what you're needing tonight, Countess dear." Without waiting for Countess Eulalie to speak, she turned and followed the trail of the music then to the massive cherrywood piano, where she raised its curved cover from over the keyboard and sat and began to play.

In those times the music of the inhabitants of New Orleans was as various as their dreams and disappointments, and the humid atmosphere was so crowded with melody that it was opined that even if one day all of the countless players and singers of it were struck silent for a fortnight, there would be enough music left over in the air that it could continue to spill down from the mists and swirling river breezes without interruption. In the Storyville district the establishments had always hired all manner of musicians, from string quartets to audacious spasm bands to sweet-potato moaners, to attract and stimulate their clientele, but the preferred custom among them was usually to employ piano players. Some of these ticklers simply played softly in the background, often hidden from the customers' view by screens or curtains; others sat in a central, visible place and sang or recited while they played, repeating familiar lyrics or improvising spontaneous, ribald commentary on the affairs of the house and its visitors; some provided melodic accompaniment to simple entertainments staged by the girls of the house; and in the roughest joints on the back side of the District, the ticklers played hot, fingerbusting music, low, grinding blues songs and sweaty stomp tunes, while the whores danced naked or writhed in erotic *tableaux vivants* and the customers howled and threw coins.

But the music of fashion in those times was the ragtime, sunny and optimistic, played with restraint but subtly tweaked in its formality by syncopation, its rippling melodies sharpened at their edges by a faint, pungent suggestion of blue tonalities, and ragtime was the music of Eulalie Welcome's favor. "She's got no patience with the spasm music and the ratty stomps," Brick had instructed Alice. "It makes her little gals too rackety and gay. And the classics get the gentlemen thinking about their wives and daughters, and it makes them shy and tight-fisted. But ragtime's got a high tone that rushes up the blood without bringing it to heat, and it keeps things moving along the way Countess likes it to be when you play it with that good steady roll like that." And as soon as Alice set her hands on the gleaming keys of the great German piano the soothing flow of Brick's ragtime rose right up into her fingers and spread out into the parlor, with its scintillating glow like the reflection of the summer sun setting across the slow-moving, dirt-brown river. The Countess, who would never recognize any music by its name or design but could seize immediately upon its flavor as it rolled across her aspirations, smiled with the satisfaction of an alligator in warm mud. "Lookityere, Mister Strap," she said when her major-domo glided into the room. "Miss Lulu White is gonna want to throw herself in the river when she loins about it, 'cause we got us a treasure like her an' all the rest of them is never gonna find the equal of it. Lookit how she sits there an' plays so fine. We got us a little *lady* to play on our pianna for us, an' she's the finest thing you ever did hoid."

The Countess called Alice her Little Lady and made certain

from the outset that the gentleman clients and the little birds understood that the new tickler occupied a special and protected position in the Mansion. "She's an artist, an' consoivatory trained," she repeated many more times than once, "an' most refined. I won't allow no foulness to come near my Little Lady, an' that best be knowed by one an' all." So formidable was her insistence on this point, and the enforcing threat of Mr. Strap, that during the first few nights that she played at the Welcome Mansion Alice was subjected to no more distractions than she had ever encountered during the months she'd spent absorbing the messages of Brick's music in the parlor of her own little brown house, and she was able to establish herself within the chamber of her concentration without disturbance. Every evening until long past midnight the music poured through her hands in steady profusion, gilding the atmosphere of the Mansion with its honeyed flow, so serene and unobtrusive that no one saw fit to remark upon the fact that from that small, light-skinned girl with her plump, scurrying fingers there issued the rhythms and tonalities of an aging, weary, colored tickler. Even outside the Mansion, in the saloons and sporting clubs where the other piano players of New Orleans gathered to gossip and show off and pass the time at games of three-card Spanish poker, though the news quickly circulated that Countess Eulalie had secured the services of a uniquely gifted performer— "A little white gal, I'm told, and playing with a fine, steady roll"—the sensation it might have caused passed by unrecorded. The ticklers were a jaded and self-centered lot, and the only novelty that impressed them was a new voice, a new sound in the teeming air, a new style that might displace them from commercial favor unless they were spry enough to adapt it to their own playing; regardless of who played it, Brick's sound was known to them and there was nothing left in it that teased their competitive desires. They dismissed Alice as nothing more than a clever imitator and turned their attention elsewhere.

But the little birds of pleasure found ways to approach Alice, and they courted her with curiosity, for they were young and excitable and always alert for novelty in their lives, and they were as intrigued by the simple dignity of her composure as they were by the incongruous artistry of her playing. Brick had told Alice: "Don't pay any notice to their talk, because they're foolish and they'll tell you tales. They get dressed up in the finery and it makes them think they're something fine. Important men come 'round and seek them out, so's they take it into their heads that they must be charming and clever. But remember this: the finery comes from the Countess, and the gentlemen always get up and go home, and they're only whores after all, those gals, and they'll never be anything better." But when they began to sidle close to her, giggling and whispering behind their hands so that the Countess wouldn't hear them defying her edict, Alice discovered that they were only girls and full of playfulness and fear and the experience of things she had never had the opportunity to consider, and although she never let her concentration be diverted from the music she listened to them just the same.

The boldest of the little birds was Grace Bonnard, a slight creature with off-center eyes and a rabbity mouth who was called Dirty Grace by the others. Even amidst the parlor's enforced gentility she behaved with a salty air of good-humored insubordination which Countess Welcome tolerated only because Grace Bonnard was the favorite companion of one of the Mansion's most influential and generous clients. "We all got our cross to bear," the Countess had said many more times than once, "an' that little Grace is my own an' my crown of prickly thorns." On a quiet evening after midnight there were no gentlemen in the parlor; only Alice and the Countess and seven or eight little birds who, even though the house was empty of customers, were not permitted to appear idle. "It don't matter the time of night," Countess Eulalie said, "Ifn a gennamens walks through this door I wants you all wide awake an' smilin' at him like it were the Fourt' of July an' he were the watermelon. Ain't that so, Grace Bonnard?" she called across the great room, not raising her voice so much as extending it, like a cat flexing its claws, so that it carried clear into the corner where Alice played softly and Grace Bonnard lounged against the side of the piano in the pretext of examining a painting on the wall. "Oh yes'm, Countess ma'am," Grace fluted, and then, as the Countess turned her scrutiny elsewhere, Grace winked at Alice and said out of the side of her mouth, "More likely it's like we was the monkey and him the *big* banana." Alice had no ear for the double-entendre, but there was something so friendly in the confiding way it was said that, unexpectedly, she smiled.

Grace Bonnard returned her smile with a look of some amazement. "Well wipe me dry," she said. She motioned to another of the little birds, a pouting, round-faced blonde with thin, painted eyebrows. "Hey Luana," she called in a loud whisper. "Hey c'mere." The blonde turned slowly and moved to the piano with a dreamy, gliding step and her head held back in a haughty way. She came to a stop near Alice's shoulder and she and Grace Bonnard faced each other in their parlor finery as regally as German duchesses, which was the way the Countess liked them to appear. "I beg your podden," the blonde murmured imperiously, and then snorted aloud when Grace Bonnard rolled her eyes and stuck out her tongue. "I seen her smile just then," Grace said, speaking low and rushed. "Seen what?" said the blonde. "Seen her grin, the Lady here."

The blonde looked disbelievingly down at Alice. "Is that a fact?" she asked, and Alice, flourishing an ascending cluster of notes that was like a tangle of butterflies, looked up at her and said softly, "Oh yes." She smiled again, ever so sweetly, and the blond little bird and Grace Bonnard looked at each other with conspiratorial delight; together they snapped a furtive glance back at the Countess and, seeing that the madam seemed to be paying them no notice, edged closer to Alice and began to whisper excitedly. "We thought you was so dicty," the blonde said. "You always look solemn as church." "Countess says tickler's suppose to be austere," Grace Bonnard said. "We was thinking that means deaf and dumb." "How you learn to play piano like that, a bitty little thing like you?" the blonde said. "I'm Baby Luana, how'd you do, and I'd admire to be able to play music like you do better than anything." "You want to hear something?" Grace Bonnard said. "Mister Balthazar Vavasseur that owns the Cotton Exchange and is my special daddy says he'd pay a pocketful of rubies to take you upstairs." "Stop your mouth, Grace Bonnard," Baby Luana said. "Don't you listen to that mouth of hers, Lady. She can't help the trash that comes out of it." "Thisun's ass smells like apple blossoms," Grace Bonnard said. "Least that's how she thinks about herself." "Dirty Grace, Dirty Grace," Baby Luana sassed. Then she straightened and turned toward the entryway, where the sound of men's voices could be heard. "Don't pay her no mind, Lady," Grace Bonnard said confidently to Alice as Baby Luana, patting her blond curls into place, moved away with a stately step toward the center of the room. "She's my special friend but she ain't got the sense God gave a dodo bird. Anything you want to know about this place, you ask me, all right? Here comes the Fourth of July." And she fixed her face into the haughty expression the Countess liked to see and went to join the other little birds, as a party of smiling, corpulent gentlemen filed into the room and greeted the Countess and the little birds with the stern bonhomie of benign conquerors. Alice noticed that she walked with a pronounced limp in her step.

Within a short time all of the Countess' little birds of pleasure had managed to introduce themselves to her and as she became acquainted with them Alice found that their voices and moods were already familiar to her, for they inhabited the voicings and sonorities of Brick's music. The only aspect of the little birds' natures that she hadn't been led to anticipate was their fear, which she quickly realized lay just beneath their bright chirping and their bold, knowing chatter like a serpent in a flower bed, and which even the brassiest and most insouciant of them could not keep from disclosing. So pervasive was the flavor of anxiety in them that Alice was puzzled that Brick, with all his gentle and accepting understanding of the world and its

158

ways, had ignored it in his instruction, but when she alluded to it he denied its import with a sour, sidelong look. "Whores got no reason to be afraid," he said flatly. "They wind the men 'round their fingers and lead them like dogs on a chain. If they were feared of it they never would have chosen that life. Whores don't have the decency to be ashamed or to worry for the Hereafter. Any man could tell you that."

His harsh pronouncement perturbed Alice but she hadn't the heart to dispute with him, for she attributed its callousness to the bitter progress of his illness in him. Its poison had stolen the resonance from his voice and the calm gleam of sympathy from his eyes just as it was consuming his muscle and flesh, so that his bones showed through his loose skin like old iron in a jute sack; even the flattened pads at his fingertips had shriveled, and he no longer had the strength or desire to approach the old, salt-stained upright that had been his confiding ally for so long. Ignored against the parlor wall, the piano seemed deflated and forlorn, a derelict vessel aground on an inhospitable shore. If Brick left his bed at all now it was to shuffle to the back yard, where he sat huddled into himself on the kitchen rocker in the afternoon sun; there, to escape the battering spasms of his pain, his mind conveyed him back into the time of those pleasant afternoons when Mimi was alive and trundling back and forth about her business with the patient, unhurried gait of a strolling porcupine, and little Alice, a shy child with fingers like pink bubbles, trailed behind her mama's skirts or lay among the blossoms on the ground beneath the chinaberry and the smoke tree, peering out from under the brim of her straw hat at the laundered sheets dancing on the clothesline. These memories pleased Brick so much that after a while he took them into his dreams and shut himself up there with them, so that he could feel the sunshine again on his forehead and his coppery hair and smile at the sound of Mimi's singsong and laughter while his pain raged away somewhere far in the distance, like a storm out over the Gulf, and he scarcely noticed any more when Alice propped up his head and fed him red beans and rice or fish stew from a bowl in the early even before she went off to the Mansion. By the end of that autumn his blues had left him altogether and the chinaberry stayed in fresh blossom day and night for him. Alice could see that his pain no longer tormented him constantly and for that she was thankful, and she continued to bring him the news from the Mansion and the marketplace and to tend to his needs with cheerful diligence, though he had become so distant from her that he seldom acknowledged her presence, even when she washed him with a sponge or lifted him from the bed in her short, strong arms and set him in a chair while she turned Mimi's old, sighing mattress and changed the bedsheets.

"Old Brick now, he's not your daddy, is he?" Grace Bonnard asked Alice one night. "Tell the truth now, Lady." Alice understood by then that when the little birds talked about daddies they weren't referring to their male parents, but Grace's question was asked in simple curiosity and Alice shook her head while she played and answered without offense or embarrassment, "No, dear, he's not." Because they knew things about life which she couldn't even guess at, she paid the little birds the courtesy of listening attentively to their exotic chatterings, and treated them with an unjudging politeness to which they responded as though she was a favorite aunt, whom they could tease and tell secrets. "I'm not saying he wouldn't be a good old daddy to have," Grace Bonnard said. "Kinda close-mouthed, maybe, but he had a kindly way about him, and he didn't seem like the whupping kind. Besides, a good tickler can always make the money. You make the money now, don't you, Lady?"

"Every man's the whupping kind," Baby Luana said before Alice could answer Grace's question. "There's not a man on this earth that don't want to give you pain sometimes, and you may as well know that. Best a woman can hope for is to find her a daddy that whups soft and seldom, and then work to keep him that way. Study on his ways, and say Yes Daddy and No Daddy and keep him sweet as you can." Luana's skin was extremely fair, and Alice had noticed that it was often bruised; beneath her powder and paint dark patches lay not quite hidden, like oyster shells in the sand, and her pouty mouth was often unnaturally swollen.

"You know that Mister Roscoe Faraday that writes in the newspaper?" Grace Bonnard asked. "A sweet little man that talks so cultured and got hands no bigger than a boy?"

"I never gone with him, I don't believe," Baby Luana said.

"Naw, he always ask for Sarah," Grace Bonnard said. "Except one time she's laying up with cramps, so Countess say to me, 'Grace dear, p'raps you likes to convoice wid Mister Faraday,' the way she does, and he smiles so sweet and talks to me like it was poetry and I'm saying to myself how this is going to be like eating cakes and candy. And in the room I'm rubbing him up and telling how fine he is, and how big and strong and all that trash the way they like to hear it told to them, and he gets to grinning and shining and ready to go, and just like that without saying Gimme that, he takes hold of my arm and bends it around behind me like this and starts to twist and yank like he's pulling the leg off a chicken. I say, 'Whoa mister,' I say, 'let up 'cause it feels like you're gonna bust it,' I say, 'Please, Daddy, that hurts me terrible.'"

"Doesn't make him any mind," Baby Luana said.

"I might as well be talking to the Chinaman," Grace Bonnard said. "He's puffing and steaming and his face is getting red like fire, and he keeps on twisting and yanking till I'm about to shout help murder and never mind about the Countess or Strap or anybody to keep my shoulder from being broke, and just then he does his shot *bangbangbang*, real quick, and as soon as he does he lets go. Mercy, that old son of a bitch. You know what he says?"

"Same as they all say," Baby Luana said.

"'You're a bad little girl.'"

"That's right," Baby Luana said.

"That's right," Grace Bonnard said. "I'm a bad girl. And me, I say, 'Yes Daddy you're right I'm a bad girl and you're my good strong Daddy,' 'cause I'm no fool, unh-uh. You remember Araby?"

"No, but I heard tell about her," Baby Luana said.

"That was a big handsome gal of partial color I always believed, though she carried on that it was all Spanish blood in her."

"I heard she lays up in a crib now, over back of the District."

"Worse'n that," Grace Bonnard said. "She went crazy one night, is what. Man bit through her skin up top of her titty, and she started hollering and commenced to hitting him with his own boot, yelling 'You son of a bitch' at him till he ran out of the room and she chased him right down the stairs, both of them buck-ass naked and dripping blood like water off the roof."

"I know who it was that bit her like that," Baby Luana said.

"'Course you do," Grace Bonnard said.

"Biting like that's the worst thing of all," Baby Luana said. "A man can kill you with a bite as quick as a snake can, Doc told me."

"Quicker than," Grace Bonnard said.

"I'd sooner take pain joy with a strap as biting," Baby Luana said.

"You ever took real pain joy off a man you wouldn't say that," Grace Bonnard said.

"Did you ever?" Baby Luana asked.

"Not like the kind I mean," Grace Bonnard said. "Countess never did permit it like that. She always said it was too dangerous, she said. She don't want that kind of reputation for the house."

"A man'll do what you let him do."

"Naw, Baby," Grace Bonnard said. "A man'll do what he *wants* to do, if you let him or not, 'cause he's the man. No difference if it's here or Germany's"

"Why'd you say Germany's?" Baby Luana asked. "Is that where Araby's at?"

"I was thinking about that poor girl that died over there last week, taking pain joy, is what. What was her name?"

"Callie, I heard."

"That's right," Grace Bonnard said. "Callie. A yellow-looking little old girl, real beat up. I seen her once or twice, I think."

"Man that did it was a policeman."

"Presink captain from the Sixth Ward," Grace Bonnard said. "Busted her back like as if a wagon run over it. Lotta policemens go to Germany's all the time. I druther lay up in a crib, I think."

"Not me," Baby Luana said. "I'll stay right here."

"Huh," Grace Bonnard said, "till they throw you out."

"I'll find me a daddy first that'll take me away."

"And beat on you without paying for it. You got no more sense than to do that, Baby."

"What happened to Araby then?" Baby Luana asked. "She gone to Jackson?" Jackson was the site of the Insane Asylum of Louisiana.

"What happened? Oh, she told them off real fine, is what. She chased that Mister Jonathan Bohannon right out the kitchen door—"

"I knew that was him," Baby Luana said.

"—and then she come marching right into the parlor pointing to the spot where he bit through her titty and says real loud, 'I ain't no ham samwich that you can take a bite out of me like that, and if you ain't gone to tell them that'—she says to Countess—'I'll tell them myself.' Countess says, 'Araby dear, you best clean yourself up, dear, and then go lie down till you gets your relaxation back,' acting all sweetly and concerned, you know, only then Strap comes in with a sheet to wrap around her and he's got that look on him that he gets sometimes—"

"Oh Lordy," said Baby Luana, "I heard it was like that."

"—and he wraps her up and takes her away so fast she's gone like smoke up a chimney," Grace Bonnard said, "and

Countess is sending downstairs for champagne as if nothing's happened."

"Oh Lordy," Baby Luana said. "Sometimes I look at him and I want to scream just thinking about it. Those yella eyes on him, Lordy. That man is pain on feet."

"Boy I was talking to out the back door the other day—you know him; he's that boy with the funny ear, that rides the fish wagon and's always telling his stories about how the Sicilians used to do—he says he seen Araby down by the docks now."

"Turning sailors in the alley for a nickel," Baby Luana said. "That's where you go if Strap turns you loose without killing you."

"Laying back on a sack of corncobs," Grace Bonnard said, "with your face in the shadow so they don't see how you've been marked."

"Find you a man that all he wants is to whup you from time to time," Baby Luana said, "but if he takes out his razor you might as well run down to the river and throw yourself in, because a man with a razor is like any animal, that once he gets the taste for blood he don't want nothing but more."

"That's the only time Strap is ever happy," Grace Bonnard said, "is when he's carving on some girl's flesh with that big old blade of his. Ain't much in this life that can scare me, but I surely fear that dead-eyed son of a bitch. He cuts slow, deep and careful. He must have been waiting on Araby, account of she was so big and handsome, and he cut her three ways: lips and eyes *and* nose. Now a man'd sooner tongue-kiss a alligator as look her in the face, and she's gone plumb crazy from it, is what I heard."

Alice listened to their stories and recorded them in her memory, but although she was often perplexed by the world they revealed to her, and even more by their defiant acceptance of their place in that world, the little birds' pain and fear never succeeded in breaching the enclosing protection of her music with its strong, steady flow, and their troubles never disturbed her in her heart. Old Patanouche had once told her that trouble always came out of the past, and Alice was confident that as long as she sustained her serene concentration on the ragtime that surged through her hands, the power of the music would lock the past and its trouble away from her like a dream banished by the golden sunrise. But then one night in the early spring, shortly before midnight when the parlor was in full gleam and she was industriously dispersing the ragtime's balm in shining currents through the chatter and hum of the gentlemen and the little birds as they courted each other in the civilized fashion to which the Countess ascribed the historical precedent of the *Bals du Cordon Bleu* of the previous century, the music abandoned Alice, and for an instant time gaped dark and empty in chill silence beneath her and dread bit into her more deeply than Strap's razor could ever go. In the blink of time between one note and the next, the keys of the huge German piano froze solid and her fingers slipped from them as if she were grasping at a wall of polished stone, and in her wrists and shoulders, where she had felt the sustaining warmth of the music's flow ever since the night she had first rested her hand on top of Brick's while he played his blues, there was only a faint aching without dimension or movement or outline or heat, which was the ache of silence. Her eyes widened and she stared down at the keys and saw them suddenly tilt and tumble upon each other in hideous disarray like bones spilled from a box and then fall away into the darkness of a widening void, and in that moment she was ejected from the present and fell back into the time she had been a little girl awakened from her sleep by a voice calling her name in slow, grinding sorrow.

In that same instant, in the little brown house on Angelus, Brick was restored to the full and complete experience of his life. An hour before, he had awakened with a jolt so pronounced that his Panama hat had tumbled from his head into the yellowed grass. Little Alice scampered to his side and picked up the hat and handed it to him, giggling, and then ran off and hid behind the smoke tree, and Mimi said to him, "La, Brick, the way you jumped, the cat must have run across your grave." She laughed and her affection was as warming as the sunlight on his face, and he yawned and stretched and felt the lazy strength of his contentment, watching the little nut-brown washerwoman going about her tasks in her steady, unhurried rhythm while the warm breezes flipped the corners of the sheets on the clothesline this way and that. He stood up and asked, "May I fetch you fine ladies some lemonade?" and as he entered the house he could hear Mimi saying, "Oh, but that's the darlingest man, isn't it?" Once inside the kitchen he heard music coming from the parlor, and when he looked into the cool, shadowy room he saw that it was little Alice at the German grand piano, playing with a fine, steady roll even though the keyboard was so large that she could not sit on the straight-backed chair but had to dance back and forth in front of the piano to reach from one note to the next. "Here, Alice dear," he said, taking her place at the instrument, "leave those old blues out in the alley, and let's play the sunshine music now." He flexed his fingers over the old, stained keys, and watched his hands swell and spread as they filled with the beloved harmonies. The keys submitted softly when he stroked them, and the music that rose out of them was as deep and peaceful as a river moving lazily through a cottonwood grove. There were no blues in him now, only bright hymns of joy for his life in its fullness, and for the times and the people he had known, and their essence swirled through and around and within him and inflated his soul with the power of their inevitably ordered melodies, until they all fused together in a single soaring chord which had no top or bottom, beginning or end, for it was constituted of all the music he had ever played or heard in his life of playing and listening to music, all woven together in an infinite, euphonious implosion of sound, and in an instant too small to measure his spirit popped through time's impenetrable wall and floated free.

No voice called out to Alice from the silence this time, and as quickly as the music had been snatched away from her it returned. Before her pulse could strike another beat the piano keys closed again into their precise, habitual order and dipped obligingly beneath her fingers' pressure, and the music that greeted her hands then and poured through her wrists and arms and shoulders was more lustrous than she had ever known any music to be, with a rich, sweet texture that surged out into the parlor with the depth and power of an ocean wave. Countess Eulalie, sitting in her huge citadel chair exchanging pleasantries with a bank president and a city commissioner, cocked her painted eyebrows in surprise and raised her head like a lion on the prowl. Even with her senses sifting every nuance of her parlor the Countess had overlooked the heartbeat's instant of silence which had flickered through Alice's steady tide of music, but the enriched sound which came after it called her to attention, and for several minutes she watched anxiously about the room, fearful that this passionate new timbre might upset the civility she decreed there. *My woid but my Little Lady's playin' strong*, she worried to herself. But for all of the fervor that throbbed in its tonality, the music never quit its ordered design, and in its flow it stayed as measured and stately as ever, and the aura of courtliness in the parlor was not overturned. Rather, the little birds and their suitors seemed to fall into a state of willful, smiling languor, and instead of flying apart, the atmosphere of gentility densified. After a spell of tingling perplexity, Countess Eulalie breathed deeply in delight, for she recognized then that on this night something ideal and sublime had been admitted into her Mansion, and like the rest of her company she feared only that it would depart too soon. "My woid," she said again, and though it was only Wednesday she sent the serving maids to fetch champagne from the cold cellar.

Alice played that night in a trance of bewilderment, unable to draw back from the insistent strength of the music or to comprehend the sudden resonance of its power, which was astonishing to her in its force and fullness, and which washed away the vision that had come to her of silence and loss and left behind in the calm center of her concentration only a tiny splinter of dread no broader than a thorn's point, and so surpassingly did the music sustain her through the rest of the night that it was not until it had finally played itself out and she had closed down the curved cover over the keys of the piano and bid good night to the Countess, who looked at her with shining eyes and said, "You are my wonderment, Lady dear," and had gone out into the mists that bore the fecund, floating message of early spring in the soil, that she recovered the memory of what she had seen, and she realized then as she hurried through the dim streets with their fading echoes of the night that although the slow, grinding voice of her sorrow had not called to her she had been visited again by its messenger, and that nothing in her life was the way it had been.

As soon as she entered the little brown house on Angelus she saw Brick in the parlor, lying on the faded carpet next to the piano bench, and in the amber-lit room she heard the after-tones of his life dwindling away like angel berries in the sun. In death, Brick's mouth had relaxed into a calm, lazy smile. Alice knelt beside him and took his hands in hers and she could feel that his music had left him and left nothing behind in his corpse but silence. She gathered him up then in her short, strong arms and carried him up the narrow stairs to Mimi's bed, where she laid him out on his back with a pillow under his head and his bare feet hanging over the foot of the bed, and she crossed his hands upon his chest so that the spatulate tips of his miraculous fingers lay flat against his bosom; then she kissed his creased forehead and returned to the parlor and by ancient habit to the piano, but when she set her hands out on the keys the blues of Brick's life did not come to her fingers. She could hear them in her head and see his times unfolding through them, and she felt their weariness and their pain and their redeeming joy so acutely in her own heart that she wept for her dear protector and the life he had endured, but no sound rose up out of the old nautical piano with its cracked, yellowed keys and salt-stained sides to express Brick's living spirit into the damp morning air of New Orleans.

When the sun had risen and the noises of the day had returned to the streets of the quarter Alice fetched a pot of water from the pump and warmed it on the stove, and she washed Brick's body and dressed it in the opera clothes he had worn on the evening of the new century. As she patted the wings of his bow tie into place she clearly heard her mother's voice, saying, "La, Brick, but you look handsomer as the king of Spanish Mexico," and she realized then that the little brown house was full of the past. At noon she went to LaRivière and rode home an hour later on the undertaker's cheap wagon behind a sorrowful old horse, with one of the undertaker's assistants driving and his helper sitting on the tailgate, and she wasn't surprised to recognize the assistant, a fat young man named Nonny No, as the same boy who'd sat on Mimi's coffin miming the playing of a slide trombone, or to discover Lizzie Bocage waiting for them on the front steps of the little brown house, wringing her long-fingered hands in bereavement, for Alice understood that she was alone now and had to bear all of her times, past and present, by herself.

"Poor darling," Lizzie Bocage cried in her mourner's voice, "oh, the poor darling." But Alice evaded the Orphan Woman's embrace of sympathy and as gently as possible sent Lizzie Bocage away. "Thank you, Miz Bocage," she said, "but I promised Brick not to mourn him, because that was his wish. I appreciate you understanding it so." "I'll pray for him, then," Lizzie Bocage said. "I'm certain he'll hear your prayers," Alice answered. "Thank you." Though Brick had requested no such promise of her, Alice knew by the unbroken silence he left behind that he required nothing further of the living, and she made up her mind to dispose of his body as simply as possible and get on with her life, which was the life he had prepared her for. She buried him before nightfall in the same cemetery ground that had taken her mother's remains.

At the Mansion that evening the Countess and the little birds were touched and solicitous in their attention to Alice, for the news of Brick's passing had been heard throughout the District and that night his memory was being celebrated by every tickler, although in their self-centered way, each of them employed his own voice and style rather than Brick's in playing his eulogy. But Alice found her consolation in the music which greeted her hands when she set them on the shining keys of the Mansion's grand piano, rising to her with the same richness and force that had taken her over at the moment of Brick's expiring; as she rode upon its powerful flow she understood that the music was now entirely her own, and she found herself examining and admiring its order and inevitability with an appreciation which had never before occurred to her, and with the clear logic of intuition she deduced that there must be a corresponding, inevitable order to her own life which the music would in time reveal to her. Her concentration remained intact, and within its safe enclosure she was able to will away the faint thorn-prick of fear she had been carrying in her heart since the previous night and adopt a trusting, patient attitude while she waited for the music to lead her on in her life.

Nor did she leave the music behind when she departed from the Mansion the next morning; instead, it conveyed her through the deserted, fog-shrouded streets to the little brown house where the lantern sat at the foot of the stairs and shed its amber light into the parlor. There, she set aside her shawl and, still following the music, seated herself at the old upright piano which had been Brick's and the sea captain's before him, and for the first time, in shy, tentative measure, Alice began to play the blues of her own life. Because she was so young, the sound of her blues was meager, and their melodies were only simple fragments that ended abruptly or were suddenly displaced by obscure, cosmopolitan airs which were the still-sequestered memories of the sea captain and his times, but Alice recognized her own voice in them, and a meter which was the pace of Brick's rhythm flow enlivened slightly by the scurrying technique of her own small hands. Although at first she was apprehensive and, remembering Brick's perpetual insistence that she leave the blues "out in the alley," she resisted their insistent pull at her fingers, before long she gave herself over to them, and until dawn arrived to cloud the parlor windows her blues rang out, proclaiming the message of Alice Beaudette and her brief time into the profuse air of New Orleans, where it could be heard by the spirits no less clearly than by any living human passing in the street outside. Then, soothed, Alice climbed the stairs to her little bed and slept the morning away.

For nearly a month during that early spring the music sustained her while she lived amidst her times without wonder or concern, in a state of calm detachment. Her blues returned to her infrequently, so that usually upon arriving home from the Mansion she went straight to her bed and slept without dreaming, and the power of her ragtime, her sunshine music, continued to flourish in the Countess' parlor with unmitigated sweetness. Its warmth tingled in Alice's wrists and shoulders with the protective stroke of comforting hands, and she was content to wait as the music bore her along at its own unhurried measure through the unfolding of her time. But then one evening as she was walking along Piro on her way to the Mansion she heard the melancholy, keening tone of Jibba's harmonica in the air, and as it had on that day in the schoolyard it seemed in its timeless yearning to address itself directly to her heart and to awaken there an answering note of sorrow which spread outward within her so quickly and remorselessly that in an instant she was overtaken by a chill dread as sudden as a summer shower. Shivering with apprehension, Alice forced herself to continue along toward the Mansion, where, amid the severely regulated order of Countess Welcome's parlor, she might recover her music and, with it, the healing refuge of her concentration, but as she passed into the District Jibba's tone continued to assail her and, casting about in fear and confusion, she noticed for the first time how garish and squalid were the streets of her accustomed route, so violent in their license that policemen traveled there in pairs with their pistols drawn, and for the first time since the night the music had led her out of her little brown house she was conscious of her own vulnerability in the world. She heard the howling in the saloons, and shattering glass, and the anguished, unruly turbulence of the spasm bands. She smelled the vivid, sour odors of blood and whiskey and urine and sweat, and she saw that the street was crowded with men of every sort who stared at her when she passed with expressions in their eyes which made her think of the little birds and their tales of pain joy, of beatings and razors administered by the hands of men who gave pain to women simply because it satisfied them to do so, because they were men. She lowered her head and increased her step, but still she could feel their eyes on her, and by the time she arrived at the Mansion's kitchen door she was terrified.

She closed the kitchen door behind her and, trembling, stood for several moments while Jibba's tone died away in her bosom. Her bewilderment did not leave her, however, for no sooner had the clamor of her fear begun to diminish than she became aware of an uproar of voices beyond the pantry door, chattering high and excited, and when she pushed through into that small serving room she discovered all of the little birds, and the housemaids and the cook and the serving girls, milling about in a gathering which spilled out through the opposite door into the dining room, each of them conversing agitatedly with the two or three closest to her in the scandalized, disbelieving tones of witnesses to a great disaster. The cook brushed past her into the kitchen, muttering, "Perdition, perdition," and was followed by the two serving girls, who seemed to be exercising a disagreement in which Alice heard one say, "It was the man's own blood," and the other assert, "It was Mister Strap's. It was all his."

As she listened and tried to comprehend this unprecedented disturbance, Alice's consternation pounded in her head like the barking of a big dog, and her wrists began to ache and tremble, for the upheaval of the Countess' regimen, with its intimations of violence close at hand, had betrayed her hope of finding sanctuary from her fear among the well-regulated order of an evening in the Mansion, and it seemed to her that now the protection of her music lay far beyond her reach. "Oh *la*, what has happened to me?" she groaned softly, and, not knowing which way to turn, she pushed through the pantry into the dining room, where she saw Baby Luana and Grace Bonnard whispering animatedly together.

"Lady, come here," Grace Bonnard said, beckoning Alice. "Did you see? Did you see him?"

"Did you?" Baby Luana echoed.

Joining them, Alice shook her head vaguely, and felt all the more disoriented in their company. The little birds looked strange to her, and it took her several moments to realize that it was because, for the first time in her acquaintance of them, they were not made up and dressed in their parlor finery. Their hair hung tangled around their shoulders and the skin on their faces was marked with blotches. Grace Bonnard's cheeks bore a sallow tinge and on her upper lip rested the faint shadow of a mustache, while Baby Luana had a mole beside her nose and was missing her eyebrows altogether, which gave her a ghostly look. Both were dressed with haphazard shabbiness, Grace Bonnard in a torn robe of indeterminate fabric and Baby Luana in a mottled camisole which exposed a pattern of bruises, yellow and purple, on her back and shoulders, and without the mask of their perfume they exuded a dismal odor that was like the smell of old shoes in a trunk. Lacking their transforming cosmetics and regal gowns, they were revealed as nothing more than ordinary small girls, whose forlorn plainness struck Alice as yet another aspect of the utter disarray which had been visited so unexpectedly upon her, but in the gleam of their excitement neither Grace Bonnard nor Baby Luana noticed her dismay and they went on chattering with the furtive ardor of conspirators, so insistently that Alice could not turn her attention from them.

"Looky there, Lady," Grace Bonnard said, pointing down at a dark, moist stain on the dining room's Oriental carpet. "Look at it. The son of a bitch bleeds real blood. I'd of never believed it, would you?"

"Keep your voice quiet, fool," Baby Luana urged in a whisper. She pointed toward the far corner of the room, where an elaborately painted standing screen masked the entry to the Countess' personal suite of her bedroom, sitting room and bath, which none of the Mansion's employees except Mr. Strap had ever been permitted to enter. "She's in there with him now," Baby Luana told Alice, "and the door's open, so talk soft, because she's in a fearsome way."

"I'd of thought it was nothing but lye water in his veins," Grace Bonnard said, lowering her voice only slightly. On her face was an expression of mean triumph. "He bled like a hog hung for slaughter," she said. "Look at it all." Alice followed the gesture of Grace's hand and saw that the stains lay about them all over the carpet, and in several places there were dark spatters on the wallpaper as high as a tall man's head. "What on earth has happened?" she asked.

"Baby seen it all," Grace Bonnard said, with an admiring look at her friend. "Ain't that so?"

"I did, Lady. I seen it all," Baby Luana said proudly. "I was in the kitchen there when the man come busting through. Sometimes I gets to feeling vaporish and cook makes me up a tonic special, you know, so's I don't—"

"Ain't that special, neither, Baby," Grace Bonnard interrupted. "It's just the laudanum Countess gets her, and it's for everybody, not just you."

"Cook makes it different for me," Baby Luana protested mildly, pouting her lips. "She knows I ain't like everybody else, and she says I deserve to—"

"Never mind that, you dodo bird," Grace Bonnard said. "Tell Lady what you seen, before you forget it all."

"My daddy owned planting land," Baby Luana said to Alice, "and my mama rode in a carriage."

"*Baby*," Grace Bonnard whispered vehemently.

"Hush, Grace. All right, all right, I'm telling it now," Baby Luana said. "I was in the kitchen with cook, when this big colored man comes to the door and busts right in without knocking and starts hollering in a real spooky voice, something about his daughter and his blood, only he's talking so strange you can't hardly tell what he's saying. He's saying things like, 'free in her blood,' and, 'set free the pain,' and, 'her pain in her blood,' and I don't know what all, because he looked so crazy and wild I just run right under the table and covered my head, woo."

"Lord help her, I wonder whose pa it was," Grace Bonnard said.

"He looked more colored than anyone here," Baby Luana said. "Handsome, sort of, but he looked like he'd been beat on regular on his head, and his eyes was so crazy it'd give you the shivers."

"Couple of the girls look like they might almost be that colored, maybe underneath," Grace Bonnard said, looking around speculatively.

"If they was that colored, Countess wouldn't have them," Baby Luana said.

"Baby, you just believe any old thing anybody tells you, don't you?" Grace Bonnard said.

Baby Luana ignored her friend's remark with a haughty toss of her head. "I'll tell you what happened next, Lady dear," she said to Alice, "if I can do it without being interrupted all the time."

Grace Bonnard snorted but said nothing.

"Cook had her big old carving knife up in her hand," Baby Luana told Alice, "and she stood right up to him and told him he'd best get out of there, old cook did, but she might as well been talking to the Chinaman, 'cause the man never even paid a mind to her, but he did stop hollering and it was real quiet there for a minute or so. And I looked out under the table and he had his head up like this, and it was like he was sniffing the air, like he was a dog tracking scent, I declare, and then I heard Countess out in the dining room, out here, and she was hollering mad and yelling, 'Who's that? Who's that in the kitchen?,' so mad the doors was rattling, and then things happened real fast."

"Tell her now," Grace Bonnard urged.

"I'm telling," Baby Luana said. "I am. Just then, soon as he heard Countess, the man took up to hollering again, and he run right out through the pantry and it commenced a terrible racket out here. Him and Countess was bawling at each other so bad you couldn't tell what either one of them was saying."

"Everybody heard it," Grace Bonnard said. "I was up in my room just getting ready to primp, and I'd of swore it was the Galveston hurricane come to blow the house down, the noise they were making. I said, 'Lorda mercy, what's that?' and I and everybody else come running down to see."

"I can tell about it myself," Baby Luana said. "I seen it all, because as soon as the man run out through the pantry I clamb out from under the table and went right after him, and I seen it all through the pantry door, when Strap put his hand on the man's arm and said to him, 'Nigger, you better go before there's trouble for you,' in that hard voice of his that makes you feel like you're falling down a well. Most times when Strap puts his dead eyes on them and says like that to some gal's pa that's come looking for her, even if they're all liquored up for courage they'll stick their tail between their legs and leave like a dog running out of the henhouse, but not that man, oh no. That man was big as Strap and just as cold and crazy in his eyes, and he just look at him so—"

"Tell what he *did*, Baby," Grace Bonnard said.

"I'm *telling*," Baby Luana said. "Strap's holding him on his arm up here, and he start to give it a shake, and the man snatched Strap's hand right off him, and he took Strap's finger in his mouth—rrr—and he bit it clean off, right down to the middle part, right down to here. Lady, it was the awfulest thing I ever saw."

"Bit it clean off," Grace Bonnard repeated happily, "and didn't that son of a bitch holler then?"

"They must of heard it all the way to Spanish Fort," Baby Luana said.

"And didn't he bleed?" Grace Bonnard said. "I come in and there's blood flying all over the place, and Strap's got his razor out and I seen him take a swipe at the fella like he's gonna lop his head off, only the fella jumped back so quick he missed him a mile, and the fella grabbed Countess then and swung her around between him and Strap, so if Strap's gonna get him he'll have to go through her first."

"He was laughing," Baby Luana said, "laughing and dancing around behind her, and he spit it out on the floor like it was a chicken bone, and he says, 'Brother, I don't want your blood—'"

"No no, he says more than that," Grace Bonnard said. "He says, 'I don't taste no white blood in you, brother.' No *white* blood. He says, 'I don't *need* to shed your blood, brother.' He's got Strap's blood all over his chin, and he's spitting it on Countess and laughing like it was all a big joke, and he said some more that I couldn't hear, on account of Strap's hollering and Countess's hollering and gals is screaming."

"He said his *name*," Baby Luana said. "I heard that. The man said something about his blood and his name, and he said his name was Trot. I heard that, Trot, and then he run right past me and out through the kitchen. If you'd of come a minute sooner, Lady, you'd of seen him go."

"There's no gal here name of Trot," Grace Bonnard said, "or anything like it."

"That don't signify anything, anyways," Baby Luana said. "I wasn't azackly always given the name of Baby Luana, either, truth be told."

"You wasn't?" Grace Bonnard said. "How was you called, then, Baby?"

But Alice didn't wait to hear Baby Luana's answer. She turned away from the two little birds and made her way out through the pantry and the kitchen and left the Mansion and its uproar, walking with the drifting, measured deliberation of a sleepwalker. Her fear pressed upon her an implacable lassitude, and as she passed along the streets and out of the District she felt removed from herself, as if she were a dozen paces behind, watching Alice Beaudette through a screen of woven smoke, and there was no sound in her except the slow groaning of fatigue, and no feeling in her wrists and shoulders except a faint, rasping tingle like the sound of a rat's claws scratching on a stone wall. She turned the corner from Piro onto Angelus, so thoroughly enclosed within her numbing dread that she never did notice that, for the first time in her life, a thin, cold thread of silence hung in the air of New Orleans that night in the place where Jibba's tone had always sounded, so that everywhere in the city time had made its changing power known and nothing was exactly as it had been.

Chapter Seven

Wild Man Blues

In the early spring the river was dark with the soil which had been scoured from the Southern earth by the upcountry floods, and the night mists in New Orleans bore a fecund scent and a faint tinge of rust red, which some said were put there by the breath of zombies awakened by the subterranean commotion of the changing season and others claimed were the traces of the blood of slaves and soldiers draining upward from the land, drawn by the gravity of the new spring moon. In that season the music of the city, the bright slicings of the cornets and the carved tracery airs of the clarinets accompanying them, always acquired a slightly muddy and effortful tone, and only the keen, plaintive sound of Jibba's mouth organ coursed overhead with its usual clarity, which sounded all the more urgent and significant, like a hound barking a bear up a swamp tree. "Listen at him," people would say. "Whenever did you hear him so excitable? Listen at him so." But in his afflicted isolation Jibba was so remote from them that it wasn't until the night that his sound ceased altogether and the news began to spread that his body had been discovered in an alley off Perdido, with its throat cut and his oatmeal-colored eyes missing from their sockets, that people recalled that in that particular season the blind wraith's tones had seemed not merely excitable but almost jubilant, in a way they'd never heard before, and the opinion soon prevailed that Jibba had foreseen and proclaimed his own death, and that became part of his legend.

One afternoon long before then, Old Patanouche had said to Alice, "I'll tell you about poor Jibba.and how he came to sound so sad and far away," and the old woman had gone on to recount the story that was often heard in the city, about a boy bugler no more than twelve years old who had gone one early spring to Tennessee with a Mississippi cavalry regiment commanded by his father, "looking so proud in the little uniform that was a copy of his daddy's, and riding on a fat little pony." Fresh from the plantations, their troop had been dispatched straight into the heart of the battle of Shiloh, where the smoke and shot were so thick that the air turned black and sang like a million hornets, and where a mortar exploded beneath the little bugler's pony and flung the boy so high into the sky that when he finally fell back to earth his skin and hair had been burned to white ash by the sun and his brains boiled like rice in a pot; the functions of sight and hearing and speech had been struck from his memory and he fell like a dry husk upon that ground which blood had turned to crimson pudding and lay there with no sensation left in him except the joy of a single small kernel of his spirit exulting in the imminent remission of death.

"But there were so many folks dying that day," Old Patanouche told Alice, "that he couldn't get through the crowd of them, and while his spirit was waiting they snatched him back, poor child." The boy was uncovered from beneath a pile of muddy corpses by a family of stragglers, the human scavengers who prowled the carrion battlefields after the armies had departed, and the daughter of the family, a girl not much older than he, adopted the little bugler as a kind of pet and succeeded in diverting him from his deliverance.

"But how could she do that?" little Alice had asked, fearfully mystified. Patanouche had turned suddenly delicate, sucking in her cheeks and rolling her eyes evasively, and witheld the answer common to the legend: that the straggler girl had distracted him with lust, employing him on herself as if he was a cucumber or a carved stick, so variously and so frequently that in ecstatic astonishment his soul had hesitated and lost sight of the way to its release. "How?" Alice had repeated. "She had her ways," the old woman had said grudgingly.

Before long the straggler girl and her family—whose other members had devised their own uses for the boy—had tired of their pet, and when one night he'd slipped free of the carelessly knotted rope with which they'd kept him tethered to the wheel of their wagon, and stumbled off into the countryside, they hadn't bothered even to miss him, let alone search for him. His wandering had begun that night and continued ever since, an endless, questing journey through the featureless chasm of time which divides life from death, calling out for his bearings with the shrill tones of the little mouth organ which some said was the bugle he had brought from Mississippi, melted and re-forged by the explosion, in sounds that made people touch their breasts in sadness and shrink from the cold wind of his solitude as he passed them by.

It must have been the busyness of the spirit community there which directed him to New Orleans ("Spirits kick up a frightful ruckus, if you can hear them," Old Patanouche said), and perhaps, when he'd felt the beckoning pulse of their presence, the boy had thought he might find a resting place among them, the souls, ghosts, shades and haunts who inhabited the dense atmosphere along and above that crescent shore of the river; but when he arrived there the spirits ignored him altogether, not out of meanness or mischief but simply because they never knew he was about, for although they maintained a participant's acquaintance with both life and death, their nature denied them the memory of the transient state that came between. On the other hand, from the night he first appeared in the midst of a spirit-calling in Congo Square, the living people of the city were aware of him throughout his decades, for he was seen and heard everywhere, a phosphorescent child with shuffling feet and eyes like boiled potatoes who moved unerringly and perpetually through the streets and alleys of every quarter of New Orleans like an apparition of conscience, rending the air with his insistent, unearthly—and, some believed, prophetic—cries, beside whose desolation the most distraught blues sounded as blithe as jigs and reels.

Someone heard the wraith's name—Jibba—pronounced by his little harmonica on that first night in Congo Square, and before the next dawn it seemed as though everyone in the city knew it, and he was known as Jibba forevermore. It was said of him that he did not eat or drink and that he never slept or even rested. Somewhat contrarily, it was rumored as well that each night he halted in the bed of a different woman, where he performed with such furious and unrelenting carnal aptitude that those women were transformed; even, in certain cases, reduced to puddles of passion-broth which then evaporated from the face of the earth. This was a rumor devised and nurtured by the women of the city themselves, and passed on from mother to daughter and aunt to niece for years without ever attracting serious notice from the men, even when, some time after Jibba's death, electric traffic lamps were introduced upon the intersections and thoroughfares of New Orleans, and it became a popular custom to say, when one's passage was arrested by a red light, that one was "caught by the Jibba," a localism derived from the women's clandestine description of Jibba's anatomy, of which they whispered that in arousal the bulb of his manhood glowed with the hot, cherry hue of iron at the forge.

The musicians had their own expression; whenever one of their number, in the course of playing a blues, developed a strain so melancholy that its hopelessness was beyond resolution, they said that that player was "answering Jibba." They considered Jibba's sound the distillation of the blues picked clean of all aspiration, and even in their bleakest moods they were loath to incorporate it into their own tonalities and figurations. The women's ribald speculations notwithstanding, the plain fact of his sojourn among the inhabitants of the city was that Jibba never felt the touch of another human body or even the warmth of another's breath, for his flesh was guarded by a palpable glacial chill from which everyone, whether compassionate or perverse by nature, withdrew in consternation. For all the sensation his surroundings ever imparted to him, he might as well have been tumbling still in the sky above the hot, bloody ground of Shiloh, an endless instant from redemption, until one evening in an alley not far from the corner where Perdido crossed South Rampart Street he was embraced by Truehart and his journey finally achieved its destination.

There was no claim of grace in Truehart's act, and no intent to bestow redemption; rather, it was like the peevish gesture of a man wiping away a cobweb from in front of his face, for Truehart was searching through time and the city for his daughter, tracking her by the sound of her music and the scent of her blood in the teeming air of the New Orleans night, and Jibba's keening was another distraction to him. Just minutes before, Truehart had run out of the Welcome Mansion, his senses so agitated by the taste of his encounter with Mr. Strap that he'd lost his bearings entirely and did not notice it by sound or scent when he and Alice, who at that moment was in flight from her own confusion, passed each other on the opposite sides of Basin Street. Inside the Mansion the echoes of the girl's music and the traces of her blood-smell had been so strong that he had exulted, realizing in an illuminated moment of clarity that he was close upon the fulfillment of his tortured life's purpose, but then the huge mulatto had interceded. Appalled, Truehart had snapped like a dog at the giant, and when the rich aromas of Strap's blood had risen up into his senses they'd obscured his daughter's spoor from him. Time and the city had tilted like a tumbling, multifaceted prism before him and in an instant he'd lost sight of his surroundings and his design, and with an instinctive, animal cunning he had fled.

On Perdido he halted and stood waiting for his purpose to return. Having escaped from the state asylum at Jackson more than a week before, by now he had been prowling in the city for two days and nights, and he was growing accustomed to the tricks of confusion time and the city played in his memory and his senses, for New Orleans was full of the obfuscating images and sounds and scents of his past, which rolled over him in waves like acrid smoke and blotted out his apprehension of himself and the mission that he had been designated by time to perform. Through his years of pain, Truehart had come to understand that he was time's instrument, that the suffering of his life had been inflicted upon him in his blood by time, and that it was time's intention that he expiate his agony by cleansing the world of his blood, in himself and in his only child, the girl who had been taken and hidden from him for so long, prolonging not only his suffering but her own.

He shook himself impatiently, perplexed by the endless profusion of the New Orleans evening, the smells of whiskey and coal smoke and river mud and hot-ironed linen, the noise of voices and pianos and banjos and trumpets and drums. Obscure, disturbing images flickered through his concentration, of razors and violins and a woman's straw hat, and a little house constructed of boards that had weathered to a dusty brown: time and the city teasing him with things he could not quite remember. The air was full of the detested sounds of the colored trumpets playing loud and hot, and full of the blues; Truehart could feel them grinding in his blood, their only purpose to divert him from his quest, and over and over he had to remind himself not to permit them to lead him off on a false, foolish trail. And while he stood there distracted, trying to deflect the confusing impulses that swirled around him, Jibba's sound sprang up in his ears and lanced into the core of Truehart's obsession like an icicle hurled from a mountaintop.

Uttering a low growl in his throat, Truehart spun around and bounded a dozen steps back along the sidewalk toward South Rampart Street. Jibba's cry seemed to him a deliberate taunt, replete with the mocking, detested inflection of the blues, another of time's infuriating ruses; but this time, at least, Truehart had been granted the opportunity to follow the ruse to its source. He halted at the entrance to a darkening alleyway between two saloons, and saw there approaching him the small, glowing figure, shuffling carelessly through the broken bottles and smashed crates, his sounds pouring out of him and pelting Truehart like hailstones, and Truehart stooped and drew from his boot top the fisherman's knife he had stolen from a wagon near the docks, and in the heat of his own madness and frustration, and with the blues seething in his blood, Truehart never felt the glacial chill of dispossession which had masked and protected Jibba's flesh ever since he had arrived in the city. Truehart threw his arm around the blind wraith's head, knocking the tarnished little harmonica from Jibba's lips onto the alley pavement, where it shattered like crystal into ten thousand tiny fragments, and in an unwilled spasm of strength he drew the serrated blade of his knife across the boy's throat, so deep and final its stroke that he cut all the way through to Jibba's neckbone, where the rasp of steel against bone sounded a note that buzzed like a bluefly in a glass bell and put an electrical charge into Truehart's hand which made him exclaim in a burst of ecstasy. If Jibba had bled then, Truehart would have bathed his hands in the wraith's blood, to celebrate the feeling of release that washed through him, his joy at realizing that he'd purged from the air of New Orleans this essence of the hated blues, but no blood rushed from Jibba's wound; only a wan, reluctant fluid that was like pine sap, which dried to a yellow crust in the cool evening air before it had traveled far enough to drip to the ground, and no sooner had Jibba's sound trailed away in a ribbon of pristine silence than it was replaced in Truehart's senses by the moan of a trumpet playing a blues called *Careless Love*, its tones bent and squeezed by the manipulation of a derby hat in front of the trumpet's bell, in the fashion first made popular by Buddy Bolden.

With a groan of angry disappointment, Truehart used his knife point to pry Jibba's smoky gray eyeballs from their sockets and, holding one in each hand, he pressed them against his ears to charm away this latest agent of his recurrent confusion. The eyeballs had the dry and lissome feel of lizards' eggs in his fingers, and while they did not succeed in excising thoroughly his apprehension of the blues in the night air, it pacified Truehart somewhat to possess them, and he was able to wait patiently for the several minutes that passed then, until the faint, familiar scent of Alice's blood came once again to his lifted nose and beckoned him to follow. When he was certain the scent was clear in its message to him, and not just another trick, he took Jibba's eyeballs away from his ears and put them in the pocket of his trousers, and set off in the direction of Angelus, confident again now that his purpose had returned.

By Truehart's own estimation, the blues were a power sent to seal his madness inside him, to uproot him from his remembered heritage and consign him to his life of pain and confusion. He had been born Obregon Vraicoeur, and his family were Creoles, those handsome, golden-skinned people of mixed blood who, although they were frequently called *gens de couleur*, were exempted by the city's statutes from inclusion among the groups designated as being "colored," a classification which in the early times was applied only to Indians and indentured Africans. When Obregon was a boy, the Creoles enjoyed the full franchise of New Orleans, permitted to circulate freely throughout the environs of that diffuse and cosmopolitan city, to vote and own real property and even to keep slaves. They were a proud, enterprising people who considered themselves the conservators of French culture in the New World, and those who could afford it sent their children back to France to study at the universities and academies there. Obregon's father, Alceste Vraicoeur, and his uncle, Archille, had gone together as youths to Paris, where for three years they had studied violin at the Conservatory, as their father had before them, and upon their return to New Orleans the two Vraicoeurs had immediately secured positions in one of the four symphony orchestras supported by the Creole community.

When Obregon was still a child in dresses and ringlets, his father gave him a half-size violin and showed him where to place his little fingers on the strings and how to draw the bow across them to induce from the instrument the sublime tones every Vraicoeur for generations had spent his life examining and cultivating. "You must understand and accept this, my son," his father told him even before Obregon was old enough to recognize music written on a lined page, and then repeated throughout his childhood, "that when dear Mozart wrote a note upon the score he had only one note in mind, with one dimension of tone and one specific duration, and no other. It is the duty of the musician, Obregon, to discover and preserve the intention of the music's creator. Not to alter, not to 'interpret.' *Interpret?*" Alceste Vraicoeur's lips curled in scorn. "Interpret Beethoven? Schubert? *Mozart?* I think not, my son, I think not. The voice of genius requires no such interpretation. No, your sacred responsibility is to *surrender* yourself to the voice of genius, to take it as your own, and thereby to keep genius alive."

Obregon's father and Uncle Archille were his first and only teachers. Respected throughout the community as violinists of the first rank, the Vraicoeur brothers were elegant, fine-featured men whose skin radiated the burnished color that had emerged from the blended strains of their gallant French forebears and the beautiful brown people of the Caribbean islands. They had dark, introspective eyes and strong, supple fingers which curled and tapered to exactly the angle and breadth necessary to forge a connection with each note in the violin's scale at its absolute center, and their souls were exalted by the purity of their unwavering devotion to the genius of the European composers they served with their artistry. From his earliest days young Obregon embraced their tutelage with grateful, unsmiling diligence, eager to prove himself worthy to assume the gifts of their sensitivity and dedication, as he had inherited the shape of their wrists and hands and their delicate, lobeless ears. A solemn, fastidious boy, he listened and studied and practiced and concentrated until whenever he tucked the violin's gentle curve against his shoulder its music sang to him in every fiber of his being and the voices of the great creators spoke clearly to him from the lined pages of their scores, expressing their designs directly to his ears, and long before he reached manhood the older Vraicoeurs agreed that in Obregon the Vraicoeur legacy had indeed been vouched safe, and preparations were made to send him to Paris to refine his talent in the salon of the same French concertmaster who had been the mentor of their youth.

But before Obregon could claim it, his birthright was snatched away from him, and from all the Vraicoeurs and the rest of the proud, autonomous *gens de couleur* too, for with the stroke of an unseen white hand the Creoles, keepers of the culture, were parted from the European heritage they had nurtured so long and so assiduously. The Race Laws of New Orleans were revised, and in new statutes of classification the Creoles were designated as colored; denied the rights of property, they were stripped of their citizenship as well as of their chattel and forced to surrender their holdings in business and real estate and to seek to support themselves and their families in the menial occupations of Negroes. Because the disenfranchised Creole community could no longer afford to support them, their symphonies disbanded. One bright morning Obregon was in the parlor, practicing a Schubert sonata whose clarity and logic on the printed score proclaimed nothing less than the beneficent harmony of God and all humanity, when he was interrupted by the sudden arrival of his father, who had left the house not an hour before on his way to spend the day rehearsing a program of Mozart. Alceste Vraicoeur stood in the parlor doorway holding his violin case loosely by its handle and wearing on his face an expression of bitter submission so anguished that Obregon's fingers went slack in dismay and his bow twisted from his hand and fell to the carpet, and in the premonitory hush that filled the room his father said, "No more. There is no more symphony." Obregon watched, uncomprehending, as his father crossed the room to the cracked leather armchair by the window, let his violin drop to the floor and, seating himself with the slow, incremental precision of infirm old age, withdrew immediately and uncompromisingly from life. For the rest of his days Alceste Vraicoeur spent all of his waking time huddled in his chair staring at sheets of blank composition paper upon which no notations had been entered and no divisions set across the crisp horizontal lines to arrest their perpetual parallel flow. Although he could occasionally be overheard sighing in his despair, he never spoke another intelligible word or sang or played another note of music in his life. His beloved violin lay silent by his chair and the horsehair strings of his bows, neatly hung from wooden pegs in a shadowed corner of the parlor, dried and parted.

Surprisingly, for he had always been the more taciturn of the Vraicoeur brothers, Uncle Archille responded to their altered circumstances with a show of ambitious resilience. "Eh," he said, "we are colored now. Still, we must eat, no?" He shrugged and smiled hopefully around at the family, which, besides Alceste and young Obregon, consisted of Obregon's mother and his sister, Camille; Uncle Archille himself had never married or indicated any inclination to establish a home of his own away from his brother's house. "Humanity has many voices, I think," he said. "If we have become brothers to the poor Africans, perhaps we may teach them to sing with our voice, and learn to sing with theirs. Music embraces every color," he declared resolutely, and, appending to his name the title of Professor, he advertised himself about in the Negro wards as a music teacher, while Obregon's mother, a shy woman with a delicate constitution, began to take in laundry.

But Uncle Archille's optimism was quickly spent. The Negroes, he found, were canny pragmatists, from whom the aspirations of an aesthetic ideal had long since been scourged and replaced by an uncomplicated esteem for mere survival in the hostile world, and although he persisted in his enterprise it soon became a burden to him. He would spend his evenings complaining sourly to his silent brother, while Obregon, unable to fathom this misery which had been visited upon them and wondering whether it would ever pass, listened from the hallway beyond the parlor door. "That fat one who came today," he heard Archille say with rising contempt. "That fat savage with his jolly smile, he pays me to teach him to read the notes on the page, to make a musician of him, he says. I show him the page, so. I say, 'The man who placed these notes here was a genius. These notes are the handwriting of a divinely inspired man. They sing with the voices of angels,' I say. The fat one smiles his smile and says, 'Fess'—they call me Fess; they are too indolent to say 'Professor,' you see—'Fess, that is just spots on paper.' Specks, he calls them, *specks*. 'They don't do nothing just lying there, Fess,' he says. 'Music is what you *play*,' he says. Ah, he is no worse than any of them, you see. They do not want to be musicians; they want to be players. They want only to make noise, without gentility or design. I tell them, 'The note is absolute. There is a single, correct way to sound the note.' I show them the note, make its sound for them in all purity, and they reject it. Reject it! They reject the A of dear Mozart! They say, 'I've got my own sound, Fess,' and then they make any sound they like. *Poum poum poum*, they sound like engines. They want to play loud, you see, everything loud. And be rich. They want to play loud and be rich and every day, my brother, it is like this. They grunt like pigs and are satisfied to call it music, so, without shame. Don't you understand what I am saying, brother?" But Obregon's father never spoke, and Obregon could only mutter fearfully and without hope.

Within a year of their misfortune's arrival, Obregon's mother and sister were taken from the household by brain fever, and the following spring his father uttered a final deep sigh and slid out of his chair and was dead before the last sheet of blank manuscript paper, scattered from his lap, had come to rest on the carpet beside him. Uncle Archille's bitterness had rooted so deeply in him that it had driven out his power of condolence. All he could say was, "What will you do now, eh, my pretty Obregon? What will you do?" It had been weeks since he had touched his violin, a Del Gesù which had been his grandfather's, for he had given up trying to impart instrumental technique and now taught only sight-reading and ear training by the vocal method known as solfeggio.

But because music was all he had ever been given to understand in his life, Obregon tried to follow his uncle's earlier example and adapt his musicianship to their reduced surroundings. With studious obstinacy he taught himself to play the guitar and the clarinet, instruments favored among the colored musicians, and with his inherited skill, his birthright of sensitivity to tonal dimension, he mastered them quickly and had no trouble finding work in that city where everyone sought music to express the feelings of their lives. He played in marching bands and in the small orchestras that entertained in the parks and the social clubs and the smoke-filled colored dance halls, playing trumped-up marches and raggy quadrilles and the syncopated stomp tunes the Negroes liked so well, and he played the simple, repetitious, maudlin music they called the blues.

For a while he was able to persuade himself that the colored music in its simplicity was nothing more than a diversion to him, that his duty, and his destiny, would eventually be satisfied in the manner his heritage required, and to that end he worked at keeping his classical skills at their peak. He practiced diligently from the written scores at home and every Monday afternoon met in chamber groups with other young Creole musicians who had been his father's associates in the symphony or were the children of his father's associates, now enduring the same hard circumstances as he. They would criticize and encourage each other, and remind each other how important it was not to let their obligations to the European masters lapse, for if the Race Laws were so easily changed in one way, who among them would swear that the same laws could not be just as easily changed again in the opposite way? Like a government in exile they plotted the restoration of their culture to its legitimate place in the city, vowing that their first restitutional act would be to bring together all of the symphony musicians to perform a program of Mozart, of Beethoven, and of Haydn and J. S. Bach and Schubert, that would last for an entire week, and the purity of its legitimacy would be so powerful that it would drive the wretched music of the Africans from the air of New Orleans altogether. Like most musicians Obregon and his friends were an unwordly lot who had no difficulty beguiling themselves and each other with their hopeful visions, and in each others' company they were easily persuaded that, if only they could survive their present troubles, the future would bring to fruition the promises of the past, a resolve which, in their innocent self-absorption, none of them seemed to notice was the inherent message of the Negroes' religion and of their blues.

Obregon, despite his doubts and fears, found a measure of peace in his association with the other Creole musicians, and even when, as the months passed on through the seasons, their optimism began to acquire an ever more desperate strain and they spent more and more of their time together articulating their fantasies and complaints, and less time actually playing their hallowed music, he was able to impose upon himself a patient determination to lead a normal life. He courted and married Mimi Beaudette, a pretty young girl whose family had known his since before the bad times had begun, and settled with her in a small house on Angelus, leaving his Uncle Archille behind in the home of his childhood, attended by a black housekeeper who sang psalms in the kitchen and refused to cook fish. In his bitterness Uncle Archille was becoming dissolute and erratic and his former elegance had decayed into disheveled eccentricity; he seldom shaved or changed his trousers, and his hair and fingernails grew like wild brambles on an unplowed field, and at odd hours he wandered about the house declaiming the solmization syllables of Guido of Arezzo in a harsh monotone punctuated by barks of scornful laughter. Obregon felt reproached and threatened by the older man's constant rancor, and could no longer endure his company. "He listens only to his own unhappiness," he explained to Mimi. "He will not acknowledge the changes which have occurred and get on with his own life. To be sure, the times are hard and nothing is what it was, but if we do not accept things the way they are—accept what *is*—then we cannot make them better." Obregon spoke with earnest hopefulness when he said these things to his new young wife, and with the instinctive cheerfulness of her nature Mimi encouraged him in his hope, but in his dark, sensitive eyes she could detect the impulses of an eroding hesitancy, some barely restrained madness, and she prayed for the strength and the constancy she would need to guard her marriage against adversity.

At first Mimi's innate good humor and loving solicitude sustained Vraicoeur and soothed the corrosive discouragement he felt every time he went out to play the music he despised in the company of musicians for whom he could feel no kinship. The black people of New Orleans, like all of their brothers and sisters in America, were hard-worn, frightened people not so far removed from slavery that they were free of its oppressing pain, who still carried in their bones the echoes of the fetid holds of the ships that had brought them to the New World and the iron chains that had bound them upon their arrival there. Their music did not aspire to any sublime order. Rather, it was spontaneous and urgent, charged with the wondering energy of survivors of a continuing peril and with the simplest claim of the living: I am alive. But Obregon felt the music's defiant jubilation as a deepening mire which threatened to smother him in its grasp, and although he continued always to play in accordance with his heritage, addressing each note at its true center in the fullness of its inherent dimensions of tone and time, he began to sense that his sound, with its metronomic rhythm and meticulous tonality, was becoming gradually less and less distinguishable from the sounds of the black musicians. A feeling of helpless panic breathed its first breaths in him, and the condescension with which he had once belittled the colored music was replaced by loathing, for the imprudent, careening clamor of its emotionalism and for the arrogance of the Negro musicians who played it so proudly and with so little art.

The black musicians, most of whom were unschooled and

not ashamed of it, played any way they could play. Their instruments—dented cornets and trombones as old as the times of the French military bands, fingerworn clarinets, homemade banjos and drums, warped, tarnished fiddles—came from the city's attics and pawn shops and secondhand stores, and the self-taught players created their own innocent orthodoxy in accordance with the insights of their feelings. They ragged the notes; they bent and blued them and played around their edges, far from their legitimate tonal centers. They twisted and altered their rhythms for no more valid or rational end, as far as Obregon could ever see, than just whim. They reproduced barnyard sounds, levee sounds, swamp sounds, African sounds. They played the blues like mourners throwing ashes over their heads without shame. In Obregon's ears their music was jungle anarchy and worse, for the attitude of the black musicians made it plain that they considered themselves to be more important than the music; they never apologized or sought to excuse their shortcomings. "A musician is nothing," Obregon told Mimi, echoing his father. "A musician is an empty vessel into which genius decants its creations. They haven't the intelligence to be humble; they aspire to nothing."

For their part the colored musicians considered Obregon typical of the Creoles who had come to work with them in the times since the Race Laws had changed, and, although he would never have thought of exposing the integrity of his violin to the indignities of tone and harmony inherent in their music, they called him Fiddler, because they could see that the name irked him. One night when he was newly arrived in their ranks he had proudly, if indiscreetly, confided to the player next to him that he had received his training as a symphony violinist. "Is that right?" the musician had replied, obviously impressed. "You a fiddler, are you?" Obregon had begun to correct him, to explain that, no, he was a violinist, which was something altogether different, but the other man had already turned away and was passing the word along the bandstand that their new young Creole guitarist, who could double on the clarinet, was a fiddle player too. Obregon hated the very sound of the word; to him it sounded like Nigger. "Look at me," he cried to Mimi when things began to fall apart from him, "I am a nigger, look. Smell me, feel my hair. Listen, I go *wah wah wah*. I am only a nigger." "Obregon, Obregon," Mimi wept for him. "You are too fine for them. You are an artist."

"I am shit," Vraicoeur said to Mimi. "I have no art. I am a nigger." The music had begun to burn in him like bile, igniting a turmoil in his nature which daily he found more difficult to contain. On the bandstand, while the music raged around him, his stomach twisted in queasiness and his lungs pressed shut in his chest, and when he came home late to his little house and lay down beside his wife the music's aftereffects would not leave him. He began to suffer headaches, brief, nightmarish spells of torment in which he felt as though his brain, like a rat in a basket, was trying to eat its way out through his skull to the open air, and when the pain of the headaches relented it left behind a low roaring sound which Obregon heard not just with his ears but with all of his senses and which, after he had examined it in his sleeplessness for several weeks, he decided was the voice of his blood. As he listened to it for night after night, he detected a gradual, accumulating change in it, and he was overcome by the conviction that the change in its pitch reflected a change in his blood's composition. His blood was dividing itself, separating into its black and white components which, because they could no longer mix, rubbed against each other in his veins like flint rubbing steel, and struck sparks. His blood was at war with itself, black and white trying to burn each other out, and Vraicoeur was being consumed by the heat of its fires. He was terrified.

His fear made him restless. He left the little house on Angelus and stayed away from Mimi for days at a time, wandering in the streets and napping in the saloons. He never practiced anymore with his violin, but instead spent his days lounging in the barber shops with other Creole musicians, unhappy violinists who had become fiddlers, violists turned banjo players, dispossessed cellists who now carried tubas in the parades. Together they validated their discontent in endless choruses of complaint and sourly ridiculed their employers and associates in the colored bands. Whenever Vraicoeur did return home he found Mimi ready to minister to his unhappiness, but her solicitude only exacerbated the state of self-loathing into which he had driven himself. On the day his Uncle Archille committed suicide by locking himself in his parlor and lighting a bonfire of violins and sheet music there, Vraicoeur beat Mimi unconscious with his fists because she said to him, "Oh, my poor Obregon, your family is gone. My poor Vraicoeur." Three days later he began to beat her again, for a tender gesture she'd made with her hands, and when she ran from him he caught her on the staircase and forced himself upon her there. Six weeks after that she told him she was pregnant and if he beat her she would leave him, so he ignored her altogether. "I am Hell itself," he said one day. "Nothing matters. I can do anything."

Several months later a man Vraicoeur knew slightly stuck his head into Monette's barber shop in the middle of a dusty afternoon, and said, "Anybody here play guitar and wants to make a dollar or five tonight? I need a guitar player tonight."

It was Willy Cornish, a colored trombone player who worked in the band led by Buddy Bolden, the powerful young cornetist whose popularity in the black community was preeminent in that season. Cornish was considered sympathetic by the Creoles, for it was reputed that he could read music and enjoyed listening to the classics, but the men in Monette's shop, wary of his connection with Bolden, greeted him without enthusiasm. Bolden was known to them as a bully, a difficult, erratic man who made no secret of his low regard for Creole musicians who considered themselves too refined to play his music the way he wanted to hear it played, and they in their turn despised him. He played with a raw, exuberant power which devastated music's claims to propriety or art. A tall, glowering man with a stevedore's heavy shoulders and barrel chest, even in repose Bolden seemed to resound with battering, primitive noise; when he laughed or shouted, his voice boomed and echoed like cannon fire, and when he played his horn you could hear it clear across the river. He played like a man possessed, flaying his lips with the force of his music until the blood ran down his chin, and he wanted musicians around him who weren't afraid to bellow and stomp and pit their own strength against his, to howl and sweat along with him in nightly celebration of his music's power.

Once, when they were playing together in a funeral parade, Willy Cornish had complimented Vraicoeur on the tone of his clarinet, and now he recognized him and smiled broadly. "How about you?" he said "You're Obregon, aren't you? I remember you. The fiddler, sure, with that nice clarinet sound. You play a little guitar too, don't you? What do you say? Make yourself a dollar tonight? Maybe five or ten, and do me a favor while you're at it. Henry Randolph's laid up over in Mobile and I need a steady guitar man. What do you say?"

Vraicoeur squirmed in his chair and said nothing. Just the thought of Bolden was enough to awaken the heat in his blood.

"What do you say?" Willy Cornish persisted, speaking gently, encouragingly. When Vraicoeur still said nothing, he looked around at the others, a half-dozen young Creoles filling Monette's chairs with their haughty disdain. "Any of you other fellows know guitar?" he inquired. "We got a little social to play for over in Union Sons Hall. It won't be anything difficult to play, just the usual old Funky Butt and all. Make you a dollar, buy your gal a new hat. What do you say? You got you a job for tonight? It's money in your hand."

The others shifted about nervously; money was always hard to come by. Vraicoeur watched them sullenly, noting the way their eyes ran back and forth between Cornish and himself as if they were judging a contest, judging him. Lately their fellowship had become strained, for they had begun to fear his moods, his sudden outbursts, and when they addressed him he remarked about them traces of the same pity that he saw in Mimi. Finally he spoke. "I can play that music," he said flatly.

197

"Of course you can," Willy Cornish said.

Vraicoeur looked around defiantly at the others. They all loathed and feared Bolden as much as he, he knew, but they had to be shown that Vraicoeur would not be pitied. "All right," he said. "I will play."

"That's good," Willy Cornish said. "It will be fine, you'll see."

Even before the band started to play that night, Union Sons Hall was crowded, and the black faces were turned up toward the bandstand like sunflowers at midday. The first tune was a fast blues, and when Bolden slammed his heel on the floor and set his horn against his lips and sounded his power, the room inflated with yearning and jubilation, and the dancers shouted and exploded into movement like the sea breaking against a rocky coast. From the very first note Bolden and his musicians poured the music out over the crowd in steady, pounding waves that sent them reeling ecstatically every which way, and with every breath he took, Buddy Bolden—King Bolden—seemed to grow and swell in the dim, smoky hall, until he loomed over the dancers and the other musicians like a tree on a riverbank. The music burst from his horn so loud and strong that the cornet drooped and waved like a flag in a hurricane, and his bandsmen trooped to his call, shouting and stomping and growling their antiphonal accompaniment to his lead, their ragged, half-realized harmonies, willing to settle for a passing approximation of tone, a transient acknowledgment of euphony, sacrificing order and regularity to that maelstrom of power given and received which whirled around the bandstand and the dance floor with such force that the entire building seemed to lift up and tilt this way and that like a dice cube passed from hand to hand.

But Vraicoeur sat transfixed and silent in the center of the storm with his guitar lying unhandled across his lap and a remote, pensive expression on his face. At the sounding of Bolden's opening phrases he'd felt himself suddenly lifted up and transported to the very heart of the African music, thrust there so deeply that its mire finally closed over his head and hid him altogether and forever from his heritage, and although his blood raged in him its heat seemed somehow liberating, its pain an inspiration of purpose. The music and the pain banished his past from him and with it his obligation to his name, and he felt blissfully freed. At last he could accept without shame the primacy of the blackness that had been imposed upon his blood, could address it directly and fearlessly, and could thereby cleanse himself of it. For an instant the turmoil of the social hall receded from around Vraicoeur and a message of destiny appeared for him, as clearly as if it were being spoken directly into his ear: *Set free all pain; I will free my blood.* He wasn't immediately certain what it meant, but the resolute, oracular authority of it thrilled him, and he drew a deep, peaceful breath and looked around the bandstand with a placid grin of contentment.

But Buddy Bolden, swinging from side to side in the buffeting gales of the music and joy, had intuited the absence of the guitar from his band, and at exactly the moment of Vraicoeur's illumination he reached the end of his chorus and wrenched his horn from his lips and rounded on Vraicoeur with the charging force of a locomotive. "Where's your playing, Frenchy?" Bolden demanded, his chest heaving with the effort of the music that had been dredged from it. "What you God damn grinning at, you dicty little shit?" He was hot with his power and hadn't the patience to be mocked at by a prissy Creole with high-flown notions of legitimacy; Buddy Bolden took his legitimacy from the roaring power of his music and the ecstasy of his crowd responding to it. But Vraicoeur only smiled back at him, unseeing, and Bolden, who had been about to take hold of Vraicoeur's shoulder, stayed his hand, for he saw that in the Creole's eyes there was a heat as intense as the heat of his own power, and recognized by it that Vraicoeur was cursed. A superstitious man, and wary of curses, Bolden drew back and pointed to the open door behind the bandstand, and roared with all the strength of his barrel chest for Vraicoeur to get his dicty Frenchman's ass off the stand.

199

The instant of Vraicoeur's inspiration blew apart like milkweed before the force of Bolden's shouted command, and Vraicoeur blinked at the interruption and looked around him, and saw that the music had stopped and the dancers were slowing and turning indignantly toward the bandstand. Bolden repeated his order as loudly as before, and now the indignation on the black faces began to turn to malice, and the seething in Vraicoeur's blood brought him only pain and confusion again. His calm smile hardened to a fearful rictus, and with his eyes locked against Bolden's he sprang up from his chair, raised his guitar high above his head and smashed it down upon the stage at Buddy Bolden's feet, where it burst apart with a hollow sound, *padoum*, and a shriek of its strings. Then, impelled by the clamor of his blood, Vraicoeur ran out the door behind the bandstand and down the outside stairway to the street, one story below, pursued by a swelling chorus of scornful Negro laughter.

Mimi was in the kitchen at the stove when Vraicoeur burst into the little brown house, and before she could say anything to him he saw the look of compassion rising into her eyes and he grabbed her neck and squeezed it with his strong hands to halt her words of loving dismay in her throat. Her soft flesh yielded beneath the pressure of his fingers, and he could feel her blood moving in her and recognized that, like his, it was heated by the abrasion of its black and white strains, rubbing against each other like dry-skinned reptiles in a tank. "My pain in you," he cried, and, intending to free her of it, to set free all pain, he pressed down harder on her throat with his thumbs. A brief instant later he found himself lying on his back on the kitchen floor, with a throbbing echo in his head and Mimi nowhere to be seen.

Vraicoeur struggled to his feet and went to the kitchen door, where he leaned against the doorframe and waited for his senses to clear. He raised his head, listening and sniffing in the air of the warm spring night, and was greeted by the rich profusion of the New Orleans atmosphere, in whose midst he thought he could detect a faint, bitter aroma which, although he could not recall ever having smelled it before, struck him as so familiar that it could be only the scent of Mimi's blood. Knowing that she was nearby, he called softly to her, addressed her tenderly as his Little Wife, but before he could explain his healing purpose for her he was interrupted for the second time that night by Buddy Bolden. This time it was not Bolden's voice but his horn which distracted Vraicoeur, playing a blues called *Careless Love*, its sound plunging through the other night-sounds to taunt and bully him by proclaiming for all the city to hear that Vraicoeur had been banished by the black musicians and thrown off the bandstand at Union Sons Hall as if he were nothing but a bothersome kazoo player. Furious and ashamed, Vraicoeur turned back into the house and raced upstairs to his bureau, where his razor lay in a leather case. He cursed himself for not having taken it with him earlier that evening.

He climbed the outside stairs at the back of the building and entered Union Sons Hall by the same door through which he'd fled, the door behind the bandstand, where the band, faced away from him toward the roiling mass of dancers, was in full cry. Vraicoeur saw Bolden's broad shoulders pulling at the seams of his box-backed coat and his neck swelling out over his soaked shirt collar. He saw the muscles of Bolden's back and haunches writhing like nests of fat serpents. Bolden's loud, mocking sound scoured Vraicoeur's nerve endings and Vraicoeur's breath backed up in his throat. He flicked his razor open like a lizard's tongue and held the sparkling blade out before his face and leaped past the drummer toward King Buddy, who turned as if he'd been waiting and pointed the bell of his shining cornet at Vraicoeur and blew a note that seemed to leap out of the horn like a fat black snake striking at Vraicoeur's eyes. Vraicoeur yelled and flinched away, and before he could recover, someone had pinned his wrist and someone else's arm was around his neck and black hands were grabbing at his legs, and he was pitched to the floor beneath a mass of outraged, vindictive blacks whose fists and feet beat their rhythms on him until he was unconscious. They threw him out into the street then, where the police were waiting to cart him away, and when he awoke and began to enumerate his injuries he discovered that the fingers of his left hand, with which he had once pressed upon the silky gut strings of his violin and extracted its most sublime tones in their absolute fullness, had been mangled during the melee, so thoroughly bent and smashed that the only sound to which they might ever aspire would be a groan of pain. He was found guilty of dangerous and malicious behavior, a colored person's crime, and sentenced by Judge Fogarty to serve not less than eight years in prison.

After three years Vraicoeur, along with a dozen other inmates, was ransomed from the state by a man who owned a turpentine camp in the Alabama pine forest, and was taken to work there. Shackled around his ankles during the day and manacled to his bunk at night, Vraicoeur spent more years at the camp than his sentencing had demanded, tending huge open vats of boiling pitch whose heat and acrid smell actually pacified him, for they seemed to create a balance between the world outside his skin and the torment in his blood which generalized his pain, and he was able to ignore it until it was a memory almost as distant from him as his family name.

It was the camp's overseer who had taken Vraicoeur's name from him and replaced it with Truehart. "There's no Frenchmens that works for me in my camp," he'd said when he'd read Vraicoeur's name on the remission list. "Boy, you all be niggers here. I'll give you a nice nigger name now, and that's the name you'll answer to, you hear?" The overseer drew a line through "Vraicoeur" on the list and wrote in "Truehart," in large letters, and held the paper out for Vraicoeur to see. "It's about the same thing, boy, isn't it?" he said. "Isn't it, Mister Truehart?" The overseer wore a Colt pistol in a holster behind his hip and always carried a weighted truncheon in his hand; when Vraicoeur sneered at the new name and reached to tear the paper from him, the overseer flicked his club like a fly whisk, catching Vraicoeur's right hand with its tip and crushing two knuckles there like glass marbles ground beneath a boot heel. "Mister *Truehart*," the overseer admonished, and he hit Vraicoeur once more behind the ear, and when he regained consciousness Vraicoeur was Truehart.

He didn't exactly forget the name Vraicoeur. He understood that Vraicoeur was the name of a person he once had been, a person whom he could consider from a distance and with a mild contempt which, because he remembered so little about him, was puzzling but not bothersome. But he thought of himself now as a colored laborer named Truehart, and accepted that his life was Truehart's life, and until he completed the term of his servitude and returned to New Orleans, the only vestiges of the past that were left to him were his headaches, which still belabored him in the night, although at widely spaced intervals, and the sound of his blood roaring its message of black and white pain, so constantly that he reasoned that it must be a natural part of Truehart's existence and therefore lay beyond explanation. Then, in the city with its sights and smells and sounds, memories began to assail him, and they were all the more disturbing because he knew they were Vraicoeur's memories, forced upon Truehart by time. He understood then that time was a trickster whose purpose he could never thwart but which he might deflect if he could discover and adhere to a purpose of his own, and he began to examine and interpret his pain again. His pain drew him back to the quarter where Vraicoeur had lived in his unhappy time, where Truehart saw Mimi and Alice and recognized them, and his blood seethed in him more powerfully than he could remember and just before the eve of the new century the message returned to him out of the teeming cacophony of the New Orleans air, borne in the tones of a vagrant blues strain: *Set free all pain; I will free my blood*. He found Mimi then and killed her, and they took him away again to the colored wing of the asylum at Jackson.

Shortly after Jibba's death a freshening spring breeze blew over from Ponchartrain and drove the rust-hued mists from the streets and alleys of New Orleans, so that the early stars of evening could be seen glistening in the crisp indigo sky overhead. The sounds in the air seemed to glisten too, as if all of the city's musicians had raised up into one of the sharper keys which Brick had said prickled up the spirit so, but as Alice turned from Piro onto Angelus she was far too preoccupied by the deadening weight of her fear to pay heed to the night's sparkle and gaiety; her head was lowered and her hands dangled numb at her sides, and her feet dragged with a reluctant shuffle that left shallow furrows in the dust behind her heels.

She hesitated in the street before the little brown house and then, conveyed by an impulse she was too distracted to question, she continued on in the same listless fashion toward the end of the street, where the tall board fence guarded the coalyard and Old Patanouche's tiny cottage sat in its dusty yard surrounded by stunted shrubs and patches of wild herbs. Alice stopped there in front of the old woman's picket gate and rested her hand on the gatepost and looked in at the old cottage. In the dim light it looked lumpish and abandoned; it seemed to list and sag at its corners and its chimney leaned precariously toward the coalyard, and Alice felt a sour pang in her chest at the sight of it. For the first time since her mother had died and Brick's music had begun to direct and enclose her life she felt the sadness of nostalgia. She couldn't recall now how long it had been since she had visited Patanouche or exactly why their times together had seemed so special and important to her, but she remembered the sweetness of special chocolate and the husky sound of the old woman's gentle voice telling her silly stories in the parlor, and Alice wondered why the times had been permitted to change so quickly and bring her such unhappiness. *I work in a whorehouse,* she said to herself in a sudden rush of shame; *oh, Gran'mère, my friends are whores.* And staring at the still face of the forlorn little cottage she was overcome by a vast silence of loneliness and she began to weep, her tears rolling slowly down her cheeks and falling onto the bosom of Mimi's old black gown.

Then she saw something move at the side of the yard, and fright sounded in her again, with a tone like a bass drum shrouded in funeral cloth, making her hands flutter. "La," she exclaimed fearfully, and stepped back from the gate, looking around her from side to side. It moved again, a low, gliding shadow blending in and out of the darkened outline of one of Old Patanouche's little shrubs, and then, as it sauntered away from the shrub into the yard, Alice saw that it was a cat, and while she watched, the cat strolled nonchalantly to Patanouche's doorstep and hopped up onto the step and sat there and slowly began cleaning its paws. "Oh mercy," Alice said in a low voice, for she realized that Old Patanouche was nowhere nearby, and because she hadn't the will to choose to do otherwise she turned and fled back up the street to the little brown house.

As soon as she stepped into the amber-lit hallway at the foot of the stairs she smelled the swamp-mud odor of Truehart, and when she looked into the parlor she saw him there, sitting on the narrow sofa and smiling at her with a harsh grin of triumph that stretched the skin over his long jaw so that it gleamed through the stubble of his unshaven cheeks like a railroad track in the moonlight. He wore a pair of cracked boots and ragged trousers that he'd stripped off a man whose neck he'd broken near the levee, and a shirt he'd stolen from a washline. The shirt was spotted and stained with blood on its front and sleeves, and in the crooked fingers of his left hand, resting in his lap, he held his knife, the tip of its long, serrated blade pointing directly at Alice's heart.

In her memory Alice heard the tone of Jibba's mouth organ and saw a flash of scarlet, and she knew at once that this was Trot; looking at him she understood why the sound of that name had struck terror into her from the first time she'd heard it, back in the schoolyard of her childhood, for he was a desperate-looking man, a man of pain, a madman. Above his grin his eyes were like the depthless eyes of a serpent glimpsed by torchlight, frozen and unseeing as they stared through her from a distance only he could measure or traverse. His face was battered, its flesh bruised and sun-darkened to a tobacco shade. His hair had been shaved to the skin, and the knife-point widow's peak was only a shadow on his brow; a pale scar slanted from its end to the swollen flesh above his left eye. His nose was flat and bent to one side and his lower lip drooped at the corner even when he smiled, and Alice noticed that teeth were missing from the side of his mouth. The only feature of him that appeared not to have been mangled by brutal hands was his ears, which were tiny and had no lobes, so that they had the cupped, delicate look of chinaberry blossoms stuck against the sides of his narrow head. Alice let her breath out in a quavering sigh of helplessness and her eyes filled again with tears, as Truehart spoke.

"Child," he said in a low soft voice. "Daughter."

She knew his voice immediately. Thick with sorrow and menace, it had spoken to her on several occasions from within her blues when she had played them recently in the early morning hours, and although she hadn't recognized it she'd understood that it was speaking to her from her own times and was not one of the sea captain's haunted voices. Now that she could see how it connected to her times, it occurred to her that in submitting to the call of her blues and permitting them to play themselves out through her she had likely summoned this moment to herself, and she understood why Brick had always warned her not to seek out the blues, for she was certain that she hadn't the knowledge or experience to defend herself. *I'm just a girl*, she said to herself through the slow roaring of her terror. *I'm all alone and I'm just a girl.*

Truehart lifted his knife from his lap and waved it at her with a lazy, unspecific gesture. The blade seemed to shimmer like a moonlit pool. "I found you, baby," Truehart said. "I been seeking you a long time, so. Lord, it's been a long, long time."

Alice couldn't move or speak; she felt as if she was buried to the neck in wet sand, watching a wave break over her head. Nothing she had ever been taught in her life—by Mimi or

Brick or Patanouche or the Ursuline sisters—had prepared her for the hopelessness of this moment. *There's nothing I can do*, she thought. *If I run he'll catch me; if I stay he'll cut me*.

"You were lost to me," Truehart said. "Lost lost lost. They held you from me."

He was a tall man, and so broad across the shoulders and chest that his head looked unnaturally small, as if it had been squeezed on. *He's bigger than Brick*, Alice thought, almost as big as Strap and even more frightening. She remembered hearing Baby Luana say: "Worst thing you can ever do is let a man know you're afraid of him. Man loves that; it's like putting raw meat in front of a dog. Course, on the other hand, it don't azackly help you much to sass back at him, neither, or he'll be whuppin' on you for that, same as. Face facts, woman ain't got much room whichever way she turn. There's only about two things you can do that pleases a man and don't hurt you, both, and that's only if he's feeling specially kindly and lets you do them." Alice was certain that he could hear her fear pounding in her, for it seemed to shake the house. The floor was heaving beneath her feet and even the solid little piano in the shadows at the far end of the parlor seemed to pulsate in time to its surging.

But Truehart gave no sign that he was stirred by it. He leaned back on the narrow sofa with the easy air of a man relaxing at the end of a day's hard work, and when he spoke there was a reminiscent tone to his voice. "Oh baby, I been such a long, long ways to find you," he said. "They taken me up one side and down the other, tried to break me. Tried to break this body, ha. You ever gone to Jackson? Did you?" He paused, pointing his knife at Alice.

"No, sir," she said. She was surprised at the steadiness in her voice, and though she spoke softly her words sounded clearly through the clamor in her head.

"Say what?" Truehart said. "Say no what?"

"No, sir," Alice repeated, raising her voice a shade. "I never did, no." The tightness in her chest eased somewhat.

"You never," Truehart said. "Course you never. Hell fire, girl, I'm your papa. I know that. No sir. Child says no *sir*. Hell fire. Is that any how to call your papa? I hear your blood, child. Talk to me. You been to Jackson?"

"No, Father," Alice said. "I never have been to Jackson, Father." Oddly, the words sounded familiar to her, as if she had spoken them before, though she couldn't remember ever having addressed her father, even in her dreams. So encompassing had been Mimi's protecting love that in all her years Alice had never felt the lack of a father or questioned his absence.

"That's right," Truehart said. "I been to Jackson. Truehart. I'm a hellhound from the hellhole, Jackson. I been laying up in Jackson all my days, till you called me back. Got chains in Jackson. Got the big stick and the iron pallet. Got crazy niggers in the hellhole. Got the rats. I'm a crazy nigger. You know why? Do you? Talk to me now."

"No, sir," Alice said, and then corrected herself. "No, Father," she said. The sound of her fear was receding, and the numbness that had immobilized her relaxed its grip on her limbs, so that the first traces of a tingling returned to her hands and shoulders. She moved her foot, a tentative step toward the parlor. The floor stayed steady beneath her.

"No," Truehart said agreeably. "You're just a child. Don't know the pain that's in you. Can't feel your blood yet, can you?" The knife dangled in his hand and swung loosely from side to side as he talked. "My blood," he said. "Vraicoeur blood, too. But baby, I feel your heat, I do. I do. Soon as you called me I could feel your heat, your pain. White blood burning in the black. We're colored, child, you and me. Soon as you called me, ha. I do. I. They held you from me, broke my body. Aw baby, I'm a hellhound. I'll set free your pain, set free my blood from you and me. See." His fingers tightened around the knife handle and brought the blade up so that it pointed at Alice again. "Got no business bearing white blood." His voice rose and thickened and he leaned forward on the sofa. "Crazy niggers bearing white blood, no wonder. Pick that up, nigger.

208

Turn it over. Set it down. Crazy nigger. Pick it up. Whoo. Talk to me, daughter. Do you fear me? Do you?" He cocked his head to the side and regarded the knife blade quizzically, turning it this way and that in the air between them.

As Alice was about to answer him she felt a familiar pressure in her hands and wrists, and for the first time since it had deserted her on her way to the Mansion that evening she was aware that her music was making its presence known to her again. She looked across the room at Brick's old piano, its salt stains glowing dimly in the amber light, and the sight of it comforted the hopelessness she felt. *As long as you have the music*, Brick had said. She took another step and crossed the threshold into the parlor, and the pressure in her hands and wrists increased.

"I don't hear you," said Truehart, still examining his knife. *Say "Yes, Daddy," and "No, Daddy,"* the little birds had said. "No, Daddy," Alice said.

"You're not a bad child, then, are you, baby?" Truehart said, his voice softening.

"No, Daddy." She walked slowly and with great care toward the piano; the nearer to Truehart she came, the more immense was the effort it took to lift each foot from the faded carpet, as if her shoes were cast in iron. Then he looked up sharply at her and she halted, scarcely an arm's length from him.

"Where are you going so?" he asked. Without waiting for an answer he said, "Don't you be going in your mama's kitchen, baby. Nothing there but harm."

"No, Daddy," she said, taking a half-step backward as he leaned toward her.

"See," Truehart said. He pressed the knife blade against the ball of his thumb until the skin there broke. As the shallow cut filled with blood he held it up for her to see. "You see?" he said. The blood spilled over at one end of the cut and traced a thin line down his thumb to his wrist. "You see my pain?" Truehart said, his voice rising again. He turned his hand over and held the bleeding cut close to his eyes, then put it next to his ear and listened to it, then brought it back before his eyes. While his attention was fixed on the small wound, Alice side-stepped softly past him. Truehart didn't appear to notice; in a high, excited voice he seemed to be talking to his thumb. "Got no business," he said, "Got no, got no. Bearing in my pain. Hell fire. I know the meaning of hell fire. I *seen* hell fire, bearing in my pain. Lord Godamercy I seen black pain, white fire. Lord. Set it free. Break this body, so. I *will* set free my blood, in you, in me. Set it free. Crazy nigger. Pick it, nigger. You know why? Do you? I killed Vraicoeur, set Mimi free. Do you know *why? What are you doing, girl?*" He sprang suddenly to his feet and held his arm out full-length, pointing his knife at Alice as if it were a pistol, as she seated herself on the piano bench, raised the cover from over the old, stained keyboard and set her fingers out upon the keys.

"I'm a musician, Father," Alice said without looking back at him. "It is what I do." As soon as she touched the keys the first notes of a sweet ragtime strain animated her hands.

Truehart cocked his head suspiciously. Ragtime was unfamiliar to him, and perplexing. He could hear blackness in it, but it was not the fearful, defiant blackness of the blues, or the wild, angry blackness of the stomp music; rather, in its restrained formality it sounded almost European. He shook his head at the faint memory of European music. "Trick music," he said disdainfully. "Whore music. I know the music, girl, and I know its tricks. Time and music, always tricking."

"Yes, Father," Alice said calmly. "Let me play for you." She commenced a second strain even sweeter than the first. Truehart waved the knife in an angry circle and waited for the music with its juxtaposed qualities of black and white to set off the seething in his blood. He was ready for that trick, and ready to counteract it. He would set free Alice's blood and his own, set free all pain. But the seething never came, for the music that rose up in Alice's hands thickened and gained strength, until it rushed from the old salt-sided piano with as much richness and force in its tonality as any that she had ever summoned out of the German grand in the Countess' parlor, billowed out into the little amber-lit room like mud spilling across the fan of the Mississippi delta, and in its flowing power Truehart lost track of the sound of his blood clamoring in him. His face assumed a passive expression and his arms hung limply at his sides, and the long-bladed fisherman's knife fell from his slack hand onto the carpet. After a while he sat back down on the narrow sofa and, leaning to the side, fell into a sleep that had no pain in it, and no malice.

While her father slept, Alice played on through the night, riding the music without effort or surprise, even when it turned, gradually, into Brick's blues and she heard the voices that she had heard but hadn't been able to play on the night Brick had died, the voices of his times. From the work songs of his father and the church songs his mother had played on a small harmonium in their West Texas homestead to the New Orleans music old and new, the sounds of Brick's life greeted Alice's hands and floated out over the quarter again. She played the stomps and sea tunes that Brick had played in Vasco Robertson's Saloon on the waterfront in Galveston when he was just starting out in his trade, so new and shiny that the whores there called him Kid Copperhead, though he'd told them his given name, which was Theodore, and she discovered a sharp-tongued woman who ran a boarding house there and permitted Brick to call her his wife, though their union was never solemnized. Sometime later, Alice found herself socializing with a trombone player, a humorous man called Hawk Lip who traveled with Brick through the Oklahoma Territory, where they played together in tent revivals by night and billiard parlors by day, and later still a jittery buck dancer named Jeremy Swift whose life ended in gunfire behind a circus wagon in Shreveport. She heard train whistles and riverboat paddlewheels and dancing feet and the hooves of horses; she heard the sighs of women and the deep groans of the flowing river and the brittle susurrus of a desert wind rustling dry mesquite; she heard the shuffling of cards and the slow bubbling of gumbo on the fire. As dawn approached she heard the voices of the Countess and Mr. Strap, and Old Patanouche and Mimi and the rusted iron axle of her laundry cart, and when she finally heard her own voice in the blues of Brick's times Alice stopped playing and let her hands drop from the keyboard. Then she looked around and saw daylight outside the parlor windows, and although his knife still lay where he'd dropped it on the middle of the carpet, Truehart was nowhere to be seen.

Less than an hour before, Truehart had risen from the couch and wandered from the house with a placid gait and a look of mild bother on his face. When he was outside he turned and looked back in through the parlor window, and in the dim light he saw the piano and, hunched over its keyboard, a tall, freckled Negro with wavy, reddish hair, whom he did not recognize and against whom he felt no animosity. Something about the scene did puzzle Truehart slightly, but as he walked away toward Piro he couldn't quite define it. At the corner he circled aimlessly, turning this way and that, waiting for his purpose to summon him. He tested the air with his nose but found no message there. On the other side of Piro, on the sidewalk in front of Tom Clare's saloon, the night bartender, Cockadoodledoo, was sweeping sawdust into the gutter, and Truehart crossed over and entered the barroom. Inside, two coal cart drivers sat at a corner table taking an eyeopener, and at the end of the bar a hefty longshoreman slept standing up, wedged into the corner between the bar and the wall, a schooner of flat beer beside his hand. Cockadoodledoo knocked his broom against the door frame and followed Truehart into the saloon. "Good morning, sir, and good day," he chirped, going behind the long bar. "Gonna be a fine day, you can tell upon my word."

Truehart stared at him with a puzzled look, as if waiting to hear more. A faint, wheedling pain began to nudge at the base of his skull. "What'll you take to start the day?" the bartender asked.

Truehart shook his head and tried to remember what he had come for; something whispered distantly in his blood, and without thinking he lifted his hand and touched his tongue to his thumb where he had cut it. "I'm looking for someone," he said.

"Hard to find 'em, this hour of the day," Cockadoodledoo said cheerfully. "Mostly folks comes in at nightfall. End of the day they wants to wet down, maybe they looking for sport and game, but first light now, they wants to be at home and not expecting callers. You better likely come looking at sundown. That's when a man expects to be found here, then."

"No," said Truehart, irritated at his inability to recall his pain and his purpose in clarity. "It's someone that lives nearby, only I can't tell"—he put his hand to his forehead and pressed his fingertips against the diagonal scar there; the whispering eluded him still—"I can't tell where anymore."

"Looky, what's his name?" the bartender asked. "I know about everybody here and near."

"Aw," said Truehart, concentrating. "Godamercy, I know. I do."

"What's he look like then?" the bartender asked helpfully.

"A blood relation," Truehart said finally. "Sharing my blood in her. My pain, yes. Shares my pain. Called Alice, Alice Beaudette. You know her, brother? They held her from me a long time. Young gal. Alice." He noticed that the bartender was looking at him with a strange expression, and added: "I'm her uncle. Uncle to the child."

At that instant, back in the parlor, Alice discovered Old Patanouche's voice in Brick's music and sent it out into the quarter, where it whispered a spell into the ears of the bartender and the coal cart drivers in Tom Clare's saloon, and Cockadoodledoo shook his head sorrowfully and put his hand to his bosom. "That child," he said. "Oh my, poor little Alice. Poor little Lady. Oh my, yes, I recollect her well. "Boys," he called to the drivers, "you all remember little Alice, don't you?"

"Lives nearby, don't she?" Truehart asked with great restraint, for the message in his blood was coming clearer to him.

The bartender scowled. "Did," he said dolefully.

"Little Lady," one of the coal cart drivers said.

"She did, and that's a fact," said Cockadoodledoo.

"Mimi Beaudette's little gal," the driver said.

"Lord of mercy, what a sorrow," said the bartender.

The mention of Mimi Beaudette made Truehart sly. "I'm a blood relation." he repeated softly. "I've come to help."

"Then you've come too late, my friend. She's free from needing help on earth. Free forever."

"Fool," Truehart whispered, so softly that he might have been talking to himself. "I'm going to find her, set her free. I love that little gal better than I love myself."

"Mister," said Cockadoodledoo, "I can see that you are urgent and sincere, but there is no burden left for poor Alice to bear. She knew the hard times, seen her mama cut down under the butcher's hand and then took the disease herself that killed her. She knew pain for the longest time, that poor gal."

"Poor little Alice," the coal cart driver echoed, and his companion said, "Amen."

"She don't know her pain," Truehart said hotly. He took a step back and cupped his hand over his ear in a listening gesture, heeding the sudden roaring in him. "I know her pain," he said, his voice rising. "Her pain is in me. Bearing in me."

"Looky, have one on the house, mister," Cockadoodledoo said quickly. "I can feel your grief coming on. You couldn't of known, could you?"

"Burning in my blood," Truehart said. "Burning all my days. Break my body." In confusion he lashed his senses from side to side, seeking the sound and scent of Alice's blood. It wasn't possible that she was dead, he knew, for his pain was still strong in him. He hadn't fulfilled his purpose; he had not set free her pain. He slapped his leg impatiently and felt Jibba's eyeballs in his pocket, and reached in and pulled them out, thinking to use them as a charm against his disorientation, but while his hand was still closed around them they turned to fine dust and ran through his fingers, and he groaned with a low and evil sound.

Cockadoodledoo extended a commiserating hand across the

bar toward Truehart. "There's sorrow all about us, brother," he said. "We're born in sin and live in sorrow, and the greater glory lies beyond. Your little Alice is at peace now, brother. She's lying in—" Truehart reached down to his boot top and finding no knife there he yelled in frustration and grabbed a chair and threw it over the bar, and then followed it with a table, and Cockadoodledoo went to his hands and knees on the duckboards behind the bar and grabbed the old cavalry Colt hung beside the taps and crawled to the open end of the bar in a shower of glass and liquor, as another chair and a full spittoon came flying into the mirror and the shelves of bar stock, and Old Patanouche's voice faded from the quarter.

"Free my blood in her, in me," Truehart cried. "Free my pain. I am the hellhound. My father cannot speak. White blood, white blood, white blood," he howled, as the coal cart drivers and the longshoreman pinned his arms and Cockadoodledoo beat on his head with the pistol until his blood burst out of him and they let him fall to the floor. When the police got there they found him lying dead in a crimson pool, and at last there was no heat in him and no clamor or pain, but only silence.

Alice stood up from the piano bench and closed the cover down over the keyboard. She went upstairs and took an old leather valise that had been Brick's from the corner of Mimi's bedroom and packed it with a few items of clothing, some combs, and a sachet which Baby Luana had given her at Christmastime. She took no mementoes of Mimi and nothing that would remind her of her childhood, which was done and gone and best left to the past. She rinsed her face in the washbasin and brushed out her long French hair and knotted it up on top of her head and pinned a black straw hat into place over it.

Without closing its clasp, she carried the valise downstairs to the kitchen and set it on the table there, and pulled a chair beneath the cupboard and stood on it, stretching high overhead until she reached the wooden box that rested at the back of the topmost shelf. She climbed down carefully and set the box on the table next to the valise and opened its lid; inside the box was her money, the wages the Countess had paid her and the cash gifts that the gentlemen had discreetly dropped into the silver urn set alongside the great German piano and the money that Brick had brought home with him and left for her, more money than she had ever counted or considered until she opened the wooden box on the kitchen table and saw the gold and silver coins and the notes of all denominations, and even then she didn't pause to count or consider it but took it by the handful from the box and stuffed it into the valise, pushing aside her clothing and packing the money beneath it in the bottom of the worn leather satchel. When she was done, there was nothing in the box except a little rabbitskin pouch tied at the neck with a thin leather string, which Patanouche had given her one afternoon before the old woman had gone away. Alice had forgotten about the pouch and didn't know how it had gotten into the wooden box beneath her money, and she picked it up and untied the string and dumped its contents out on the tabletop and saw that it contained several twists of paper and a wizened brown root with a vaguely human shape to it, which had a length of twine wrapped around its middle, and without knowing why, she put one of the twists of paper into her purse and returned the others along with the root to the rabbitskin pouch and retied its top and stuffed it deep into the valise with the money. Then she closed the valise and snapped its clasp shut. She wrapped a shawl around her shoulders and with the valise in one hand and her purse in the other she left the little brown house and walked to the river, where she bought a ticket and boarded the *Lydia V*, a steamboat of the Winsted Line, sailing at nine that morning for the upriver ports.

All this she did with the unhesitating, tranquil pace of a sleepwalker, without plan or calculation but simply responding to a certainty within her that this was what she had to do before Truehart shook off the drowsiness which Brick's music had given him and returned to threaten her again. Later, while she stood at the rail on the steamboat's deck and stared down into the dark brown currents of the spring-swollen river flowing back toward New Orleans, her understanding would begin to deepen, and her resolve. She would feel the strain of the boat's engines vibrating in the deck beneath her heels and the massive rolling of the paddlewheel behind the boat's stern, and their reverberations would sound in her heart, a slow, grinding movement bearing her forward in her life. And in her thoughts she would hear her own voice speak clearly to her for the first time, no longer distorted by the enveloping safeguards of her childhood: the cheerful, pragmatic innocence of Mimi Beaudette; the whimsical magic of Old Patanouche; Brick's music with its solid, buoyant flow; the mercenary watchfulness of Countess Eulalie Welcome in her parlor full of whores and lechers and well-dressed brutes. In her own voice Alice resolved to close them all away behind her, to hide them even from her memory, for reminiscence bore messages to the past and the past, she understood, teemed with spirits eager to bear pain and fear into the present, where there was already plenty for a woman of mixed blood alone in the world. *I must not play my blues*, she said to herself. *I must leave my blues* . . . She paused in her thoughts, realizing that she had been about to form the words, "out in the alley." . . . *behind*, she said to herself, finishing the thought with an emphatic nod.

Alice spent the rest of the morning calculating and deciding, while the riverboat strained northward against the muddy current and the spring breezes blew across the deck. She was confident that the music in her was her own now, and that in its power she possessed the means to make her way without having to seek the violent protection of a man, although she must never be careless of men or assume that they would respect her simply because of her skill at the piano. She was certain too that she was fair enough of skin and feature to be able to pass as a white person, although she thought she might be safest in that regard if she took herself to one of the Northern states, where she had heard that white and colored mingled freely. She would speak with the soft, cultured accents of the Countess' parlor, and bear herself with dignity and concentration, and she vowed that she would never, in love or anger, call any man "Daddy." She would leave the past in New Orleans and never return to it, and her life, she decided, would be a great adventure.

As midday approached, the sun's light began to fall upon the portion of railing where Alice stood, and she gathered up her purse and her valise and prepared to move on to a better-shaded part of the deck, near the bow. Before she left the rail, however, she took the twist of paper from her purse and tore it open and shook it out in the wind, which seemed such an altogether natural act to perform that it never occurred to her that the decision to perform it had been made for her by Old Patanouche more than two years earlier, just before the eve of the new century. A sprinkling of herbs scattered from the paper into the wind and were blown aft of the steamboat and settled to the surface of the river, where they formed a thin line that ran from bank to bank across the water like the trail of a pointed stick dragged through dry sand, and then rose up in a cloud of steam as dense as the night mists of New Orleans and formed a curtain that blocked Alice from the sight of her past. But she never noticed the barrier, for she had already let the torn paper slip from her fingers and turned away from the rail and was walking toward the bow, facing north into the present.

PART III:
NEW YORK—SAND SPRINGS
1903–1919

Chapter Eight

Troublesome Ivories

Now, Mama played the ragtime and she played it fine and very legitimately, because ragtime was supposed to sound legitimate that way. For a spell there it was the hottest thing around and every bit as popular as the others that came after, hot things like the Charleston and swing and the rock and roll. People played ragtime on the parlor piano, and the sheet music sales for a popular rag could make its composer a wealthy man and quite well known, and the professional players were very much in demand. There were ragtime shows traveling back and forth around the country on the black circuit and the white, and before she settled down with me in Sand Springs, Mama was on the road with an outfit called The Joseph Selson Ragtime Orchestra and Minstrel Display.

She kept a poster picture of the Selson orchestra in an old trunk in her bedroom, stashed down in the bottom with some other old stuff like her old straw hats and her voodoo root, that as far as I know she only used the one time, when she was calling me back from the dead. See, I knew about the things in that trunk because once in a while when I was alone in the house I used to sneak in and rummage around, you know, just being a curious kid and all, and once I found that old photo there I used to like to go back and look at it from time to time, and I'll tell you why.

Now, there were thirty-three musicians in the photo, standing in two rows, and they were all dressed as if they were going to the opera, the Diamond Horseshoe, with the gents all done up in wing collars and the old soup and fish, white ties and tail coats. There were five women among them, wearing dark, heavy-looking gowns that left their shoulders bare and white gloves to their elbows and little chokers around their necks, and Mama was all the way over on the left in the back row, beside the potted plant, she looked so pretty and *so* serious. She was short and on the plump side, but in the picture she was carrying her head way up and stretching out her neck and with her hair rolled up on top of her head the way she did she looked almost as tall as Joe Selson himself. Well, at least she was as tall as that potted plant, ah-ha. I never knew her age at all, but I'd bet money that she wasn't any more than sixteen or seventeen when that picture was taken. And then, down in front there were seven boys and girls in blackface and wooly wigs, sitting on the floor, and they were the minstrel display and probably did comedy sketches and sang coon songs. Coon songs was what they called them then, those black-face songs about eatin' de watermelon by de levee, and they were a popular part of just about any vaudeville or variety show you ever saw, black or white. Mercy, it does seem an embarrassment, doesn't it, but that's what those times were like.

Joseph Selson himself stood front and center, holding his baton in both hands, and just in case you missed him, there was a cameo of him, too, up in the corner of the picture, with his name printed underneath. He was a tall fellow with a big gut on him, had his mustache waxed up at the ends and his hair in waves like wings on top of his forehead, and you could tell by the expression on his face that he was in charge of that outfit. He had that leader look, all right. Oh, I practically memorized that photo at one time, when, you see, I was feeling the lack of a daddy particularly hard and I took it in my mind that perhaps

222

my pa, Mister Anthony Mayhew Winslow, had been a musician that Mama had met on the band. She had never said that he was, you understand, but on the other hand she'd never said he wasn't, either, and I guess I must have thought I could pick him out of that crowd if I looked hard enough. So I studied on it and studied on it every time Mama left me alone in the house, but I never did find my daddy in there, just a bunch of old road musicians and Lord knows I've seen plenty of them here and there in my day.

There were tin-pot preachers in those times who stumped around preaching against the ragtime, because they said it made the young people loose and crazy with its syncopation, and there were people like Alfred Calhoun who called it nigger music that was going to turn us into a nation of darkies, but it was only music, you know, and it never fired a gun at anyone. It had its little syncopations, all right, and its little touches or chromatics, and that was probably curious and upsetting to somebody whose idea of proper music came out of the hymn book at the Methodist meeting, but if you listen to most of those ragtime tunes you'll wonder what the fuss was all about. It's pleasing enough to hear but by and by it doesn't really go anywhere or tell you about its soul, and that's why it sounds pretty rinky-tinky to us now, and old-fashioned. People didn't go in for telling their soul then, at least not white people, and the black musicians who devised the legitimate ragtime for the white people to hear seemed to know that and composed their tunes with a white sound and made it formal so. Everybody knows about Mr. Scott Joplin's instruction that you should stomp the ragtime without taking your foot up off the floor, and that was probably so as not to scare off the white people, you know, and make them fearful of Negritude. That was one of Alfred Calhoun's favorite words, Negritude, one of his two-bit specials that he used to cuss about when he and the loafing society were having their high-level discussions there in the barber shop.

Now, when the black musicians were playing for each other,

that was a different story, you understand, and they stomped plenty and ragged those tunes till they were about to fly apart. I recall hearing Jelly Roll Morton playing rags and stuff in New York, uptown, and he was supposed to be old-timey then, what with all the new stuff that had come along, but, mercy, Mr. Jelly was lively as a cricket and that old scoundrel could *swing*. I shared a taste with him in the kitchen between sets and asked him about New Orleans, figuring to find out if he'd remember hearing about Mama there, but all he wanted to talk about was shooting pool in Texas and he was such a headstrong talker that I never did get him turned around and headed where I wanted to go. He had that accent, though, and he called me Lay-on, the way Mama pronounced my name, with that French sound, and that pleased me so and gave me the old nostalgia tickle.

Mama played with a nice rich sound and she had excellent time, steady and safe as Fort Knox gold, and she knew a few little tricks and extra effects around the keyboard, little trills and grace notes, to cover up the fact that her hands were too small to bridge twelve or even ten keys and she was using false fingerings most of the time. And that was nice, it made the music ripple when she played. But she played with a conservative style altogether, a white style, even when she was just messing around on her little piano in the parlor at home, and she never improvised or ragged and she certainly never stomped. She did surprise me from time to time, though, and there were things about her that make me curious to this day. For an example, there was this one time when I was on the road playing a dance or a show and before it started I was warming up my clarinet, getting my reed wet, and I was playing this little warmup piece I used to play, which was a funny little nursery tune Mama used to play for me at home when I was very small, a little tinkle-tinkle that ran up and down the scale, top and bottom. There was one old fellow in the room with me there, an old black fellow, and when I played that piece he popped his eyes and started chuckling fit to bust a gut, and he told me that the last time he'd heard that song it was in a cathouse back in New Orleans and it was a naked dance that, you know, the piano player would play and one of the whores would do a shimmy to it without her clothes on, to stir the customers up. Well, I still wonder about that. If I ever catch up with Mama in the by and by, that's one something I mean to ask her about, ah-ha, I do.

And then there was another time, when I heard her playing the blues, which was so mystifying to me that I've never been able to swear I wasn't just dreaming it, because even though the blues belong to everybody and they're everybody's business, like it says, my mama was not a blues player, no sir. Mama was an old-fashioned lady, you see, just like her name, and something like the blues would have been too lowdown for her soft little hands to get next to. All you had to do was listen to her ragtime and you'd know that. Except then you say, "But she played you a naked dance, didn't she?," and I've got to say she did. Yes, she did.

I was asleep anyway when her blues came stealing in on me, and you notice I say I *think* they woke me up and made me shiver, they were so sad and scary to me. It was as if I was overhearing Mama sobbing in the dark. You see, I didn't recognize that kind of music then, because I never had heard it played, and all I could think was how unhappy it sounded, and I just lay there in my little bed and I didn't know what to do. I thought about all the unhappy things I'd ever seen or thought about in my life until I was practically crying out at the pain of it, and that music just kept playing and playing, so soft and lonely and sad like that and it never let up, there was no end to it that night.

Now, the thing about the blues that's most important is the thing that was lacking from them that night, and that's the resolution that always comes in somewhere along the line. You play diddle-a-*bip*, and then you play diddle-a-*bop*, and the *bop* resolves the *bip*, you see? And that goes to say that, bad as things are, they'll work out by and by. You have the same thing in the verses of the blues songs, in the words, you know, saying how the sun is going to shine someday in my back yard and like that. The idea is that there's always a reason to be hoping, which is an idea that comes out of the slave times when they couldn't believe things were as bad as they were, they just had to think something better was in store or else they might as well jump in the river and drown there. That's where the blues came from in the beginning of them, and people who think they're not about anything except feeling sorry for yourself are only listening with half an ear, because if the blues have anything to say, it's, "Go to Hell," and, "Look out, I'm coming back up." And I'll tell you something: I already knew that about the blues that first time I heard them that night, only I didn't know I knew it. It was a lesson I had learned from a raggedy old gentleman called Bub the Fire Eater.

I already mentioned about the only time Mama ever struck me. That happened when I came home one day and she was there in the parlor playing, and I asked her if she was playing nigger music. Well, her hand flew up and smacked me across the face so fast it surprised us both, and then we both started to cry, because she understood I didn't mean anything by it and was only repeating something I had heard someone else say, and that was true, you know, I was. Most likely it was Alfred Calhoun or his boy Roger that I'd heard saying it, but it could have been another, too. Mama apologized then and said she was so sorry, and I said I was so sorry too, and she made me swear with my hand on my heart that I would never say "nigger" again. I did that but it puzzled me, because it was only a word and you heard it spoken here and there and meaning a lot of different things. There was a licorice candy, for example, that we called nigger toes, and on the Fourth of July the bigger boys lit up nigger chasers. What else? Well, we played Catch a Nigger by the Toe in the schoolyard, and there was a flower we called a nigger daisy, it must have been a black-eyed Susan, and in the marshes by the lake there was a way the grass grew that was called nigger heads. You see, it was a word that got around, and it didn't mean anything special to me because, although I was eight or nine years old, I had never seen an actual living nigger. There was no such person in Sand Springs and I'm not sure there ever had been.

But I told you I was a curious and adventuresome pup, and I was that, right enough, and I decided to get out and see what it was that made my mama so upset that she'd have come up alongside my chops like that so fast, and I knew where to go looking, too, because the story was all over town. Every small kid in Sand Springs knew that down in Carlowsbridge there lived a creature called Bub the Fire Eater, who drank kerosene oil and ate burning coals that made his eyes and his teeth glow in the dark, and we knew he liked to burn up little kids with his breath, *whoo*, because it was something that mamas used to tell their fry when they got rambunctious around the house. You know: "If you don't quit that this minute, I'm calling Bub the Fire Eater, and he'll come and burn you to a cinder, you hear?" Probably the same as their own mamas told them. Who knows how those old stories get started? But the thing that was most important to me was that this Bub was a nigger, and that was most well known. So you see, the first chance I had I lit out for Carlowsbridge to find him.

Now, it was a good ten miles to Carlowsbridge, and I'd never been all that way by myself before then, but I knew the way well enough, because there was only one road out of Sand Springs in that direction and that was the Carlowsbridge road where the trolley ran, down along by the river, and that's the way I went. Put a chicken leg in my cap for lunch and run right off. I believe it was the late spring or maybe early summer.

I didn't hop the trolley because I didn't want my friend Ripley's daddy to see me, who was the motorman on that line, but I snagged a ride on a baker's wagon and told the boy driving it that I was going to visit cousins, and when we got there I hopped off and started exploring. My, I had a wonderful time and saw some sights, too. Now, you understand that Carlowsbridge is just one of those little old rundown riverside cities like you find anywhere and forget you ever saw it as soon as you clear the city line. You know the kind I mean, where everyone says good night and goes home at sundown and they turn off the lights and put the sidewalks to bed. But coming down from Sand Springs, that place looked as big and lively as Gay Paree to me, and I just wandered around with my jaw hanging down and taking it all in. People were all dressed up the way we only dressed on Sunday in Sand Springs, and I saw men wearing jewels in their lapels and women with fancy hats and veils over their faces, and automobiles, so many automobiles. I saw a chicken run under one and just disappear, leaving not so much as a feather behind, and I saw a bunch of streetcorner boys no bigger than myself and they were all smoking cigarettes and talking loud, and then I ducked down an alley and there was a fellow sleeping on the paving stones there and singing in his sleep, and I thought, Mercy, what kind of a place is this? I looked in the store windows, and one them was filled up with fish, big fish, looking practically alive, and then in another there were skinned lambs hanging up by their hind feet and rabbits, you know, with the fur still on their paws. There was another store that was full of nothing but clocks, and when I went by they all struck the hour, all at the same time, and there was a barber shop with six chairs and a mirror practically as long as the side terrace at the inn. Oh, and there was a candy store there, oh my, that just about broke my poor little heart. I'd never seen all that much candy before. I stood and stared through that window at all that candy for the longest time, trying to calculate, you know, which kind I liked best and how could I get some of it for myself without actually stealing it, and that was a knotty problem, all right. My favorite was the ribbon candy, and they had miles and miles of it, but I liked the jellies, too, and there must have been a ton of those, not to mention all the chocolates. Mama used to bring home chocolate from time to time when she went down to Berde Bros., which was the department store where she demonstrated the sheet music, and I liked chocolate just fine.

Well, I was standing there and talking to myself about

228

candy, and the day was getting on, and somewhere about that time this big old policeman came right up beside me and said How d'you do to me, and that was Constable Ambrose Burnside of the Carlowsbridge Finest. He said he'd been noticing me on his rounds and he wondered if I was lost or needed some assistance, because, he said, he knew most of the young fellows in Carlowsbridge and he knew I wasn't one of them. He said he could see that I was a visitor newly come to his fair city, and he spoke to me in a serious and kindly way and that flattered me, because it sounded like the way grownup men talked to each other, you see, so it put me at my ease with him. I told him I wasn't lost, and that was no lie, and he invited me to stroll with him, and said he'd show me some sights of interest in the city, and I couldn't refuse to go along, being that I was just a little sprig like that, so I did.

He wasn't as big as Henny Vaughan, but he was a big man, Constable Burnside, and even though he walked slowly I had to hop some to keep up with him on his rounds. We chatted away like a couple of gents, and I felt quite like the man of the world, you know, peregrinatin' on the boulevard and swappin' tales like that. I told Constable Burnside some stories about Sand Springs and he was so polite and pretended he'd never heard any of them, and he asked me about Uncle Pedey Donker, who he said he remembered from the last Fourth of July parade when Uncle Pedey had stood up in the carriage and hit the driver with his ear trumpet, and about Chester MacIntyre who was the constable in Sand Springs and a good friend of Constable Burnside's. He told me how he and Chief MacIntyre had hunted down a convict together up in the hills above the west shore of the lake, and I told him I knew for a fact that Chief MacIntyre carried a pistol that could drop a grizzly bear at fifty paces, and I asked him if his pistol could do that, and he said probably not quite, and on and on we went like that. And by and by without quite thinking about it I let it slip that I'd heard tell of somebody called Bub the Fire Eater, and that he sounded like an interesting sort of a person to see.

Well, my friend Constable Burnside got altogether serious when I said that, and he said, "Did your mama tell you Bub would come and burn you up with his breath if you were naughty?"

And I said, "No sir, not my mama."

And he said, "But you did hear that from someone, didn't you?"

And I had to admit that I had heard that story, yes.

"Mister Winslow," he said, which was what he'd been calling me, "Mister Winslow, that's a lot of awful foolishness that little boys' mamas have been spreading about poor old Bub for years and years, and there's not a whisper of truth in it, you have my word. He's nothing but a harmless old nigger that works in the coalyards and lives in a shack there without comfort or friendship, and I'd consider it a favor to myself if you and all the children who come about wanting to stare at him and call him names would have the kindness to leave him be. Would you do that for me? Would you ever?" And he stopped and bent over in front of me and looked me right in the eye, so close I could smell him.

Well, I was just mortified, displeasing him like that, and eye to eye with him I said that I would do what he asked, and when he stood back up and clapped me on the shoulder and said, "Good lad," to me I was ready to keep my promise and go on along his rounds with him as if nothing had changed between us, but then we turned a corner and there was the trolley depot right up ahead. I realized then that he had been guiding me along that way and that he was going to send me home, and, sure enough, he led me right up to the front of the trolley and called up Hello to the motorman, Mr. Threadgill. Threadgill said, "Hello, Ambrose," to him and, "Hello, Leon," to me, and Constable Burnside said, "Mister Winslow has been visiting with me as my guest, Mister Threadgill, and now I believe he's expected home for his supper. I'd appreciate it if you'd extend to him every courtesy of the line."

My ears just burned, because I knew I'd been steered

around like a puppet on a string, you know, treated like a little kid, and I was so embarrassed and angry I couldn't even look that Judas constable in the eye when he shook my hand and said good-bye. I was so down about it that it didn't cheer me a bit when the conductor on the car, Dib Gallagher, let me ring the signal bell for him, which was ordinarily a privilege, and when the trolley stopped at the Peterson Tannery a couple of miles up the road where there was a crowd coming off the day shift, I slipped off the back step and hid behind a gatepost until it was gone on its way, and then I crossed the road and hopped down the riverbank and made my way right back into Carlowsbridge. I was going to find that coalyard and see that Bub for myself, you see, and not take anybody's word for anything, no sir.

Now, I didn't want to run into the constable again, so I lurked around the outskirts of town until it started to get dark, and then I followed the railroad track where it ran along by the riverbank, and by the time I found the coalyard it was night and the stars were out and I was having second thoughts. I'd been on my feet all day, you understand, and had nothing to eat since breakfast except a cold chicken leg and some water from a pump, and I was only a little cuss, after all, even if I was full of adventure most of the time. I got to that old coalyard and shinnied under a loose board in the fence and once I was inside the yard, oh Mama, I got spooked. That place looked like the end of the world. It looked like the other side of the moon. It was nothing but huge piles of black coal, mountains of coal as far as my eyes could see, with little pathways running between them and cinders on the ground that made a crunching sound every time you put your foot down, and it was smoky with coal dust, and so dark and quiet I figured there couldn't be anything but dead things there, or things that ate fire and spit out flame. I was expecting to see dragons and zombies jumping out of every shadow, and since the place was nothing *but* shadows, I could feel their breath on me from every direction. I kept dodging these things I thought I felt moving around in the darkness there, and it wasn't any time at all before I'd lost track of the fence and scarcely knew which way to go. And then, oh my, I heard footsteps. Big old slow-moving footsteps, just like a zombie would make.

Lord of mercy, didn't I run then. Up this way and down that way, it didn't matter to me where I went just so long as I was going as fast as my little legs could move under me, and every time I'd stop to get my breath there'd be another noise of some kind and that would set me off again, until finally I was fit to collapse and the only thing I could think to do was to haul myself up one of those big piles of coal and hope they wouldn't consider looking for me there. And that's what I did, climbed right up to the top, and when I got there I lay down across it and put my face down and started to cry, and wish that I'd never gotten myself into this scrape, which was worse than all the other scrapes I'd ever gotten into put together. But then, while I was crying and carrying on in my unhappiness up there, out of the corner of my eye I saw a light that seemed to be coming up from the ground on the other side of the pile, and I heard laughing going on, and once I stopped sobbing and my breath was coming softly to me again I eased over very carefully until I could just peek around and see what was there, and that's where I finally saw Bub, right down below.

There was a patch of clear ground there in the middle of the coalyard with a little campfire burning in it, and I saw four men sitting on the ground around that fire with their shadows dancing on the coal piles behind them. Three of the men were all in a bunch on one side of the fire, and they were white men and they had their backs to me, but I could tell from their voices and their clothes that they were rough characters. They were passing a whiskey bottle back and forth and laughing and cussing and cutting up, and on the other side of the fire from them was the man himself, the one I'd come to see, old Bub the Fire Eater and my very first nigger.

Now, I could recall one time that I'd gone to a sideshow at a circus or a traveling fair, and I'd seen a poster outside a tent

232

where they said they had a giant man-eating alligator from the banks of the Nile River, and on that poster it had a picture of a huge green creature with fiery eyes and a tail like a freight train, and the top half of a black man was sticking out of the creature's mouth looking so frightened it was comical, with his eyes popping and his hair standing up and his big red lips gaping wide open, saying Oh, and he was drawn with paint so black there was nothing else you could see about him except his shape. Well, Bub was just as black as the fellow on that poster, but there was nothing comical about him. He looked dark and dirty and miserable to me, wearing clothes that were nothing but a lot of rags that seemed as if they'd been stuck to him with pot paste, and when he opened his mouth there wasn't a tooth in it, and his eyes were dull and sleepy and sad, and all brown where they should have been white. And right behind him was his home, which was just a shack no bigger than a two-hole privy, made out of scrap lumber and tin, with a torn blanket hanging down over the door. He wasn't eating any fire, either, not then, but he was pulling on his own whiskey bottle and swaying back and forth on the ground like as he was riding on the roof of the trolley going full out on a bumpy track.

The three white men must have been drivers, you know, on the coal wagons, and as I said, they were having a high old time, which all seemed to be at Bub's expense. They kept saying Nigger this and Nigger that, and telling jokes where nigger was the punch line, and that made them fall all over themselves laughing. Every so often one of them got up and went around to Bub's side of the fire and clapped Bub on the back so hard he almost toppled over and called him A Good Old Nigger, and then the white man staggered back around with his friends and they'd hoot some more and pass the bottle. And Bub never really said anything, but he grunted a lot and mumbled from time to time, so that it looked as if he was even drunker than they were, and now and again he smiled, but not like he was sharing the others' jokes. Just a goofy little smile that didn't have anything to do with anything.

Well, it made me sad to see it. I was just a kid but I knew meanness when I saw it. I knew Alfred Calhoun was a mean man, and those white men were behaving as meanly as he ever did and maybe more. They were taunting that poor old man in a nasty way, like boys poking sticks at a sick dog in a cage, and he had nothing to defend himself with, and that saddened me so I didn't even want to watch it. I turned away and started to edge myself back over the coal pile, and I would have climbed down and started to see if I could find my way home, but just then I heard a whistle and a voice shouted, "Yay, Bub." It sounded excited in a different way, so I turned back to get a last look and I saw Bub push himself up from the ground and stand there in the firelight, swaying a little but not as much as he had when he'd been sitting down. And then he started to chant.

I couldn't hear any words in his chanting that I recognized, but the rhythm of it caught my ear. It was slow and steady and his voice was low and soft, and it seemed a soothing thing to hear, and he started to bounce a little in time to it and then he started to dance. At first he just shuffled there, stirring up the coal dust with his feet, and I noticed that he didn't have any shoes on and his toenails looked golden and pointed like claws in the firelight. Then he shifted and began to thump his heels on the ground, and every thump kicked up a little cloud of dust and cinders that got bigger and thicker until it surrounded his legs all the way up to his knees and you couldn't even see his feet through it, and Bub jumped straight up in the air and danced on the top of that cloud, this way and that, very easy and graceful, while the cloud got bigger and thicker still. When it covered the fire, he danced forward over the flames and reached down through the cloud and picked up a glowing hot coal the size of a crab apple with his thumb and forefinger and tossed it in the air and began to juggle it from hand to hand, flipping it higher into the sky with each toss, and the higher it flew the hotter it glowed, until it was as white as any star and trailing a tail of sparks behind it like a comet. Bub gave out a whoop and flung that ember so high in the sky that it disappeared among the stars up there, and then he snapped his bare heels together with a noise that sounded like a branch breaking in the wind, and he spun around and jumped clear over my head to the top of the tallest coal pile in the yard. I laughed in wonderment and looked back over my shoulder at him, and I saw him reach up and pluck a star from out of the Milky Way and smash it against his forehead and scatter the sparkling blue-white pieces all over the coalyard and beyond. And then he was off, leaping from peak to peak across the yard, gathering stars and hurling them down to earth and replacing them in the sky with nuggets of coal that he lit with his breath and tossed high in the heavens, and when he jumped over me I rolled over on my back to see and the earth and sky changed places. I found myself floating up above the coalyard and Bub was way far beneath me, grinding the coal to powder with his golden toenails and sweeping it up in clouds that filled the empty space between me and the ground, and the clouds held me up as I fell into them and I began to glow like a star, and the next time Bub went by he wound a line of sparks around me and spun me like a top, and I laughed and laughed, I felt so light and free, and I rolled across the coal piles until I was so dizzy that I had to close my eyes and curl up into a ball, and when I did that I stopped spinning and everything got dark and quiet again and I felt fine and so happy, as if I was sleeping in my own little bed.

I woke up in Constable Burnside's arms, and he was carrying me to his house. When we got there he tried to scrub me off some before he put me on his spare bed, but the grime from the coalyard was too much for him, so he just spread a canvas sheet and I slept on that and didn't soil Mrs. Burnside's clean bed linens. In the morning Mrs. Burnside took a turn at trying to wash me, with lye soap and a stiff brush, and she rubbed until I thought my skin was going to come off, and then when I got home Mama plunked me down in a tub and took her turn, too, but, you know, weeks later I was still finding little bits of coal dust on me.

Now, you might say that I dreamed the whole thing, and I

suppose it could be so, but I couldn't swear that it didn't happen like that. It was real enough to me at the time. I was just a kid, you see, and I didn't have the full picture yet concerning what was possible and what wasn't. Men had just started flying in airplanes then, and that sounded almost too fantastical to be true, and in the time following Halley's comet there were plenty of wild stories going around that people promised had really happened when it passed overhead, like infants who were born with the power of speech and black sheep who'd turned white overnight, and trees that split open and revealed statues of Jesus or Napoleon. And it was well known among the young fry in Sand Springs that Uncle Pedey could defy gravity as easily as he defied Alfred Calhoun, ah-ha, and that once at the Carlowsbridge Fourth of July he had risen off his chair on the speakers' platform and sat there five feet up in the air, easy as you please. And then there was supposed to be a place in New Jersey where a horse climbed a ladder and dove from a diving board into the ocean, and when Fritz Larrabee, who had a farm in Sand Springs, heard about that he went to Henny Vaughn and told him that if he'd build the diving board, then he, Fritz, would train any of his farm animals to dive into the lake. Cows, pigs, goats, Fritz said it made no difference. "The man's enthusiasm is quite bewitching," Henny told us. "To hear him describe it, a person would think the cow was cousin to the otter." When Henny turned him down, Fritz told him he wasn't progressive, and that hurt Henny's feelings, because he was always looking for new ways to amuse his guests. That was why he built the big pier with the ballroom on it, so that the guests could do the fox trot and the other dances that were up-to-date when the ragtime lost its popularity. You see, there were plenty of things going on that I couldn't have explained, but I didn't doubt that they were so.

And don't forget, my mama came from New Orleans, where there's something mystifying going on all the time in the way of hexes and odd disturbances that you can't quite put your finger on; and even though she never talked about those things, she did have her little voodoo root that she'd brought along with her, and that's another thing I mean to ask her about in the by and by. Now, I should say that I didn't know back then that it was a voodoo root. I thought she'd healed me from my drowning with home medicine and mother's love, and that shriveled-up old piece of wood she kept in her trunk was just a good-luck charm like a rabbit's foot or a lucky penny that she'd held onto because she was superstitious or sentimental or some such. It wasn't until later when I was out on the road and got to know some of the New Orleans fellows and heard them talking about haunts and curses and the heebie-jeebies as if it was all as natural as sunshine that it occurred to me that Mama had been in touch with what they called the mysteries. I got tight one night in Omaha with a trombone player named Kalson, we were sharing a taste and talking about this and that, you know, and I remembered that root and described it to him then, and he jumped right up from the table. He turned around three times and spit on the floor and crossed his heart, and he said to me, "Winslow, your mama was a voodoo lady and that there was a voodoo root she had." He asked me did I ever see her sticking pins in it or holding it over the candle flame, and I told him I never did, but I told him about my experience with the drowning and he said, "Uh-huh, moicy me. You've been charmed, my boy. You're gonna live forever." Well, I hope he was wrong about that because of all the questions I still have to ask her that she never had the time to answer in this life, all those things she never got around to telling me.

So you see, maybe my visit to old Bub the Fire Eater was a dream, but then again maybe not. Maybe it was voodoo. Whichever it was, it had a nice kind of lesson in it that left me feeling good for my pains, and that's what the blues are supposed to do. But the night I heard Mama playing blues in the dark, the music she played didn't make me want to smile. It sounded so lonely and lost to me, and it never did reach up to grab at the stars. It made me think of the lake, where it was deep and dark and cold.

People said that in its deepest places the bottom of the lake was covered with huge granite boulders, as big as houses, that had been shaken down out of the glaciers, and in ancient times the Indians around there had believed that there was an ice spirit named Sikanteh who lived in a castle down among those stones, which was how the lake got its name, you see. The Indians had their legends about people who fell into the lake and disappeared and then came back years later, no older than when they'd left, who'd been living in Sikanteh's castle underneath the water, and even in my time you heard tell of strange things sighted or heard in the mist, fishermen who'd seen arms beckoning out of the water or heard a woman's voice raised up in sorrow, and I thought of those things, too, when my mama played her blues. After a while of it I got up out of bed and walked out of my room, and when I got to the top of the stairs Mama stopped playing and came out into the hall, and I said, "Mama, are you all right?" Well, she said, "Oh yes, I didn't mean to wake you, darlin'." And I said, "Mama, that music sounded so *sad*." She said, "La, I was just feeling sleepless and playing soft to settle myself back down, so you go back to bed now and I won't disturb you with it anymore." And that was the only time I ever heard her play the blues.

That happened in the late winter or the early spring, just around the time I turned sixteen, and it was only a little while after that that Mama started slipping out of the house early in the morning and going to the lake shore by herself. I remember the first time I heard her go out I heard the front door close and I hopped out of bed and watched her out my window. She went straight across the road and into the thickets there and then I couldn't see her in the mist, and I got quite alarmed by it and didn't know what to do. She was gone about half an hour and when she came back I asked her where she had been. She said, "Oh la, nowhere at all. It seemed such a soft morning I thought I'd treat myself to a constitutional before breakfast."

Well, that was all the more puzzling to me, because Mama had always avoided the out-of-doors as much as she could, and particularly in the daytime. She'd always said that fresh air made her "florid" and she never went out into the sun without wearing a big hat or carrying a parasol to shade her skin, which was very fair, you know, and very fine-textured. I asked if I could walk along with her the next time she went, and she looked startled but said she supposed so, and the next day I made sure I was up early enough, and we walked together along the lake road until we were within sight of the inn, then we turned around and walked home and that was that and I hadn't learned anything from it, so I tried a different approach. A couple of mornings later she looked in on me and asked did I want to go walking with her and I said no, but as soon as the door closed I hustled into my clothes and snuck out to follow her. I crossed the road and tippy-toed through the woods and I came upon her standing beside a tree on the bank of the lake, and she wasn't moving a muscle but was just standing there looking out into the mist that rose up off the water in the early morning so thick that there was nothing to see out there and sometimes you couldn't tell where the mist ended and the water began, it was so heavy. But the curious thing about her was the way she was holding her head, and that was just like the way I'd seen her looking on the morning I woke up after I fell through the ice and drowned. She had it pulled in like that, and her shoulders hunched up as if she was waiting to be struck, and although I couldn't see her face from where I was watching, I was certain that it had that same expression on it, as if she was listening to something from far, far away.

Well, she kept going out like that all that spring, on mornings when the mists were heavy, and I stopped worrying about it after a while, you know, I thought it was just something she was doing and she must have had her reasons for it. But one morning at the beginning of July I glanced out my window after she'd gone and I saw a man standing out there in the road, and he was looking into the woods on the other side of the road, right at the spot where she always went.

He was a tall man, with shoulders so broad they made his

head look too small for the rest of him, and he was dressed in city clothes, with a dark suit and a derby hat and big heavy black shoes like you used to see policemen wearing. He was smoking a cigar and just standing there as if he was waiting for Mama to come out of the woods, and for some reason the sight of him gave me a fright. My window was raised and I stuck my head out and called to him, said, "Hey mister. Hey there," figuring to ask him his business. But he jumped real sudden, like as I'd startled him, and took right off toward the inn without even looking up at me, walking fast, and by the time I'd got my trousers pulled on and was downstairs and out the door he was way out of sight.

Mama came out of the woods on the other side of the road then, and said, "I heard you call, darlin'. Is everything all right?"

I said, "Mama, there was a man here just now."

Well, she stopped stockstill and drew a big breath and let it all out in a rush, and she looked this way and that as if she'd lost her way, and I said, "Mama?," and she said, "Here? Was he here? At the house?"

"No," I said, "he was out here in the road."

"Oh la," she said very softly, and then she asked me, "Was it a tall man?"

"He was pretty tall," I said. "He had big shoulders and a derby hat, and he was smoking a cigar."

"What were his ears like?" she asked me then.

I thought that was an odd question, and I said, "What do you mean?"

"Did you see his ears?" she said.

"No," I said, "I didn't notice them. He had a hat on."

"What was he doing here?" she said. "What was he doing?"

And I said, "He wasn't doing nothing, really. He was just standing here and looking hard over that way, where you were."

She let out another breath then and seemed to relax, and she said, "It was probably just a guest from the inn, out taking the air. I'm sure I don't know such a man."

"He was dressed like a city man," I said. I didn't tell her that I knew all of the inn's guests by sight and had never seen that man among them. You see, I was working at the desk that summer, so I got to see them all, coming and going. I supposed it was possible he had checked in late the night before, after my shift was over, but I didn't really believe it, because I had worked past ten and folks didn't usually travel that late at night.

She shook her head and that listening expression came back to her face, and she said, "Oh la," a couple of times, but when I asked her what was wrong and who did she think it might have been, she didn't want to talk about it then. She told me to ask her about it another time and she'd explain it all, which was a thing she said to me so often in our times together. I believe she meant it, though. That's something I've always believed.

Chapter Nine

American Beauty Rag

Six of the eight doors along the second-floor hallway had panes of frosted glass set into them, whose filtered glow, augmented scarcely at all by the dim light which escaped the stairwell, provided the only illumination in that shabby corridor, and although it was a warm and sunny June day outside, Lady experienced a decided chill as she paused on the landing while her eyes accustomed themselves to the gloom. The air, she noted, was stale with the lingering smells of soot and cigars and scented powder, their dismal, musty odors reminiscent of old dressing rooms, and from somewhere among the upper stories of the building she could hear a soprano voice attempting a tune in an unsteady waltz tempo, accompanied by a piano with a sour, metallic tone.

She looked up and down the hall and located the door she was seeking, but as she approached it she heard from inside the room the sound of a man's laughter, booming with a raucous authority that made her flinch, and she halted and for a few seconds busied herself patting down her dress and straightening her little straw hat and plucking at the white lace at her cuffs. While she was thus engaged, the door clattered open and a tall blond woman stepped briskly into the corridor. The woman's face was heavily painted in a theatrical style, and she wore a day outfit colored in vivid hues of green and yellow and a hat upon which blossomed a cascade of ostrich plumes, but although her brightly rouged mouth was stretched wide in a jolly grin, her eyes sparkled angrily, and as she swept in a perfumed rush past Lady she muttered, "Whew, *Jesus*." A few steps down the hallway, however, she stopped, turned and stared back at Lady. Looking her up and down with an insolent expression, the woman said, "My my my. Rudy'll fancy you, all right, little one. But take a tip, and be careful how far you go with him, 'cause he's a poxy bastard. Just don't tell him I said so, okay? Ta ta, dearie." She turned and rustled away toward the stairs, as another burst of barking laughter tumbled from the room.

For a moment Lady considered following the blond woman down the stairway and returning to her room at Mrs. Standcumbe's. There was an indecisive feeling in her hands, and her concentration was quite unsteady. Her thoughts turned constantly to her baby son, Leon, whom she'd left in Polly Schofield's care; she'd told Polly to be sure to move the little basket away from the window if the sun started to fall upon the baby's face, and if he awoke and was hungry to wet his lips with sugar water, but she knew that Polly, an unemployed actress, had a somewhat scattered disposition and enjoyed sipping cherry brandy in the early afternoon.

But before she could persuade herself either to stay or to leave, there appeared in the open doorway a small, sharp-faced man with bulging eyes who exclaimed, "Well well well, hello indeed, my buttercup. Step right in here and let's see what you got, okay?" He leered at Lady with a proprietary air and took a step backward into the room, beckoning her to follow him.

Lady stiffened her shoulders and raised her head, so that she stood at her full height. "I beg your pardon," she said. "but are you Mister Augustiner? The notice in the newspaper said to see Mister Rudolph Augustiner. Do I have the correct address?" She did not move to follow the man into the room.

"Yah, that's me," the man shouted, taking another step

backward. "The original Augustiner. You must be the new gal in town. Do you have a name, buttercup?"

"Lady," she replied. "I am Lady Winslow. I have come to audition for you."

Augustiner looked her up and down with careless familiarity. "Audition, hah?" he said loudly. "All right, audition. Come on in. What d'ya do, anyway? What's your specialty?"

Lady took two steps forward to the doorsill and looked into the room, which was small and dismally inhospitable, with a low, stained ceiling and cracked plaster walls of a brown tint. The only furnishings were a short-legged table, two straight-backed chairs, a plump settee and, near the window, a battered upright piano whose keys were the color of concrete and whose sound, Lady realized immediately, she had no desire to hear. "I play the piano," she said without special conviction. "I am a musician."

"Oho," Augustiner said. "Kitten on the keys, hah? Like to tickle the ivories, do you? Come in, come in. Don't be shy, let's be friends. How about singing? Do you sing?"

"I do not sing," Lady replied. "I am—"

"Dance, then?" he rattled on. "How are your ankles? Let's have a look at the ankles, all right? I'll tell you what. Red. I see red on you, bright red. You let me dress you in bright red, something you can lift up in front, maybe I can use you."

Lady clutched the handle of her parasol tightly in her fist and repeated, "I am a musician, Mister Augustiner. I do not display myself." Frustration began to twist in her throat. *Why don't they listen?* she asked herself. It was the third time in a week that she had been invited by a prospective employer to show her limbs. If the other two could be taken for examples, Augustiner's next move would be to grab for her skirt front.

And indeed, he took a step toward her, spreading his hands wide. "Musicians I can always get, sweetheart," he said. "Musicians grow on trees in this town. But a soubrette, now, with a pretty ankle and a plump *poitrine* like you've got on you, that's what I need more than anything right now. Let's give

244

Rudy a little look, hah? Just a peekaboo for Rudy." He cocked his head to the side and winked saucily.

"I think not, Mister Augustiner," Lady said. "I appear to have been mistaken in coming here." She felt the warning heat of anger on the back of her neck and she raised her parasol before her and took a step back from the doorway.

Augustiner's sauciness did not flag. He whistled softly, and winked again. "Spunky, aren't we?" he said. "Oh me oh my. You must have yourself a nice old sugar daddy, all right. But I tell you something, buttercup. If you don't need me, I don't need you. Rudy's got all the girlies he can handle, don't you fear. I'll tell you something else, too, and you can—"

But there was nothing more that Lady wanted to hear from Rudolph Augustiner. She turned away from the door and hurried to the stairway. "Be damned with them all," she muttered to herself as she descended. "The men be damned." Anger and dismay filled her eyes with tears, and as she rushed headlong out of the building onto Broadway, she was greeted immediately by a shout of "Hey sister, over here," from a driver perched high on the seat of a horse-drawn furniture van passing slowly in the congested street. She lowered her head and ploughed forward without any thought for the direction she was taking, for she wished only to escape the attention of the men she saw all about her on the busy thoroughfare, and at the first corner she turned onto the side street, which was slightly less crowded, and, still muttering to herself, headed east toward Fifth Avenue.

More than a year had passed since she'd landed in Saint Louis and moved straightaway into a furnished room in a white neighborhood not far from the downtown district. She'd told the landlady that she was Lucy Jones, and then immediately regretted the carelessness of that improvisation, for the name had no distinction whatsoever; but although she'd spent the better part of three days fretting about the matter, she'd been unable to discover a satisfactory alternative, and the puzzle of it was still unsolved when, in response to a notice in the newspaper, she went to audition for the management of the Joseph Selson Orchestra, a traveling ragtime and minstrel show of—the notice proclaimed—international repute, at present in rehearsal for its annual summer tour of the midwestern and northeastern regions of the country.

Captain Joseph Selson himself sat nearby on the stage of the empty ballroom where the auditions were held, and he listened intently while she played through two somewhat elementary rags and then a more ornate piece. The rehearsal piano was a worn-out upright with scarred sides and loose pedals, and a twanging quality in its sound which echoed to and fro around the ballroom and came back at her from a dozen different directions. It startled her at first, but before she reached the modulating passage at the end of the rag's second strain she had made allowance for it in her concentration, and the music flowed from her hands then into the tired piano with a sparkling lilt that enlivened its voice considerably. Although she had not consciously designed it so, her music now seemed to bear a more brittle tone and rigid meter than Brick's ragtime had, and its feeling was lightened by a strain of superficiality which had never diluted his playing, for this was proper ragtime in the legitimate style favored by the white players; still, she played it with spirit and precision, and struck each note cleanly upon its center, and when she had finished the third of her pieces, Joseph Selson thumped his carved walking stick enthusiastically upon the stage floor and said, "Bravo, young lady, bravo," and she could see the small retinue of managers and copyists who stood about his shoulders smile and nod approvingly among themselves.

"Thank you, sir," she said, and tilted her head at Selson, and he beckoned her to come and stand before him. He was a big, thick-necked man with a heavy black mustache that was waxed and shaped in such a fashion that its points stood up like sentinels above his mouth, and his bearing was imperiously remote. When he spoke it was with the rumbling tone and orotund diction of a stage tragedian, but his eyes were not unkind

246

as he measured her with his gaze, and although she held herself stiffly and returned his look with an expression of guarded reserve, she did not feel threatened by him.

"That was a prodigious display, my dear," he said. "Bravo to you, bravo. If I hadn't beheld you at it with my own eyes, I'm not at all certain that I'd have accepted a report of such formidable artistry in one of your tender years. I do believe that I can find a place for you in my show. I do indeed."

"I know I appear young," she said, keeping her voice low and steady, "but I am nearly eighteen, sir." As she had when she'd first met the Countess, she increased her years by a couple.

"Be that or not," Selson said, "my instinct is to present you as a prodigy. My instinct tells me that my audience would respond most favorably to you in that guise. I mean no disrespect, my dear, but your appearance is, I should say, surpassingly youthful."

She met his gaze head on and said forcefully, "I am not a child, Captain Selson, and I do not choose to be displayed as one, if that is what you intend. I am a musician, sir."

"I never thought otherwise, my dear," Selson answered.

"Then hire me as a musician, Captain Selson," she said, "or I'll simply wait until someone comes along who will."

Joseph Selson raised his eyebrows in surprise and shook his head. "Well well well," he chuckled. "Oh my oh my." For several moments he indulged himself in private amusement, while she waited silently. Then he said, "I admire your spirit, young lady. I have the feeling that you might negotiate your affairs as skillfully as you manipulate the piano keys. Most skillfully indeed. Tell me, my dear, what is your name?"

"Lady," she said, and then, without taking the time to think about it, "Winslow." As the second name escaped her lips, she recognized that it was a name which she had seen three days earlier when she'd descended the steamboat's ramp. It had been painted in tall blue letters on the side of a dockside warehouse, and without stopping to consider it, she had thought it quite elegant. Now she found that she enjoyed the sound of it altogether, and she repeated it for Joseph Selson, pursing her lips around it appreciatively, her new name: "Lady Winslow." The next time she passed by that warehouse, she saw beneath the tall "Winslow" a slogan printed in smaller letters: *Winslow Brand—Favorite Snuff*. But by then three weeks had passed and she had accepted her new name so wholeheartedly that it seemed as though Alice Beaudette had been only a childhood acquaintance, and Lady Winslow giggled at the advertisement and continued on her way.

"Ah," Joseph Selson said approvingly, "Aha. Lady."

"It is not a title, Captain Selson," she said. "Lady is my name."

"Still," Joseph Selson had said. "Still and all, who would have to know?" He'd looked at her inquiringly, and she'd answered him with a smile and a shake of her head, and said, "I'm sure I couldn't say."

He'd favored her then with a proud grin. "Bravo, Lady Winslow," he'd said. "Now tell me, have you ever been to New York City?"

"No sir," she had replied, smiling brightly at him, "but I'm quite certain I would like to go."

Now she felt thoroughly betrayed by her decision, and she was thrown back to the unhappiness of her first weeks of traveling with the Selson orchestra, the previous summer. One of the pillars of her new independence had been her assurance that in her music she possessed the power to impose a barrier between herself and men's innate need to inflict dominion and pain upon a woman, against which the Countess' little birds had warned her time and time again. But no sooner had the Selson tour commenced than she recognized how fragile a defense her talent was against their self-absorption and their brute confidence. Everywhere she turned, in the railroad carriages, the hotel lobbies and boardinghouse parlors, the alleys outside the stage doors, she was challenged by their preening condescension, their doggish arrogance, and most of all, by their loathing. It was palpable to her, the hatred she felt emanating from the men, and distressing. "It's because I'm free," she reasoned. "They cannot abide my freedom, can they?" "You may as well relax and enjoy it, Lady dear," Kitty Flowers, one of the older women in the troupe, told her. "Men are men, bless 'em, and they just want a taste from every cup. Don't take it personal. A man'll slip around with just about any kind of gal, except maybe new widows and those that are in the family way, and even then, I've known a couple of fellows . . . No, I hate to tell you, honey, but you are bait for the wicked. Wisht I had your fine skin myself."

But Lady did take it personally, for in choosing the way of her future she had accepted that she would be free to function in a world ruled by men, and now she was forced to acknowledge how unconsidered that acceptance had been. The problem of it became an obsession, over which she labored day after day, while the tour progressed up the Mississippi and across the flatlands by the southern Great Lakes, and all along the way the men hovered about with their hot expectancy shining and their contempt in constant display. Until she could devise a means to hold them at bay, Lady knew, she would never be able to appreciate a moment's peace, or savor the independence of her life.

The troupe was in Hammond, Indiana, in the middle of a week's engagement at the Opera House there, when she awoke one morning and found her decision fresh in her mind. The solution to her dilemma, she saw, was to compromise with the men's needs. To relieve herself of the burden of their hatred, she would convince them that she was not so free that they needed to fear her. She would present herself to them not as an untamed Miss, but rather as Mrs. Winslow, a widow, and if they questioned the legitimacy of that fiction she would answer them with the irrefutable proof of a child, a baby. Surely, Lady told herself, no man was so remorseless in his need for conquest that he would exercise his hatred against a widow raising her baby alone in the world. For the rest of the week she turned the decision back and forth in her mind, until, at last, she could accept it as a pact with herself, to signal whose ratification she went that afternoon to Hammond's only department store and purchased an ounce of perfume and a large bar of violently scented soap.

And what had it come to? she asked herself now. Her anger had begun to abate, but in its place she found a deepening perplexity, and the dismay of having to acknowledge that if her stratagem failed, she had no other to take its place. Whatever could she do? She looked around as if seeking an answer to her problem, and saw that she was on a tree-lined street of brownstone residences, in a neighborhood she did not recognize. As she passed out of the protecting shadow cast by a small but abundantly leafy beech she remarked that she had been so upset by her truncated audition with Augustiner that in leaving she had neglected to open her parasol, and, ducking her face away from the sunlight, she stopped on the curb and began to fiddle with its clasp.

While her attention was occupied by the parasol, a large, closed touring car turned the nearest corner and advanced toward her, and when it was only a few yards away a man stepped off the opposite curb and began to cross the street, on a route intended to intersect with the car's progress at the point of its off-side rear wheel fender. The man's given name was Benjamin Glasgow, but he was known in his own society as Benny the Fall, for his occupation was to throw himself against the sides of passing vehicles and then to feign injury, with the object of obtaining compensation from the vehicles' owners. Benny chose his quarry with a careful and practiced eye and confined his trade to the conveyances of the wealthy, upon whose impatience he had learned he could quite profitably depend. As a youth he had hurled himself beneath the hooves of carriage horses, but his maturity had coincided with the beginnings of the automobile age, and now he operated exclusively among the motored set.

250

Benny waited until the slow-moving auto was just past him and then darted out into the street and came alongside from behind, on the side opposite the driver, and he was about to commence his artistry, when by chance the driver spotted him on the edge of his eye.

The driver was an elderly man named Houlihan, who was, like Benny, a graduate of the horse-drawn age, during whose final years he had been the principal carriage driver for the family of Antioch Peterson, the industrialist. When the Petersons had recently switched to traveling in automobiles, Houlihan had grudgingly adapted himself to their altered requirements and become a chauffeur. But he'd never been as comfortable behind the wheel of an auto as he had behind the footboard of a carriage, and in times of excitement he sometimes forgot himself and asserted the habits of his earlier occupation, as in this instance when, upon glimpsing Benny's sudden approach, Houlihan shouted, "Whoa, haw" and pulled hard upon the steering wheel as if it were the reins of an eight-horse team, meanwhile bracing both feet against the floorboard forward of the steering column. Since his right foot was resting against the auto's accelerator at the moment of this reflex, the principal consequence of Houlihan's action was a sudden increase in the vehicle's speed. The car shot away to its left and jumped the curb, missing Lady by scant inches and leaving Benny in the middle of the street, still poised for his dive, and came to a loud halt against the stone steps of the nearest brownstone.

Lady barely had time to dodge as the auto leaped past, and when she did, her foot slipped off the curb and she fell backward against the trunk of the beech tree, hitting her head there with sufficient force to stun her. She staggered and fell to her hands and knees on the sidewalk, where the first person to arrive at her side was Benny the Fall. "I set this one up, sister," he hissed in her ear while making a show of helping her back to her feet. "If you know what's good for you, you'll split your take right down the middle with me, or I'll see that you never work this town again."

Lady shook her head uncomprehendingly, for her senses were quite scrambled, and the only thing she could say was, "Oh my. Oh my." Benny started to repeat his message, but quit abruptly when he was joined by Houlihan and a tall, pale gentleman who had been the passenger in the auto, and when each of them took hold of one of Lady's arms to steady her, Benny moved to the next corner and disappeared as quickly as if he'd melted through a crack in the sidewalk.

"Are you all right, ma'am?" Houlihan asked Lady. "I'm frightful sorry. The creature simply ran away from me." He turned his face to the passenger and repeated, "It got away from me, Mister Edgar. It did." The old chauffeur's face was ashen with worry, and the passenger, seeing that, spoke comfortingly to him. "It's all right, Houlihan," he said. "I'm sure there's no damage done, honestly, I am. Why don't you take a look at the auto and see if you can see if . . . I don't know. See if we're stuck there or if we can get home in it, or see what you can see. I'll look after this poor woman."

Houlihan touched his cap and turned away to examine the car, while his passenger assisted Lady to the steps of the next house along the street and helped her to seat herself on the second step. He removed his hat and bent down in front of her and looked closely into her eyes, which were beginning to regain their focus. "Can you hear me?" he said, in a high, reedy voice. "Can you hear me, miss?"

Lady blinked several times and then answered softly, "Yes. Yes I can."

"Well, I'm certainly glad to hear that," the man said. "How do you feel?"

Lady reached up and touched the back of her head where it had struck the tree. There was a spot of pain there, but it seemed that her hair had cushioned the blow somewhat and there was no blood or swelling. She did have a slightly queasy feeling in her stomach, however, and an ache along the left side of her neck. "Let me collect myself for a moment, please," she said. "Then I'm certain I'll be all right."

"Fine, yes," the man said. "I'm sorry. Of course." With an embarrassed expression on his face he straightened up and stood before the steps, shifting awkwardly from foot to foot and turning his hat over in his hands as if he couldn't decide whether or not to replace it on his head. He had thin, sandy hair which lay lifeless against his skull, and his skin was a pallid shade. His lips were thin and pale and his eyes looked as though they would at any instant fill with tears. He was in all ostensible respects a most unattractive man, and yet his concern for Lady seemed wholehearted, and the halting quality of his manner bespoke a shyness of spirit to which she felt herself responding gratefully, for she sensed that she need not fear him. She sat there for a few moments, and the queasiness she'd felt began to subside, though the ache in her neck persisted.

The chauffeur returned from his inspection, touched his cap and said, "There's no great damage as I can make out, Mister Edgar. A crack in the headlamp and some scratches on the near side varnish is all I see, and I should be able to back her away from there clear."

The man replaced his hat on his head then, and said, "Oh, Houlihan. Very good. Very well. Thank you. Let's . . ." He turned back to Lady, and immediately removed his hat. "Miss," he said. "Madam, I . . . please permit me to let you take my automobile. That is, I would feel much better about this if you'd let me . . . or let my chauffeur, if you'd rather . . . accompany, er, drive you home. May we do that?"

Lady smiled gently at his earnest discomfiture and shook her head. "That won't be at all necessary, sir," she said. "But I do thank you for the kind offer. I haven't far to go." She started to stand up, but found when she regained her feet that she was still unsteady on them, and she touched his arm for support while a *petit mal* shivered through her.

"No no," the man cried as she braced herself against him, "you must not. You mustn't even try. Here, you come with me.

253

I insist, absolutely, I do. I insist." He helped her along to his auto and carefully assisted her into the spacious back seat, where she let her head fall back and immediately fell into a light but adamant slumber.

She awoke in a large room which she did not recognize, and found herself lying on an upholstered settee with a blanket covering her, and she lay there for a few minutes, looking around and trying to remember how she had gotten there and whether she had ever been there before. The room had a ceiling as high, it appeared, as a church's, marked across at regular intervals by heavy beams, and its walls consisted almost entirely of bookshelves packed row upon row with polished leather-bound volumes. There were several thickly stuffed chairs and a small writing table, and hardly more than an arm's length away from the settee was a piano as vast and impressive in its size as the German grand piano at the Countess' Mansion. None of it looked familiar to her in the slightest, but before her curiosity changed to worry the door to the room opened and the tall, pale man looked in. Seeing her awake, he smiled shyly and said, "Oh, well. Hello. I'm sorry."

Lady sat up and swung her feet down to the floor. "Leon," she said, for the first thought that came to her then was of her son. "What time is it, please?" she said. "Where am I? How long have I been here?" Remembering her collapse on the sidewalk, she turned her head from side to side, and was relieved to find that she felt no dizziness, and that the pain in her neck had lessened.

The man stepped cautiously into the room and stood just inside the door. "This is my home," he said. "I didn't know where else to take you, I'm afraid. If you like, I . . . do you feel better?" His voice had an irritating, whining tone, but, as before, the shy eagerness of his solicitude was reassuring.

"Yes," she said. "Yes, I do. Thank you, but how late is it? I'm afraid I cannot stay here. My son is waiting for me, my baby."

"Oh, it hasn't been long," the man said. "Not so long." He

fumbled in the pocket of his waistcoat and pulled out a watch, and fumbled some more getting its cover open. "It's two twenty-five," he said finally. "Houlihan will drive you straight home. I'm terribly sorry. I didn't know where else—" He fell silent as Lady stood up, and watched her apprehensively, as if he expected her to fall again.

"You've been very kind," she said. "I really must get home to my baby now."

"I'm . . . my name is Peterson," he said, rubbing the back of his head with his hand. "Edgar Peterson. I . . . this is my house. Is there anything I can do for you before you, er, before you go?"

"Why yes, I believe there is," Lady said. "I believe I should like a drink of water, if you would be so kind."

"Oh," he said. "Oh, yes. Certainly." He lunged out the door, hitting his elbow against the frame as he went, and when he was gone Lady tried to tuck her hair back into place and brush the dirt and wrinkles from her dress, with only some success. When Peterson returned with a pitcher of water and a tumbler, she accepted them with a grateful smile. She drank enough to soothe her throat, then, setting the tumbler aside, she said, "Mister Peterson, my name is Lady Winslow, and I thank you. I am in your debt, sir."

"Lady," he exclaimed, his voice climbing.

"It's not as it might sound," she said. "It's a name, not a title."

"Oh," Peterson said. "My. Certainly. I understand, a name, like Emily, or Alice. Oh, not"—he hastened, for something had flickered in Lady's expression—"not that I'm making a joke of it. Please understand."

"I do," Lady said. "I understand entirely."

"You seemed perturbed," he said.

"I have had a perturbing day," Lady said, and she poured herself some more water, and without considering why she was doing it, she told him about her recent encounters with Augustiner and the others, and the extreme frustration they had caused her.

Edgar Peterson listened without interrupting, becoming more visibly agitated as her story unfolded. "Why, that's a terrible thing," he said when she'd finished. "I've heard of Rudolph Augustiner. He owns Augustiner's Gardens. But I never would have dreamed. The man's a bounder. They're all bounders. Missus Winslow, you are a brave woman to submit yourself to that sort of ordeal. It must be terribly upsetting for you."

"Alas," Lady said. "It's what I do, Mister Peterson. I am, after all, an entertainer." She gathered up her hat and purse and parasol from the nearby armchair on which they lay.

"But my dear . . . but Missus Winslow," Peterson said. "That's no reason. A person . . . a woman . . . no one should have to be subjected to an ordeal like that. No, that's quite wrong."

"Now, Mister Peterson," Lady said. "Now now. Don't upset yourself, I beg you. If it hadn't been those men, it would just as likely have been someone else. It's not an uncommon attitude among gentlemen in that business."

Peterson shook his head persistently. "No," he said. "You are an artist, Missus Winslow. You deserve better."

"That's kind of you," Lady said.

While she pinned her hat into place upon her head, Peterson paced in a small circle by the door, and when she was finished and said, "There. I'm ready now, Mister Peterson," he said, "One moment, Missus Winslow. Please. Let me offer . . . let me suggest . . . I have an idea."

"I really must see to my son," Lady said, somewhat impatiently.

"Please," he repeated. "This is quite important, I feel, and I think it might be just the answer. New York . . . this city . . . it just isn't the place for a woman in your position. Alone, I mean, and with a child to raise. I . . . oh dear, how shall I express this?" He frowned in dismay and moved behind a large armchair as if seeking shelter there, and addressed her across its high back. "Please don't take offense," he said. "I'm not a person who lectures . . . I'm not comfortable . . . I wish to advise you of something."

"Mister Peterson," Lady said, "I am listening."

"I . . . my family," he said, "own a hotel . . . a resort hotel, an inn, in the country. It caters to an entirely respectable trade, I assure you. If you . . . see here . . . would you accept an offer of employment there?"

"In the country, you say?"

"Yes, in Carlowsbridge . . . Sand Springs, really . . . on the shore, at Lake Sequantus. The Sequantus House. Have you heard of it?"

Lady shook her head, and said, "I don't think so." Seeing a cloud of disappointment cross his face, though, she added, "I may have, Mister Peterson. I have only recently arrived in this part of the country."

"Of course." He smiled. "Well, I can assure you . . . please trust me, I beg you . . . a small town, a healthy atmosphere, and there's a house nearby that I know is not occupied. You and your child could . . . you would be so much safer there than in the city, Missus Winslow."

"May I think about it for a while?" Lady asked. "It sounds most entirely generous altogether, but I should like to think about it."

"Please," Peterson said gratefully. "Please do."

Two days later, looking out the window of the railway carriage as the train bent around a curve above the bank of the Hudson River, Lady thought: *We shall be safe now.* She turned and smiled down at her baby son, asleep in his little basket on the seat beside her. Leon was as pale as a chinaberry blossom, with a flimsy cap of downy black hair, and she marveled at the delicacy of his eyelashes and the coral glow of his tiny ears. When he had been born, in her room at Mrs. Standcumbe's, and the midwife had held him up for her to see, she had laughed and wept in triumph at his pinkness, for she had feared that some spirit from her past might have slipped into the baby and darkened his skin, and as she took him to her breast she had whispered, "Oh my baby, my baby boy, my baby, baby boy." And although it had been winter still and the hawk wind was rattling the window in its frame, she had been warmed by her pride and her contentment. Now she bent over him and spoke softly, saying, "We are safe now, Leon darling. We shall protect each other now, and we shall always be safe."

She wondered then for the first time how she would explain herself and her life to him. What would she tell him about his father when he asked her? Surely he would want to know about his father some day. How would she ever explain to him that she wasn't even certain herself who his father was. It might have been one of several men: a salesman in Elkhart; a banker in Fort Wayne; a minister's son in Sandusky; a railroad man in Buffalo; another man, any of several, along the route of the Joseph Selson Orchestra's summer tour. For more than a month she had become Baby Luana and said Yes Daddy to them; accepting only pale men with straight, light-colored hair, she had encouraged them with a whore's boldness, yielded to their grasping hands and their wheedling mouths, and with the forbearance of an instinct she'd never known she possessed she'd lain beneath them and said Yes Daddy to them while they moaned and shuddered and, bangbang, they did their shot night after night, until she was sure that her purpose had been fulfilled. How could she hope to make her son understand that she had undergone the pain of that to ensure that in her life she would never have to fear pain again? Riding beside the sleeping infant in the train to Carlowsbridge, Lady decided not to yield to the perturbation which that question made her feel, and instead she continued crooning softly to her son, "We shall be safe, little Leon. We shall be safe from now on."

She changed trains in Albany, and arrived in midafternoon at the Carlowsbridge depot. There she was met by an automobile and driver from the Peterson estate, and conveyed straightaway to The Sequantus House, where she had been told the manager, Mr. Vaughan, was expecting her. As the car turned onto the lake road the baby awoke and Lady held him up to the window and exclaimed, "See, darling. See how the waters shine so, and see the mountains, la. So many beautiful things to see, Leon darling, in our new home."

Chapter Ten

S. O. L. Blues

Edgar Peterson was his son. Antioch Peterson's only male issue, and don't you think that didn't gall the old man. Fact is, it killed him. He married late to begin with, and then expected to start breeding sons right off. Wanted boys to run alongside of him while he was thrashing back and forth across the continent. Teach them what he knew. Give them everything he'd taken or built. "I am a man," Antioch Peterson said, "and by damn, I shall have what's mine."

By the time he came here his first wife had already been sent packing. Didn't breed fast enough to suit him. The next one was Edgar's mother. A tall, thin woman, pale as marble. Edgar favors her still. Maybe even paler now, in his present condition, but he always was a skinny stick. Funny eyes. Watery, shifty. Funny way of talking, too, as if he didn't expect you to listen to him. Awkward fellow. Awful awkward. Hurt you to look at him. It's just damned hard to believe that a woman like Mrs. Winslow would get herself involved that way with a lukewarm customer like him. Doesn't matter how many people might have thought she was, they never came up with any proof. Only questions. That's what Orrie heard and saw up in the woods, was questions. Rumors and gossip. Two detectives, best they could come up with was rumors and gossip.

That's getting ahead of the story, too.

Edgar's birth killed his mother. Don't think Antioch Peterson ever forgave him for it. Named him Edgar as an insult. Burst into the room just as the doctor and the midwife were closing her eyes. Mamie Gobel was the midwife, Henry Donker's cousin. Said Antioch Peterson was shedding ice from his clothes and steam from his brow when he burst in. Said his eyes were rimmed red and there was a mark of frostbite like a drop of cream on the end of his nose. It was the dead of winter and he'd just that minute arrived back from the Northwest Territories. He'd been mining ore in ice caves, come back by dog sled, horseback and rail. When he saw them pull the sheet up over his wife he roared so loud it bent up the corners of the roof. "Damn me," he cried, "this is unconscionable."

The doctor tried to explain. Said it was a weakness in her heart. He was a New York doctor.

"Weakness," Antioch Peterson said. "Damn weakness. Weakness is betrayal." He turned away and started to leave the room, run all the way back to his ice caves, only Mamie stepped into his way. She had the baby in her arms. "What's this?" Antioch Peterson asked.

"Your son, Mister Peterson," Mamie said. She folded back the swaddling cloth so he could see the infant's face clear.

He looked at the child for no more than a second, mad as a hornet, and waved it away. "Bother me with this," he said. "I've just lost a damned good woman, and you bother me with this. This newt. This egg. What's this to me?"

"It's your son," Mamie repeated.

Antioch Peterson squinted and bent over the bundle she held. He put his face close to it, seemed to sniff it like a grazing animal. The child opened its eyes. Even then they were pale and watery. He started to cry, made little mewing noises. Antioch Peterson flinched. He turned his back on the baby. Said, "Bah. Let the clergy take him. This will never be a man I'd trust to pull my fat from the fire."

The doctor said, "The child needs a name, Mister Peterson. Had you chosen a name?"

"Name?" Antioch Peterson said. He didn't give it a moment's thought. "Edgar," he said. "Call it Edgar. It looks like a damned Edgar." His distaste for the name was clear. "I can make a better one than that," he said. "Damn me." Drew back his fist and punched the door. Then he left the room and the castle.

He came back in less than a month with another wife. She bore him a daughter, so he sent her packing, too. Took another wife, as if he was pulling cards from a deck, looking for the queen. Or the jack. She lasted six months and then left of her own accord. Couldn't take it, Antioch Peterson's urgency.

We watched them come and go. Watched Edgar, too, right from his birth. Even as a baby he was quiet, fearful. Flinched whenever he heard his father's voice in the house. It's a huge place, a castle. Antioch Peterson had it brought over from France, stone by stone. Put it back together there behind the hill. Kept Edgar in the north wing, himself in the south. Ignored the boy. A quarter of a mile and three dozen rooms between them, but every time Antioch Peterson cleared his throat Edgar would flinch. Had an Englishwoman to take care of him, Mrs. Spence, but the maids, the servers and cleaners, were Sand Springs girls, and Bertha Graaf was his wet nurse.

The last wife was a Scandinavian girl. Her father was one of Antioch Peterson's farmers. She was blond and healthy and built like a breeder. Had six brothers, too. That must have impressed Antioch Peterson. Married her in the chapel on the estate and before the wedding feast was over he had her up in the south wing, putting her to the test. He was a bully fellow but she was up to it. Encouraged him, kept him at it. Lord, three and four times a night. They said you could hear him bellowing lust all the way to the stables, said the floors trembled with it. He plowed his seed into her for forty nights. The whole wing stank of their rut. Must have amazed even him, how he kept at it. He wasn't a young man.

Finally it broke him. His obsession did what no wilderness or wild animal or rival had been able to; it brought Antioch Peterson down. The effort of it burst his heart. Took three male servants to lift him off his widow. They laid him out naked on the oak table in the banquet room, and in death he looked like a creature brought in from the hunt, a wild ox or a buffalo, huge and shaggy. Antioch Peterson had admired the buffalo, said he could see eye to eye with it. "I believe I'm kin to the great bison," he'd said. "Damn me if I'm not. I'm a buffalo in shoes." They brought Edgar in to see the body. The boy took one look and buried his face in Mrs. Spence's skirts. Didn't cry, he just whimpered. He was only three years old, too young to realize his own part in it.

They placed Antioch Peterson's remains in a marble crypt in a shallow glen, up in the northeastern corner of the estate, and when they sealed the door the power of him was gone, still. That's when we started looking for him. But all that we could hear in his stead was the murmuring of the accountants.

Edgar was the sole human heir. The wives and the daughter were given some cash and that was all. As women they had no recourse and they accepted that. Mr. Fitzroy Bobwit saw to it. The only one of them to raise a fuss was the last one, and that was her father's doing. Right after the estate was settled out, he and three of his grown sons went to see Bobwit in his office at the tannery, yelling about their due. "My girl deserves better," the father shouted. You could hear him all up and down the halls.

Bobwit never raised his voice. He was dry as a soda cracker, explained Antioch Peterson's intentions as if he was reading it out of a ledger. The girl was allowed to take nothing from the estate except what she'd brought to it. The cash settlement was handsome, generosity of the Peterson Trust. No other provision for her in the will.

"They weren't married two months," the farmer shouted. "Peterson didn't have time to write her into the will."

"Mister Peterson did not serve time," Bobwit said. "Time

served Mister Peterson, and it's my observation that if he wanted something done there was time enough to do it. There's nothing more to be said on the matter. Good day, gentlemen."

The farmer tried to argue. Stood his ground. Bobwit called the factory guards. One of the farmer's sons had to be carried out by the others. Nobody saw the family leave the estate, but the next morning their cottage was empty. Not a sign that they'd ever been there. Only time they were ever spoken of, it was to show how efficient the Peterson Trust was. Not powerful, just ruthless. Men are nothing but fuel and fodder to its working.

Edgar Peterson was raised by the Peterson Trust. He lived his boyhood in Antioch Peterson's castle with no one for company except servants. Stayed indoors like a little hermit, read a lot. Mr. Fitzroy Bobwit used to visit twice a year from New York. He always brought a carload of books with him. It was all Edgar ever wanted. When he went off to Harvard University he took a dozen wooden crates with him, all filled with books. Took a servant with him, too, an old Bavarian named Klaus.

At Harvard Edgar was a goat, the butt of everyone's pranks. The Peterson Trust couldn't protect him from it because many of the other lads were as rich as Edgar and a damn sight livelier, had trusts of their own and real parents. They locked him out in the snow, cut up his clothes with scissors and filled his trunk with horse manure. Servants were supposed to be neutral, safe from the hijinks, but a bunch of Edgar's classmates made off with old Klaus one night. They stripped him naked and smeared him all over with bootblacking and left him in the middle of the town green in Concord. Hung a sign around his neck that said: *I'se Marse Edgar's Darky. I'se a Good Ole Darky*. When the Concord police brought the old fellow back to Harvard, Edgar tried to laugh it off. Said it was a lark. Took the side of his own class, even when Klaus quit, and then he wouldn't pay Klaus his last week's wage. Said he gave insufficient notice. Replaced him with a Sand Springs man who'd used to haul wood for the fireplaces in the castle. William

Snow. It was a shameful thing, and it stuck in our minds. Later on in life Edgar got a reputation for charity. In New York he was known as a philanthropist and a liberal man. Never refused when a museum or a library or a symphony orchestra came looking for money. Gave to orphanages and shelters for the homeless. Helped establish a university for Negroes. Alfred Calhoun always called him "His Highness the Nigger Lover." That was why. Some believe that was his connection with Mrs. Winslow, that he did her a kindness. An act of charity. Maybe, maybe not. But that's getting ahead of the story again. The fact is, remembering Klaus, most of us found it hard to think of Edgar Peterson as a charitable man.

About the only friend Edgar had at Harvard was a fellow named Osgood Blackthorne. Came from a mercantile family in Boston, lived on Beacon Hill. Zenas Blackthorne and Sons, Import–Export. They'd been merchants and traders in Boston since the time of the British. Speculated in all manner of goods, tea and molasses and timber and hides. Tobacco, cotton, shoes. Slaves, too, in the slave times. Blackthornes were an ugly bunch of skinflints, counted their pennies every night at bedtime. They wore black and served mutton and boiled potatoes at the Sunday table. Servants slept on straw pallets.

Osgood Blackthorne never joined in the pranks played on Edgar. Wouldn't have, anyway. Didn't have a playful bone in his body. Blackthornes smiled about as often as snow falls on Panama. Courted Edgar as a matter of finance. Ambition. The Blackthornes' fortune wanted tangibility. All it consisted of was ledger balances, bills of lading, promissory notes. It shifted about between agents and brokers and sea captains, and it was at risk to wind and tide, supply and demand. Their goods were always in transit, value anticipated, payment due. On the other hand, the Peterson fortune was solid, visible. Land, buildings, livestock, ore, rails and rail cars. Antioch Peterson had liked to put his hands on things. Osgood Blackthorne was inclined that way, too. He had a sister, Electa. She was as shy and friendless as Edgar, and no more attractive to see. A thin girl with a worry crease between her eyebrows and a mustache she did nothing to hide. Osgood played marriage broker, invited Edgar home to Beacon Hill for Sunday dinner, seated them next to each other. Blackthornes ate in silence after old Amos Blackthorne said the grace, didn't look at each other. Edgar felt comfortable there in the bosom of their family, cold as it was. Went back every chance he got.

They wed right after Edgar graduated from Harvard, in the Methodist church on Beacon Hill. Blackthornes lined up in their pew like crows on a fence rail. Mr. Fitzroy Bobwit stood up with Edgar. William Snow sat upstairs with the servants. Said Edgar told him, "I've never been so happy, William. I'm truly happy." Bobwit took a good look at the Blackthornes and went back to New York and changed the locks on the safes.

After they were married, Edgar divided his time between Sand Springs and New York. Had a house there that Antioch Peterson had left him. Occupied a whole city block on Fifth Avenue. Pursued his avocation for philanthropy and collected rare volumes. But Electa Peterson seldom left the estate. She spent her days doing the things women do, pressed flowers and embroidered samplers and wrote in her diary. Spruced up the castle, too. Got rid of a lot of Antioch Peterson's things, the animal hides and the guns and spears. Hung lace curtains at the windows and paintings on the walls. Brightened it. Every Christmastime she handed out baskets of food to the farmers and their families. A smoked ham and a fruitcake and a gallon of apple cider in every basket. They came in through the kitchen and she met them in the servants' dining room, shook everyone's hand and wished them a Merry Christmas in her shy voice. Never looked anyone in the eye. Most of them, that was the only time they ever saw her. She didn't go outside much.

They had two daughters, born three years apart. Alice and Elizabeth. They were lively girls, inquisitive. Nothing like their parents. From their earliest years they roamed around the estate and explored it with a bully spirit that put us in mind of old Antioch himself. They climbed and rode and swam in the

266

brooks, as active as boys. They laughed and made mischief. Made it possible to think more warmly of Edgar and Electa, who were so shy and solemn. Stiff as statues, the way they looked the night the stable roof burned.

It was shortly after Electa Peterson had come to the castle. Not many had seen her. There was a storm that night, thunder and lightning, and a bolt hit on the stable roof. Made a great crashing noise and set fire to it. Everyone fell out to fight it. Seemed as if that bolt hadn't even faded before the stable yard was filled up with men and boys carrying ladders, axes, buckets. In a matter of minutes all the horses were out and safe. Another minute and the flames were out and the rain was taking care of the smoulder. Someone looked back up at the castle just as another stroke of lightning lit up the night. Saw Edgar and Electa standing up there on the verandah in their nightclothes. The thing is, they weren't standing together. Stood at opposite ends of that long porch. Looked pale and stiff as marble statues. But that was before the girls were born. Those that worked up there said Edgar and Electa became quite tender with each other as the years passed. Said they were kind and respectful of each other and their daughters. When Edgar was away in New York, Electa wrote to him every day, and received a letter from him in return. Those letters are probably still up there, but if that detective found them she didn't seem to find any significance in them. Too busy looking for gossip, probably.

Electa Peterson died in the winter of 1916. The diphtheria took her. Two days later the older daughter followed her. Alice. Edgar was unconsolable. Never saw him express an emotion stronger than discomfort. Now he grieved. Blackthornes came out from Boston, took the younger girl back with them. Took a lot of Electa's things with them, too. Her diary, for one. Edgar thanked them for their kindness and took off in the other direction, went West. Followed his father's trails, roamed the wilderness as diligently as he'd sealed himself inside the castle when he was a boy. His clumsy feet carried him over mountains. His wet eyes squinted across prairies and forests. Looking for something to give him solace. When he didn't find it in the West, he came back East and joined the Expeditionary Force. Went to France.

Several local men and boys answered the call. Most of them saw action in France, of one kind or another. Uncle Pedey's great-grandnephew Samuel Donker shot down a German airplane with his rifle, got a medal for it. Horace Thurman, who used to help out Saturdays behind the counter at his father's store and never seemed to know how many pennies made up a nickel, was promoted to a commission in the Quartermaster Corps. Spent a year and a half in Paris and came back a wealthy man. "Boys, I saw some amazing things," he told us. "The Frenchman'll eat insects, you know, and frogs. Why, if I had all the frogs I plonked with my slingshot on the marsh when I was a boy I could open the biggest restaurant in Paris. That's not all. I saw men wearing skirts over there. And the Frenchmen, they're crazy about niggers. I watched the Hellfighters Brass Band parade down the Champs Élysées and the French gals were throwing their underclothes at them. Every man in the Hellfighters is black as the ace of spades and they play ragtime as fine as you ever want to hear it played. They've got a drum major named Robinson who used to be a vaudeville dancer, and when they saw that boy strut, those French gals were like dogs in heat. If I was that shine, I don't think I'd ever want to come home from Paree. Of course, I didn't do so badly myself, boys, once I learned to parley-voo."

Edgar Peterson was commissioned to an artillery battery. Spent six months at the front and then he lost his will. That's what the doctors said. He lost his will. Happened to a lot of men. Some of them, it didn't take more than a week in the trenches before it happened to them. Those trenches were cold and wet even in August. There were rats everywhere, and the smell of dead flesh, human and animal. The only color you ever saw on the battlefield was gray. Earth was gray and so was the sky, even when the sun shone. Wood and water were gray. So were the soldiers there. Didn't take more than a week or two, a man turned gray all over, lost his will. The army called it shell shock.

The rats, now, they were gray to begin with. They thrived on it, sat just out of reach and watched. Got fat eating corpse meat. Smug and alert. Thing you noticed about them was, they never got caught in the gas. If there was a gas attack the rats just disappeared. When it was past, they were back, just like that. You didn't see them go, never found out where they went. The gas was like a liquid, heavier than air. Blew across the lines like a tide and filled everything up. Trenches, shell holes. Yellow-green color. When it was gone you'd see little puddles of it left behind. Little wisps like tissue paper. You'd swear you could hold them between your fingers. Men tried. Took off their gasmasks and tried to eat it. Shell shock.

Edgar Peterson must have forgotten about the rats, or he would have known the whistles were blowing a false alarm. Had a lot of those. All it took was a patch of mist lying low to the ground. Better safe than sorry. But he was asleep in his dugout when the whistles blew. He woke up, sat up and reached for his gasmask. Kept it close at hand in a niche carved out of the dirt wall. Soon as he touched it the mask moved. A big rat jumped out from behind it and reared up on its haunches. Probably it'd been chewing on the straps, eating the body salt and hair oil. They did that. Edgar had a tallow candle on a crate beside his cot. That was his light. It shone up on the rat, made its teeth glisten yellow. Made its shadow dance on the wall behind it. Must have looked like the Devil. Had its front paws up, as if it was going to jump on Edgar, grab him.

Edgar stepped back. When he did he upset his candle, knocked it off the crate. The dugout went pitch black. Edgar heard the whistles blowing outside. He thought the gas was coming. But he could still see the rat. Huge, snarling rat. Couldn't choose between them, the gas or the rat. Never thought to remember that if the gas was really coming the rat wouldn't be there. The lieutenant who shared Edgar's dugout found him like that a couple of hours later. Had his hand out, reaching toward the niche. Not a muscle moving. The rat was still there, chewing on the straps. It took the medics a week to persuade Edgar to put his hand down and sit in a chair. He never has gotten his will back.

They brought him back to Antioch Peterson's castle that winter, a couple of months after the Armistice. He rode in a wheelchair. Had a doctor and two nurses with him, or one nurse and one woman who pretended to be a nurse, as we found out later that same spring. Shortly after they brought him back Mrs. Winslow went up to the castle. It was the first time we ever saw them together. That's certain. The only time. She played the piano for him and left after about an hour. Edgar Peterson just sat in his chair by the fireplace, never said a word. Can't say he even noticed her.

He's sitting up there still. They feed him and wash him and dress him as if he was a big toy doll. The business of the estate and the affairs of the Peterson Trust go on around him the way they've done all his life. They never needed him and he never had anything to bring to them. Never had the power in his whole being that his father carried around in his little finger. He just sits there, day after day. Still trying to choose between the rat and the gas. Doesn't make a damn bit of difference. Never did.

Chapter Eleven

Save It, Pretty Mama

Well, I kept an eye out for that fellow with the derby hat when I went to work at the inn that day, but things were awful busy right then and I have to admit that after a while he did slip from my mind. We were all in an uproar getting set up for the big Fourth of July gala that Henny had planned, you see, and there was no time to be just lurking around looking for a man in the middle of all that hubbub and running about. I was an assistant manager at The Sequantus House that summer, having commenced with that title only a week or two before, when school let out. During the fall and winter I'd shot up like a sunflower and filled out to my full growth, and Henny had looked at me one day and said, "Saints in Heaven, Leon, but you're practically a man now. It's time we started teaching you the hosteler's trade in earnest." And my, that suited me fine because it was, you understand, the stamp of approval from that man that I admired so much.

When Mama first brought me to Sand Springs I was small enough to tote around in a basket, and she used to carry me over to the inn and set me down right beside the piano while she played her recitals, and then when I was a little bigger and starting to run the rugs, you know, creeping and crawling, she'd leave me with the ladies in the laundry or one of the service pantries, where I wouldn't get under the guests' feet. Once I got a little mobility of my own, though, I started exploring the place and seeking out the secret parts. I especially enjoyed sneaking under the big verandah there on the side of the inn where the driveway came in, where I could peek out through the lattice at the guests as they arrived in their automobiles or else, if they were coming by train, in the inn bus that picked them up at the station in Carlowsbridge. Except in the cities, the roads weren't paved then, and people riding in those old touring cars went all dressed up in those canvas outfits to keep the dust off their clothes, with big long coats and hats and goggles over their eyes, and gloves with gauntlets that came all the way up their elbows, and it was fun to see them like that, they were like knights in armor, and then they'd take off their dusters and their goggles and just like that they'd be ladies and gentlemen come for a visit. I found that to be a wonderment and most entertaining.

In the afternoons when the sun was on the other side of the inn, the men would line up in the rocking chairs on the verandah and read their newspapers and snooze and chat about this and that, just whiling away the time. They were all rich men, you know, tycoons and all, and back then rich people showed off their prosperity by eating and getting fat, and when they all got going on those big old rockers right up over my head it sounded like as I was sitting under an industrial engine with those big wheels a-turning, with the floorboards rumbling and the men talking bully in their deep voices about their mines and their factories and their money and things I couldn't understand but they sounded very powerful and impressive to me, those men. I figured someday when I grew up I'd get to sit up there like that and smoke cigars and tell everybody how rich I was, ah-ha, and I'm still waiting to do all that.

But the thing that was most interesting to me about being around the inn when I was just a boy like that was how every day was different from every other day. All that coming and going. New people turned up every time the bus came in from

272

the station, and old ones that you'd gotten used to seeing around just disappeared from one day to the next, so that it was ever so much more interesting than, for instance, Calhoun's shop, where you saw that same old tired crowd every time you went in and you knew everything about them you'd ever want to know. Excepting Uncle Pedey, of course, because you never quite knew what that old fellow was likely to come up with next. But being around the inn made me feel up-to-date and, I suppose, sophisticated in my own little way. You can imagine how tickled I was when Henny told me, "You know this place as well as I do myself. It's time you learned how to run it." Mama took me down to Berde Bros. and bought me a suit and an Arrow shirt with a stiff collar, and when she looked me over in my new outfit her eyes got all fluttery and she said, "La, but you're handsome as a king, I declare." Duke Ellington with all his closets full of tailoring never felt as elegant as I did then, I'll bet.

They call spring the season for freshness and promise, you know, when the bird is on the wing, and I don't think any spring in my time ever seemed as promising to me as that one, however which way I looked. The First War was over and all of our Sand Springs boys had come home safe and unharmed, except for Fritz Larrabee's son, Damon, who'd had part of his foot shot off, and Mr. Edgar Peterson, who was laid up from shell shock, but then we didn't really think of him as belonging to the town, you see, except as someone to gossip about. Alfred Calhoun used to call him "His Highness the Nigger Lover," and that was enough to make me feel kindly disposed toward the man in my thoughts, but I can't say that his condition grieved me. Calhoun was meaner than ever that spring, too, because the Carlowsbridge road had been paved over and his old customers were buying Model T Fords and driving down to the county seat for their haircuts, and Henny guessed he wouldn't stay in business for too much longer, which suited me fine and good riddance to Calhoun, ah-ha.

I'd won myself a spot on the town baseball team, playing at

first base and in the outfield, and after the first game of the season I'd had my first taste of beer and swallowed it down and thought it was swell, most refreshing. I was feeling quite newly mature, you understand, and sure of myself. I had a little crush on a pretty gal named Sarah Ann MacIntyre, who was the constable's niece, and she was letting me take her hand and walk with her after school, out where the wildflowers grow, mm-hmm, and that was giving me some serious feelings and getting me to wondering about the future.

At the inn they'd been working since March on the new pier, getting it all squared up in time for the grand opening on the Fourth of July. They'd sunk the pilings for it and laid the deck down that last September after the season ended, and all spring a whole army of workmen had been putting together the dance pavilion out at the pier's end. That pavilion was Henny's pride and joy, and whenever he talked about it he lit right up like a candle, because he was certain it would make the inn the talk of the whole East Coast, you see it was altogether the most modern attraction. It was round in its shape and its roof came to a peak like a circus tent, and it had glass walls all the way around it, so that when you were out there at night, he said, "You'll feel as though you were borne upon the waters in an enchanted crystal ball, tripping the light fantastic high amongst the starry firmament." Or some words along those lines. Henny had an Irishman's soul and he enjoyed the sound of words, so when he got to plugging one of his projects like this pavilion he shined them up like a barker at Barnum and Bailey's, and don't spare the optimism, brother. He'd been jumping every which way all spring with his plans for the gala, running up and down the lawn from the inn to the pier and back again a hundred times a day, waving blueprints and diagrams around, putting together the menus and arranging for the fireworks and the banquet seating and every detail of it all down to the folding of the napkins and the placement of the citronella candles in the gardens, to keep the mosquitoes away. I don't think he'd slept a night through since the New Year, he had so much going through his head, but he was a happy man those days, and his energy had everybody at the inn all sparked up.

Henny had booked us a society orchestra from New York, led by a man named Roscoe Fitts that I've never heard of before or since, and they were going to play for the gala and then stay on through the summer providing the entertainment at the pavilion. He told me they knew all the latest syncopated stuff that the smart set in New York liked to dance to, like the two-step and the fox trot, which were dances that had been made popular by the Castles, and a brand-new thing called The Versailles. He said they played the music folks were calling jazz. Well, jazz, ah-ha. That was a funny new word then, you understand, that I'd only heard for the first time quite recently, and when I'd asked Mama about it, did she know what it sounded like and all, she'd acted quite strangely and gotten short with me, said, "I'm certain I don't know what you're talking about, and I don't care to be discussing it." That struck me as being odd, because at her job at Berde Bros. she was playing all the new sheet music that came up from New York and Boston, so she must have heard something about it, but if she did she wasn't letting on that it was so.

Mama had been acting strangely all spring anyway, and that was the only thing about that season that was just a little off the beat, you know, out of tune with all the gaiety and goodness I was feeling. And it wasn't just that she'd played the blues that time, or the way she was going out and standing by the lake that way. Her whole personality got a little sad then, and it seemed as if she was spending a lot of time sighing and looking off into space and just being melancholy. But she wouldn't talk to me about it if I said anything, and I guessed maybe it was just some woman's thing like those vapors I'd heard about that she was going through, me being so newly mature about that sort of business, and so I was making the effort to be understanding with her and going on about my own affairs as if nothing was wrong, which mostly nothing was, at least for a while.

Well now, that day before the gala was as busy as any I

could remember at the inn. Folks were coming in from all over and there was all sorts of extra help around that had been hired to set up and serve at the banquet, which was going to be an affair lasting the whole afternoon, outdoors on the side lawn by the gardens, and the fireworks people were down by the shore rigging up their displays and the workmen on the pier were laying on the finishing touches and polishing the glass, and of course Henny was racing around like a one-armed paper hanger making sure that everything was going to be as perfect as it could be. The way he moved around it was like as there were ten of him, and you could hear that big baritone voice of his coming at you from every direction, and I don't think he lit down for a second the whole day or would until it was all over, but at the end of the afternoon when I was finishing up my shift at the desk and preparing to go home for supper he popped up in front of me and asked me could I join him for a little stroll and a chat, as if the time was his to kill. "There's something I'd like to discuss with you, son," he said, "that's of a personal nature, if you'll spare me a few moments." There was a hitch in his manner that seemed almost shy when he said it, and he kind of ducked his head, and I couldn't imagine for the life of me what it could be about but I'd never have refused Henny anything I owned in the world, you know, so I said, "Sure, Henny," and followed him right away.

He led me out the side door and across the terrace and didn't say much more than, "Let's go this way," while we were walking down the lawn to the pier. There was a rope strung between the railing posts at the shore end of the pier to keep folks from wandering out there before the official opening, and we stepped over it and strolled out toward the pavilion in a leisurely way, just a couple of gents taking the air at supper-time, making talk about the fine weather we were having and did we think the Red Sox would repeat their championship this season, the kind of things gents talked about. The workmen had all gone home and there was nobody else about but the two of us, and our footsteps hit on the deckboards with a nice, satisfying kind of sound, deep and solid.

It was a clear evening and the sun was still hanging up above the mountains out beyond the lake, so that that side of the pavilion was lit up like polished gold from its reflection on the glass, and on the other side you could see the hills and the lake shore on the windows as clear as life itself. And then as we got closer to it, I could make out our own reflections approaching and I was struck by the happiness of seeing how closely matched we looked there, side by side, for I was nearly as tall as Henny by then and nearly as broad across the shoulders. Henny had begun explaining to me some of the arrangements he had made for the gala and the order of the program planned for the next day. "Your mother's recital will commence after the banquet has been cleared," he said, "but not until the company has had the opportunity to stretch its legs and digest a bit, for I don't want there to be a great lot of milling about while she plays. She deserves their attention, after all. If it weren't a matter of the public's taste, you know, I'd have constructed the entire event around her and made it a concert such as you'd see in the great halls in the city. But they won't sit still for that anymore. They must have their dancing, and it's my business to serve their whims. I hope you understand that, son, that it's not my own preference where she's concerned in the matter. I'm required to keep abreast of the times."

Well, it puzzled me to hear him talk that way, because the way he said it, it sounded like an apology, and I didn't see any reason for it. Mama knew rightly enough that ragtime was going out of fashion but I'd never heard her complain about the public's taste like that. If she'd had a mind to, she could have spruced up her act by performing some of the newer material, but she just kept plugging along in her old-fashioned way, so I figured it wasn't a matter of any much consequence to her, and even though that dance band had been booked up for the pavilion, she was still going to keep on doing her little evening re-

277

citals in the garden, because Henny was much too loyal to suggest that the time for them was past. But before I could come up with anything to say about it to him, he'd changed the subject anyway, and was calling my attention to the flagpole on the roof of the pavilion. "Tomorrow we'll hang the Stars and Stripes there in honor of the occasion," he said, "and then I've acquired a lovely long banner of silk that'll fly on the ordinary days. It's scarlet and has a white S upon it for Sequantus, a lovely thing. I'd considered putting a lamp up there, you know, some sort of a revolving beacon such as you'd find on a lighthouse, but then I said to myself it'd never be as gay as a colorful pennant in full flight upon the breeze, don't you think? Here, step this way now."

The pier's promenade deck came to an end at the pavilion doors, but there was a narrow walkway that circled around the outside of the pavilion, which was to be used as a staging for the window cleaners, or an emergency exit from the pavilion if it ever came to that, and Henny led me over to the shaded side and onto that little walk, where we went in single file with our reflections at our shoulders in the glass. I couldn't see inside the building because the curtains were drawn all the way around and I was hoping that was where Henny was taking me, because I'd been hearing his descriptions for months of what it was going to look like when it was finished, but the last time I'd looked in had been a couple of weeks before, and while I'd been impressed by the size and shape of it, you understand, the windows had been covered with canvas and the decor was mostly still in crates, and the floor was littered with machinery and carpenters' tools and whatnot. It'd had the look of a warehouse about it and not any enchanted crystal ball, and I'd decided then that it would be more fun to wait and see it as it was supposed to be seen, so I'd held off on going back in the meanwhile.

Around at the back of the pavilion there were still some carpenters' supplies stacked up on the walkway, some boards and rope and a couple of nail kegs, and we had to turn sideways and step carefully to get around them. Henny put his hand on the wooden rail and almost lost his balance because it made a cracking noise and started to bend away from him, and he said, "Judas Priest, mind you don't lean there. It's not properly attached at all. That's one of the things they'll have to finish up when they come back day after tomorrow. They'll be clearing out this extra lumber, too. I must remind myself to be certain that this is clearly closed off so that none of the guests wander back here by mistake. The last thing we want tomorrow is a tragedy." I didn't pay it a lot of mind when he said that, though, because I was looking over the side at the water, which was a good thirty feet below us, and I said, "I could dive off of here. I've dived off of cliffs this high." And Henny said, "Aye, it's deep enough, but you have to be careful of how you enter the water. If you land wrong on it, it's like landing on pavement, and it can give you a hell of a great wallop. When I was a lad in New York we used to swim in the river off the piers, don't you know, and I've seen fellows knocked unconscious who hit the water wrong." "I wonder if Fritz Larrabee's cows would jump from this high," I said, and Henny chuckled and said, "Ah, you remember that, d'you?"

Well, we kept going like that all the way around the pavilion, and it was as pleasurable a stroll as I could imagine, but I did have to wonder what Henny had on his mind. It didn't seem likely that he'd be taking this time away from his busyness just to breeze with me about swimming and Larrabee's diving livestock and such, because that was the sort of breezing we could be doing any time on any day, and not just on the eve of his grand opening and gala. But I kept right up with him, just getting a little more curious as we went, and eventually we were back in front of the pavilion and he said, "Would you like to see it now?" I said I would, yes, and he opened the door and held it for me while I passed on inside. There was a little entry space there and then you came upon the curtains, which were closed tight, but we found the opening in them and Henny said, "Just go in and wait a second now." I slipped through and let the curtain fall closed behind me and it was pitch dark in there, so I just stood and in a very short while the chandelier lit up and my oh my. The chandelier was all crystal and sparkling and as big as a cloud hanging down from the center of the roof where it came to a point, right over the middle of the floor. The floor was all hardwood and waxed so slick and shiny you could part your hair looking in it, and all around the outside of it there were little whitewashed café tables and chairs, with potted plants set in among them. And there was a stage at the far end of the room that was already set up with chairs for the orchestra and a big black grand piano on it, and the front of the stage was hung with bunting, you know, in red, white and blue, and so were the crossbeams up overhead. And then all around the outside of it were the curtains, and they were crimson colored and shiny as new satin, and I walked out in the middle of the floor and turned around and around taking it all in until I was dizzy from it. Mercy, it was the grandest thing I'd ever seen. It was so big, you know, and so elegant, and I hadn't even seen the best part of it yet.

Henny stuck his head in through the curtains at the front and asked me, "What do you think of it, lad?," and all I could say was, "Oh gee, Henny. Oh gee." And I recall we both started to laugh then, and Henny ducked back out again and straight off there commenced a great rumbling noise and the floor began to tremble, and I said, "Hey," because for a minute there I didn't know but what the whole thing was starting to tumble down around me. But then a beam of light fell across me from behind, and I turned around and saw the curtains moving apart and the sun bursting in through the opening, and I looked about and the curtains were parting in four places, front, back and sides, and they continued to slide back like that until they were drawn up around the four big supporting pillars and there was nothing between them except the glass, which was so clean I expected to feel the wind on my cheek. And it was just the way Henny had always said it would it be, you know, like as I was in a crystal ball, floating there with the mountains and the hills and the lake all around me and up at the end of the lawn the inn. It just took my breath away. "Ah, Henny," I said. "Ah, Henny, gee." And that was eloquent enough to express my feelings, all right, ah-ha.

Well, Henny came out on the floor with his arms open wide and he was practically prancing, he was so pleased. He was beaming like a kid on Christmas morning. "Isn't this a piece of work, Leon?" he said. "That's what it is if I do say so myself, a piece of work. The engine for the draperies came all the way from Chicago, and it took us four days to assemble it, me and the engineers. I was up until this dawn making the last connections myself. It's a piece of work, and no doubt about it." He put his hand on my shoulder and we stood there and gaped at it together for a few minutes, and then we sort of drifted over to the stage, Henny guiding me along by the arm, and when we got there we hiked ourselves up and sat on the edge of the stage and gaped some more, looking back along the length of the pier and up at the inn, which was shining in the sun like the snow on the mountaintops. "All of this," Henny said. "All of this."

We sat there for a few minutes more without saying anything, and then Henny started to fidget, you know, picking at his cuffs and dusting off his trouser legs, and when he began to talk his big voice was very soft and low and he talked straight down at the floor. He started out by saying, "My father was born in Ireland, son, in a hut so small it'd fit through the door of this. He left his home and came to New York to escape the famine, and he found work as a porter at the General Putnam Hotel and worked at that until he died in a streetcar accident. I was nine years old when that happened, and still in short pants, but I was the oldest child of five and the family needed supporting, so I went to work myself at the Putnam, working below stairs as a bootblack and a scullery boy for pennies a week. Pennies, mind you. But I was observant and ambitious, and I was honest, and I was able to advance in the hosteler's trade by dint of my willingness to work and to serve, and so advance I did. I was a night manager at the Strathcona Court when Mister Bobwit hired me to run this house, and I think I've run it well. I think I have. And by God, I love the old place. I do. I've given it everything I have, perhaps more than it deserves. Perhaps . . ." He paused and I waited.

"You see, son, my point is this," he said after a few seconds. "I've had a rewarding life, and I'll not deny it, but it's taken its toll in sacrifice as well. I've had precious little time to pursue certain of the amenities that some folk take for granted. The amenities of the heart, you might say. The things of tender spirit." He paused again and cleared his throat, and I looked over at him and noticed that the back of his neck was getting red. "No, damn me, that's not true," he said. "It was my own choice. It was what I chose. A man's got to take his medicine, and no excuses." He looked up at me out of the corner of his eye with an angry look.

He seemed to be waiting for me to speak, so I said, "Yes sir."

"I blame no one but myself for it," he went on. He lowered his gaze to the floor again. "I had my chance and I made a botch of it. Plain and simple, that's what it was. A great botch. Misperception and misunderstanding. I mistook myself, tried to be something I wasn't. I was too young to know any better. But I took my medicine. I did. I swallowed my shame and got on with my life. That's what I did. My life is here. This is my life, my work. This is what I'll be remembered for, if I'm remembered at all. The past is dead and gone. A man's got to get on. You see, I'm at peace with myself. My work speaks for me. And I think I've earned a second chance. There's no one who'd deny me that, not any longer. You can see the justice in that, can't you?"

I hemmed and hawed over that, because I couldn't imagine what he was talking about or leading up to, and Henny nodded and said, "Very well then," as if we'd settled something between us. He took a couple of deep breaths and cleared his throat some more and then he said, "You're not old enough to've ever drunk whiskey, are you, son?" I said, "No sir," and he said, "Quite rightly, too. There'll be plenty of time for that in its time." Then he leaned away from me and looked me up and down, and I felt myself starting to blush because he seemed so scattered and confused in his manner that it was upsetting to me.

After he'd inspected me for a while, he said, "You're a fine-looking lad, Leon, a fine lad. Your father must have been a tall man."

I said, "I don't know."

And Henny said, "Damn me, of course you don't. Forgive me. I'm not stating this at all well."

"Yes sir," I said.

"Do you have any notion at all what I'm driving at?" he said. "Is it at all clear?"

"Well," I said, "no sir."

"Damn me, I knew it," he said. "Of course you don't. I'm talking like a perfect ninny. Let me put it this way. The point is that in my time I've come to be able to recognize quality. I have every confidence in myself that I can distinguish between the true coin and the counterfeit where a person's substance is concerned. Do you see? Substance shines through. Stand up, lad. Stand up." We both lifted down from the edge of the stage and Henny turned and faced me and grasped my shoulders, and looked into my eyes with a grave expression on his face, like as he was sending me off to war, and he said, "Before I say another word, I require you to pledge me your confidence. I must have your solemn promise."

Now, I still didn't know what he was going on about, so I said, "What do you want me to promise, Henny?"

And he said, "I'm asking that you promise on your word as a man of honor that you'll say nothing to your mother about this conversation. If she should ask you directly, I'll not want you to deceive her, to be sure, but I pray you otherwise not to report what I'm about to say to you. Will you do that?"

"Well sure," I said. "All right."

"Your word, then?" he said.

"Yes sir," I said. "I promise."

"Good lad," he said, and he squeezed my shoulders with his big hands and gave me a little shake, but he didn't let go of me, and his eyes got wider and wider, and his voice started to raise up, and he said, "Straight out then, it's this. It is my intention, and mark you, Leon, I want your permission to pursue it, it is my intention, I say, once the grand opening has been seen to and the festivities are done with, it is my intention to approach your mother, Missus Winslow, and request that she join her hand to mine in marriage."

Well, I could hardly believe my ears, you know, when he said that, and the blood rushed up into my head and my chest filled up and my hands and knees started to tremble, because that was the finest thing I'd ever heard and the most wonderful news, and I just stood there and shook and said, "Oh Henny, oh Henny," about a half-dozen times, with my voice going up an octave every time.

And Henny grinned at me and said, "I've not inquired of her on the matter in the slightest way, you understand, but I believe that after all the years of our friendship I do not displease her. And for me, I can deny myself no longer. She is the most remarkable woman in every aspect of her being that I have ever beheld, and if she should accept me I would be the proudest and happiest man in the world. I'd devote my life to her, lad. Do I have your permission?"

I flung my arms around him and tried to lift him right off the floor, and he hugged me back and chuckled and said, "I'm taking this to be your blessing, son." And I said, "Oh yes, Henny, oh yes."

Now, I can't tell you how I managed to keep that from Mama during supper, except that I ate fast and skipped right out afterwards and took a walk through the woods, and when I got back I yawned a lot and said I thought I'd turn in early, since I had to go down to Carlowsbridge first thing in the morning for the baseball game, and she only seemed a little bit curious and said, "My, but you seem in fine spirits tonight," without pressing me on it. Then I went up and lay across my bed and didn't get to sleep until way past midnight, being too tickled to even shut my eyes, because at last I was going to have a real daddy, and not just that but it was going to be Henny Vaughan, you see, and though I can't remember what they were I'm certain that when I finally got to sleep that night my dreams were sweet. And you know, I'd forgotten all about that man in the derby hat, who I'd seen in the road only that morning.

The next day was a lovely warm day and everything went so nicely. I mentioned about the baseball and how I did, and then when I got back and checked in to work at the inn everyone was as gay as could be. I didn't see Henny to speak to but he passed by a couple of times and gave me a big wink and a smile, and I knew it was all solid with him and it couldn't have been any finer with me. I was just buzzin' like a bee.

I was working an evening shift that would keep me behind the desk from noon until ten, with time off for supper and a chance to duck outside for the fireworks, which were going to be shot off once it got good and dark and the orchestra was taking its break, and Mama stopped in to see me a little while before sundown, on her way down to the pavilion. That was the very last time I saw her alive. Oh my, it was. She was wearing a white gown that night with a high neck and long sleeves, and the collar and the cuffs were trimmed with white lace, with the cuffs cut a little short above her wrists the way she liked them, so as they didn't interfere with her hands when she played, you understand. And she had a broad-brimmed hat on, too, that was white and lacy, and when she came into the lobby through the French doors from the west side of the inn, the sun was setting behind her, and it lit her up like an angel with a halo. She was so pretty to see, and I said, "Mama, you look beautiful," and I've always been glad I told her that.

She smiled when I said it, and batted her eyes at me a little, the way she did when she was flirting with Uncle Pedey, and she said, "Thank you, darlin'. Do you really think so? La, but I feel gay as a Dutch tulip tonight." And then she said, "Have you seen Mister Vaughan about? I must have a word with him," and I started to blush and grin when she mentioned his name, and she said, "My, what did I say? You're grinning like a madman."

I started to turn my head away, but she put her hand on my cheek and looked me in the face, and said, "Is it a secret, darlin'? Do you have a happy secret?" I was afraid she was reading my thoughts, and I pulled back my head and said, "Aw no, Mama. It's just a fine night, is all. Isn't it a fine night?"

Well, she cocked her head over to the side and studied me for a second, and then she gave my cheek a soft little pat. She had very soft hands for a piano player. The tips of her fingers were flattened out the way they get when you spend your life pressing on the ivories, and they were strong and so quick she could drop an egg from waist high and still catch it before it hit the floor, which was something I saw her do in the kitchen one time, but they always had that softness that felt so gentle whenever she touched me like that, those little pats she liked to give. "Well," she said, "I'm certain we shall tell each other all about it later on."

"Tell each other what, Mama?" I said, being all innocent.

And she said, "Why, la, whatever there is to be told, darlin'. Whatever there is to be told." And that was the last thing she said to me, because then she turned away and gave me a little wave and left the inn.

Some time later I stepped out onto the side terrace and had a look down toward the pier and the pavilion, and it looked just splendid. Darkness was just coming on and the lamps along the pier had been lit, and more lamps around the lawns and gardens, and inside the pavilion all the little café tables had candles on them, so it looked like a big glass jar full of fireflies. I could hear Mama's ragtime rising up from the pier and I remember thinking how rich it sounded, you know, much richer than she usually played. The tonality seemed to be fuller, if you know what I mean, more harmonic, and there was a gliding to her rhythm that I wasn't accustomed to hearing. I didn't know but what it might have been just the way the pavilion took the sound, the acoustics of it, but I thought it sounded fine and I meant to tell her so. Then I heard a commotion going on back in the lobby and I went in to see, and it was the society band going through on their way down to the pier, all dressed in their tuxedos and toting their instruments, there must have been twenty-five or thirty of them. They were joking and cutting up, and I stayed behind the desk to keep an eye on them, you know, because those traveling musicians were always known to be disreputable and Henny had told me to be sure and watch that they didn't make any mischief around the guests or steal the curtains, ah-ha, or the like.

The next time I went out was to watch the fireworks, which went on and on and filled up the sky in their magical way, and then finished up with a huge American flag on a frame on the lake shore and rockets bursting overhead, and everybody cheered and waved sparklers, and right after that Tom Hart came in and relieved me at the desk. I went down to the pier then and looked in on the pavilion, which was jam-packed with people enjoying themselves, drinking beer and wine at the tables and dancing the new dances all over the floor. The chandelier had been dimmed down somehow but the light from all those candles reflected off the glass and it was hard to see outside, so I didn't exactly get that enchanted floating feeling I was looking for, but there was enough excitement anyway for my young taste, and I stood around and listened to the music and watched the dancers and wondered if Sarah Ann MacIntyre and I would be bouncing around like that some day, with our arms around each other so. I certainly did hope so.

I spotted Henny sitting at a table near the doors with Mr. Bobwit and a couple of other men, and I was a bit surprised that Mama wasn't there with him. I waved to him and he got up and came over to me and patted me on the shoulder and said, "Splendid occasion, son. It's a proud night for us all." Then he put his head close to my ear and said, "You've not said anything to her, have you?" I shook my head, and he said, "Good fellow. Keep it secret for another night, and I intend to ask her tomorrow. Can you do that?"

"All right," I said, "but is she here now? I don't see her."

Henny said, "No, I've not seen her myself since she left the stage. She played magnificently tonight, simply magnificently. You should have heard the cheers."

"I thought she'd be with you," I said. "She said she was looking for you."

"She must have missed me in the crowd," Henny said. "I've been entertaining Bobwit and his friends. They're from the Peterson Trust, and they're most impressed."

"I guess she just went home then," I said.

I stayed around and watched the dancing for a while longer and then I went home by the path through the woods, and as soon as I entered the house I could tell that she wasn't there. It was just something I knew, and right away it alarmed me. I called out for her and ran through the house and looked in every room, and then I went out in the yard and called for her there and into the woods around the house. When I didn't get an answer I went inside and fetched a lantern, and I went back along the path to the inn, thinking she might have fallen in the woods along that way, and then I went back home along the lake road. I didn't see a trace of her or hear any answer to my calls. I went across the road from the house and down to the lake shore where she'd been going in the mornings, but she wasn't there either, and then I remembered the man in the derby hat and I began to suspect that he'd done something to her, some foul play, and I ran back to the inn and found Henny. He was still at his table in the pavilion, and I grabbed his arm and said, "Henny, I can't find her. She's not at home and I'm worried."

Well, Henny jumped right up and we went back to the house together, going through the woods again and both of us shouting for her, and when we got home I told him about the man and how he'd stood in the road watching after her. When I described him, Henny said he recalled that he'd seen the same man hanging around outside the kitchen door at the inn the week before but that he'd been too rushed with his other affairs to stop and ask the man his business. "If any harm's come to her, I'll find him," Henny said, "and break him in two." His anger made me more fearful than ever, and I said, "Oh Henny, what will we do?"

"We'll keep searching, son, and hope there's a reasonable explanation for her absence," he said. "Since she's not here and it's too dark to be combing through the woods, we'll start at the inn. Perhaps she's at the inn."

But she wasn't at the inn. Henny and I spent the rest of the night going through the place from top to bottom, all the closets and the storerooms and the odd little hiding places I knew, everywhere except the guests' bedrooms. Even in his urgency Henny couldn't bring himself to disrupt his guests, you see. At dawn we still hadn't found her, and we were standing on the side terrace and talking about getting up a search party to go through the woods when I happened to look down toward the pier, and in the first rays of the sun that were shining through the pilings under the pier I saw something white, and I said, "Lord of Mercy, Henny, look there," and we both started running down across the lawn to the shore.

Mama was there in the water under the pier, floating face up with her long hair drifting free around her. I recalled that when I was just a little boy she used to let me help her brush out her long hair, and I started to moan and cry at the sight of it so, floating in the water like that. The lace on one of her cuffs had snagged against the side of the piling and she was just shifting back and forth in the water, bumping against the piling as the little lake waves pushed against her body, and the sunlight was falling directly on her face, which was something she had never let happen when she was alive.

The water where she was floating wasn't even knee-deep on me, and Henny and I waded in together and pulled her sleeve loose from the piling, and then I lifted her shoulders and he took her feet and we carried her back onto the shore and set her down on the grass at the bottom of the inn's lawn and knelt down beside her and just looked at her. There was no question she was dead. Her skin had a gray shading in it and her lips and eyelids were dark blue, and so were her fingernails. And on the side of her forehead where the little fine hairs began there was a dark bruise several inches long, where the killer had hit her with a stick or a club before he threw her off the pier into the water. We didn't say anything. We were both too choked by our grief to speak words, so we just rested there on our knees beside Mama's body and cried big hot tears, and after a while I picked up her hand and pressed it against my cheek and felt how cold it was and how it had already lost its softness, and Henny kept brushing her hair away from her face and stroking it on the ground. I don't know how long we stayed there like that, but at some time we heard voices from up at the inn, and so we picked her up and carried her home along the lake road, back to our pretty little house in the woods.

Chapter Twelve

The Entertainer

On the morning of the Fourth of July, Lady awoke just as the sky began to show a soft orange band behind the eastern hills. From her window she saw that a thin layer of mist lay over the lake, but she did not trouble herself to go out on this morning; instead, she tied a dressing gown over her nightdress and went downstairs to the kitchen and made herself a cup of chocolate. She carried it to the parlor and sat on the sofa there and sipped the chocolate and thought her thoughts, and after a while, hearing Leon stir overhead, she returned to the kitchen and set some water to boil. When it began to steam in the saucepan she went to the foot of the stairs and called, "Leon darling."

"All right, Mama," he answered in the deep, loud voice he had acquired so recently that she still wasn't accustomed to it.

"Good morning to you," Lady called, "and good day. I am about to put your eggs in the water."

"All right, Mama," he repeated. "I'll be right down."

She dropped three eggs into the boiling water and cut four thick slices of bread and put them on a plate, and shortly Leon came clattering down the stairs and burst into the kitchen, wearing his flannel baseball uniform with the felt letters S. S. on his shirt front and the grass stains so unyieldingly embedded in the fibers of his knickers that Lady was sure that not even Mimi Beaudette with all of her soaps and potions could have removed them. "I've got to hurry," he said. "We're taking the early trolley. Have you seen my cap? I can't find my cap."

"Good morning to you too," Lady said, cracking the eggs open and scraping them out into his bowl. "Do you have a kiss for me this morning, or don't you think Mister Ty Cobb kisses his little mama before he goes off to play his games?"

"Sure, Mama," Leon said. He bent down and touched the side of her forehead with his lips. "Have you seen my cap?" he asked again.

"If I'm not mistaken, it's there on the porch with your glove and your shoes," she said. "Now sit down, please, and eat your eggs before you do another thing. Sit." She placed the bowl and the plate of bread on the table, and after a brief, silent show of impatience Leon sat and began to spoon strawberry jam onto his bread and his soft-boiled eggs, while Lady fetched a bottle of milk from the icebox and poured her son a glassful. "It's going to be a fine day today," she said. "I'm so glad the weather is favoring us, aren't you? It would be such a shame if it wasn't perfect for the gala tonight, after all the care and effort Mister Vaughan has put into it. I'm quite looking forward to the festivities, aren't you? This is going to be a very, very special day for us, I think."

Leon mumbled something around a mouthful of bread and stirred more jam into his eggs. For some reason he seemed inordinately interested in the process, because he kept his head lowered over his bowl and wouldn't meet Lady's eyes with his, even when she bent down beside him and said, "What do you see in there? Are you telling your fortune? If it's wealth and romance, I hope you'll share some with your little mama. I do so enjoy wealth and romance, you know." His face reddened suddenly and he began to cough, and Lady straightened up and patted him on his shoulderblades, resisting with some effort her desire to lecture him on the folly of trying to swallow an entire mouthful in one gulp. "There now," she said. "There there."

He stopped coughing and took several deep breaths. "Sorry, Mama," he said, and then finished his eggs, wiping the bowl clean with the breadcrust. As he stood up from his chair he drank off the last of the milk, but when Lady said, "Wait," and reached to clean the white mustache from his lip, he turned away to the porch, saying, "I've got to catch that trolley. I've got to."

"All right," Lady said. She shook her head forbearingly. "It's always such a pleasure conversing with you in the morning," she said. "Sometimes the stimulation is more than I can bear."

"I'll see you later, Mama," Leon said from the door. "G'bye." The screen door slapped shut behind him as he jumped to the ground and ran off into the woods toward the Sand Springs road. Lady watched him go, and when she could no longer see him she went back into the kitchen and made herself another cup of chocolate. She hummed quietly to herself, a simple melody from her childhood whose words she could not remember, although she felt she ought to, for it had been one of the songs her mother had sung to her in their yard behind the little brown house. She smiled at the memory of the back yard, with its soapy ground and the chinaberry and the smoke tree where she used to hide among the fallen blossoms.

Leon returned shortly before noon, booming with excitement about his ball game. He washed himself off at the pump, struggled into his white shirt and his suit and left in a rush to take up his post at the inn. After he'd gone, Lady toweled her hair and brushed it out for the second time. It still wasn't dry, so she left it hanging loosely down the back of her robe and went to sit beside an open window in the parlor, where a warm breeze rustled through the drawn lace curtains, and after a while she moved over to the lowbacked chair in front of the piano and, almost without thinking, began to play the blues.

She played them softly that afternoon and without fear, and as they recalled her times for her she was pleased by them, and the voices of her life made her feel whole and confident. She had begun to play her blues again in the late winter, not long before Leon's sixteenth birthday, and at the same time she'd begun to dream, something she hadn't done since her childhood had ended with Mimi's burial. In both instances, she was impelled by a despairing apprehension that the past had finally discovered her, for she'd heard pronounced a word that she'd forgotten she even knew, and it had resonated in her like harsh spirit laughter: jazz.

She had been sitting that winter morning at the little demonstration upright in the piano showroom at Berde Brothers, leafing through the newest sheet music and thinking about Edgar Peterson, who had recently been brought home to his father's castle, when Claude Davies, the gramophone salesman, had strutted up to her side and favored her with a well-practiced wink. He was a young Carlowsbridge man who fancied himself a sophisticate, for he owned two check-patterned suits and a red necktie and he'd recently grown a thin mustache, which he stroked incessantly with the side of his index finger. "Howdy do, Professor," he said. "Sure do hope your dance card's not filled today."

"Good morning to you, Mister Davies," Lady replied without looking up from the scores. She regarded him as a nuisance, although a harmless one.

He bent closer and pretended to look over her shoulder at the music, a new song by the Broadway songwriter Irving Berlin. "Looks like a humdinger," he said. "Some swell jazz, if you'll pardon my French."

Something turned over in Lady's chest then, and she looked up sharply and exclaimed, "Mister Davies! What did you say?" At that instant, with a clarity that made her gasp, she heard the voice of Grace Bonnard saying, "... I was jazzin' with my daddy ...," and she felt her face redden with heat.

Claude Davies, appearing not to notice her consternation, grinned wickedly and said, "Yup yup, some hot stuff from Dixieland, all right."

Lady stood up from the piano bench, and without excuse she turned to go to the lounge. Her only thought was to find a place where she could be alone and try to collect herself from the midst of the turmoil she felt.

But Davies stepped along right beside her. "Trip your pretty toes into my parlor, why don't you, Missus W.," he wheedled. "Something new has come in, and I know you'll want to bend an ear at it, you being a musician and up to date with all the latest stuff. I'd fancy your opinion on it, because between you and I, I think it's swell." His hand hovered just over her shoulder, for although he prided himself on his irresistibility to women he hadn't quite the brass to bring himself to touch her.

"Mister Davies," Lady protested weakly, but she was too enervated by anxiety to withstand his insistence, and she permitted him to herd her into the gramophone department and stand her before the golden, lily-shaped horn of the Victor demonstrator. He wound the crank, tested the point of the hardwood needle and said, "Tell me if this ain't the hottest thing you ever heard." He released the lock and lowered the needle carefully upon the rim of the spinning black disk. As soon as it caught the first groove, Lady stiffened and bit her lip to keep from crying out in surprise, for the music that issued forth to her ears from the faint distance of the bottom of the acoustic horn was the music of a New Orleans spasm band playing a ratty old tune, a sound she'd thought she'd left behind forever. It sounded far away, like an indoor social at the other side of the quarter, but there was no mistaking it for anything but what it was, with a stabbing cornet asserting the lead voice and a trombone swooping around it, and the blue, piping squeals of a clarinet shrilling in the breaks like Jibba himself calling across the night mist. It was colored music, and it had followed her across time and distance and finally caught up with her. She looked about in dismay.

"It's the newest craze, Missus W.," Claude Davies was saying, "and it's going to be a panic, you mark my words. I can see you think so too, eh? This ditty here is called *The Livery Stable Blues*, and the bunch that's playing it calls themself the Original

Dixieland Jazz Band. Sounds like a bunch of coons with kazoos, don't it, but I tell you it's hot stuff with the real feeling, all right. Did you ever hear the likes?" He patted his foot on the carpeting and wagged his head from side to side with self-conscious abandon, and when the record ended, Lady turned without a word and hurried from the store, gathering up her overcoat and hat and purse as she went.

She knew that she had no proper reason to have been so surprised by the phonograph record, for there had been signs for a long time that that music was abroad. She had first detected it in the newest scores more than two years before, and ever since then she had been trying to ward it off by playing the new tunes as she played her ragtime, with the precision of a rectitude that denied every memory of the harsh, stomping colored music of her childhood. From the morning she had left New Orleans, she'd put that music behind her and adopted legitimate ragtime as the voice of her independence, confident that its propriety would hide her from Truehart and the pursuing vengeance of his madness. Now, it appeared, the power of that propriety had worn thin, and in the new music her past had been gathering close about her.

That same night, for the first time since she and Brick had buried her mother, Lady dreamed. In her dream she was back on Angelus, standing beside the dirty coalyard fence at the closed end of the street, with the thick, gray mists tumbling around her, obscuring from her sight everything except the fence itself and the dim outline of Old Patanouche's gate. From Patanouche's yard she heard the thin wail of Jibba's harmonica approaching her in the mist, and gradually she saw his childish figure take shape behind the gate. But when he got close enough that his features could be seen, she saw that it was not Jibba at all but Leon, and the melancholy sound issuing from the little harmonica he held pressed to his lips was not Jibba's sound but Leon's, Leon's blues, so profound in their sadness that Lady tried to reach out, to embrace and comfort him. But she could not lift her arms; strong hands held her wrists and pinned them tight against her sides, and Leon slipped past her and continued along into the mists on Angelus without ever seeming to notice that she was there, until the fog closed around him and he was gone.

Lady awoke then, and discovered that she was sitting at the piano in her parlor, and her blues were rising up from the keys through her fingers with the swirling profusion of coal smoke, bearing to her the voices and sounds of New Orleans as clear and unmistakable as if she were little Alice Beaudette again and back in the parlor of her little brown house, playing on Brick's old, stained upright. On her first waking impulse she thought to snatch her hands away from the keyboard and leave the piano, to halt her blues before they spread back into the spirit world and called its attention to her, but she found that the feeling of the music was too comforting in her wrists and shoulders to relinquish, and that she was more curious to discover what messages the music contained than she was afraid of their content, and so she kept on playing.

It was only the second time since she'd left New Orleans that she had played her blues. The first had been more than three years earlier, on the night after Leon had drowned, but that time, in her fear for the boy and in the effort of tracking his spirit through death's timeless regions, she hadn't permitted herself to consider the content of the music as she summoned it, and when she was done and Leon had been restored to her she had closed the lid down over the keys and prayed that she'd never have to resort to her blues again. For weeks after that, Lady had lived in unabating fright, shying away from shadows and jumping at sudden noises. She'd been certain that True-hart, having tracked her by her music, would appear in her parlor as he had before, and that this time her own music would not be the proof against his madness that Brick's had been. Only when the first thaw of early spring arrived and he still had not come was she able, finally, to persuade herself that she'd been granted the grace of a single night's reprieve, no doubt by the same powers which had enabled her to recover her son. But even then she had relaxed only gradually, and in the three years since, she'd been more pertinacious than ever in guarding the formality of her music, lest some quirk of her true nature slip out and betray her safety and her happiness.

But now, on another winter's night, the blues sang beguilingly to her and calmed her fears, and with curiosity she heard them unfold. She exclaimed softly to herself as the old voices passed through her parlor—Mimi and Brick and Old Patanouche and the Countess; and some newer voices, too, that she never would have thought to associate with the blues, which had seemed to belong only to that part of her time when she had been Alice—Edgar Peterson, Henny and, finally, Leon. Her son emerged into the flow of her blues in a melody that was not as forlorn as the sound she had heard in her dream but seemed nonetheless to be markedly more somber than she would have judged by the evidence of his nature, and she replayed it with concern, examining it to see whether she could discover the source or intention of this melancholy. While she was turning it this way and that, running it through the different registers of the keyboard and augmenting it with alternate harmonies, she heard Leon's footsteps on the floor upstairs, and she halted at once and got up from the piano.

Lady went out into the hallway, and looking up, she saw him at the top of the stairs, wearing a red flannel union suit that she'd bought for him only two months before, which was already inches too short on his arms and legs, and the sight of him so grown and husky and handsome gave her a pang of happiness and regret. His hair was tousled and his face rumpled by sleep, and he peered down the dim stairway at her with a worried expression and said, "Mama, are you all right?"

"Oh yes," Lady answered him. "I didn't mean to wake you, darlin'."

"Mama, that music sounded so *sad*," Leon said in his newly deepened voice.

Lady paused, wondering how much to say to him. He was almost sixteen and as big as most grown men, and she knew that before much longer she would have to begin to tell him about her past and his. But she quickly decided that this was neither the time nor the place, so she fluttered her hands about in her vague way and said, "La, I was just feeling sleepless and playing soft to settle myself back down, so you go back to bed now and I won't disturb you with it anymore."

"Are you sure, Mama?" he said. "It sounded awful sad."

"Why, mercy," she said, "aren't you a harsh critic in the middle of the night, though?" She affected a bright smile for him.

"All right," he said. "Good night, Mama." He turned back toward his room.

"Good night, sweet darlin'," Lady said. When he was gone she went back into the parlor and sat again on the lowbacked chair before the piano, but she kept her hands clutched in her lap while she thought about her son, and did not touch the keys.

She wasn't at all certain how to tell Leon the story of their lives. For as long as they'd been together she had made it a habit to evade his questions with promises and fancies, knowing that his innocence would be his protection against the past, as well as a bulwark of her own safety in her identity as Lady Winslow. But she understood that just as she was obligated to him for having safeguarded her, so was she required by the conscience of her love for him to redeem that obligation eventually, by presenting him with the truth of his life, his heritage and history, lest he be surprised some day by an agent of a past that he'd never known existed; lest Truehart or another vengeful spirit like Truehart's catch him unawares. His sixteenth birthday would be the time to start, she decided; it would be her special gift to him. She would sit him down in the parlor and with the lamp turned low and her piano nearby to ease her, she would begin: *Darling, it's time I told you about your mama and her times. . . .*

The two facts which would be hardest to impart to her son, Lady knew, were the facts of his paternity and his racial heritage, which were also the two fabrications indispensible to her imposture in the world. They had kept her free and independent in her time, and to disclose them would risk not only the recrimination of Leon's misunderstanding but also the loss of their protection for herself; the screen of resolve that she had erected between herself and the past would be finally pulled down and she would be cast back into the same condition of vulnerability which had driven her from New Orleans in the first place, so that she might as well have never bothered to flee.

And yet, she asked herself, how effective had her resolve been? For months now, omens had been informing her that some sort of confrontation with the past was approaching. The inevitability of it was unquestionable, and hastened not just by Leon's maturity but by other portents, such as the letter that had come so unexpectedly the previous autumn from Edgar Peterson, written from the Front. She could no longer ignore the signals of them, or the responses they stirred up in her own feelings.

Before she'd opened the letter, she'd stared at his name on the corner of the envelope and tried to imagine what it might contain from him, or why he should be writing to her at all. In all the years since he had so kindly sponsored her journey to Sand Springs, she had actually seen Edgar Peterson only twice. On the first occasion, three or four years after she had moved to Sand Springs, he had come to call upon her in her house, merely for the purpose, he said, of ascertaining that she and Leon were well, in a spontaneous gesture inspired simply by the fact that it was a fine spring day and he had been out riding in his automobile on the lake road. She had served him coffee in the parlor and they had chatted pleasantly about innocuous matters, and then he had left. The other time had been at the inn, where he'd been on the terrace with a party of gentlemen when she passed by. He had seen her and had bowed in her direction, and she had answered his bow with a nod and a smile, but they had not spoken. That had been shortly before his wife and daughter had died of the diphtheria and he had so abruptly departed for distant places. And now she had received a letter from him, written from the Front. Puzzled, she opened it at last, and in reading it her puzzlement turned to uneasiness.

My dear Mrs. Winslow,

I hope this finds you well. I write in haste and, I fear, without especial grace, for which I beg your indulgence. I find I am constantly fatigued by my present circumstances and surroundings, and frequently lack the concentration upon affairs by which the amenities of manners are guarded safe. I did, however, wish to relate to you an interesting occurrence which brought you, for reasons which I shall tell you presently, to my mind.

I was in Paris recently for a weekend's leave, a blessed respite from the battlefront. On that Sunday afternoon I was strolling near the Tuileries, enjoying the feeling of the sun upon my face, when I heard a clamoring nearby, toward which I saw several people turn and begin to run. I became curious and, although I did not run, I followed them in the direction of the sound, which, as I came closer, revealed itself to be the music of a brass band, and playing with a marked *esprit*. As I turned the corner, I beheld them there upon the avenue, marching south, and I saw that every musician in the band, and its drum major and its commanding officer (for it was a military band, with every man in it wearing the same uniform as I) was a Negro, that this was the celebrated 369th Infantry Band, directed by Mr. James Europe, who has recently been prominent in New York's musical circles.

Mrs. Winslow, my heart exulted at the sight of them. What style they had! What precision! How jubilantly they strutted along the route of their march! I confess my eyes filled and my chest swelled with pride at their evident high spirits, and I felt in some way recompensed beyond measure for my meager charities to their people.

But more than the sight of these men, so jubilantly patriotic, what moved me (and inspired me, dear lady, to write this letter) was the music they played as they marched, for it rang with the same lightness of spirit which elevated their steps. I shall not try to describe it in any more detailed a fashion than that, because I have neither the ear for music nor the facility with words which might imbue such a description with the ring of life. I can say only that its exuberance was unsurpassed, and in no time at all the route of their march was lined ten-deep with cheering Parisians, to whom such a display in the midst of their travails was tonic.

Mrs. Winslow, the music they were playing was the ragtime, the same music to which you bring your own bountiful talents, and in hearing it, I recalled you and knew that I must pay you my humble respects and assure you of my continued friendship and admiration. Should I return safely from this terrible conflict, it would be my pleasure to call upon you and convey these selfsame assurances in speech which I now commit to paper.

Dear lady, I am,

Most humbly yours,
Edgar Peterson

Uncomprehending, Lady read the letter a second time. What was she to make of this? It was at once so guarded and so yearning a communication, and perhaps nothing more than the scattered feelings of a man distracted by the awful pressures of the battlefront, but the aspect of it which made her hands tremble as she read his words was its reference to the Negro musicians he had encountered and to his "charities to their people." Lady was suddenly gripped by the notion that he intended in an oblique way to remind her by that of his charity to her, that he had by some instinct or acquired information divined that she herself bore the blood of slaves, and that he had been merely indulging her in her attempt to pass. She wondered then whether, if it was so transparent to him, her white disguise was as easily penetrated by others. She remembered the colored chauffeurs at the inn, and tried to recall how they had looked at her. Had their expressions betrayed special understanding? She thought of Calhoun's description of Edgar as "His Highness the Nigger Lover," and wondered now whether the vicious barber intended that epithet against her as well, as the object of "His Highness'" love. She had been overhearing Calhoun in his irresponsible rantings for so long that she had come to accept them as the meaningless rituals of a bitter man. What if she were wrong in that estimation?

For the rest of that autumn she had borne an awful weight of apprehension throughout her waking hours. No longer secure against their implications, she flinched every time she heard Calhoun's tirades against Negritude rising up into her studio from the shop downstairs, and when she played the new sheet music at Berde Brothers, each dotted quarter note and minor harmony seemed to shimmer with an ominous glow, like the amber lamplight reflecting from the blade of Truehart's knife.

That winter Edgar Peterson had come home, and after submitting herself to a period of delay and compromise, Lady had gone to visit him at his castle. She wasn't at all certain what she expected to achieve by the call, but it seemed to offer the prospect of some sort of illumination to apply to her darkening fears, and so she borrowed a car and driver from the inn and rode one afternoon up the long gravel road which was the driveway of the Peterson Estate.

It was an altogether inauspicious March day, chill and dank. Overhead the low sky was the color of weathered slate, and because the first thaw had recently arrived, the fields surrounding the driveway were bare and muddy, dotted here and there and in the hollows by clumps of dirty snow and gray ice, and the tall, leafless elm trees which lined the drive looked like the charred survivors of a consuming fire. The vast house itself, the castle, seemed as if abandoned; from the outside there was no more indication of vitality within than might be discerned on the granite face of a mountain cliff. Yet when Lady stepped out of the auto beneath the vaulted porte-cochère, the front door of the house opened immediately, and she drew her breath in fright when she saw in the doorway a huge black man in servant's livery, as tall and scarifying as Mr. Strap. She had to force herself to climb the stone steps and say, in as evenly modulated a voice as her will could fabricate, "My name is Missus Winslow, and I have come to visit Mister Peterson. Is he at home, please? It is quite important that I see him."

"Mister Peterson is indisposed, madam," the man answered from his great height. "He is receiving no callers." His manner was as distant and correct as Strap's, too, but Lady saw kindness in his eyes and the softness of humanity in the creases around his mouth, and her fear abated.

"I had heard that he was not well," she said, standing her ground. "That was why I wished to visit. Perhaps I could give him a measure of cheer."

The butler shook his head and was about to speak again when a stocky woman in a nurse's uniform joined him in the doorway. "What's this about, then?" she inquired in a belligerent tone, her voice carrying a slight brogue. "I can feel the draft in the sitting room, if you don't mind."

"My name is Missus Winslow," Lady said to her. "I am a friend of Mister Peterson's and I thought I might bring him a bit of cheerfulness while he recuperates. Do you think I could see him, please, nurse?"

The nurse stared boldly at her for a moment, and then said, "Why I suppose you might. Indeed, you may. That will be all right, Luther," she said to the butler. "Please come in, ma'am, Missus Winslow. Please do." She held out a hand and ushered Lady into the hall. "I do hope you understand," she said as she led Lady down a side corridor hung with heavy draperies and dark oil paintings, "that Mister Peterson is quite thoroughly indisposed. I'd not want you to take fright from it. He looks healthy enough in his person, but in his condition he is quite removed from communication, and when you're speaking to him you'll get no response."

"I had heard that," Lady said. "I expected something of the sort." In fact, the rumors regarding Edgar Peterson's condition had stated that his shell shock had rendered him speechless, but in her consternation she had hoped that she might devise another means to communicate with him. "I wonder if I could spend some time alone with him," she said.

"Ah," the nurse said, turning her head and smiling. She had a broad, healthy face, with red cheeks and cheerful eyes. "Ah, no," she said, "I'm afraid that it's a question of his safety, you see. Someone must be in attendance. I do hope you understand."

"Very well," Lady said.

She found him in a large sitting room, seated in a plush, highbacked armchair before a fireplace which contained a sizeable blaze, into whose flames his eyes stared with unmoving fixity, even when she called out, "Good afternoon, Mister Peterson, and good day to you," in forced cheer and crossed the room to his side. The nurse turned her attention to one of the bookshelves along a side wall. "La, Mister Peterson, how very well you look," Lady said, bending forward to see his face. He was well-scrubbed and closely shaved, and his hair was neatly parted and combed flat, but his expression was as vacant as a bolt of uncut cloth, his mouth hanging open and his eyes unfocused as they regarded the fire's dance.

She tried for several minutes to elicit from him some sign that he was aware of her presence in the room, speaking of this and that and laughing at her own words, and, once, touching his arm. But it was all without effect; she might as well have been gossiping with one of the display mannequins at Berde Brothers. She was tiring of the effort and beginning to accept the futility of it when she noticed for the first time that there was a grand piano at the far end of the room, and, still chattering gaily, she went to the instrument and played a ragtime piece. When Peterson didn't respond to it, she played another, but this time she loosed the reins of her propriety somewhat and, acceding to an unexpected memory of previous times, she let her hands escape outside the legitimately prescribed boundaries of the piece and gather to it some of the warmer sonorities and more exuberant fillips of syncopation that she associated with the playing of the ticklers, and she became so caught up by the emotion of them and by the exigency of her need to communicate with Edgar Peterson, that she played that way for more than a half-hour, until, finally, the realization of what she was playing turned back on her like a reprimand and she stopped short. Throughout the recital she had been watching his profile intently, ready to note the first signal from him that he could hear her music, but it had never come, and now she felt defeated and a bit hopeless. "Oh dear," she sighed. "Oh la."

"That was splendid, ma'am," the nurse said, leaving the bookcase and going to Peterson's side, where she smoothed the blanket that lay across his lap and made a slight adjustment of his cuff. "That was played as well as any professional could have played it."

Lady did not try to enlighten the woman concerning her profession, but said only, "Do you think it had any effect? Do you think he heard me at all?"

"I'm certain of it, ma'am," the nurse said. "No living creature could be insensitive to such charming melodies, if you don't mind my saying so, ma'am."

"Well then," Lady said with forced hopefulness, "perhaps I'll come back another day and play for him again."

"I'm certain that would suit us all, ma'am," the nurse said cheerfully.

But when Lady went again to the castle two weeks later she was told by the butler that Edgar Peterson was asleep in his bed, and she departed without seeing him, and not long after that she was assaulted by the recorded music of the spasm band, the jazz. She put off her attempt to communicate with Edgar Peterson then, and turned instead to addressing her own times. On a late winter's night she began to dream again, and to play her blues.

The next day, as soon as Leon had left for school, she hastened to the piano and spent the morning playing the blues again with particular concentration. She was searching in them now for Trueheart's voice, by which she hoped to determine whether he had discovered her, to measure the closeness of his threat. For some reason, it had not appeared the night before, nor could she locate its sound on this day, and, with mounting perplexity, she sought forward and back through her times for it, until evening approached.

She spent another week then, looking for Truehart whenever she found herself alone with the opportunity to play her blues unheard, and then the week after that. Leon's sixteenth birthday came and went, but in the sudden urgency of her search for her father, Lady put aside her plan to divulge herself to her son, at least until she could capture Truehart's sound and measure its threat. The feeling grew in her that now he was close by, and that his sound's absence indicated that he was eluding her deliberately as he stalked her, but as the weeks passed and the custom of addressing her times grew in her so did the comfort she found in having her life complete around her. The past no longer menaced her. Her blues were becoming a consoling ally, and day by day, with an unobtrusive naturalness, her apprehension of Truehart turned gradually to impatience. As spring came and the countryside began to warm to the ascending sun, she discovered that now she wanted him to appear. She wanted to confront him with the wholeness of her life, and, with the power of her own blues, to face him down and then send him away forever.

No longer content to seek him only in her music, Lady took up the habit of searching for Truehart in the heavy morning mists on the lake, for the mists reminded her of the teeming night fog of New Orleans and she felt that they might amplify the messages of her thoughts as she called to him. All that spring she went out in the early hours of daylight and stood on the bank of the lake, willing Truehart to appear, until finally, yesterday, she heard Leon call out from the house, "Hey mister."

Leon's description of the man he'd seen in the road was frustratingly sketchy. A tall man with broad shoulders. A derby hat. City clothes. Lady couldn't press him too closely on it, though, because she had decided not to confide in him until she had seen Truehart and disposed of him by herself; then she could open up her life for her son, and be certain that when Leon took possession of his past it would bring him no bodily pain. So instead of badgering him with the hundreds of questions that sprang into her mind, she had feigned indifference. "It's probably just a guest from the inn," she'd said, and hoped that Leon didn't notice the excitement that sang through her like a trumpet's call, the thrilling certainty that it was Truehart at last, that at last her time had come.

By the late afternoon her hair had dried, and she closed the lid over the keyboard of her parlor piano and went into the kitchen and ate a light supper of cold smoked shoulder and new potatoes before going up to her bedroom to dress for her evening's recital. She brushed her hair out carefully with long, steady strokes, and then, her hands following the familiar designs of habit, rolled it and pinned it into place on top of her head. She rubbed a light coating of rouge into her cheeks and lips and thickened her eyelashes with a preparation of frankincense and mastic, then put on the white gown she had chosen to wear to the gala. She smoothed the bodice tight around her and plucked at the neck and cuffs of the gown until the lace there stood out smartly, and then she stepped to the middle of the room and looked at herself in the full-length mirror that stood near the foot of her bed. While she was turning this way and that, she suddenly remembered a phrase from the little tune she had been humming that morning: *Baby's gonna be a rich man's bride*. She giggled. Who'd ever have me? she asked herself facetiously, for she was secure in her commitment to remain single all of her days. Although there had been men in her life whom she'd respected, and one or two she'd regarded as friends, she hadn't yet met the man whose belonging she wished to become. Humming Mimi's little song, she fetched her pretty white hat and left the house, and took the path through the woods to the inn.

As had long been her custom, Lady commenced playing the

first of the evening's rags softly and without flourish, so that the music emerged from the piano with a shy, deliberate sound which rippled delicately as it made its way outward to summon her listeners' attention before returning to reassure Lady in her concentration. Then, as the flow of it began to tingle in her shoulders and wrists, the texture of the music brightened slightly; acquiring the momentum of confidence, her hands began to lift and stride upon the keys, hitting each note on its center and making it ring with a sweet, silvery tone, and embellishing the rag's lilting phrases with little figurations that sparkled and danced like the reflections strewn across the crinkling surface of the lake by the sun perched on the mountains above the western shore. This was ragtime the way she had played it ever since she'd left New Orleans, blithe and celebratory, its cadences forthright in their steady progress and its tonality as crisp and transparent as the streams that tumbled from the hills into Lake Sequantus, with scarcely a trace in it of the honeyed density that had once gilded Countess Welcome's parlor with its soothing lassitude, back in the times when the music had still been Brick's and all she'd ever had to do was to set her hands out upon the keys in order to ride its easy flow from dusk till morning.

Lady knew perfectly well that the ragtime had fallen out of fashion and that soon it would be a relic, quaint and curious, like a bustle or a beaver hat. As long ago as the previous summer she'd sensed that the inn's guests had become merely polite in their heed to her playing, and this year their lack of interest was unmistakable; even when she raised up into a sharper key and increased her tempo by a turn, they continued to murmur and exclaim among themselves and shift restlessly in their chairs at the café tables set around the pavilion. Ragtime had lost its power to entice them with the promise of surprise. Its syncopated cross-rhythms and its blue chromatics, which had once seemed so agitated and startling, were passing into common usage, and now the smart set had embraced with their favor the livelier styles of dance music, the jittery city energy of the two-step and the fox trot, and the music whose name had frightened her so that winter, the jazz. She wondered whether, once she had banished Truehart, she might make use of the new music in her playing, and in the boldness of her new resolve she could think of no reason why she shouldn't.

As the last of the sunlight withdrew from the pavilion, and the mountains melted together in shadow on the far side of the lake, two theatrical spotlights were illuminated in focus upon Lady. The curtains behind the stage had been left closed and, seated at the black grand piano in her sparkling white gown, she shone in the setting of their crimson velvet like a pearl in a jeweler's case, eliciting from her audience appropriate whispers of admiration. She sensed now that she had summoned their attention, and she rewarded it in her next piece by permitting her hands to sweeten the harmonies slightly more than was called for in the composition, and then, midway through the second strain, she was startled by the recognition that that sweetness bore the disinctive flavor of Brick's music, which she thought she had been cleansed of when she had played out his blues for Truehart, long ago. She smiled to hear the familiar warm tonalities, and her hands scurried among the keys with the excitement of discovery and artfully blended Brick's music to her own, so that its formality was softened by a tone of wry tenderness. The audience hushed altogether, and smiled expectantly.

The brightest smile among them belonged to Henny Vaughan, who was seated at a table near the doors, with Mr. Fitzroy Bobwit and two gentlemen from New York who were employed in an executive capacity by the Peterson Trust. From the moment Lady had arrived on the stage Henny's attention had left his companions entirely, and he watched her with shining eyes and a grin so intense that midway into the first rag his jaws began to ache. *Magnificent,* he said over and over to himself. *She is nothing short of magnificent.* As soon as she had finished playing, he vowed, he would take her to a quiet spot—perhaps the garden—and present his proposal to her. If it hadn't been for his overpowering happiness, he would have cursed himself then for having waited so long, but instead he only grinned all the more brightly and clenched his fists to contain his excitement.

She played three more rags in the fashion which combined Brick's voice with her own, and in each succeeding one the sound of her playing gained another measure of density, until at last it rolled out through the great pavilion with a muddy, lazy flow and a golden hue sufficiently flavorful to have made Countess Eulalie herself smile and say, "My, but my Lady's playin' richly tonight." As though mesmerized, the audience attended upon every note. Then Lady turned to a slow piece.

Its composer had not designed the piece to strike a somber mood, but in Lady's hands it became a blues, and while she had not intended it so, several of the voices of her own blues appeared and addressed the uncomprehending audience, to whom only the desolation of their sound was apparent, and none of the redeeming humanity. Even Henny suffered a moment of perplexity in the midst of his pride, for one of the voices of her time that Lady inadvertently called upon was his own, and although he did not honor it with the claim of recognition, it set off an echo in his heart whose nature he could not fathom. For her part, Lady followed the progress of the blues through her hands in a state of rapturous concentration, and played more than a dozen choruses of the piece before her mood eased and she noticed that the hush which had fallen upon the pavilion was a hush of despair.

She finished the piece then as quickly as she could, and before its final notes had faded into the peaked roof overhead, she kicked her heel twice on the stage and swung into a lively, martial-sounding rag which she played with such surpassing optimism and joy that before the end of the first strain the crowd had been shaken from its melancholy and was on its feet and clapping along in time to her strutting measure. She played it three times through, with each chorus sharper and more spirited than the one before, and finished with a bright smile and a flourish of her hands in the air.

The cheering that filled the great room then exceeded any acclamation she had ever experienced in a lifetime of performing, and she waved happily into the lights and stood and made a shallow curtsey. On her way to the steps at the side of the stage she curtseyed again, while the audience continued to holler and applaud, and she waved once more as she began to descend the short flight of stairs to the pavilion's floor.

Below her as she descended, she could see several men waiting in a group at the foot of the steps, wearing tuxedos and carrying musical instruments, and they were applauding too. One of them shouted, "That's how to stir 'em up, sister. That's giving 'em the old razzmatazz." Lady smiled about her in an unspecific way, for the spotlights were still strong in her eyes and she couldn't see who had called out, and while she was looking toward the glass wall along the near side of the pavilion, she caught sight of a man's silhouette which fit against her memory and caused a sudden rush of fright in her bosom. It was a tall man, with shoulders so broad that his head looked undersized upon them, and he was slightly more than halfway between her and the doors and moving purposefully toward her through the crowd, and in fright she closed her eyes and saw a bright scarlet flash in the darkness.

Truehart!

Her eyes still closed, she stumbled on the bottom step and would have fallen headlong to the floor if a young trumpet player had not caught her neatly around the waist and propped her upright. "Whoops, m'dear," he laughed, and then, grinning self-consciously, released her. She steadied herself with a hand against his chest and stepped back from him. "Oh, la," she said faintly. "Oh dear." The optimism of her recent resolve seemed suddenly years from her, and she felt fearful indecision winding like a serpent around her heart. This was not the place to meet him; it was not what she had planned. She had expected him to come for her in her parlor, when she was alone; all of her purpose had been founded upon her anticipation of that, and upon her confidence that she could meet him there and use her blues to banish him. Her life depended on it. Why was he here? She looked again quickly in his direction, and saw that he was coming closer, struggling through the crowd. "Oh dear," she repeated, fanning her face agitatedly with her hand as she turned this way and that.

"Are you all right, ma'am?" the young trumpeter asked her.

"Oh yes," Lady said. "It's only . . . oh my, don't you think it's close in here? I declare, I do feel somewhat overcome." She had it in mind to keep the young man near her, for surely Truehart would attempt no violence if someone was near and watching her in the crowd.

"You need some fresh air," the trumpeter said. "Here, there's a side door back here somewhere, I think. This is some place, isn't it?" He guided her to the end of the curtain that was hung along the curved wall behind the stage, and pulled at it. "Look there, see?" he said, pointing into the dark space between the curtain and the giant panes of glass. "See the door back there? There's a little walkway out there. You go out that way and take some air. It will clear your head. A body needs a clear head, and there's nothing for it like fresh air."

Lady sidestepped along the narrow aisle between the curtain and the glass, through which she could see the silhouettes of trees on the near shore and the flickering of the lake's rippled surface behind the dim reflection of her own pale face and white gown. She paused for an instant and stared at her ghostly image, and then was interrupted again by the voice of the young trumpeter, who still held the curtain's edge and was watching her progress. "Is everything all right?" he said. "Do you see the door?"

"Oh yes," she answered vaguely, and, collecting herself, she continued on until she reached the door and pushed it open. The night air was mild and fragrant, with a soft breeze which stirred against her cheek as she stepped out onto the walkway that circled the pavilion. She pushed the door closed and leaned back against it. *I must not be afraid,* she told herself; *I must concentrate and be calm.* She breathed deeply of the sweet summer air.

Against her back and on the soles of her feet she could feel the murmurings of the festive pavilion vibrate, but the presence of the gala crowd did not reassure her. She wanted only to be back in her little parlor, with the lamp casting an amber glow and the familiar measures of her blues rising into her wrists and shoulders to comfort and protect her with the solace of her life. Somehow, before Truehart could stop her with his broken hands and his flashing knife, she had to make her way to her house in the woods. Only there would she able to gather the composure to meet her murderous father.

She hadn't been on the walkway for more than two minutes, and her indecision still held her fast, when she heard a sound from just behind her head. Someone was knocking softly on the other side of the door. Lady bent her knees and pushed back more firmly against it, and a voice called low to her, in scarcely more than a whisper. "Missus Winslow," it said to her. "Missus Winslow, I must speak to you." It wasn't the voice she remembered as being Truehart's, but what of that? Perhaps that was why she'd been unable to find him in her blues this spring; perhaps he'd taken on a new voice. She didn't answer. "Please, Missus Winslow," the voice said. "I only wish to speak to you."

Lady held fast, and in a minute the knocking ceased and the voice called no more. She turned her head to the side and saw his tall shadow on the other side of the glass wall, gliding off toward the front of the pavilion like a shark in a tank. She realized that he would have to pick his way through the crowd to get to the entrance doors, and that if she moved quickly enough she could get there before him, and without pausing to think about it further she stepped away from the door. On her first step, her foot hit against the end of a stack of pine boards and she was thrown off balance.

She exclaimed softly and stumbled sideways toward the railing, and threw out her hand to grab it. With the unerring quickness which had been her good fortune, her fingers closed firmly around the rail, but when the weight of the rest of her body followed against it the upright support gave way with a snapping sound, and before she had the time to consider it, Lady found herself dropping toward the dark, rippling surface of the lake, still clutching in her small, plump hand a segment of the pier's railing. When she struck the water the impact of her fall flung her hand up into her face, and the short piece of hardwood hit the side of her temple like a blow from a vengeful hand, and she was unconscious even before the lake's cool waters began to penetrate her heavy gown and haul her beneath the surface. The very last sound she heard in her time was a high squeak like the chirp of a piccolo, which gradually deepened and spread through and around her and became her own note and the sound of her spirit's release.

Chapter Thirteen

Something Doing

Nowadays Uncle Pedey's about as lively as old cowflop. Spends his days sleeping up against the back wall in Calhoun's. Mumbles and makes little fizzing noises like the new soda pump at Hart's Pharmacy in Carlowsbridge. Fighting redskins in his dreams, back on the Ohio frontier. People've come to think of him as not much more than a piece of old furniture, cracked and sprung in the seat. Folks forget what a sharp eye and nimble tongue he had when he was a young man.

He went off to the Ohio territories in the first place as a trader, not a soldier. He was just a pup when his parents died and he lit out of here with a tinker he met in Carlowsbridge. Rode the tinker's wagon to Utica, hooked up there with a merchant's representative going West. Sold blankets and whiskey and farming tools to settler and Indian alike. Slick as they come. They say he could charm a bear sow into giving up her cubs, sell a cup of water to a drowning man. Came back to Sand Springs ten years later sporting a scar on his neck that he said he got from an Indian arrow and another on his belly from an angry husband's knife. Said he stood right beside General Harrison at Tippecanoe. Said the General got so excited he talked in tongues and mounted his horse backwards.

He had his own emporium right here on Main Street, next

door to the bank. Sell you anything from a family Bible to a keg of rum. Dynamite, horsecollars, whale oil, window glass, women's hats and gloves. More stuff than you can find at Berde Bros. Married three times. He was our most prominent citizen. People say he was bright enough to've been a preacher or a politician if he'd wanted. Uncle Pedey claimed he hadn't the constancy for the one occupation or the cussedness for the other, without saying which was which.

Nowadays he doesn't make much sense to anyone, or even care to try. Lives in his own world most of the time. Once in a while, though, he perks up. Lifts his head, looks you in the eye, says something that if you think about it, it seems like he's known all along what's going on. Maybe more than that. Sometimes you'd think the old fellow was blessed with second sight. Take the morning John J. Byrnes came into Calhoun's for the first time. Soon as he was inside the door, before he'd taken off his hat or said a word to anyone, Uncle Pedey had his head up and was looking him up and down as if he was measuring him for a suit of clothes, sharp as can be. Sang out loud and clear, so we all could hear it. Said, "Pursue her at your peril, sir. The fairest flower will not wilt." Of course we all thought it was just more of his nonsense, and in a minute his chin was back down on his chest and he was snoring again. Wasn't till later, afterwards, it struck us what he'd said.

John J. Byrnes. We didn't know his name then. He was just a stranger come in for a shave. Figured him for a drummer at first. Most strangers you see in town are drummers. He was a tall fellow with black hair and a long jaw and broad shoulders. Big hands, too, thick fingers, knuckles like river stones. Tough-looking customer he was, wearing city clothes. A dark suit, common cloth, and a derby hat. When he came into Calhoun's, Harold Wales was in the chair. The stranger, Byrnes, didn't say anything. Glanced over at Uncle Pedey when the old man spoke, but didn't seem to pay any mind to him. Picked up a *Police Gazette* and sat down in the chair by the door.

Alfred Calhoun finished shaving Harold Wales, patted some

talcum on his cheeks and dusted him off when he got up from the chair. Said, "Next," as if everyone in the place was waiting to be worked on by him. Harold Wales paid him his dime and bid us all good morning and left. Alfred said to the stranger, "Next. You're next, mister."

Byrnes lowered the *Gazette* from in front of him and looked at Alfred with a question on his face, but he still didn't say anything. Alfred said, "If you're waiting for these niggers to move, mister, you've got a long wait before you. They'd sooner cut their own throats than spend two bits in my joint. They just come in to keep out of the sun, or the rain, if you like. They couldn't tell the difference. A shave's a dime, haircut fifteen cents. What'll yours be?"

"Very well, then. I'll be wanting a shave," Byrnes said. He had a high-pitched voice, with some Irish in his accent. Touch of brogue. The other one, the woman in the nurse's uniform, had the same way of speaking. He stood up and took off his jacket and hung it on the rack. Some sort of fraternal key on his watchchain. Couldn't make it out. When he took hold of the ends of his tie to undo it, Alfred said, "There's no need to remove your collar, mister. I do a neat job and my methods are up to date. Sit yourself right up here."

Byrnes paused for an instant. Looked at Calhoun in a calculating way. Then he shook his head and pulled the bow undone, dug at his collar button. "It's for my own comfort," he said. "A man must follow his custom, don't you think?" Alfred only grunted. Didn't argue the matter, though surely it went against his own custom to stand for contradiction, no matter how slight or well meant. He's usually the most contrary of men, Alfred Calhoun. We sensed that the stranger had scored a point on him.

He didn't talk much while he was in the chair, but then it's hard to converse with steel scraping around your neck. Alfred tested him with the usual questions. Was he new to Sand Springs? Yes. Was he here on business or pleasure? That depended. Did he plan to stay long? Perhaps. What line of business was he in? This and that. Was he staying at the inn?

"What inn would that be?" he asked. As if he'd never heard of the place.

"Why, that would be The Sequantus House," Alfred said. "Our internationally acclaimed lakeside resort and gathering place of the upper crust." His sarcasm was plain in his voice. Byrnes looked at him with that same calculating expression as before. Then he said, "Oh. Oh no, I'm not." He had blue eyes, very pale blue. Seemed to make Alfred uncomfortable when he looked at him, because Alfred didn't say anything else. Just finished the shave, wiped him clean and powdered him and pumped him upright in the chair. Byrnes jumped out of it with a lighter step than you'd have guessed, a man of his size. Didn't fumble with his collar, either. Man with hands that big, you'd expect him to have trouble with his collar. Combed his hair in the mirror and lit a cigar, stuck a dime on the counter next to the cash register. All done neatly, no waste motion. Brisk. Alfred looked sour, watching him. Byrnes didn't seem to mind. Said, "I thank you kindly, mister . . ."

"Calhoun," Alfred said. "Alfred Calhoun, my lord." Still being sarcastic. Things had been going badly for him since they'd paved the Carlowsbridge road.

Byrnes didn't seem to notice Alfred's irony, though. He just nodded pleasantly and said, "Mister Calhoun it is, then. Good day to you, Mister Calhoun. Good day, gentlemen." Set his derby hat square on his head and left the shop.

Soon as the door closed, Sebron Porter snuck over to the window to watch him. Saw Byrnes cross the street and enter the bank. "That's a smart-looking fella, right enough," Henry Donker said. "Looks like a city man. Wonder what his line is."

Bob Marshall leaned over and said, "Probably safety razors," just loud enough so Alfred could hear him. "I heard that, you son of a bitch," Alfred said. The surest way to get his goat was talking about safety razors. Just then Uncle Pedey spoke up.

Second time that morning and the sun hadn't even burned off the dew yet. "Save my lady," he shouted. "Damn all the Philistines, she's going down. Save my lady." His leg was jerking and he started swatting around in front of his face with his hand as if there were flies there. "Ha-ha," Alfred Calhoun laughed. "Fight 'em off, you old coon. Kill 'em all."

After a while Byrnes came out of the bank. Stopped on the street corner, looked this way and that. Joined his hands behind his coattails and just stood there, taking it all in. Alfred stood next to Sebron at the window. "Look at his shoes," he said. "I'll tell you something, boys. When I was in Schenectady all the policemen wore those big heavy brogans like that. That man's no drummer, boys, you can mark my words. If that man's a drummer I'm king of the jigaboos. Look at his shoes."

Byrnes spent the whole morning there on Main Street. Went in and out of all the stores. Just looking, passing the time of day. In between times he rested out on the sidewalk. Smoked his cigar. Didn't seem to be in any rush. The more we watched him, the more it seemed Alfred had come onto something. The man did look like a policeman walking a beat. Solid, unhurried. Then just before noon he got into a Ford car and drove away on the Carlowsbridge road and we didn't see him again that day.

Next morning, though, he was back for a shave. First thing. Little more talkative. Asked questions about property. Farms, houses, river land, lakefront. Asked who owned them, what they sold for. No answers of his own, mind you, just questions. We still hadn't found out his name. "He's not selling, boys, he's buying," Alfred said after he left. "I'll tell you something else, too. He's not spending his own money. He's somebody's agent. You see if I'm not right." Whatever he was, Byrnes didn't look so much like a policeman to us anymore. Uncle Pedey slept through his arrival, but after he was gone the old trooper woke up and hollered, "Save my lady," again.

Make a long story short. He came in every morning that week. Had a shave, asked a few questions. Hunting and fishing, farming, the factories. He asked about them all. Never said his name. Paid his dime and left. Uncle Pedey was in a terrible froth all week. Jumpy as a cat whenever Byrnes was around.

Two things he never mentioned, though. The Petersons and the inn. Didn't strike us as odd until afterwards, both of them so prominent. We found out he knew plenty about them. He'd been up at the inn more than once, hanging around the garages and the kitchen, chatting with the help. Watching them work on the new pier. Walking in the woods there and along the lake road where it runs past the Collins house. Spying, it turned out.

He didn't have to spy on Edgar Peterson. Had the woman do that for him, Edgar's nurse. We saw them together, keeping company, but we didn't make anything of it. Explained it away. We were so sure he was here to buy land or property for a rich man. Didn't know but that he'd buy something of ours. She was a hefty girl and kind of plain. Big face, apple cheeks. Not homely, but not pretty either. Brown hair rolled up in a bun at her neck. Thick legs and big feet. Looked like a worker. Spoke with a brogue like his, Byrnes's. Saw her get into his car on the Carlowsbridge road, not far from the end of Peterson's driveway. No mistaking either one of them. His broad shoulders, derby hat. Her nurse's cape, headdress. Saw them again in Carlowsbridge. They were leaving the Bijou together after the evening performance. That time she wasn't wearing her uniform, but it was her just the same.

Another thing we might have noticed. Did notice. Didn't make enough of it. Happened at the beginning of the next week. Byrnes asked Alfred for a haircut. Bob Marshall snorted so hard his chair bucked off its front feet, but Byrnes paid no mind. Sat in the chair, let Alfred wind the sheet around him, said, "I'm given to understand, Mister Calhoun, that you've a room upstairs that you let out for commercial purposes. Might I inquire whether it's available at present?" Very cool, as if he was talking about the weather.

Alfred stopped his shears in midair, as if he'd been frozen.

An awful confusion went on in his face. Must have stood there for two minutes like that, calculating so hard you could almost see the smoke come out his ears. Finally he said, "At present, sir, it is rented, but only through the week. If you're interested, sir, I could have the space available to you by Monday next." It was as sweetly as we'd ever heard him speak, and he was grinning like a baboon in a banana tree. For fifteen years he'd insisted Mrs. Winslow was only there temporarily. Been saying all that time he was going to boot her out first chance he got. Guess you couldn't call it treachery, then. Alfred just figured time was finally rewarding him. Still, it wasn't a pretty sight to see, the way he groveled for that stranger. No other word for it. He groveled. "Are you interested, sir?" he asked.

"Hm?" Byrnes said, as if he'd already forgotten his own question. "Oh, aye," he said, "the room. Perhaps I am."

"Might I ask what your purpose is, sir?" Alfred said.

"Business affairs," he said. "I was thinking I might want an office in a central location."

"Oh, sir," Alfred said. "This is a lovely commercial space, sir. I've been at this spot myself nearly twenty-two years, sir, and I can vouch for the location. It has two windows, sir. Takes the daylight very nicely, you'll see." Byrnes said nothing, so Alfred pressed on. "Would you like to see the room, sir?" he asked.

Byrnes said, "I mayn't, may I? You said it was occupied."

"No bother, sir," Alfred said. "She's not about on Mondays. I can slip you right in and she'd never know it."

"That doesn't sound exactly ethical, Mister Calhoun," he said.

"The woman's a bother to me, sir," Alfred said. "An endless bother ever since she moved in."

"Do you mean to say she lives there?" he said.

"No no, sir. Not on your life," Alfred said. "No, she conducts what you might call a music academy up there, sir. A conservatory. She instructs the little children, sir, and the women who'd be better off minding to their affairs at home."

All the while he talked, he took little snips at Byrnes' hair. No pattern to it, though. Alfred was too agitated.

"Perhaps not, then," Byrnes said. "I'd not want to be responsible for a piano teacher's eviction. I consider music a grace, myself."

"As do I, sir," Alfred answered him, quick as could be. "As do I. If you ever want to see tears in Alfred Calhoun's eyes, sir, all you have to do is sing one of the old ballads, you know the ones I mean. But this woman, sir. Winslow is her name. Calls herself Missus. She plays that ragtime music, sir. I find it abominable. You're a gentleman of the world, sir. I can see that. Surely you agree that that colored music's a slap in the face of decent people. Negritude is staining the Republic, it's well known. Henry Ford himself has said so. Her being up there has driven away loyal customers that I've served for years."

"I don't understand," he said. "Do you mean to say that the woman is colored?"

"Ha," Alfred said. "Who knows what she is? Oh, her face is fair, sir, fair as you please. But who can see the color of her blood, hey? That boy of hers, he's a regular burrhead, if you catch my meaning. Tough as wire. She's not from our parts. Came here like a fugitive, a runaway. Babe in arms. Said she was a widow, sir, but if you ask me, I'd say she never was a wife."

"That's a hard thing you're saying, Mister Calhoun," Byrnes said.

"She's a hard woman, sir," Alfred said. "She trades sharp. Deals with men in a way you don't see a proper woman deal. If she was a proper woman, sir, she'd have herself a husband to serve. She don't. She rules a man. I'd black her eye, sir, if she was mine and spoke up to me the way she does. I'd show her who the ruler was in the proper order of things, I would." He'd quit cutting Byrnes' hair altogether and was pacing back and forth. Waving his hands in the air. Red as a beet. "I'll tell you another thing, sir," he said. "I've seen niggers in my time, don't think I haven't. I learned my trade in Schenectady and saw plenty of them there. There was a bootblack at the railroad station there that spoke with the same kind of accent she has. I knew it the first time she opened her mouth. I said, That woman talks just like that old shine in Schenectady. Damn me if I didn't."

Byrnes watched him in the mirror. No expression on his face at all. Said, "Whyever would she have come here? Meaning no disrespect to your town, but it would seem an odd place for a woman such as you're describing to want to settle."

"Ah," Alfred said. "You've made a common misunderstanding, sir. She don't belong to the town. She's at the inn. It's a different place entirely, sir, different sort of person. Once you've been here awhile, sir, you'll see what I mean. A richer crowd, sir, too rich for our blood. Things go on there, sir, that would shame a decent person. It's just the place for a rich man's doxy like her." He calmed down some. Started back in at cutting Byrnes' hair.

"I see," Byrnes said. "You mean she's a kept woman."

Alfred said, "Have you heard the name Peterson, sir?"

"Peterson," Byrnes said. He appeared to think about it. Play acting, it turned out. "Would that be the same Peterson whose name is on all the factories?" he asked.

"The same," Alfred said. "The very same. Edgar Peterson brought her here, set her up at the inn. His Highness the Nigger Lover, I call him, and not just because he gives his fortune away to coons, either. His father was Antioch Peterson. You may have heard of him, sir."

"Perhaps," Byrnes said.

"There was a man," Alfred said. "I never saw him myself, mind you. He was before my time. But we all know the stories. He was a real bull of the woods, old Antioch Peterson. A man's man, sir. He died in the saddle, if you catch my meaning, sir. What a way to go, hey? Not that his son's cut from the same cloth. A damned milksop, Edgar. Couldn't even carry the old man's eggs, if you catch my meaning."

324

"I'm afraid I don't follow you there, Mister Calhoun," Byrnes said.

"How's that, sir?" Alfred asked him.

"There must be some life in him if, as you say, he's keeping a woman as spirited as your music teacher seems to be," Byrnes said. "Did you say he fathered her child? The man must have some fire in his furnace then, hey, Mister Calhoun?"

Alfred backed down a bit then. Said, "Well now, I've never been certain of that, sir. No sir, in all fairness, that's not something I'm certain of. I wouldn't exactly say he kept her, no. She does seem to've made her own way, right enough. No, I think if you asked around, you'd find that he, that Edgar, didn't have a great deal to do with her, in all fairness. No, my own opinion, sir, is that he brought her here for someone else, one of his rich pals, most likely."

"Do you mean then, that there's another who visits her?" Byrnes asked.

"No sir, not that neither," Alfred said. Still backing off. Don't know exactly why, unless he figured that Byrnes, with his rich man's connections, might carry the slander back to someone who'd take offense. "Nobody that we've ever seen, sir," he said. "Anyways, it's too late for Edgar Peterson," he added. "He's long past that. The war got him, they say. The man's nothing but a lump now. His Highness the Lump, hey sir?" He seemed uncomfortable saying it. Stopped talking.

"I see," Byrnes said. Didn't say anything more until Alfred took the sheet off him. It was an awful haircut, one of Alfred's worst. Looked like tree blight on Byrnes' head, but he didn't remark on it. Did up his collar, tied his tie. Said, "Concerning the room upstairs, Mister Calhoun. I'd like to slip in and have a look at it, just to have an idea of its dimensions."

"Oh yes sir," Alfred said. "Yes sir. Go right up. Stairs are back there, through that door."

"I'll not disturb any of the woman's effects," Byrnes said.

"She'll never know you were there, sir," Alfred said. Dusted off Byrnes' shoulders. "If it suits you, sir, we'll make an arrangement that won't displease you, you have my word."

Uncle Pedey was sitting up in his chair. Quivering and sputtering as if he'd been dipped in the lake. Pointed his finger at Byrnes' chest. Byrnes stopped, looked at the old man. Uncle Pedey said, "Pursue her at your peril, mountebank." Byrnes smiled at him.

"Pay him no mind, sir," Alfred said. "The old coon's lost in the woods, cracked."

Uncle Pedey's hand was steady as a rock, pointing at Byrnes. Said, "Keep clear of my lady." We thought he was just having a spell.

Byrnes took a cigar out of his pocket. Said, "Here you be, old trooper. You look like a man that enjoys a good smoke."

Uncle Pedey pulled his hand back. Shook his head. "Judas," he said. "I'm versed in treachery. Don't mistake me."

"Henry, shut the old son of a bitch up," Alfred said. "Don't mind your manners with him, sir. He's nothing but hot air. Go ahead on up."

Byrnes put the cigar back in his pocket, passed on through the door. In a minute we heard his footsteps overhead. He walked around the room, stopped several times. Might have opened a drawer. She had a dresser up there. Kept music in it. Might have been one of the windows. None of us said anything except Uncle Pedey. Looked at Alfred as if he wanted to skin him alive. Said, "Murder and treachery. Murder and treachery." Said it a good dozen times. Each time his voice got softer. Finally dropped off. Started to snore. Byrnes came down after some twenty minutes. Said, "Thank you, Mister Calhoun. I'll be communicating with you presently." Left the shop.

We watched him get in his car and drive off toward the lake. Then Bob Marshall said, "You know, Alfred, the man didn't pay you for the trim." Alfred looked on the counter. Sure enough, there was no money there. "Can't say I blame him," Henry Donker said. "Man looked like a half-skinned squirrel. That was an awful cut you gave him." Alfred didn't rise to it, though.

326

Said, "He'll be back, boys. Never you mind. He'll be back sure, and when he does I'll be rid of the whore at last." Uncle Pedey groaned in his sleep, and the rest of us got busy with our newspapers and *Gazettes*. Nobody said anything about how raw Alfred had talked to the stranger about Mrs. Winslow. Guess he'd been talking that way about her for so long we forgot to notice. Should have. Disservice to her.

That was on a Monday. Byrnes didn't come to town the next day, and the day after that was the Fourth of July and we didn't look for him. Everyone went down to Carlowsbridge for the celebration. Our town team beat the Carlowsbridge nine in the morning. Leon Winslow played right field for us, had a double. Our volunteer firemen got beaten in the muster and so did the Carlowsbridge Engine Company. Team from the Peterson estate beat them. Had their own pumper and ran through the hose-and-ladder drill like monkeys going up a tree. Only one other old soldier in the parade with Uncle Pedey. An old bird that'd ridden with Rough and Ready Taylor in Mexico. Next to Uncle Pedey he looked spry enough to've run beside the coach. On the speakers' platform Uncle Pedey raised both arms, shouted, "Surrender! They're killing the women!" Knocked his hat off. By the time Henry retrieved it and put it back on Uncle Pedey's head the old man was asleep. Ox roast in the afternoon. Sack races, relays, pole climbing, greased pig. Sideshow had a fat lady and a boy with alligator skin. Fireworks at dusk. Streetcars ran late bringing everyone back. That night someone saw Byrnes at the inn, out on the pier. We never did see him after that. Didn't see the woman either. Next day her room at Peterson's castle was empty, cleaned out.

We didn't pay much notice to that then. Too many other things going on. That same Thursday morning we heard Mrs. Winslow was dead. Day after that it was Leon and Henny Vaughan. All of them, gone. Awful business, we all agreed. Two tragic accidents, one after another. Bad luck comes in bunches. Even Alfred Calhoun felt badly. Wouldn't talk about it. Behaved like a guilty man. Suppose in his intentions he was.

We forgot about Byrnes. Never occurred to us he might be connected. Then a couple of weeks later Henry Donker's cousin Orrie Tilden showed up in town. Told us what he'd told Chester MacIntyre, the town constable, and what Chester told him. Odd story, raises questions we probably shouldn't ought to ask.

We don't see Orrie in town very often. He's kind of a hermit. Nothing wrong with him, mind you. People see him, think he's eccentric. Fact is, he's quite smart. Reads a lot, prefers poetry to people. Not unfriendly, just partial to his own company. Feels at home in the woods. He lives in a cabin he built out past the end of the logging road that runs up the east shore of the lake. There're eight or ten fishing camps along there owned by city men, most of them from Albany. Summers, Orrie hires out as a guide, boatman. Makes himself enough cash to buy a few books, and flour and salt and lard for the winter. Hunts his meat, runs trap lines, trades the skins, burns the tallow. Got everything he wants.

Orrie stopped by Calhoun's to see Uncle Pedey, pay his respects. Always has a kind word for the old man. Says we should pay better attention to him. "You have to be patient with the old," Orrie's fond of saying. "Think of the years he's seen, bless him." We asked him what brought him to town. Said he'd come in to ask Chester about the Winslow woman, how she died. Seems he'd come across some funny business up the lake. Involved her. One thing about Orrie. Once he gets talking, he'll talk. Comes from living alone, most likely. Told us this story.

Orrie said that one day three, three and a half weeks before, he'd smelled smoke along the logging road. Traced it to one of the camps there, belongs to a man named Beresford. Albany man. Surprised Orrie. Didn't think any of them would be up till after the Fourth. Walked in to see if they wanted him for guiding, handiwork. Shutters were open, chimney smoking, tire tracks in the grass but no car there. Went up on the porch, knocked. Nobody there. Went down to the shore, hollered. Same thing. Beresford's boat was still hauled up and covered with canvas. Orrie decided to come back later. Before he did, though, he went up on the porch again, looked in at the window. What he saw puzzled him.

There was no sporting gear inside, fishing or hunting. No guns, no tackle, no boots or waders. Just a black suit hung on a peg, and an overcoat. One bunk made up. Suitcase at the foot of it. Pair of heavy black shoes with high tops and thick soles of leather. City shoes. Table had been pulled over next to the window. Stacks of paper on it, looked like business letters. Written on a typing machine. Two books there, a ledger and a little book in a purple cover, looked like a woman's diary. Little gold clasp on it. Ledger had a name printed on its cover. Letters big enough to read through the window. John J. Byrnes, it said.

Couple of other things on the table, too. Cigar box. Inkwell and three or four pens, couple of pencils, ashtray. Orrie wondered for a minute if it might not be a poet staying there, writing his verses in the little purple book. Tickled by the thought. Whoever it was, it didn't look to be just a drifter. Now and then a drifter'll break into one of the camps, set up housekeeping. Orrie's run off a bunch of them. Never saw one yet with a diary, he said, or a ledger and an extra pair of shoes. Figured it must be a friend of the cabin's owner. Went on about his business.

He went by again that same evening, though, after dusk. Lamps were lit, Ford car pulled up alongside the porch. Heard voices. Now, Orrie's no sneak, mind you, but there's not one person in a hundred that if he comes on two strangers talking won't stop and listen to a word or two. He just stood there by the foot of the porch steps, didn't have to go any closer. Window was open, voices carried. Couldn't help hearing.

It was a man and a woman. Woman sounded edgy. Kept saying, "I've had enough of it," and, "Let's be done with it." Called the man Mr. Byrnes. He called her Tessie, tried to calm her down. Told her she was doing a good job, said, "You're a good soldier, Tessie."

Hard to tell what they were talking about, except that Edgar

Peterson figured in it, and so did some woman. "It was plain enough they meant poor Mister Peterson," Orrie said. "She kept talking about Eddie, or Petey, calling him that, and saying how he was just sitting up in that drafty old castle and how, in his condition, he'd never tell them or anyone else what they needed to know. My land, the poor fellow. The way I hear it, he's gone so far out of his mind he can't even read, and the man's got thousands of books. Imagine it. Thousands of books, and he can't read a word. I don't care how rich he is, you have to feel for a person in those circumstances. I certainly do.

"As for the woman, they never did mention her name, so it didn't strike me until after, who they were talking about. But that Byrnes kept saying he wanted to have it out with her. Those were his words: 'Have it out with her.' He must have said it a half a dozen times: 'I'm going to have it out with her.' He said, 'It's the only way.' He said he couldn't find anything out about her past, no matter where he looked. It was as if she didn't even have one, he said, meaning a past. Said he'd have it out with her.

"Well, I wasn't there long. No more than maybe five minutes. Then the woman said, 'I've got to be getting back before they miss me, begorrah,' and he said, 'Right you are, Tessie me gal'—you see, they both talked like the Irishman in the vaudeville—and I heard them starting to move around in there, in the cabin. I didn't want them to walk out the door and catch me standing there gaping like a ninny on the steps, so I just went around the side. But I looked back when I got there, and I saw them come out the door. He was a big fellow with broad shoulders, wearing a derby hat and smoking a cigar, and she was a nurse, wearing a cape and a nurse's headpiece. Just before they got in the car, the man said, 'I saw the boy, and you can't tell anything by looking at him.' Then they got in the car and drove off, and I went on home. I thought it sounded like a curious business, all right, but it wasn't any of my affair, and I put it out of my mind. At least for a while I did.

"The next morning, I went up into the mountains, up behind Rose Notch, like I always do, this time of year. I fished a little in Dixon's Pond there, camped awhile, and when I come down my head was clear and I was ready to go to work. I looked in at the inn, thought I'd say hello to Cousin Sally, and that's when I heard about Missus Winslow and her boy and Vaughan. Drowning and fire, my land. Death and destruction. Well, I remembered something I'd heard those two say in the cabin that night, talking about the woman and Edgar Peterson. That nurse had said that when the woman had come to call she'd played for him, for Peterson. Said she'd played beautifully, and the man—Mister John J. Byrnes—he said then, 'And so she should. It's her profession.'

"That was one thing they'd said that I remembered, and there was another thing, too. One of them—I think it was Byrnes—said something about the rumor that she'd come in his car, only he said there was no proof of it. His car, meaning Edgar Peterson's, I could tell. Well, as soon as I remembered that I guessed I knew who the woman was that they were talking about, all right, so I came straight in to see Chester, told him the whole story, everything I saw and heard."

"I'll be God-damned," Bob Marshall said. "John J. Byrnes, hey? We thought he was here buying property. That's what Alfred said, didn't you, Alfred?" Alfred just pulled a face, didn't say anything.

"I don't get it," Henry Donker said. "What's it got to do with the fire, anyway?"

"Why, you nitwit," Alfred Calhoun said. "How in hell do you even manage to tie your own shoelaces?"

"Go to hell, Alfred," Henry said. "When did you get so smart all of a sudden? You thought he was—"

"Henry," Orrie said. "It was Missus Winslow they were talking about."

"Plays piano, Henry," Bob Marshall said. "Came to town in Peterson's car, you get it?"

"Oh," Henry said. Looked real thoughtful. "Oh. Oh sure. Oh, I got that, Orrie, sure. I did. What I meant was, it was an accident, all of it. Wasn't it? That's what everyone says. Accidental drowning, accidental fire. Do you mean it wasn't?"

"Shut up and let him tell it, why don't you," Alfred Calhoun said. "Go on, Orrie. What'd Chester say when you told him?"

"Said he already knew about the man," Orrie said.

"Go on," Bob Marshall said. "He did?"

"Yup," Orrie said. "Chester said the man came into his office his first day in town, and presented his credentials. Professional courtesy. Told Chester his name was John J. Byrnes, and he was a licensed private detective from Boston, had a letter from the Boston police, bona fide. He told Chester he was investigating a matter for the Peterson Trust, and he said he hoped he could count on Chester's confidence. Chester told him he could, as long as there was nothing illegal involved, and started to ask him a few questions, sound him out a little more. Well, Byrnes shut him right off, told Chester that if he wanted to know any more about it he should get in touch with Mister Fitzroy Bobwit and ask him his questions. Said he'd told him all he was at liberty to say about it."

"Oh my," Henry said.

"Yup," Orrie said.

"I'll be God-damned," Bob Marshall said. "Mister Fitzroy Bobwit. Well, that's that, isn't it? If that man says it's an accident, that's what it'll be, Bobwit. If he says black's white, then—"

"Shut your mouth, you damned fool," Alfred said. "Don't you ever know enough to shut your mouth?" He looked unhappy as could be.

"Those poor people," Orrie said. "My land. Those poor people."

Just then Uncle Pedey woke up. Lifted his head up, said, "Mind your filthy ways, Alfred. My lady's coming through today." Looked about with a big smile, working his gums around as if he was milling grain.

"Aw now, damn it, Henry," Alfred said. "I thought you said you told the old coon."

"Of course I did," Henry Donker said. "I did tell him."

"Then why don't he give it up?" Alfred asked.

"Speak up, Alfred," Uncle Pedey said. "What's he saying, Henry? Is he slanging my lady again? You're a dog, Alfred. Don't be a dog all your days."

"Aw, Henry," Alfred said.

"All right," Henry said. "I'll tell him again, but I don't guarantee he'll get it clear." He started to get up from his chair.

Orrie stopped him. Said, "Let me tell him, Henry." Went over to Uncle Pedey and crouched down in front of him, looked him in the eye. Said, "Hello, Uncle Pedey. It's Orrie. Orrie Tilden." Didn't raise his voice much.

Uncle Pedey said, "Of course it is. Howdo, Orrie. D'you see my lady?"

Orrie said, "She's not coming in any more, Uncle Pedey. There was an accident. She's dead. Yes sir, she is. She's dead, Uncle Pedey." Spoke real slow. Every word clear.

"Nonsense, Orrie," Uncle Pedey said. "You never saw more life in any woman. Take more than Alfred's slander to do her in, you bet. I'll stand up for her. I always have."

He had, too. Cracked as he was, he always had spoken up for her. More than the rest of us could say. We liked her fine, only nobody ever spoke up for her. Might have made a difference if we had.

Orrie stood up. "All right, Uncle Pedey, I'm going now," he said. "You take care of yourself." Uncle Pedey didn't say anything. Worked his gums around some, then went to sleep. Just like that. Orrie said, "I think he knows. I'm pretty sure he does. He's not going to say so, though."

But a little while later Uncle Pedey groaned in his sleep, and then said, "They're killing the women, damn them. Stop them. They're killing the women." And a big tear ran down the side of his nose and fell in his whiskers.

Oh, Didn't He Ramble

The body was laid out in the parlor in a fine coffin with polished sides and brass handles, held up by two sawhorses and draped with black cloth, and we set out four black candles in tall candleholders at the corners of the coffin, and some others around in the room. The undertaker had done a proper job of restoring the right color to her eyelids and her lips, and he'd covered up the bruise on her forehead with powder, but he'd rouged her cheeks too heavily, and her hands, which he'd crossed on her chest, were so stiff and still they were nothing like as they'd been in life. Looking at her, I could tell that there was nothing of herself left behind in that body.

The undertaker had her laid out by the early afternoon, and Henny and I sat down side by side on chairs at the coffin's foot and stayed there for the rest of the day and on through the evening. Some folks came by from the inn to share condolence with us, and a couple of women from Sand Springs that she'd taught piano to, but we were alone for most of the time, and we just sat there, thinking our thoughts, and didn't have much to say. It was a hot day and quite muggy, and when night fell the insects started banging against the wire screens on the windows, and once in a while a little breeze would drift in and the lace curtains would stir and the candle flames dance, but that was the only movement in the house. Finally, sometime around about midnight, I was starting to nod, so I stood up and told Henny I had to get some sleep. He said, "Go ahead, son. I'll sit with her a while longer and then I'll be going. I could use some rest myself." His voice sounded thick and his eyes were blood-shot, and there was a raw patch on his lower lip where he'd been gnawing on it all day.

"You could stay over here," I said, and then it occurred to me that that would mean he'd have to sleep in Mama's bed, and that didn't sound right to me somehow, but he said, "No, I'll rest better in my own bed and come back in the morning." I said, "All right," and, "Good night, Henny," and I dragged my-self upstairs.

When I was passing by Mama's room I had an idea, and I went in and opened up her old trunk and got out that voodoo root, with the notion that in the morning I'd slip it into the coffin and she could be buried with it. Not for its magic, you understand. I didn't know about that yet. I just thought she might like a keepsake in the hereafter, and that old root was something I knew came from long out of her past. It was just an idea I had. I put it in the pocket of my trousers so as I wouldn't forget, and then I went on into my own room and fell across my bed, and I didn't even have the time to kick off my shoes before I was sound asleep. And then I had this dream.

I dreamed I heard music playing downstairs, so I got up out of bed and went down the stairs and looked into the parlor, and I saw Henny playing the piano, making music that sounded like a little bit of ragtime and a little bit of my mama's blues. The coffin was there in the middle of the floor, but it was empty, and Mama was on her feet and waltzing with some man I'd never seen but who I recognized, only at that moment, you understand, I couldn't say exactly why I recognized him or who he was, and I was puzzling on it because it seemed to be some-thing I had to know. I could feel the importance of it. He was very tall, as tall as the man I saw in the road, but I could tell it wasn't the same man. This one was tan-skinned and his face was handsome in a hard way, close-shaven and with a long, sharp jaw that had a sort of a shine along its edge. He had the smallest ears I'd ever seen on a grown person, and on the top of his forehead his hairline came to a sharp point there, you know, what they call a widow's peak. He had a frightening grin on his face, with no kindness or joy in it at all, and his eyes were black as coal, you couldn't see anything in them, and he was dressed in evening clothes and wore a cape with a red lining. He waltzed Mama around so fast that her feet came right up off the floor and her skirts were flying, and they went around and around the empty coffin, with the music going faster and faster, and then I noticed that they were knocking the candles over and the lace curtains had caught fire. But I couldn't do anything myself to warn them, I couldn't move or cry out, and they didn't seem to see the flames or the smoke. They just kept on waltzing around and around while the smoke in the parlor got thicker and the flames jumped up the curtains and spread into the walls and windowframes.

And then, just like that, I was awake, and Henny was shaking me from side to side and shouting at me. He was saying to me, "Get out, Leon. Get out. The house is on fire. Get out." It was so like my dream I couldn't think, you see, but then I smelled real smoke and saw it seeping along in the hallway outside my door, so I jumped up and Henny and I ran downstairs to the front door, and as we went past the parlor I saw that it was full of smoke and flames were licking up the curtains and the windowframes, just like in my dream.

Well, we got clear of the house and turned around to look, and I asked Henny what had happened. "I must have dozed off," he said. "I don't know. I don't remember. The wind must have come up and knocked over a candle, maybe one of the curtains caught it. I don't know. God, I don't know. The whole window was afire. Oh God." There were smudges on his face and clothes and a burn on the back of his hand, and inside the house I could hear glass breaking, and flames were dancing in the parlor window. "We have to get her out," I said. "We have to get the body," and I started back toward the house.

But Henny grabbed me and held me back. He shouted, "You can't do it. You'd never make it."

"I have to," I said. "I have to get Mama out of there."

"Then I'll do it," Henny said. "You stay here and I'll fetch her out."

"No," I said, and I struggled to break out of his grip, because he had me wrapped up in a bear hug and I couldn't even raise my arms.

"Stop it, Leon," he said, and he released me then, but before I could recover he hauled back his fist and hit me right over the ear, and I was stunned and sat down hard on the ground. Then he turned and ran back to the house, and I was still trying to get my senses back when he ran right in the front door, into a cloud of smoke so thick that I lost sight of him immediately.

"Henny," I called out, and I tried to get up on my feet, but my legs were shaky and I stumbled sideways like a drunk, and just then there was a roaring noise and the parlor window burst and flames shot out of it, and in the midst of the flames I saw the face of the man I'd seen in my dream, with that fierce and frightening grin on it, and I was as certain as if I'd heard it spoken to me by my mama's own voice that that was the face of the man who'd killed her. For some reason I touched the outside of my trouser pocket then and through the cloth I felt the voodoo root, and I pulled it out and threw it at that face in the flames, and an instant later the whole windowframe fell back into the fire and the house began to collapse, the walls buckling and the second story falling down upon the first.

The rush of sparks and flame was so hot that it drove me backwards across the road, and from there I saw lights approaching from the inn, lanterns and automobile headlamps. I'm not sure what I was thinking of, I was in such a panic, but I know I didn't want anyone to see me just then, so I backed into the woods and down to the lake shore and I took off to the west, toward the marshes where the lake ran off, and I was on the run. The next night, south of Carlowsbridge, I jumped up out of a ditch next to a curve in the railway line and grabbed a boxcar in the middle of a long train that was just picking up speed and bending west toward the Hudson River and whatever was out there beyond it.

If anyone had asked me, those next couple of days, I guess I'd have said I was tracking that man. But nobody did and that was just as well, because the truth is, I didn't know what I was doing or where I was bound for. I was all alone, you see, and starting fresh, making it up as I went. I even sounded different, without Mama's sound to tune myself by. I had to find a sound of my own, and my own time.

Tim Parks

Loving Roger

'A tight, disturbing novel . . . mordantly illuminating on the
way love contains the seeds of vindictiveness and hatred.'
Observer

'Extremely compelling . . . the human observation is witty,
acute and sensitive . . . absolute authenticity.'
Sunday Telegraph

'With his chillingly elegant prose and frighteningly deadpan
narrative, Tim Parks has written, not a whodunnit, but a
brilliant whydunnit.' *Today*

'A tale that is cruel, upsetting and compellingly credible.'
London Standard

Flamingo